The Art of You

Costa Family

Brittney Sahin

EmKo Media

THE ART OF YOU

Copyright © 2024 Brittney Sahin

Published by: EmKo Media, LLC

Editors: Michelle Fewer, Cindy Shafley

Proofreading: Judy Zweifel - Judy's Proofreading

Cover Design: Mayhem Cover Creations

Photography: Ren Saliba

This book is an original publication of Brittney Sahin. Authored by Brittney Sahin.

In accordance with the U.S. Copyright Act of 1976, the scanning, uploading, and electronic sharing of any part of this book without permission of the publisher constitute unlawful piracy and theft of the author's intellectual property. If you would like to use material from the book (other than for review purposes), prior written permission must be obtained by contacting brittneysahin@emkomedia.net Thank you for your support of the author's rights.

This book is a work of fiction. Names, characters, places, and incidents either are products of the author's imagination or are used fictitiously. Any resemblance to actual persons, living or dead, business establishments, events, or locales is entirely coincidental. The author acknowledges the trademarked status and trademark owners of various products, brands, and/or restaurants referenced in this work of fiction, which have been used without permission. The publication/use of these trademarks is not authorized, associated with, or sponsored by the trademark owners.

Ebook ISBN: 9781947717428

Paperback ISBN: 9798344214818

❦ Created with Vellum

Music Playlist

SPOTIFY

Unchained Melody - The Righteous Brothers

The Door - Teddy Swims

Hungry Eyes - Eric Carmen

Let It Burn - Shaboozey

Ring of Fire - Johnny Cash

Yours - Post Malone

Bulletproof - Nate Smith

I Like It - Alesso & Nate Smith

The Painter - Cody Johnson

Crashing (feat. Bahari) - Illenium

Any Love - Dermot Kennedy

Highway - Shaboozey

Enter Sandman - Metallica

I've Had The Time Of My Life - Bill Medley & Jennifer Warnes

Chapter 1

Isabella

Hudson Yards, New York – October 2025

"Bella, you good?" Hudson's deep voice cut through my closed bedroom door, but it wasn't enough to jar me from my current, freaked-out state.

I couldn't answer. Nor budge a step from where I stood by my bed like a Disney ice sculpture, chills flying up my spine in the sparkly dress. I was probably as transparent as glass, too.

My jaw muscles continued to shiver as I stared at the photo resting on my palm like a shard of broken glass, one flinch away from cutting me.

"Something wrong?" His follow-up was the gentle nudge in the ass I needed to open my mouth and talk.

If I didn't answer him, he'd walk in and find me exposed. Well, not physically, but emotionally. "Uh, hold on."

"Hold on to what exactly?" His smart-ass response finally pulled my attention toward the door and away from the picture.

"The zipper. I'm just having issues with it." The lie nearly fractured apart on my distressed tone.

"Callie said you were dressed and ready." He didn't waste time calling me out on my bluff.

He was right, though. My sister-in-law had already helped me, leaving my room less than five minutes ago. Five minutes before I'd set eyes on the wicked blast from my past still searing the skin of my palm.

Forcing my feet to move, I went to the nightstand and hid the picture between two issues of *Golf Digest*. Reading about golf, or watching it on TV, was my therapeutic version of sleep noise.

With the evidence of why I was a nervous mess out of sight, I slowly spun around to face the 1930s bespoke door. My designer had chosen to keep a few of the original elements of the almost hundred-year-old home during the remodel. Now I was regretting my decision not to suggest a lock.

And at the sight of the porcelain knob turning, Hudson's patience apparently gone, I outstretched my arm as if I could telekinetically stop him. "Don't come in or you'll see me naked."

"I don't believe you." Contrary to his words, the knob stopped turning.

My brain was still lagging, so I blundered my way through the lie and said, "Last-minute decision to use the bathroom before we go. You have to take the whole dress off or risk peeing on it." It was no wonder the man would never see me as more than his best friend's sister. Because, you know, discussing urinating on a ball gown was uber attractive.

"So, you need me to get her back up here to help you?"

I framed my face between my hands, checking to see if my skin felt normal to the touch.

"Or are you so stubborn you're fixin' to spend more time trying to wrangle it in place yourself?"

You could take the man out of Texas, but not Texas out of the man. At least he'd distracted me again. The color should've returned to my face by now. I needed to confirm what I hoped would be true—that I no longer looked like Casper's cousin from an Italian mother.

"Too stubborn," I finally called back, holding the skirt of my dress so I didn't trip as I shuffled over to the antique mirror on the wall.

"Of course you are," he grumbled loud enough for me to hear. His face was probably parked an inch away from the door, and it was likely taking all of his restraint not to open it.

"I really am on the verge of success." *In hiding my nerves, at least.*

Dropping hold of the luxurious fabric, I checked myself in the mirror that once belonged to my Sicilian grandmother. The ghost staring back at me was the opposite of what I wanted to see.

My sister's brown eyes beneath my dark brows observed me like I was a story just waiting to be told. Bianca was the writer in the family, but I highly doubted even she'd want to tackle the mess that I was and bundle it up into something worth telling.

Of course, my prologue started with her death. So, she couldn't exactly pen anything, now could she?

I peeked back at the magazines, thinking about the photo again, and . . . *I'm failing. How am I going to act normal tonight?*

"From the sounds of the commotion downstairs, everyone is here now. They'll be waiting on us."

On me, you mean. My attention swung back to the white paneled door and my shoulders hunched forward. Hand to my stomach, the little beads and crystals of the bodice poked into my palm like thorns from a rose. Doubt they'd draw blood the way that photo nearly had, but I had to do something to pull myself together.

There were lives on the line, and I couldn't let what was wedged between those two magazines risk tonight's mission because my focus was now collapsing under the pressure from my past.

I needed a way to get through this without the truth leaving my mouth. If Hudson or my brothers knew about that photo, they'd pull me off the op tonight. They'd go through with the mission because they had to, but then something might go sideways because they were distracted, and I couldn't let that happen.

I had to adjust and find a new way forward to get through this night.

I walked barefoot to the door, mentally preparing myself for the face-off. "I need help."

"So, I take it you want me to get Callie after all?"

"No, you can help me." Resting my hand on the knob, I closed my eyes, my heart rate pulsing in my ears.

"I don't think it's a good idea for me to help you get dressed." That deep, husky tone felt richer and more indulgent than the dark chocolate I'd polished off an hour ago. While golf put me to sleep, candy was my go-to for a pick-me-up.

I finally opened up, letting him know there was no risk of seeing his best friend's sister indecent.

Given my current state of mind, what I hadn't been ready to experience upon seeing him, never mind so dramatically, was lust. But I fell headfirst into the feeling, forgetting tonight's objective and the distraction between the magazines.

Standing before me was the six-foot-two definition of handsome. Long legs were encased by perfectly fitted trousers. A pressed white shirt stretched along broad shoulders. He was leaning forward, his suit jacket draped over his shoulder in one hand, with his other palm wedged against the doorframe, his bicep flexed. His thick brown hair was slicked back, and I was dying for a lock to escape so I could reach out and brush it away from his forehead.

But it was the two blue pools of trouble now staring at my face that had my stomach all fluttery.

Photo? What photo? Emergency mission? What mission?

One hot look from this man could melt the polar ice caps ten times faster than the burning of fossil fuels ever could.

He shoved away from the doorway and put on the jacket, never losing hold of my eyes. "Seeing as you tackled the dress problem, what do you need my help with?"

I blinked my way from his eyes to his mouth and licked my lips, time traveling back to our one and only kiss that happened the last week in May.

To keep with our couple cover during an undercover op in Rome, I wound up kissing him. What I hadn't anticipated was for him to turn the moment into a French one. His tongue had cruised between my lips and met mine. I'd been left dizzy, lightheaded, and desperate for more.

I'd attempted to see if "more" might happen between us. There'd been a gas leak at my place, and I bunked at his apartment for the weekend. I'd embarrassingly gone so far as to traipse around in a bikini to sunbathe on his balcony, wearing my sexiest one, too. You would've thought I was a nun in robes with a crucifix around my neck the way he'd treated me.

"You ready?" my brother Alessandro yelled from downstairs, and my attention took a sharp U-turn back to the problem at hand.

"One minute," I called back, eyes returning to Hudson's as I did my best to remember what I'd planned to say to him.

"Bella?" The only person to ever call me that had a tendency to rob me of my precious brain cells whenever he said my name while locking eyes with me. Holding me prisoner right now, in fact. "You nervous about tonight? Is that what's going on?"

I almost snapped my fingers at my side as my thoughts finally clicked in place. *Nerves.* That was what I'd planned to ask him to help me with. Hide my issues in plain sight with some version of the truth. "I'm nervous about the mission. I don't normally go out in the field with you." I turned toward my bedroom, unable to look at him any longer, worried he'd get an accurate read on me and know I wasn't being honest.

"Going solo may raise suspicion. Although I rarely attend my father's political events, when I do, I never go alone. It's, uh, well..."

His reputation regarding his dating life wasn't unknown to me, and I was rather curious how he planned to dig himself out of this hole.

Whipping around, I found him still in the hall, as if there was an unspoken rule about him not being allowed to cross the line into my bedroom. Maybe there was, and I just didn't know it. I wouldn't put it past my brothers to have their own version of the seven deadly sins as guidelines for things Hudson could never commit when it came to me.

"It's expected that you always have a date with you?" I politely offered a reason when he couldn't seem to cough up the truth—that he was a playboy like Alessandro once was.

"Something like that." He fingered the knot of his tie, rotating his neck. "But, uh, if you're uncomfortable going, you should sit this op out."

"No, no." My gaze skated over to my bed as I murmured, "I want to come."

"And I want you to come." There was a subtle rasp of sexiness in his tone that had me biting my lip.

The number of times I wanted that man to make me come, yeah, well, I'd lost count.

Brows drawn together, he grumbled, "I meant, I want you to come to the party."

I smiled. *Holy hell, I'm smiling right now despite the chaos in my head.* "Of course, what else could you possibly have meant?" It was hard not to antagonize the man when he'd gone out of his way to act allergic to me lately.

He braced both palms against the doorframe. "If you want to *go* to the party, then how can I help you with your nerves?" Great, he'd stricken the word *come* from his vocabulary now.

"I suppose there's nothing to really be uneasy about. I'm just going as your plus-one." Hudson had been pretty clear in emphasizing the words "plus one" when reviewing the mission details. *Not* attending as his date or girlfriend. "No weapons allowed inside, and security is as tight as a frog's ass, right?"

"Speaking frogman language now, are you?" he drawled.

"Frog *woman*, you mean?" I winked, trying to play off casual when I was anything but. "Anyway, I overheard Constantine refer to frogs and their derrières when reviewing the mission details earlier." I circled my finger in the air as if winding something up with it, nerves getting to me all over again. "I forgot about the whole 'SEAL and frog-nickname' thing."

At least he was smiling now, and I'd diverted his attention. "Yeah, security will be tight. No weapons on the premises outside of security personnel. But if someone tries to breach, Constantine is on overwatch, and we have two others on lookout with him as well."

"Right. Okay." Fidgeting with the skirt of my dress, I kept

my eyes on the floor and asked, "And will we cross paths with your father tonight at the party?"

Hudson moved away from the doorframe but remained in the hall. "He'll more than likely keep out of sight until the op is done. You know, just in case security isn't as watertight as a frog's ass." The touch of humor catching in his tone stole my eyes his way. "We'll be fine. You won't be anywhere near the danger. Only reason I'm letting you go."

My brothers will be, though. But that was par for the course for them. "And if danger shows up anyway? You know, since danger rarely comes with a party invite."

"What is it you're not telling me?" he asked before I barely finished my words. He pocketed his hand as if trying to fight back his desire to reach for me.

That assessment was more than likely in my head, though. *If only.* I was a non-committal number to this man tonight. His plus-one for an op and nothing more.

"I'm good. Solid. No longer worried. Super tight now. Like that frog and his ass."

My nervous rambling sent the man across that invisible red line and right into my room. "Bella."

I shooed him away with a flick of my wrist. "Don't *Bella* me."

"I'll do it to you all day and night if I have to," he said gruffly before rolling his eyes at how sexual that wound up sounding. Did to me, at least. "Stop smiling at me like that. You know what I meant."

I reached for my lips, discovering I was grinning like a schoolgirl whose pigtails had been pulled by her crush. "Mmmhmm." I sighed, lowering my hand to my side.

One signature scowl of his later, he pleaded, "You *sure* you're fine?"

"I am now. Promise."

The Art of You

Needing to end this conversation before I told him the truth about the origin of my nerves, I searched out my heels so we could leave. Spotting them by the bed, I hastily went over to the sparkly shoes. Even doing my best to be a vision of poise and grace, I still lost my balance. Clearly, I wasn't God's favorite Costa and needed to embarrass myself.

Hudson was at my side in a second, his arm swiftly settling against my back, keeping me upright.

I slowly peeked up at him from over my shoulder, and we quietly stared at each other. Just breathing. Simply existing.

There were so many truths on my tongue dying to slip out, and none of them had to do with that photo. The most painfully obvious fact fighting for freedom was that I didn't want to be his plus-one tonight. I wanted to be his plus-everything.

"You okay?"

I forced a nod, trapping every last thought in my head, saving them for another time and place. You know, for an alternate universe where we could be together.

I finished putting on my heels, and only once I had my balance did he let me go.

"You look nice, by the way." There was a strange dryness to his tone. Like it took all his energy to rip the compliment from his mouth. And with that, he abruptly left my side, went to the window, and parted the curtains. "Enzo has the Porsche parked out front. Surprised he's letting us take it."

Me, too.

Letting the curtains fall into place, he turned around, scanning the room as if only now realizing he was in the sacred space where I slept. Where I got undressed every day. Took care of my own personal, and pleasurable, needs. Did all the things one did in a bedroom.

He cleared his throat. "You'd think when they remodeled

they'd have put the primary bedroom on the other side so there'd be a view of the river."

"Right, a view of the Hudson River from a home in Hudson Yards, where I'm now standing in my bedroom with a man named Hudson."

I'd been swimming in a sea of reminders of this man at every turn. It was no wonder I couldn't get him out of my head, even when we weren't at the office or all of us hanging out at the bar he owned. A bar called *Hudson's*, of course.

I was met with a look that could penetrate steel as he joked, "Can't get rid of me, huh?"

"I never want to." That bit of pure truth floated on a breath between us.

Hudson opened his mouth to respond but never had a chance to say whatever was on his mind, because we were no longer alone.

"You two good?" Constantine's voice echoed around us and into the four chambers of my heart, causing it to skip a beat.

Our attention jerked toward the doorway where my brother stood, his muscular frame filling out the space. Although he'd be on comms tonight, he was still sporting a suit in case anything did go sideways and he had to make an appearance at the party.

"I asked him to go over the mission details again." The words barreled from my mouth fast, my nerves propelling me forward to eat up some of the space between myself and my brother.

For a moment, I was sixteen again, and Constantine had come home earlier than expected on leave from the Navy, catching me making out with my boyfriend. A boyfriend who called later that night and broke up with me. And why wouldn't he? Constantine told him if he were ever alone in my

The Art of You

bedroom again with me, he'd remove his ability to grope me by cutting off both of his hands.

Heaven help my brother's future kids when they began dating.

"You worried about something?" Like all of my brothers, the subtle notes of an Italian accent floated through Constantine's voice whenever he spoke. Sometimes his accent was absent altogether. But then there were moments like now when it became much more pronounced.

I shook my head and started babbling. "Tonight will be super easy. Well, my part, at least. I just need to go as Hudson's arm candy. Easy peasy."

But really, it would be as simple as simple could be. Minus the heart pitter-pattering going on, the chills down my spine, the picture between the magazines, my smorgasbord of feelings that were all over the place right now, and my pulse still firmly cemented in my ears. You know, despite *that*.

"You'll never be arm candy." Hudson's words had Constantine shooting him a funny look.

Yeah, well, his comment earned a what-the-hell one from me, too.

"Not what I meant." Hudson grimaced before peering at me. In an almost somber tone, he clarified, "There's just a lot more to you than being a beautiful woman."

Well . . . damn. Then I remembered we weren't alone and glanced at my brother to see if Hudson's words ignited stars in his eyes like they did in mine. That was highly unlikely. Well, unless they were laser-guided throwing stars.

Constantine zeroed in on Hudson in the same questioning way I'd seen him do toward all my past boyfriends. They were best friends. Why wouldn't he want his best friend as a brother-in-law?

Okay, I was jumping the gun there, but still.

"We should go," my brother stated, then mumbled something in Italian under his breath.

Being the only sibling born in the U.S. meant I had no accent, and my Italian was subpar compared to my parents and brothers. But I still spoke it, and it only took me a second to rewind his words and translate them.

Don't make me kill you one day.

So, you know . . . *that's great.* I rolled my eyes, giving Constantine the proper amount of time to translate that expression.

He grunted and turned to the side, gesturing for me to get my ass moving. The man acted like my father, even though our dad was very much a part of our lives. "A word," he said to Hudson, but from the corner of my eye, I caught Hudson lifting his chin like a directive.

"Someone needs to help her down the stairs so she doesn't trip." Hudson's gentlemanly gesture was appreciated, but I was doubtful it would earn him extra points from my overbearing brother.

Constantine hollered down to Alessandro for an assist. "Give us a second," he requested once I was in the hall, closing *my* door to *my* room and leaving me out of the conversation.

"That man drives me nuts sometimes," I muttered as Alessandro met me at the top of the stairs and offered his arm.

"He makes us all crazy, trust me." Alessandro shrugged. "Guessing he had issues with you being alone in your bedroom with his best friend, huh?"

I shot him a look over my shoulder. "He remembers I'm thirty-two, right?"

"Doubtfully."

Callie was waiting for us at the bottom of the stairs. "Everything okay?"

"From what I can tell, Constantine's just being an *idiota*."

The Art of You

Alessandro let me go and hooked his arm around his wife's back, drawing her tight to his side. The man couldn't go a second without touching her if they were in the same room, and I loved that.

My gorgeous, sweet sister-in-law proved that alleged cold, dead hearts could be revived. Because Alessandro had once believed that organ in his chest was long gone, but everything changed once she came into his life.

"I still can't get over you in that dress." Callie clapped her hands together near her mouth.

"Thank you for raiding your closet and bringing this ball gown with you. Most of my wardrobe consists of jeans and tees with inappropriate sayings."

"And that just makes me love you all that much more." She shifted free of her husband's hold to reach for my forearms and lightly squeezed, continuing to appreciate the gown. "It was made just for me, but it looks even better on you."

"Surprised I didn't need to stuff socks in the built-in bra to fill up the top," I said with a chuckle, and Callie let go of me and flicked her wrist at my joke. But really, she was way more endowed there than I was.

"That's an Ella McAdams original," she added, and my brain short-circuited for probably the third time tonight.

I'm wearing Ella's dress? I'd met her and her husband at Callie and Alessandro's wedding in Nashville in August, but my family already had a history with Ella's husband.

Not only did Enzo know Jesse from some past-life "employment," but he'd been the one to break the news to Enzo last year that our sister Bianca's murderer wasn't quite as six feet under as we'd all thought. Thankfully, her killer was now, but . . .

Shit. That was definitely not what I needed to be thinking about right now. So much for all that hard work to compartmentalize my thoughts and push forward for the sake of the mission tonight. Gone, gone, gone. Nerves firmly in place once again.

"Anyway." Alessandro with the award-winning redirect, somehow recognizing I needed a subject change. Maybe he did, too.

Fortunately, Enzo provided a much-needed distraction. He casually strolled into the foyer, dangling a slice of pizza between his fingers. "You two can't keep your hands off each other."

"Like you're any better with Maria," Alessandro reminded him, and Enzo chased away a smirk with the back of his hand.

Both Enzo and Alessandro had flown in for this last-minute op. While Callie had been able to make the trip with Alessandro, Enzo had to leave his wife back home in Charlotte since she was pregnant with twins. He'd been hesitant to be away from Maria, but Hudson—who was spearheading this operation—had promised the mission would be quick. Hudson had accepted the job as a personal favor for his dad.

"Why are you wolfing down pizza right now?" Alessandro asked Enzo after he'd devoured the slice in practically two bites.

"Can't operate on an empty stomach," Enzo said around a mouthful, brushing the crumbs on the sides of his black fatigues.

He and Alessandro were in military clothes, charged with handling the dangerous behind-the-scenes work while I went as Hudson's plus-one to the fancy A-list political soiree at some big campaign donor's home in Scarsdale.

"Don't worry, I left you a slice." Enzo winked at our brother before directing his attention to the stairs behind me.

Ah, the eldest has returned. Hopefully he didn't lay into Hudson about being in my bedroom.

The fact Hudson didn't make eye contact with me as he came down had my concerns rebooting. But at least I was once again distracted from the OG problem of the evening: the mystery photo.

Enzo reached into his pocket and tossed his keys to Hudson. "No scratches." Although Enzo didn't live in New York anymore, and we'd converted his former home in Chelsea into the new headquarters for our off-the-books security company, he'd kept his beloved Porsche in the city to use whenever he visited.

"I'll be on my best behavior." Pretty sure there was some double meaning from Hudson on that, especially when Constantine nodded at him.

I bit back a resigned sigh, then went through the motions of hugging everyone goodbye as if I were going off to war instead of to a party.

"I'll be just down the block from the location," Constantine promised in my ear during our quick embrace. "I've got your six. No worries."

"Thank you." I patted his arm and faced the door, finding Hudson holding it open with his back.

As we started for Enzo's metallic-gray Porsche by the curb, Hudson commented, "It's just a quickie, no sweat." He abruptly added, "You know what I mean." How many times had that phrase left his mouth tonight?

"But do I?" I teased.

"Just get in," he ordered, fighting off a smile.

Maybe you aren't so allergic to me after all?

He extended his forearm so I could keep my balance and duck inside, but with the odd feeling we were being watched—and *not* by my siblings—I stole a look at the building on the other side of the street.

Chills scraped over my skin, goose bumps forming there.

"Something wrong?" Hudson asked as the curtains on the fourth floor swooshed closed.

"No."

I'd barely squeezed the word out between my teeth before he helped me inside. Hand on the roof of the car while holding the door open, he stared down at me. "You sure you're okay?"

Eyes on the road ahead so I wouldn't lie straight to his face, I whispered, "Absolutely."

Chapter 2

Hudson

Scarsdale, New York

I'D BEEN DREADING this assignment ever since my father made the request for help two days ago. I not only hated attending political events, but willingly bringing Bella into the lion's den, armed with only a tie and fake-as-fuck smile, didn't sit well with me.

What made it worse was that I had to watch Bella bite her tongue at every turn, knowing she could school every one of these political types who tried to educate her on matters of world affairs. As much as I wanted to let her unleash that gorgeous mouth and roast them like the pigs some of these men were, we were there for an operation. So, if she could nod, politely smile, and behave, then I'd find a way to do the same.

But if our target didn't arrive soon, I had a feeling I was one conversation away from losing my self-control. If another asshole spoke to Bella like she was just my arm candy with a box of rocks for brains, he'd be eating his teeth instead of caviar.

Bella tugged on the sleeve of my suit jacket, and I lowered

my gaze to my arm in mild amusement. "Yes?" A smile cut across my face, probably the first legitimate one of the evening.

"What if we dance? Maybe it'll keep the piranhas away," she offered softly, pointing her big brown eyes at me.

I glanced around the room, deliberating the benefits of putting ourselves out there as the third couple to get lost in the music. If dancing would keep me from decking a guy until our target arrived, it wasn't such a bad idea.

Without waiting for my answer, Bella let go of my sleeve and began moving from side to side. Swaying her hips. Dragging her hand sexily along the line of her collarbone as she closed her eyes. I'd known her for a long time, and she'd dance to anything, never giving a damn what people thought, even if she didn't have the best rhythm.

I couldn't take my eyes off her, a woman who fit the phrase "born to stand out" to a T.

Putting my hands on her, especially in public, was the last thing I should've been doing, but it was also the only thing I wanted to do.

Selling myself on the idea that if I let her go it alone I'd look like an asshole, I stepped forward and hauled her into my arms. A bit too abruptly, because based on her eyes startling open and her hands flying to my chest, I'd caught her off guard.

Holding her hips, I rasped, "Is this what you wanted?"

She nodded as if in a trance. Made two of us.

My hands went to the small of her back in an entirely too possessive way, drawing her closer.

She leaned into me, lifting her chin to maintain eye contact. Neither of us were dancing, just coasting through the moment as if we were alone. Everyone and everything were now background noise.

The desire to drag my knuckles up the column of her throat

and along her jawline, encourage her mouth to open for me, had me locking my hand into a fist at her back.

The seconds added up as we stayed in this position, and it was only when the band changed songs that she pointed out in a whisper, "We're just standing here."

Right, the dancing thing still needed to happen. *Not* the eye-fucking that was going on now. Behavior I'd worked so hard not to do in her bedroom earlier.

And shit, once Constantine hacked the security cameras, he'd have eyes on us. I didn't need to catch hell from him tonight. Not that he'd lectured or warned me in her bedroom. He said nothing about his sister at all. Honestly, he and I both knew he didn't need to. It was what he didn't have to say that I still heard loud and fucking clear. His sister was off-limits.

I didn't need Constantine to remind me I was bad for Bella. I was well aware of that.

"You've got this. Just step side to side. And maybe act like you don't hate being this close to me." She smiled.

"Not sure if I'm that great of an actor," I teased back, finally moving with her.

Her hands were still on my chest, and she circled one around my tie and gave it a little tug. "You're downright horrible."

I dipped my chin, focusing on her eyes. "Oh, you can read me that well, can you?" That came out entirely too flirty. I was on a motherfucking roll tonight of what *not* to say to and do around my best friend's sister.

She nodded in response, then licked her lips, continuing to test my patience. To test my willpower to abstain from driving my fingers into her thick hair and fisting it while dropping my mouth over hers.

She rotated her hips, keeping hold of my tie while knocking her pelvis into my crotch.

I shot her a stern look. *Fucking naughty.*

At some point, I deserved to be sainted. Or knighted. Or whatever the hell it was called when a man had temptation in his face 24/7, but still behaved himself.

"You know how many times Bianca and I watched *Ghost*?"

I had no idea where her question came from, but it was very much like Bella to pluck random topics from the air and turn them into conversation centerpieces. But then it clicked. The song playing was "Unchained Melody" from the *Ghost* soundtrack.

"Thought that movie was from my generation, not yours." Unlike her, I grew up in the '80s, and I needed to remember that ten-year age gap as yet another reason not to give in to whatever I'd been feeling lately.

"Pretty sure it belongs to all generations." She finally let go of my tie, sighing. "Don't worry. My sister waited until I was old enough to let me watch it." Still dancing in place, bumping into my crotch again as some cruel form of punishment, she continued her story, "I'm also pretty sure ninety percent of the population had a crush on Patrick Swayze back in the day. I know I did." Her soft, slightly nervous laugh managed to penetrate my suit jacket. It rolled right over my skin, and a strange feeling of some-fucking-thing flew up my spine. "You give off the same vibes as him."

I had no idea what that meant, so I kept quiet.

"But can you *dirty* dance like him?" She lifted her brows a few times.

To be honest, just dancing like this with her was making me forget why we were at a fifteen-million-dollar home in Scarsdale. Forget lives were on the line if everything didn't play out perfectly tonight. Of course, the two of us didn't have to do much more than just exist at this time and in this space for the operation to unfold as planned.

And now I was tempted to sling her arms over my shoulders, slip my hand behind her back, and show her I could dance like Swayze. Not only would that make front-page headlines and give my father's campaign manager a heart attack, but it'd also give Bella the wrong idea about us.

"You changed movies on me. Thought we were talking about *Ghost*," I deflected before I also forgot we could only ever be friends and colleagues. Before I gave in to desire, creating heart attacks and heartbreak.

"Guess neither now, because the song changed." A cute, lopsided smile stole over her lips. "But Elvis is playing, so if you'd like to move your hips like him, I'll happily back up and give you the floor to do so." She batted her lashes a few times, and the Bella I'd known for years was front and center, a stark contrast to the nervous woman I'd found on the other side of her bedroom door tonight.

She was sweet, funny, charming, and for the past several months, a motherfucking tease to my senses. Quite literally, all of them.

Sight: The woman was an Italian goddess, so that one was easy.

Smell: The medley of perfumes she rotated between each day of the week. Of course, she never stuck to one. But she always smelled so good I had to fight the temptation to sniff her wrist or kiss the side of her neck.

Hearing: As already established, her laugh.

Taste: She'd kissed me for "the sake of a mission" in Rome, and I'd been savoring that memory ever since.

Touch: Did now count? Having her in my arms.

Intuition: That unspoken sixth sense—knowing I'd only break her heart if I threw logic out the window—intervened and pulled me away from her, ending the dance.

"You okayyy?" She'd repackaged my question to her outside the Porsche by tacking on her typical dramatic flair.

Constantine popped over the comms in our ears as if on cue, letting us know he had eyes on us.

The moment fully broken, I immediately stepped back from her as she gently shoved away from my chest.

Our comms were currently muted, so I searched out the camera on the ceiling and gave him a nod, acknowledging him.

Eyes back on Bella, I answered her with a partial truth. "I'm fine. I just need a drink." I leaned in and mouthed, "You know, for the sake of appearances." I followed up my words with a wink, hoping she wouldn't see right through me. To realize that ever since that kiss in Rome I'd been on the verge of losing control when she was near me.

"Okay." She smiled, then requested, "Aperol spritz for me, please."

We made our way to the cash bar that overlooked the lit-up courtyard outside, where a few men in suits were gathered, smoking cigars and probably discussing their stock portfolios.

After handling Bella's order, I set my sights on the bottle of Macallan Scotch, hating myself for having the same taste as my father, but not enough to stop myself from asking for a double. Neat, just like the governor liked. Not that I planned to indulge, given I was working.

I paid the bartender, offering a generous tip, then turned to see Bella scanning the room while sipping her cocktail.

So much for our drinks only being props.

Once I had my scotch, I gave in and took a healthy swallow, nearly dropping the glass when I could've sworn I saw an old SEAL teammate.

No, not possible.

I focused on the crowded corner of the room, feeling like I'd seen a ghost even though he wasn't dead.

"Are you sure you're good? Did I say something while dancing to upset you? Like, do you have something against Patrick Swayze?" Her tone was more teasing than anything else, and she saved me from nearly falling into the past, to my last deployment in Afghanistan.

I shook my head. Not really an answer but it was the best I could do. I looked around the room again for a man whose name hadn't been on the guest list, or I'd have sure as hell noticed.

Losing my mind. I focused back on the beautiful woman before me. "Nothing against Swayze, no." I lifted my glass to my mouth, then hesitated, deciding drinking was a bad idea after my hallucination, and the glass should remain nothing more than a prop in my hand.

"Well, glad you don't have anything against him. I might have to unfriend you on Facebook if you did," she said softly.

"I don't have Facebook," I reminded her, taking two seconds too long to realize she'd been joking. *I'm still strung-the-fuck-tight.* Walks down memory lane could do that, though. Especially remembering anything from 2010.

Bella set her free hand on my forearm while angling her head. "I'm going to ask you again, so don't get annoyed. But are you okay?"

"What? You think I'm lying the way you were to me by the Porsche?"

She rolled her lips inward as if worried her thoughts were conspiring against her, and she might slip and tell me the truth. Tell me the real reason she'd taken so long with the zipper in her bedroom.

"Exactly what I thought," I admitted, then set aside my drink, too tempted to toss back the rest of the scotch in an attempt to help block out the memories from my past I couldn't quite shake now.

Bella placed her drink on the bartop table next to mine and pushed up in her heels to whisper in my ear, "I need a distraction so I'm not so distracted by something else so I can focus on the mission. Does that make sense?"

Somehow? Perfectly. Losing both my mind and control, I banded my arm around her waist and slid my hand up to her bare back, allowing my palm to move higher beneath her hair and to the nape of her neck.

Eyes on mine, she breathily said my name as I continued to caress her skin like we were two lost souls searching to be found and completely alone in space. She shuddered beneath my touch, arching into me. *Responding* to the connection, the same as I was.

"Oh, I see what you're doing," she murmured. "I asked you for a distraction, and you're giving me one."

That wasn't what I'd meant to do, but she was right. Consider us both distracted.

"You two okay?" With those three words in our ears, Constantine splintered us apart, breaking a moment we couldn't have.

I cleared my throat, backed away from her, and discreetly tapped the device well-hidden in my left ear to unmute it. "She's nervous about the op. Calming her down."

"Yeah, well, the target is here. Not in the room yet, but on the property," he let us know, unable to hide the suspicious bite to his tone.

"Roger that." Muting our conversation again, I set my hand on the bartop table, waiting for our target to make an appearance. When my eyes fell back to hers, and I found her staring off into the distance with a lost look, I couldn't help but press. "Tell me why you needed the distraction."

"I thought we established I—"

"We established nothing." I heaved out a deep breath,

worried about her secrets, remembering what happened when the last female Costa kept a secret from me.

Now Bianca was dead, and if she had opened up to me fourteen years ago, maybe I could have helped her. Maybe she'd be alive and happily married, living her best life.

When she continued staring everywhere but at me, I asked, "What's wrong?" My words were gruff. Like two harsh sounds poking through the stuffy, political air.

Her shoulders sagged from the weight of whatever lie she was no doubt about to offer. "Just felt like I was being watched earlier when we got into the Porsche."

There was a hole the size of Texas in that one sentence. "What do you mean?"

"I mean exactly what I said."

"You do know what I used to do for a living, right?" But I didn't need to have trained at Quantico and been an FBI agent to detect her lie. "Don't forget what *we* do now." No rules or red tape when questioning people in this new line of work with her family at our security company.

She locked her arms in a defensive position across her breasts. "We shouldn't be discussing this now. Tonight isn't the time for this conversation, especially not here."

I opened my mouth to protest, but, from my peripheral vision, realized we had incoming. The ambush happened quickly, catching both of us off guard. A woman neither Bella, nor I, would want to swap words with, stopped before us.

Dealing with businessmen and politicians and keeping my mouth shut was one thing. Talking to a reporter and behaving? *Not happening.*

Concern for Bella had me taking a protective step around her, hoping to block this vicious woman from bothering her.

"Do my eyes deceive me? Is *the* Hudson Ashford stepping into the limelight and attending one of his father's events? Been a year, at least, since you've shown your face at one of these parties." Kit offered her hand, knowing damn well I wouldn't shake it.

Ignoring the journalist, I checked my watch as Constantine popped into my ear. "She's now inside with her three security detail, and they're a match to the names on the guest list we already cleared. But if we have eyes on her . . ."

Then so do the bad guys. They would definitely have tapped into the surveillance cameras the same as Constantine.

I discreetly touched the device hidden in my ear, unmuting it so Constantine would be able to hear me as well.

"Hold position for now," he directed.

The last thing I wanted to do was hold this position and talk to a reporter.

"Isabella Costa. Wow, I almost didn't recognize you all dressed up like that." Kit's words knocked me back to the new problem at hand. "Feels like yesterday you found your sister murdered. What's it been? Fourteen years now?"

Before I had a chance to determine the best way to handle this thorn in our sides, Bella sidestepped me, facing off with the reporter.

"Did you know I'd be here tonight?" Bella asked, a visible tremble moving through her. "Was it you earlier? Did you do that?"

"Do what?" I shot out in alarm.

"I don't know what sick game you're playing, but crawl back into the hole where you came from and leave my family alone." Bella abruptly turned, lifted the skirt of her dress, and started to walk away.

I zeroed in on Kit, pulled in two directions, knowing damn well this one didn't deserve more from me than a quick question. "What in the hell did you do?"

Kit shrugged, watching Bella as she cut farther away from us heading to the opposite side of the room.

I was about to lose the ability to remain a gentleman and keep my mouth closed, creating a situation that'd require "cleaning up" by my father's campaign manager. To say Kit and I had gone head-to-head a time or two in the past was an understatement. Unable to stop myself despite the fact we were drawing attention, I ordered, "Leave her alone, or so help me."

She casually reached for my scotch, clearly knowing it'd been mine. Exactly how long had she been watching us?

"Maybe you need a drink to calm down. Take the edge off so you can give me an exclusive on your relationship with Isabella Costa." Her eyes narrowed on mine. "Tell me, is she sleeping with you to gain favors for her family with the governor? Were you sleeping with her sister back in the day, too?"

My head nearly exploded before Constantine's words pounded into my ears. "Walk away before we both lose it." He followed the order with another directive. "It's time to move in on the target."

I would've told off this woman if it weren't for the voice of reason in my ear.

Without giving Kit another second of my time, I forged a path through the crowded room. Quick, determined strides carried me Bella's way.

It was go time.

We had a life to save.

The sooner we got the hell out of the party, the better for all of us.

Chapter 3

Hudson

"It's time," I told Bella even though I knew she had to have heard her brother's order over comms. "You okay?"

Her shoulders sloped forward, and she couldn't shake free the worry creases around her eyes. "Of course."

I let her lie go for now since we had a mission to complete. One problem at a time. I was still working hard to dial down my heart rate after the confrontation with Kit. Her name hadn't been on the guest list the last I'd checked it out.

"Got her in your sights?" Constantine asked once we'd entered the foyer.

"We do," Bella answered, which meant she'd already unmuted her comm.

The "her" in question was Carla Aldana, the Spanish ambassador to the United States, and the reason we were here tonight.

Carla's daughter had been kidnapped from her dorm at Sarah Lawrence College a few nights ago. In typical fashion, the abductors demanded Carla not reach out to the Feds or her daughter would die. So, here we were.

The Art of You

Bella and I lingered by the two sweeping marble staircases, waiting for our cue from the ambassador. Knowing Constantine wouldn't be the only one with eyes on us, we had to play this out just right or things might go bust for Alessandro and Enzo's part of the op tonight.

Rafael, the ambassador's head of security, brought his wrist to his mouth and began discreetly talking into his mic. His eyes cut across the foyer, and he gave me a light nod of recognition.

I gently squeezed Bella's arm. "Ready?"

"Yeah, I think so." Not exactly a confident answer from her. Damn Kit for being there.

I took a second to check in with Constantine and asked, "How are things looking for Alpha Team?"

"Three minutes out from moving on target," Constantine said, which meant Alessandro and Enzo had located where the ambassador's daughter was being held. "Buy the guys some time. They'll be fast-roping in soon."

"Roger," I confirmed in a low voice as Rafael approached.

The Spaniard opened his palm. "*Señora* Aldana requests a word with you two in the library."

"We'd be honored to speak with the ambassador. My father should be arriving soon as well." Those last words were meant for the eavesdroppers at my left, anxious to put eyes on my dad since it was his party after all, and he was still MIA.

I took Bella's hand in my own, suddenly uneasy at the fact I was unarmed even though I knew going into the night that'd be the case. My Glock was currently a useless piece of polymer and steel in a lockbox in the Porsche's trunk.

Three doors down, we joined the ambassador in the library as prearranged. We'd already done our own background checks on everyone attending the party, including the ambassador's people. I should've been comforted by the vetting and the fact that my father's security team had thoroughly swept the place before the start of the party, but I wasn't about to let my guard down.

Carla gestured to Rafael to close the double doors, and once he did, her other two security detail protectively flanked her sides.

I avoided looking up at the security camera in the corner of the room, doing my best to act ignorant to the fact it was there, and that we were presumably also being watched by the assholes who took the ambo's daughter.

"Quite clever of the FBI to come to you for help, Mister Ashford, but it was unnecessary." Carla's green eyes were sharp on me as if we were the only people in the room. "However, I do hope you start coming to more of your father's events to support him. I'm sure he'd like that."

Well, that low blow hadn't been part of the rehearsal, but props to her for keeping up with the act of a passive-aggressive diplomat. "Oh, I'm sure he would. But tonight, I'm here for you, not him."

Carla's gaze moved to where I held Bella's hand. "Well, as my government told the Bureau when they reached out, my daughter was not taken." Eyes back on me, she continued, "Her roommate was confused and should not have called the police. My men picked her up from campus and escorted her to our embassy in D.C." She opened her palms. "Would I be at a party if Lola had been abducted?" She was quite the actress, managing to put on a show for the cameras while knowing her daughter was in danger.

"You would be if her kidnappers told you not to seek assistance from the Feds. To act like business as usual," I cut straight to it. "This party has been on your schedule for months. You were already in New York visiting from D.C. when Lola was taken, and they more than likely threatened to kill her if you were to change anything." That was the truth.

Now time for some acting myself. "They probably also told you that as long as you pay the ransom, and don't bring in the Feds, they'll let your daughter go. My guess is the exchange is taking place tonight, somewhere nearby." I released Bella's hand and shifted up my jacket sleeve, checking the time on my watch. 23:28. "Criminals are excellent at keeping their word, so I can see why you'd trust them."

"And hypothetically speaking, let's say you're right about everything," Carla said as I adjusted my jacket sleeve back in place, her accent thicker that time. "You don't think these alleged kidnappers would believe the FBI would truly stand down even if a diplomat ordered them to, now do you? Wouldn't they suspect you're a plant by the Bureau?" She went to the desk and set her back to it, locking her eyes on me and her arms over her gold dress. Her security entourage followed her over. "Wouldn't they believe your last-minute attendance tonight is to try and thwart their efforts? They'll assume the Feds are close to the party, waiting so they can catch them once I have my daughter back."

"One minute," Constantine shared, letting me know I needed to buy Alessandro and Enzo sixty more seconds.

"You know they'll never let your daughter go, right? You'll pay them, and they'll either want more from you, or they'll go ahead and kill her." My words had Carla blinking her focus all the way down to her heels. This may have been a charade to stall and buy my guys time, but my words were still the truth, and she was clearly doing her damnedest to keep herself together given the circumstances.

"Fortunately, as I told the FBI and you tonight, my daughter is safe at the embassy." She heaved out a deep breath, then stood tall without leaning against the desk for support.

"Right." I scanned the faces of the three men who had her six tonight. "So, you're saying I really did come to this party for nothing. And no ransom drop-off is happening near here." Well, it wasn't actually, but I needed the kidnappers to believe I thought that.

"Your being here doesn't have to be considered a waste of time." She shot me a polished diplomatic smile, then nodded at Bella. "You're here with a beautiful woman, might as well enjoy your time together. Have a drink. A dance?"

Bella looped her arm around mine, remaining quiet, but I knew her heart had to be racing as we waited for good news over comms.

"Also, as I said before, I'm sure your father would enjoy your company. Well, whenever he gets here, at least." That light laugh from her had to be fucking tough. I couldn't imagine being in her shoes.

"Alpha Team is moving in on target now," Constantine announced over comms. "The second possible target was acquired on my end as well. Hold for more."

That second target had me sweeping my gaze lazily over to the security camera. Whoever else was watching us now had no clue they were seconds away from coming face-to-face with death.

Carla gestured toward the doors. "So, shall we return to the party?"

"The ambo's daughter is safe." At Constantine's words, Bella squeezed my arm in relief.

I immediately shared the news, "Your daughter is okay. My team has her."

Carla cupped her mouth, taking a few faltering steps forward. The two guards at her side caught her, preventing her from crumpling to the floor as she let the tears she'd been holding back fall freely. She was a mother before us now, not an ambassador.

"Gracias. Thank you." Carla swiped at her tears with the backs of her hands, working to collect herself.

"I don't understand." The security guard at her left, Eduardo, said something in Spanish, which I roughly translated as, *Why didn't you tell us about the real plan?*

Rafael answered for her, also in Spanish. From what I understood, while he'd been in the know about the events tonight, apparently her other guards hadn't.

"We clear here?" I asked Constantine while her security personnel continued with their heated chat.

"Overwatch took out two men who came for me after I killed their tech guy in the van down the street." He paused, sounding only mildly breathless from the altercation. "In my defense, he tried to kill me first."

Sure he did. "Any intel in that van to suggest how many guys they have on-site here?"

"From the looks of it, only three were transmitting from their secure line, including their comms guy in the van. We should be clear, but heads on a swivel just in case."

"Roger that," I responded as the doors flung open. On instinct, I protectively hauled Bella around behind me but went at ease seeing my father.

"I just heard the news Lola's okay." He went straight for Carla, pulling her into his arms as Rafael shut the doors to any potential eavesdroppers.

Based on the way my father was holding her, with their bodies flush, I had to assume they were more than just friends, which was why she'd gone to him for help when her daughter was taken in the first place. *And* why he'd turned to me for a private assist, bypassing the Bureau so the ambassador didn't risk her daughter's life by working with them.

"Everything is good. Three tangos on-site down, but I'd keep your security detail on alert in case we have any more assholes outside," I told my father, even though it was obvious Constantine had already texted him. I just wasn't sure how much he'd had time to share.

My father let go of Carla and faced me, working the knot of his tie loose. "I made a call to the FBI director and let him know that only one agent was privately tasked with the rescue on my behalf." He slapped a hand over my shoulder. "But you were not involved tonight. We clear?"

"Yeah, got it." I didn't exactly make it a habit of letting my former employer know what I did for a living since technically taking justice into my own hands wasn't entirely legal.

"The guys are about to hand over Lola to your Fed friend," Constantine shared.

Special Agent Adelina Cattaneo was the only one I'd pulled in from the Bureau for help. We'd remained in contact ever since I'd turned in my badge years ago, and I trusted her.

"Your daughter will soon be in FBI custody, and you can meet up with her." I tipped my head at Carla. "You did good. I can see why you're in the job you are."

My father drew Carla tight to his side, the same way I had Bella. I quickly read the, *Don't ask,* look in his blue eyes. No worries there. Who he dated wasn't my business.

"Diplomacy doesn't always work, which is why I'm grateful to have people like you helping out." Carla patted my chest, then glanced at her security team, shooting the two guys who hadn't been read in on the mission details what I viewed as an apologetic look.

"You keep anyone alive for questioning?" Eduardo asked me.

"My brothers kept two of the kidnappers alive," Constantine answered, and I relayed the information.

"Why? You want a sit down with them?" I asked Eduardo.

"These men think they could get away with taking *Señora*

Aldana's daughter, so yeah, I do want to *talk* to them," Eduardo hissed.

"Well, that's not up to me." Something about his tone and the look in his eyes rubbed me the wrong way. "We won't be babysitting these assholes for too long. You'll have to talk to the Feds about that." I started for the door and Rafael stepped around us, beating me to the punch to open up.

"This stays out of the press, yes?" Carla called out.

"Of course," my father piped up for me before we made a quick exit from the library and started for the front of the estate.

"You have eyes out front?" I asked Constantine. "We all set to move out?"

"I'm back in position, and from my vantage point," he let me know, "you're good to go."

Once Bella and I were outside, I followed her gaze, finding another reason aside from Eduardo to be uneasy. There was an unfinished conversation Bella and I still needed to have about the woman in the doorway.

Kit held up her phone and took a picture of us.

Just great. I was a second away from doing something stupid—taking her phone and throwing it into the fountain out front—but Bella tugged my arm.

"She's not worth it," she pleaded, and I slowly turned as the valet came over.

"You sure?" I asked while mindlessly handing him the ticket.

"Listen to her, she's right." Constantine needed to get out of my head and clear of my conscience.

"Unless you're worried about a photo of us ending up online that claims we're dating?" Bella kept her voice low as if her brother wouldn't overhear her.

"If you're good, I'm good." Well, I still didn't feel "good," but hopefully once I had Bella safely back at home, I'd be more relaxed.

"Nice job in there, by the way. Should've been an actor for a living." That was Marc in my ear that time, transmitting over our line for the first time tonight. He was one of the SEALs Constantine had brought in for overwatch.

"Yeah, I deserve an Oscar." Most of what I'd said in the library had been a version of the truth, though. Carla had to carry the burden of acting unaffected and keeping it together. While we'd run through the plans with her over a secure line before the party, preparing her as much as possible, pulling it off with her daughter's life at stake was quite different.

"Once you're safely out of here, and we handle the bodies we racked up here, I'm going to meet up with the others and wrap up those loose ends," Constantine announced, which was code for: delete evidence of our involvement tonight.

"Yeah, okay." I thought back to the exchange with Eduardo in the library, deciding my gut was rarely wrong about people. "I know we checked out the ambo's security team, and we cleared them, but she chose to leave two of her guys in the dark tonight, and I trust my instincts more than I do background checks."

"You think this was an inside job?" Bella asked.

"I don't know, but I'd rather be overcautious and have those two guys followed tonight just in case," I said before scanning the area, ensuring the ambo's people weren't within earshot.

"Agreed. Marc and Malik can tail them," Constantine confirmed as one of the valets pulled up in the Porsche.

"I'll get Bella back home now."

"Stay with her until we know more." I was about to remove the device from my ear before he issued one more order. "But there's no need to walk my sister to her bedroom. I'm sure she can find her own way just fine."

Chapter 4

Hudson

"You really think one of her security guards helped the kidnappers?"

I glanced over at Bella in the passenger seat. "Just a hunch. Hopefully, I'm wrong." Eyes back on the road, I merged onto the Bronx River Parkway to head into the city and get Bella home.

I'd let Callie walk Bella to her bedroom so she didn't trip in her dress, but I'd be parking my ass on the couch downstairs for as long as it took until I knew everything was good.

I rested my free hand in my lap, curling my fingers into a fist. At least now I had the comfortable weight of my Glock at my back, hidden by my suit jacket.

Bella tapped at the screen on the dash, turning on music. If that put her at ease, I was all for it. "Oh, Teddy Swims. I love this artist." She leaned back in her seat, drumming her nails on the skirt of her dress, seemingly more at peace.

"So, your nerves from *before* are gone?" I couldn't help but press.

"Mmmhmm."

"That's not an answer."

"Close enough to one," she chirped.

The challenging little hitch in her tone had me easing up off the pedal. She was still hiding something from me, and I was fairly certain that something had to do with the reporter.

"I can't let this go, and you know it. First, you mentioned being watched. And then that thing happened with you and Kit. What's really going on?"

After a few moments of only Teddy Swims's voice between us, she finally gifted me with hers. "How about you start first? Something had you distracted at the party *before*hand, too. What's the story there?"

There was only one person in all of human fucking history who could turn the tables on me and get me to bend to their will, and it was the woman parked next to me with pouty lips and expressive light brown eyes.

Not today, though.

"Okay, okay. To be honest, running into Kit tonight made me feel better."

I faked a laugh. "Didn't look that way."

"Realizing she was behind it . . ." She let her words trail off, leaving me hanging.

I gripped the steering wheel tighter than necessary. "Behind what?"

She looked away from me. "We should save this conversation for later. But if you want to talk about your issues, then by all means, go ahead."

"The mission was a success. Lola's alive and safe. And, hopefully, all the bad guys in connection to her kidnapping are now either in custody or dead. If not, we'll deal with it." I shook my head. "So, the only immediate issue I need to deal with is sitting next to me."

We didn't need to talk about my problems when she *was*

The Art of You

the problem. Testing me at every turn since our op in Rome. And I was failing miserably at keeping my mind from going there. To all the fucking *theres* that could ever be involving this woman naked and in my arms as I made her come.

"Seeee."

Whenever she elongated a word like that, I couldn't help but wonder how a breathy and dragged-out *yes* would sound coming from her mouth instead.

"If you were okay, you wouldn't be snapping at me." She pointed at the front window. "And you should have your eyes on the road and not on me so you don't kill us, thank you very much."

I pinned her with one of my signature looks—the kind I used to get criminals to talk during interrogation. Somehow, the dark expression seemed to have the opposite effect on her.

Did she realize she was tracing her thumb along the line of her mouth? A mouth I'd thought about doing some problematic things with. I was getting close. Really, really damn close to actually snapping, and not in the way she'd said I'd done.

I was on the verge of begging my best friend's sister for just one night. One hard, hot fuck. One opportunity to get whatever this was clear from my system so I could stop wanting her all the damn time.

I mean, God help me, how much more could I put up with from her and not give in?

I still had no clue how she'd spent a weekend at my place a few months back without her winding up beneath me in my bed. Without me tearing off that fucking string bikini she insisted on strutting around in. She even went so far as making us grilled cheese sandwiches in those two little triangle scraps of hot pink, like it was the most normal thing in the world. The number of times I had to stroke my cock in the shower so I didn't ask her to sit on my face was—

"Hudson." She reached for the hand on my lap and patted it, too damn close to discovering the bulge that'd formed while I was lost in memories of that weekend. "You seem tense."

"You're making me that way." Double meaning fully fucking intended. "Just tell me what's going on." I did my best to wrestle the conversation back to her issues and away from mine. Maybe I really did have more than one. There was no discounting the fact I'd have sworn I saw someone I used to know at the party. No way it would've been him. And he definitely hadn't been on the list. But that uncertainty lingered, pulling at my focus, and my sanity.

"Eyes on the road, not on me. Remember?" She returned her hand to her lap, thank God. "The weather is shit—"

"The weather is just fine." That was a lie. I could feel a storm coming, not that I'd admit it. "Now talk."

She peeked out her side window, searching for something that wasn't there, like my patience. "Well, it feels like rain is coming."

"It does, does it?" I finally relaxed my grip on the steering wheel, realizing I was white-knuckling the thing.

She straightened in her seat, hands now chasing up and down her arms as if cold.

I reached out to turn on the heat as she shifted in her seat again, the slit in her dress parting and exposing her entire leg. My hand went still on the control panel, and I momentarily forgot about the road and the heat.

"Hudson. Where are your eyes supposed to be?"

Not on your legs.

At her gasp, I jerked my attention to the road ahead, realizing I was close to swerving into the oncoming lane. Thankfully, no one was there.

And I was done talking about the damn weather. "You've

yet to answer me," I reminded her, trying to get things back on topic.

"Oh, was there a question you asked?"

The sass in her tone took effort that time. I knew her well enough to know she was faking that bit of attitude to dodge whatever it was she was scared to share.

Before I had a chance to demand an answer from her again, my phone rang, and I couldn't forward this one to voicemail. It was Special Agent Adelina Cattaneo, the one I'd called in for help at the last minute for the kidnapping case. The music stopped so the call could come through over CarPlay.

"Hey, everything good? Lola okay?" I asked Adelina upon answering, hating Bella had earned herself more time to evade our conversation.

"Yeah, she's a tough girl. She owes you all her life," Adelina was quick to respond.

Having moved to the U.S. later in life to attend college, her Italian accent was more prominent than the Costas'. She'd become a citizen with one goal in mind: become an FBI agent to help find her sister who'd been kidnapped when she was three. Sadly, she never found her twin, but she'd saved a lot of other lives working for the Bureau.

"Will you catch hell from your boss for not giving him the heads-up about the op tonight?" The last thing I wanted was for her to get into trouble.

"Not much he can say. Your father's got my back. Plus, in the director's eyes, this is a win for the Bureau. He can act like the FBI really saved the daughter of a high-profile diplomat and all that. You know how that goes."

"Yeah, I don't miss that shit," I admitted. "Did my team give you a heads-up about my concerns regarding the ambassador's security detail? It's only a gut feeling, but we should keep an eye on them. Dig deeper into their backgrounds since we're not under the gun to save Lola now."

"I think it was Constantine Costa who called me. He's, uh, an intense one, huh?"

"To say the least," I said while glancing at Bella. She was staring out her window, making it impossible to get a read on her.

"You alone right now?" Adelina asked tentatively.

No, the sexy bane of my existence is with me.

I'd swear Bella heard my thoughts. She shifted in her seat and rolled her eyes before flicking her wrist toward the road. There was a wreck up ahead.

"No, I'm with Isabella Costa," I finally remembered to answer. "She attended the party with me. You know, for appearances' sake." Thankfully, nothing went sideways tonight, and Bella had never been at risk.

"Ah, I see," Adelina mused, probably reading more into my comment than she should have.

I got off the parkway to take a back road so I could avoid the standstill traffic.

"Well, when the dust settles from all of this, let's get lunch. There's something I want to tell you."

"A good something?" I never knew when it came to Adelina.

"Definitely a good something."

Thank God for that. The woman deserved it.

After we exchanged a few more words and ended the call, I pulled up Google Maps on the dash to find a new route.

When I was all set, Bella began scrolling the music app for another channel. "I know she's FBI, but how well do you know her? You two sound close-close."

Was that jealousy in her voice? Not that there was anything to be jealous about. "We were at Quantico together,

The Art of You

then assigned to the same FBI field office here in New York. We stayed friends after I left the Bureau." Not on any kind of deep level, though.

Adelina didn't know my secrets, and I didn't know hers. She didn't even know I was running private security ops on the side until yesterday.

In truth, though, I didn't really make it a habit of having female friends, especially after Bianca died. The only exception I'd made was sitting next to me now.

Bella and I had never been that close when she was younger. It probably had to do with our decade age difference and the fact I'd been away in the Navy a good chunk of her life. She'd wound up spending a few years in London for work also.

When we were finally living in the same city again, she'd become busy dating assholes that had me wanting to throat-punch them on the regular, which meant I had to do my best to avoid her and her boyfriends as much as possible.

But lately? Lately was a different story. With her now thirty-two, that ten-year age gap felt like it'd been whittled down to only a handful of years. The math didn't need to math, it was just true; I no longer felt that much older than her.

The biggest transformation in our relationship started when we began working together. Side by side. All. The. Fucking. Time. I couldn't avoid her. She was always there, invading my space. Personal and private.

I was now as close to her as I'd once been to Bianca, maybe more. And that terrified me. Bianca's death gutted me. If I were to lose Bella for any reason, I'd never recover.

"Oldies again it is," Bella said after adjusting the radio, settling on a new station playing "Hungry Eyes."

"Kill me now if music from the eighties is considered oldies." *Because I am not that old.*

"Okay, we'll rebrand the beats and call them classics," she

said decisively, and I could work with that. "So, um . . . does Adelina work kidnapping cases or counterterrorism like you once did?"

"Kidnapping. Her sister was taken when she was three. They were twins. Not identical."

"Oh God. That's horrible." The pain of her own past had to be crushing her now. "She never found her sister, did she?"

"No." *Her sister is most likely dead.* My stomach wrenched, and I couldn't help but say the first thing that came to mind. "Your nerves earlier, they have something to do with Bianca?"

She immediately looked off to the right and away from me.

"Dammit, Bella."

"If I tell you, I'm worried you'll slam on the brakes and turn around and go back to the party."

That definitely had me slowing down, and I checked the rearview mirror, ensuring no one was on my ass, ready to plow into us at my abrupt change in speed.

I'd only been going forty since we'd yet to get back onto the main road, but as Bella had called it, it was now raining hard, making visibility borderline shit.

I flipped on the windshield wipers to full blast. "And why will I turn around?"

"Because you'll want to go and yell at Kit for what she did to me. Then you'll make a scene, and your father will lay into you, and she'll get the story she clearly wants." She balled her hands into fists, resting them on her thighs. "Eyes. Road."

"What story? What'd she do?" I was on the edge of insanity, and I was slipping fast into the depths of totally losing it if she didn't talk soon.

"Ugh, fine, but first you have to promise you won't head back to the party." She twisted on her seat to face me.

"Do you want me looking at you or the road?" I shot back, growing tenser by the second. "Make up your mind." I'd meant my words lightheartedly, but they came out more demanding than I'd intended.

"At a total stop would be preferable."

"Fine." We were in the middle of nowhere, and according to the dash synced to my phone, we had a weak cell signal. Against my better judgment, I pulled over to the side of the road. "Okay. Now talk." I parked, took my foot off the pedal, and turned toward her so she'd have my undivided attention.

I waited for her to talk, listening to the swishing sounds of the windshield wipers as Eric Carmen's voice faded out.

My patience collapsed when she closed her eyes instead of parting her lips to talk.

"Bella—" I cut myself off when a call came through from Constantine. Frustrated, I turned toward the display and answered it with a harsh, "What?"

"I've been trying . . . reach . . ." *And* signal lost, dammit.

I tried getting through to him two more times but the call wouldn't even connect. "We should get out of here. This conversation will have to wait." I caught sight of the panic in her eyes before she faced forward, holding on to the side handle.

"I got you, don't worry," I promised as I shifted into drive.

I barely had time to get us on the empty road before catching sight of the soft glow of headlights coming around a sharp curve up ahead.

"Oh my God," she cried out. "They're coming right for us."

"Brace for impact," I yelled, doing my best to dodge a direct hit by aiming for the side of the road.

Avoiding a collision completely was impossible, but instead of a head-on, the other vehicle sideswiped us. With the slick roads, no amount of weight I put on the brakes or steering wheel would keep us straight, and we spun in the other direction.

From the corner of my eye, I hissed out her name, realizing she'd slammed the side of her head into the window at the abrupt movement to the right.

"Bella," I hollered again, on the verge of reaching for her, but my intention was derailed when we were hit again.

Like hell was this a weather-related collision. Everything happened fast. The seat belt jerked my body, catching some of my weight, but my head whipped forward anyway. I turned the moment before my face made contact with the steering wheel so I didn't break my nose.

I barely registered the fact my airbag didn't deploy, but Bella's did. From my peripheral view, I noticed hers had ballooned out, keeping her face safe.

My head was spinning. Blood slid down the side of my face, hitting my eyelashes. I tasted it in my mouth as I tried to understand what happened.

I did my best to look over at her as my ears rang, a feeling of nausea gathering in my stomach.

"Bella, are you—" My words died when we were hit a third time, the other vehicle slamming into my side of Enzo's Porsche. I brought my arm up in front of my face, hoping to avoid hammering it into the steering wheel again. We flipped and slowly rolled over onto the roof.

Everything went black for a second or two as my mind tried to process what happened. It took me a moment to understand we were hanging upside down, our seat belts still holding both of us in place.

Twisting my head, fighting the violent pain in my skull, I worked to put eyes on Bella. "Are you okay? Bella?"

Her arms were hanging limp, and she wasn't moving. She'd lost consciousness, and based on how I was feeling, it was likely I wouldn't be able to keep my eyes open much longer, either.

The Art of You

I had enough experience with head injuries to know what was coming.

"Bella." I went to reach for her arm, but my 9mm fell from the back of my pants, sending me quickly securing hold of my Glock instead.

I began to replay the last several minutes in my mind, trying to focus. Constantine was calling to warn us about something, and I had a feeling that *something* was now outside the car.

Fighting with every last breath I had to stay awake, I waited for the person to come into view so I could handle them.

But the dizziness from the crash had my eyes falling closed despite my resistance to stop it. Everything became a blur.

And I was no longer in the car. Not even in the country.

Fucking hell, the crash and multiple hits to the head sent me back to the last place I wanted to be. To Afghanistan.

Chapter 5

Hudson

Eastern Afghanistan – Summer 2010

"I'm sure you're planning to re-up again, but we miss you." Bianca's soft voice floated across the line. "All of us do." She had three brothers, but I might as well have been her fourth with how much she worried about me.

"And when was the last time you gave Constantine this speech? He's coming up on his eighth year soon." Dodge and deflect, because how could I tell her the only way I'd ever leave the military outside of retirement was in a box? She'd think there was something wrong with my head. I mean, maybe there was?

"Last week," she said with a light laugh. "He had the same response. Swerved free and clear of the conversation like you just did."

I leaned back in the desk chair, eyeing the most recent photo Bianca had sent me with her letter. It was of her and her little sister at a bookstore. Bianca was not only a prolific writer, she was an avid reader. "How's Isabella doing? Keeping out of trouble?"

"Izzy's a typical seventeen-year-old."

I frowned. "And that means?"

"Rebellious. And before you ask me to elaborate like Constantine did, believe me, you don't want to know. You'll hijack a jet and fly here to lecture her."

Enough said. Wouldn't stop me from worrying about Isabella, though.

"I've got it covered, don't worry. Alessandro, too, now that he's back in town. We'll keep her in line."

"From the sounds of it, you're both failing." I straightened in my chair when a new email on my AOL account popped up. A message from my father. "I should probably get going."

"Yeah, of course. Well, thanks for checking in. Want me to tell Izzy anything for you?"

"Yeah, tell her if she doesn't straighten out, both Constantine and I will wind up in trouble for going AWOL when we come home to talk some sense into her."

"Copy that. Talk soon. Be safe."

"No, *you* be safe. I'll be dangerous." That was probably from a movie. Or maybe a book. I read a lot, too.

I ended the call, then let the mouse hover over the email, not quite prepared to open it up. My father only reached out when he needed a favor. He was a senator now, and I knew he had his political sights on something even bigger, but why'd bigger always seem to come with a cost?

Just do it. Get this over with. I clicked open the email after my pathetic pep talk.

Hey son, I didn't know how to tell you this when we last talked, so I'm doing it now. Your mom is keeping something from you. She doesn't want you to know while you're deployed, but I don't think that's the right move, so I'm telling you.

The cancer came back. Stage 4. The doctor said she has four to six months left.

Before you sign your papers, I thought you should know that.

Call me when you have a chance.

I reread my father's email, gripping the arms of my chair, my vision going blurry. Shock kept the tears at bay, but I barely had time to reach for the wastebasket before I threw up my dinner.

"We finally got the orders. We're spinning up now. Get your . . ."

I lifted my head from the trash to look at my team leader staring at me from the doorway. "Bad sushi."

"We don't have sushi on base." Matt lifted his hands up onto the doorframe, bracing against it as if trying to hold himself back from storming in. "What's wrong?"

"I'm fine." I set down the trash basket.

"So, what you're saying is you're the opposite of okay?" He lifted a brow, calling my bluff. Quite easy to do with the stench of vomit in the room.

Eight long days, and even longer nights, of waiting for our marching orders to go after a Taliban leader, and now of all times they came down. *This can't be happening.* I faced my desk and closed my laptop. "We're rolling out right now?" I spun around in the chair and stood.

"Yeah, as of five minutes ago, and we need you. We're

The Art of You

already down a man since Golf Team borrowed our EOD guy, and ISR detected a cache of weapons and explosives scattered all over the place at the target location."

I tried to slide back into operator mode and focus, but my father's words pounded into my skull. The reason for me to stand down tonight and not re-enlist was just emailed to me three minutes ago.

"Listen, we have that new guy now," Matt went on when I'd yet to answer. "He hasn't spun up with us yet, but from what I've heard, he's damn good. I think he should fill in for you as our lead sniper. Devon was first in his class, like you. He can be on the long gun on overwatch tonight instead. But I still can't do this without you, and if we don't move in tonight, we lose our HVT."

I hung my head, my stomach squeezing, on the verge of being sick again. "I'm not sure my, uh, head will—"

"It'll be where it needs to be." He was leaving me no option. He had Command up his ass, and they had all of Congress up theirs, so I didn't blame him.

"Yeah, okay, just give me a second."

"To remember you're an elite operator? One of the Navy's best?" Matt lowered his arms to his sides, crossed into the room, and slapped a hand over my shoulder. "Don't forget it. Got it?"

"Roger that." I closed my eyes, waiting for him to leave. The second he was gone, I clawed at my hair and took a knee. Memories scraped through my mind of the last time Mom was sick. I'd just completed Hell Week at BUD/S when the call came from my father. My parents were divorced, but like today, my mother always tried to protect me from any kind of pain, while my father was the one to rip the Band-Aid off and cut me with the truth.

I took another minute or two to pull myself together,

splashed some water on my face and rinsed out my mouth, then found the team prepping for the mission.

New Guy was doing a weapons check, and he was the first to look at me when I entered the room. I went over to him, ignoring the stares of the rest of Echo Team, knowing they could read my fucked-up state from a mile away. As for Devon, we'd barely spoken two words since he'd joined us on base, so he wouldn't realize I was off.

"Sorry, Ashford," New Guy apologized. "I'm not trying to replace you, I—"

"It's fine. Most of us just go by first names here." I did my best to breathe. To try and let go of the battle warring inside me about my mom. Shake it off for tonight, at least. "You want me to call you Devon or by your last name?"

"Anything is preferable to New Guy." He flashed me a smile.

"Fair enough." I took a knee by the gear as Matt came over to us.

"We'll be flying to the Y tonight. No choice with the terrain around the target." Matt lifted his hand to silence my protests before I could even start. "I know, I know."

"The troop chief took a helo to the valley to patrol ahead of time," New Guy—shit, *Devon*—tacked on.

The fact Matt trusted him over someone else on the team to be on overwatch meant I ought to put my faith in him, too.

"If we've got squirters, we'll know about it," Matt said. "We learned from what went wrong last month. It's why we do the AARs."

Before I could speak up, Alfie, Echo Three, joined us, stroking his auburn beard. "You, uh, good?"

My first impulse was to tell one of my closest friends on the team that I was far from it, but I caught Matt's head shake, a quiet order to keep my mouth shut.

I dragged a palm along my jawline and looked around the room, knowing one wrong move from me downrange could get someone on Echo killed. So, I did what I knew was my responsibility to do. I defied the chain of command and broke my silence. "Actually . . ." I avoided eye contact with our team leader. "Just found out my mom's cancer is back, and I don't think she's going to survive this time." My gaze bounced back and forth between Alfie and the others as I admitted, "So no, I'm not even close to being good."

Chapter 6

Hudson

Present Day

THE FIRE RAGED, destroying everything it touched as I ran into the mouth of hell.

"Alfie," I called out, choking on the smoke. "Matt, are you—"

"Wake up. Hudson."

"... must be ... a nightmare."

"At least he's speaking. That's a good sign, right?"

"He's moving, too. He keeps ripping off his oxygen mask in his sleep, so that..."

At the sound of the familiar voices, the fire extinguished. The building was no longer ablaze, and I wasn't in Afghanistan. Instead, I was walking alone through a pitch-black room. *Where am I?*

"Hudson, can you hear me?"

Alfie? No. No, that's not you. Matt?

"Hudson, you've been in an accident. Can you hear us? Do you know where you are?"

I didn't recognize that voice.

But wait...?

I slowly blinked, opening my eyes. My left one hurt a hell of a lot more than the right. Like I'd smacked my face into a wall or a—*steering wheel.* The memories from what happened surged forward, making me gasp for air as I tried to sit but failed. My body wasn't just weak, it was... drugged?

My eyes squeezed closed again. While my mind tried to drag my ass back to that inferno in Afghanistan, I did my best to stay present in the room and on the bed.

"I'm here with you." The soft voice that came next shocked my eyes open, ripping me from the past with violent force.

"Bella?" I rolled my head to the side, searching her out. The lights were too damn bright. "Are you okay?" My hand went to my chest at the pressure there. My heart would fly free on its own accord and leave me a pile of useless limbs on the bed if I'd hallucinated her voice and she wasn't really with me.

"I'm next to the bed. I'm covering your hand with mine now. You feel me?"

Bella.

I about choked out a sob hearing her voice, knowing she was alive.

Chills racked my skin, and I began to shudder.

"What's wrong? Why is he trembling so hard?"

It was her again. My Bella. No. Not mine. But...

"I'll up his pain meds, that's probably why he's—"

"No, don't," I begged, reaching into thin air, worried this was all in my head and I was somewhere else. The land of fucking Oz for all I knew.

"You'll be in pain," the same someone who'd wanted to drug me warned. "And the shaking won't stop otherwise."

"I don't care about the pain." My eyes were closed again. When did that happen?

"Go get the governor and tell him his son is awake." Another voice I didn't recognize. "Do you know who you are?"

"The Tin Man without a heart." I laughed. *Fuck*. The doctor doped me up anyway, didn't he?

"Easy on the drugs. He said he doesn't want more." A deeper voice hit my ears that time. Italian.

"Constantine?" I muttered, trying to piece my broken thoughts together.

"Yeah, it's me. Alessandro and the others are out in the hallway." Constantine's grave tone pierced through the hazy fog as my teeth stopped chattering. "They'll only let a few of us in here at a time. A nurse is getting your dad now."

"And where's Bella?" Did I imagine her voice, or was she really there? "Is she okay?"

"I'm still here. Holding your hand. I'm now touching your face. Can you feel me?" Her words had me finally opening my eyes, and I found heaven staring back at me in physical form.

My throat tightened with regret at the sight of a light purple mark around one of her eyes. "You're hurt." She was in a hospital gown, her right arm in a sling. Panic set in, and I tried to sit.

"Easy there." She rested her good hand on my chest, encouraging me back down.

My head hit the pillow, which felt no different than asphalt. "But your arm. Your eye."

"I'm not that bad, I promise. And my arm isn't broken or sprained; it just hurts. My arm must have been bent awkwardly when the bag went off. The sling removes some of the pressure."

I didn't believe her, and she must've read the look in my eyes because she pulled her arm free from the sling and moved it around to prove she was telling the truth. She couldn't exactly hide the wince when securing it back in the sling, though.

"I'm mostly just sore. Banged my head on the window, which is why I think I lost consciousness. You took a far worse hit than me since your airbag malfunctioned and didn't deploy."

Malfunctioned?

"Trust me, Enzo will look into that when he's allowed near his Porsche." There was a hell of a lot more to that statement from Constantine. I assumed he'd expand on his words at some point.

"Just glad it was mine that was defective, not yours." If anything had happened to her, the devil could go ahead and have his way with my soul. I'd have no need for it. "I'm so damn sorry."

"Don't you dare apologize." A few tears fell. "We were hit. This is not your fault. It's mine. I'm the one who should be sorry. I—I distracted you."

I reached out for her hand, finding my arm mummified, wrapped in gauze. It didn't feel jacked up, but . . . *Right, I used it as a shield to protect my face since my bag didn't go off.* Of course, I knew I'd have reached out to guard Bella instead if she hadn't had the cushion. Self-preservation would come second to her.

"You're sure you're good?" I asked again, ignoring her ridiculous apology that she didn't owe me.

She nodded, and at her silent answer, Constantine spoke up. "Izzy slept a good eight or so hours. Once she was cleared, she wouldn't take no for an answer and marched right into your room."

Yeah, I could see that. So stubborn.

"But if I had concerns about her health, I'd strap her ass down, and you know it." Constantine was also stubborn, and that was the only thing reassuring me right now she really was okay. Like hell would he let her be standing next to me if not.

But why were the two of them staring at me like the dog they never actually owned died? My head and face may have hurt like a motherfucker, but I knew them well. Drugs or not, I could read them, and something else was wrong. Far worse than bruises and a defective airbag. "What's going on?"

"You had a few nasty hits to the head, so we took precautions to ensure there was no internal damage. You've been asleep for about twelve hours, but the scans show you're in the clear," the doctor said from somewhere in the room.

I wiggled my toes, ensuring I had feeling down there and that my spine hadn't been jacked up. While it hurt to test everything out, I could move just fine. So, I was pretty sure I'd be able to walk out of there when the doctors eased up on the drugs.

"How much do you remember *after* . . .?" Constantine let that last word hang heavy in the air, as if it were supposed to mean something.

After what? After we were hit and flipped over? "I remember pulling onto the road. Someone came around the corner ahead of us, and . . ." *Then what?* I shut my eyes, trying to grab hold of the memories. "I think we were hit again. Maybe two more times." *What the hell happened after?* "Who did it? Do the police have them in custody? Drunk driver, or just driving too fast in the bad weather?" *But that wouldn't explain the multiple hits.* The drugs didn't dull my headache, and the harsh pain in my skull made it difficult to try and recall more. I was forgetting something important.

"Finally, you're awake." That voice definitely belonged to my father. If I were the Tin Man, he was behind the curtain pulling all of New York's strings. Only, in all reality, there were still others behind the puppet master.

Why am I thinking about this?

My dad skipped right over concerns for me. Not that I expected it, but he didn't even offer an, *I love you*. Instead, he cut straight to questions. "Do you remember what happened after the accident?"

There was that word again. *After*. It spun around in my head, searching for somewhere to land. "Why don't you tell me since I clearly can't recall." I opened my eyes and stole a look at Bella, curious how much she remembered. She lightly shook her head, letting me know we were on the same hazy page of don't-know-shit.

"Don't feel bad. It's not uncommon after an accident to forget some of the details, especially with such a traumatic hit to the head and face." The doctor seemed to care more about my overall well-being than dear old Dad. "You both blacked out long enough to give everyone a scare. Really is a miracle you two aren't in ICU, or worse."

Or worse? No, when it came to Bella, "or worse" was an unacceptable and illogical concept I'd never tolerate.

"Now that you're awake, I'd like to run a few more tests, though," the doctor said. "While he's talking coherently and moving just fine despite the accident and pain medicine, I should—"

"Tests will have to wait," my father cut him off, barking out orders like the man was his campaign manager instead. "I need to talk to my son alone." He rounded the bed and planted himself between Bella and Constantine. Suit jacket gone, red tie loose around his neck, he'd gone almost ghostly pale.

"I'm not leaving." Bella remained glued to my side, standing firm in her decision to stay.

I could barely look at her without feeling gutted. I didn't save her from injury, which meant I must not have reacted quickly enough or we wouldn't be in the hospital right now.

My pain wasn't just taking a back seat at the sight of her injuries. It was in another country, on a train heading for *I Don't Give A Damn About Myself* land because I almost lost her.

"No, the tests *can't* wait." Constantine's declaration shocked my father, pulling his eyes from me. I doubt even the governor could go head-to-head with my best friend. "Hudson needs time to wake up before we start talking more about what happened." He may not have been blood, but he gave all the fucks my dad didn't seem to give about me.

"And what exactly happened that I'm not ready to hear about?" I tried to sit. Still no luck. Because Constantine was right. The drugs were being obnoxious, and so were my apparent head injuries.

"Run your tests," Constantine bit out the command, ignoring my father's order, eyeing someone else in the room, presumably the doctor.

"My brother's right. He needs time." Bella gave my father her mopey expression: sad eyes and a downturned bottom lip. To say she'd used that expression on me a time or two, turning me to putty in her hands, was an understatement.

"Fine. I'll hold off the Feds and make some calls." My father had his phone to his ear before leaving my side.

The doctor attempted to shine a light in my eyes, and I waved him away. "Wait." I focused on Constantine, too curious to be left completely in the dark before I was given that time I supposedly needed first. "Just tell me why you look like someone died."

Constantine squeezed the bridge of his nose, closing his eyes. "Because last night, someone did."

Chapter 7

Hudson

"I'm not going to sleep. The doctor told y'all three times now my brain is A-the-fuck-okay, so talk."

"Based on that sailor's mouth coming back, I'm going to have to agree with you." Bella had the uncanny ability to unfuck any bad situation with her humor. When she threw a smile on top of it, I might as well throw in my hand and fold.

"Yeah, okay." Constantine joined Bella at my bedside. She hadn't left me alone for a second. He quickly glanced at my father, who was standing before the window, quietly observing us. "You want to fill him in, or do you want me to?"

"Go for it." Dad's attitude wasn't lost on me, even if the drugs were still kicking around in my system, just not as strong as they were before.

Facing me again, Constantine began, "Last night, when I tried to get ahold of you, your phone kept going to voicemail, and then when you answered—"

"The signal died," I finished for him, remembering more of the pre-crash situation, but still recalling nothing about the *after*. And could I? I'd been lights-out, apparently. "Let me guess," I said, putting two and two together now that I had an hour to stew and wonder what happened, "one of the security guards was dirty. I thought we were having them followed just in case?" At Constantine's firm nod, more pieces clicked. "Someone ditched their tail, so you were calling to warn me. Who was it? One of the ambassador's security detail? That's who hit us, right? And they died?" Must be why we're still alive if they caused the wreck. They could've easily taken us out after that since Bella and I lost consciousness.

I resisted the urge to allow that horrific scene to play out in my head. *You're alive. You're safe. We both are.*

"They think what happened to you was probably an accident due to the bad weather. The driver lost control of their vehicle and spun, which is why you were hit multiple times," my dad piped up. "If it were on purpose, they'd have had their lights off so you wouldn't see them coming and be able to avoid them."

Lost control, my ass. I kept my attention trained on my father for clarity, unsure if he had plans to give any.

"Right, because if an asshole wanted to cause a wreck in the pitch black with shit visibility from the rain, they'd be able to see their target without headlights? Use night vision, then?" Constantine had a point. Sarcasm warranted and then some.

"The police are wrong about the accident." I may not have recalled what happened afterward, but I remembered the gritty details from before. "They came around the bend, and I narrowly dodged a head-on collision. They still clipped us, though, which sent us into a spin." More and more was coming back to me now without the drugs as potent. "They rammed us two more times after that. Let me make something perfectly clear, they hit us on motherfucking purpose." My jaw strained as I stared at my father, trying to lift my head. "Please be sure to use those exact words when speaking to the police."

My father refused to look me in the eyes as he ignored my statement, opting to carry on with the bullshit official version of events. "Well, it's not the police making that call, it's the Feds." Then he killed me with his next words. "They're handling the case because we're dealing with a double homicide involving two of a diplomat's security personnel."

And there it was. Not one death, but two.

Chills rolled down my aching spine as I pulled my hand away from Bella's touch, curling my fingers inward as I tried to latch on to something. A memory. Anything. *Homicide?* "Details." I clenched my jaw. "Just get this over with. Tell me everything you know." They couldn't charge me with vehicular manslaughter. The fuckers hit us, not the other way around.

Without waiting for my father to control the narrative, Constantine took the lead on filling me in. "The ambassador's security team split up into two vehicles. Malik followed Rafael and Carla's Tahoe, and Eduardo and the other guy, Chris, were tailed by Marc. They were both supposed to be heading into the city where Carla planned to connect with Special Agent Cattaneo to see her daughter."

That all tracked, but I could tell the minute my father took over what he was about to tell me wouldn't. "Eduardo texted Rafael there was an issue with the SUV, so they were swapping it for Chris's truck, which he'd left at a gas station not too far from the party. We confirmed the F150 was registered in Chris's name. And according to Rafael, Chris had been sick earlier in the week, so he drove up from D.C. separately from his team. He came a day after the ambassador was escorted to New York but the night before the kidnapping took place."

Sick my ass.

"That text from Eduardo when they pulled off at the gas station was the last Rafael heard from them." I'd swear my father had aged fifteen years since the party last night.

Made two of us.

"Marc called to let me know Eduardo got off the parkway and went to a busy gas station. Eduardo and Chris went inside and then he lost them," Constantine picked up where my father left off.

"They got the drop on Marc?" That was hard to believe.

"Hell if I know how, but they abandoned their SUV in the parking lot, which checks out with what Rafael told us they'd planned to do. Marc didn't know they'd planned a vehicle swap for an F150, so he had no reason to suspect anything. But Eduardo and Chris had to have known they were being followed since they made an effort to sneak out of the gas station to get into the truck."

It sucked, but it made sense.

"While you were asleep, we tried to hack the cameras at the station to see what went down, only to find out they'd conveniently been off for that time period." And the bad news from Constantine kept coming.

"Great, these dead assholes have an alibi as to why they were in that truck so it wouldn't look suspicious." None of this was good, but bottom line, they died, not us. And the FBI could call it an unintentional accident all they wanted, it didn't change the fact I was innocent in their deaths.

Constantine's spine straightened, only for his shoulders to roll forward from exhaustion. Doubtful the man had slept. "I'm assuming they found you because they tagged the Porsche while you were inside the party. I don't buy the story the Feds are selling about them taking the same back road as you to bypass traffic on the parkway, and they just happened to come across your path."

"Let me guess," I said under my breath, "the Feds didn't find evidence of a tracker?"

"No," he was quick to answer me. "The second I realized I couldn't get ahold of you, I tracked your location through Izzy's phone and sent the local police the coordinates to find you."

"It gets worse." That was the last thing I wanted to hear from my old man. "They didn't die from the accident."

"Way to bury the lead." I'd targeted my dad with my frustration. "How'd they die, then?" What in God's name was everyone keeping from me?

"They found two nine-millimeter slugs in Eduardo's chest. Same for Chris. Both hit from about ten feet away. Both double-tapped just left of center. Their sidearms were still strapped." Constantine may have been speaking, but my attention was fully focused on Bella as he shared the shocking news.

Someone had a Glock on that road while I was un-fucking-conscious? All the things that could've gone wrong last night played out in real time in my head, like pages of a book flipping fast and uncontrollably.

Scene by scene.

All horrible and bloody.

She's alive. She's safe. I had to drill those words into my head so I didn't have a heart attack.

"We don't know who killed them. The truck was left abandoned, and the rain washed away any evidence of a possible third person there." My father's use of the word "possible" stole me free of the hellhole I'd been in—the *what-ifs* and *what-could-have-beens* running rampant in my brain—and back to him. "The question is," he said rather steadily given the subject, "why not also kill you and Isabella? Even if this person was in a rush to take off into the woods, they'd have had time to take you two out, especially if you were unconscious."

"You're telling me those two men were executed, and we

have no proof anyone else aside from me was there to pull the trigger?" *Is that what you're saying?*

"Unfortunately." My father rubbed his eyes. "I'm hoping your saving grace is the fact that when the police arrived, they found you unconscious and still strapped upside down in the Porsche."

I processed everything he'd shared, trying to wrap my head around the information. "Just tell me it wasn't my Glock used to kill them." I uncurled my fist and looked down. "Any residue?"

"They swiped your hands. Isabella's, too. No residue. Your tox reports were also clean." My father blinked, and I knew the moment he connected the dots of what I'd admitted. "Wait, you were carrying?"

"Of course I was carrying. The lockbox I'm sure the police already found in the trunk will be empty because I, uh, was holding it when . . ." *Shit.* A new memory unlocked. After the accident, I'd been prepared to take a shot *if* needed. "So you're saying the police didn't find my gun there when they arrived?"

My father shook his head no. "No murder weapon, which is another reason I don't think they'll charge you yet." He quickly removed his phone from his pocket and held it between his palms, probably itching to call two people. First his campaign manager, then his army of attorneys.

"Redact the word *yet* from your statement, *sir.*" Constantine was always going to bat for me. When my father didn't answer him, he focused back on me. "Your hunch about Eduardo and Chris was right, or they wouldn't have come after you. They had to be insiders. They were probably hoping to catch up with you and force you to take them to the men we had as hostages so we couldn't turn them over to the FBI. They didn't want them giving up their names in an interview."

My father's exasperated sighs and overall agitated

The Art of You

demeanor were starting to grate on me, but they didn't seem to bother Constantine at all. He went on with his theory, ignoring my father completely. "There had to be a third person in that truck with them, someone they met at the gas station, but we can't prove that since the cameras were off."

"And maybe this third person realized Eduardo and Chris intended to take out his buddies instead of rescuing them, so he surprised them alongside the road and killed them," I added, following his line of thinking, in agreement. "He kept us alive to come after us later, figuring he could force us to locate his detained friends. He didn't want anyone to know he'd been there, which meant he had to leave the truck."

"Or maybe he even followed them in his own vehicle but had no time to drag you all away," Constantine noted.

"But Eduardo and Chris didn't know about the real plan, right?" Bella chimed in. "They had no clue Lola was being rescued by our people, so they wouldn't have had the foresight to tag the Porsche during the party."

"But if they had someone on comms outside, who wasn't on the guest list for us to vet, and they were transmitting—"

"They'd overhear what happened in the library, and they'd have time to send someone to locate my Porsche and set the plan in motion," I finished for Constantine. "So, how do we prove this? Because from where I'm sitting, it looks like the Feds want to accuse me of manslaughter. They'll say I assumed they caused the accident on purpose, considered them threats, and shot them in cold blood." *No way I killed them, right?* "Was my window even down? Broken? I mean . . . I could take those shots even upside down if I had to." *To protect Bella, no doubt in my mind. I was unconscious though. I mean, I was, right?*

"They found one of those emergency tools on the ground. The kind you use to puncture glass and cut through a seat belt.

Based on the evidence, the window was broken from that and not during the crash."

At Constantine's words, I closed my eyes. "The only way I did that is if they were an immediate threat to Bella. I wouldn't have shot to kill unless I had to." I let go of a deep breath and opened my eyes, remembering the lack of residue on my hand. Another saving grace. "No way I hid the gun and washed my hand free of the residue, then managed to get back into my seat upside down just in time to lose consciousness before the police arrived. It sounds ridiculous even saying it, let alone doing it."

"We'll figure this out." Constantine folded his arms and gave me a firm nod, letting me know he believed I didn't kill those men.

"All I know is that we can't let the media get wind of this. It'll cause too many headaches for all of us." My father, always the politician.

"What does the ambassador think about all of this?" Bella, sliding in with the all-important question I'd been too focused elsewhere to ask myself.

My father faced her, undoing the top button of his shirt. There was something in his eyes, a look I'd seen from him a few times in the past. He'd honed his abilities to lie over the years to the point I could barely detect his bullshit anymore, but every so often, if his emotions got the best of him, the mask fell.

What is it you're keeping from me?

Before I could press him, he answered Bella's question. "Carla's already back at the embassy in D.C. with Lola, and her main focus is on being with her daughter. She's obviously relieved her kidnappers are now in FBI custody as well."

"And Rafael?" Constantine asked with a quick follow-up. "Tell me he's still around to answer questions."

"He went back to D.C. with Carla, but he answered the Feds' questions before he left. She didn't want to travel without

The Art of You

him, though. He's the only one she trusts from her team right now." When my father undid his second button, I couldn't hold back any longer.

"What aren't you telling us?" *There's something, I'm sure of it.*

"Nothing. This just doesn't look good for any of us." He waved me away as if that quick dismissive gesture would shut me up.

I knew him well enough to know I'd have more luck prying a seal from a shark's mouth than information from my father if he didn't want to talk.

"Don't forget, you came to us for help," Constantine pointed out in case my old man chose to ignore the favor he'd called in to us.

My father brushed him off and gestured toward the window. "The media is camped outside. I'm sure someone in the Bureau will leak the full story to the media anytime now."

And there it is. It was possible he wasn't keeping secrets, just interested in keeping his job. He was worried about negative headlines impacting his reelection campaign.

"I assume your brothers turned over the two men they kept alive to the FBI a long time ago?" *Like, before we knew we'd need to interrogate them ourselves.*

"Yeah, and I doubt the FBI will confirm whether or not Eduardo and Chris were working with them," Constantine responded.

How the hell did I let myself get in this situation to begin with?

"Unfortunately, given my son is involved in this mess, the Bureau won't share details of an ongoing investigation with me. So, I'll probably know after the media does."

So, we'll be on our own to figure this out. I held my jaw at the sudden burst of pain radiating there, and a new memory unfolded in my mind in the process. Bella had been about to share what Kit had done to upset her. A reporter was why I'd pulled over to begin with.

Bella fidgeted with her sling, staring at my arm, once again appearing to be lost in some type of stupor. She'd been mostly quiet throughout this conversation, offering her support simply by standing by me, and I was grateful.

"And how much do the media know?" I honestly didn't care about the grief they'd cause my father, only the headache they might cause for Bella and her family.

"That you were in an accident on the way home from my party. That's all for now, but it's already too much," my father answered. "I need to get you out of this hospital as soon as possible."

"You think the Feds will let us go home?" Bella asked, her voice still as fragile as glass.

"I'll make sure of it. After all, you're technically in this mess because of me, right?" My father's sarcasm was frustrating, but not too shocking. "To help explain how you got mixed up in all of this, I had to let the FBI know you were working with Agent Cattaneo to rescue Carla's daughter. But without the murder weapon, and no witnesses to rely on, the Feds don't have anything to hold you on. Plus, you were out of it when the police arrived."

"I'll see if Alessandro can look at last night's security footage from the party," Constantine suggested. "Hopefully, there's an angle of the parked cars to see who may have planted a tracker on the vehicle. If Alessandro can't hack the system from afar, he'll have to head to Scarsdale and handle it on-site."

"Handle it quietly. I've promised the director there won't be any interference from you all with this investigation, and I don't need to give them more ammo to lock up my son."

Right, that'd ruin your chances of reelection. I kept my

sarcastic thoughts to myself for now. "You *do* know I didn't kill those men, right?" I didn't need to remember what happened after the crash to know that truth deep down in my bones. *Their blood isn't on my hands.* "You believe me, right?"

My father's brows stitched together, and his quiet nod instead of a resounding yes about broke my heart.

Chapter 8

Isabella

"I've told you a hundred times and I'll tell you a hundred more. Hudson would never shoot someone unless it was in self-defense. And even then, he wouldn't shoot to kill. He'd keep the bastard alive for questioning." Bastards, in this case.

I covered myself with the blanket as I sat upright in bed, glaring at the federal agent holding a coffee mug that said, ZEN AS F*CK. Did he steal that from a nurse or bring it in from the office just to get under my skin? Probably the latter.

This was the third round of questioning this afternoon. Federal agents had taken turns from my hospital room. I couldn't believe they were treating us like the bad guys here, recycling the same lines repeatedly but in a different way as part of their obnoxious game of Gotcha.

I hadn't lied. Not once. I'd told them word for word everything I remembered. Well, I'd excluded why we'd pulled off to the side of the road in the first place, but I didn't see how that was relevant to their case.

"Back off. I told your people no talking to my daughter

without our attorneys present." Dad to the rescue, armed with his favorite asset, his right-hand man, Constantine.

The agent lowered his mug to his side but didn't flinch or back away beneath the death stares of my dad and brother. "She didn't request one. We're just having a casual conversation."

Casual my ass. I couldn't even remember the name the agent had provided, but he was perpetuating movie stereotypes about the FBI, which pissed me off. "I want to see Hudson." I sounded like a kid begging for her mother, throwing a tantrum. But who could blame me? This whole thing was a confusing and blurry nightmare.

My father's jaw worked overtime as his loafers carried him farther into my room while he muttered a few choice words in Italian I hoped the agent didn't understand.

"You can't buy your way out of this mess like you did for your sons years ago." The agent lifted his chin, eyes sweeping to Constantine as he returned to his casual sipping, testing me so hard. "I'm friends with the AG. I know about that backdoor deal you made for your sons."

I'd only recently learned about that. My father had ensured my brothers never saw the inside of a prison for murdering who they'd believed had killed Bianca.

"We saved the ambassador's daughter last night and stopped her abductors from getting away. Why don't you focus on that? Maybe thank us instead." Constantine began methodically rolling one sleeve to the elbow. "You need to leave my sister alone." I heard the "or else" I knew he wanted to say but couldn't.

I was pretty sure threatening bodily harm to an FBI agent was an arrestable offense. Leave it to my brother to always be the responsible one and think about consequences, even if it pained him to do so sometimes, like now. He'd be no help to any of us if he tossed an agent out on his ass, even if that'd be a lovely sight to see.

"My sister already told the Feds everything she knows while our attorneys were present." Constantine worked on the next sleeve, rolling it up to expose his corded forearm. This was an intimidation tactic by him. He couldn't hit him, but he could quietly act like he just might.

"Special Agent Cattaneo should lose her badge for helping your family." Sip, fucking, sip. I was about to get up and snatch his cup and shove a little ZEN up his ass. "And as for the governor . . ." He let his opinion of him hang, but it was clear he hadn't voted for Hudson's dad in the last election.

"Get out," was all my brother said, managing to remain calm.

"You don't think it's possible those two men lost control of their truck during the storm—"

"And rammed into them multiple times?" Constantine reminded him, cutting off the agent. "Don't forget the fact their truck was going the opposite direction they should've been headed if they were truly going to the city as they told their boss."

The Fed ignored my brother's point and rolled right past it and back to the crime scene. "Even if they caused the accident on purpose, it's possible Hudson still reacted quickly and put two in both their chests to protect himself and Miss Costa here."

Another Fed had offered that same theory an hour ago, and I'd already objected to it. "And then, what?" I shot out in irritation before my brother could answer. "Hudson crawled out the broken window and miraculously managed not to cut up his hands on the glass so he could hide his gun? Somehow stayed dry walking through a downpour to stash it in the woods? Oh yeah, then used the rain to wash his hands of the residue before crawling back over the glass to get into the Porsche so he could defy gravity and strap himself in upside down? Let's not forget, pass out in the nick of time before the police arrived."

So help me, if this prick wanted to start with me like this after the day I'd already had dealing with these ridiculous questions, I'd stamp LFG on my forehead. *Because yeah. Let's. Fucking. Go.*

"So, Hudson was, in fact, armed last night? Was it his gun that killed those two men? The lockbox found in the trunk was empty, so you're saying he had the nine mil on his person during the accident?" He pulled out the "gotcha" card on me, and I was too embarrassed to look at my brother or father after walking right into the trap he'd set for me. "Tell me, Miss Costa, at any point did you see a nine millimeter in Hudson Ashford's hand? Lying to a federal agent is a—"

"Yes, but that's because—"

"So, you're confirming he had one of his four registered Glocks with him last night?" His question pounded right through me, punching me in my good eye. At my hesitant nod, he went on, "If there really was a third person there, why wouldn't they leave the literal smoking gun in Hudson's hand? Why not frame him?" If I had to hear this shit one more time, so help me.

"Because it wasn't Hudson's Glock they used to kill those men. They'd know ballistics wouldn't be a match, so the *other* man there had to get rid of it." I'd dug this ditch, and I had to get free myself. "Given our team helped take down kidnappers last night, do you blame him for wanting to be armed?"

"That hole you're digging is about six feet deep. Looks like I don't even need to give you a shovel." Dark eyes studied me as he drank his coffee. I hoped it was bitter and tasted like ashes. "Hudson was first in his class in Sniper School, and given his service record, I'd go so far as to say he could hit a target drunk, or even unconscious." The smug bastard even mimed air quotes around his last word.

"You can shove those assumptions"—I included my own air quotes—"right up your—"

"Izzy," my father cut me off, which was probably for the best.

"Seeing that you're familiar with Hudson's record, and you're obviously aware he's a former FBI agent, do you really think he'd shoot to kill if their weapons weren't drawn?" Constantine countered, drawing his arms over his chest and standing his ground. "As it is, my sister offered you more facts than necessary to prove your story doesn't add up, and you know it."

The agent's jaw tightened. "Maybe there was a third person there, someone who took the gun from Hudson, which is why Hudson never had to crawl across broken glass or get wet." He mimicked Constantine's firm stance. "Tell me, Mr. Costa, where were you at the time of the accident? Did you cover for Hudson? Or did you shoot those two men?"

Now this was a new accusation, and while it had me fired up and ready to fight again, Constantine barely flinched or reacted. Instead, he pivoted the conversation in a whole new direction. "You have something against Hudson, don't you? Or his dad, maybe? A vendetta. This is personal."

That or you're in on what happened last night, too. I wasn't sure who to trust at this point.

"From where I stand, your family, as well as Hudson, are in shit's creek without a paddle." He set aside his mug on my rolling cart.

"It's up. *Up* shit's creek." I'd been a hot mess of tears and distress earlier at the sight of Hudson in that bed, not to mention feeling guilty for distracting him with my issues before the crash, but now? Now I was stuck in LFG mode, ready to go to bat for everyone I loved.

The agent didn't press Constantine on his alibi, which told me he already knew exactly where my brother had been, and it was nowhere near that road. He'd simply been trying to goad us into more *oops*-admissions like I'd done with Hudson's gun.

The agent went over to the blinds and parted them, peering out at the street and probably at the reporters.

I'd already peeked myself a few too many times, curious if Kit was with the herd. Damn that woman for being the reason I'd been so mentally off last night. But I had to reserve thinking about that problem for another day.

"Someone will pay for what happened last night." The agent's casualness was about to send me over the edge.

"So as long as someone goes down, it doesn't matter if it's the right someone, I take it?" I arched my brow, waiting for him to face me and lie.

"Or in your eyes, is Hudson the perfect person to take the rap for this precisely because of who his father is? Someone doesn't want Ashford getting reelected, is that it?" Constantine circled my bed, tightening the space between him and the agent while also creating a buffer between me and the man I wanted to push out the window he was so intently focusing on. "Rumor has it that the attorney general of New York is a friend of yours, and he's planning to run for governor next year. I'm guessing he may be motivated to resolve this case in a certain way."

Well, damn. Constantine had done his homework in the few hours he'd been away from the hospital.

The agent dropped the blinds and turned toward the room. "Even if you may have helped Ambassador Aldana's daughter, you did so without a badge. You think I don't know the other bodies your men racked up during that unauthorized operation to save Lola Aldana?"

Oh, I could smell this agent's bullshit from two counties over. He was gunning for Hudson, and it had everything to do with the governor.

He took a step toward Constantine, the scowl on his face and ice in his voice anything but composed and professional. "You think you're above the law, but you're not, and one way or another I'm taking Hudson down. If not for this, then for something."

And there it is. He knew Hudson wasn't guilty. Hell, a ten-year-old could've figured it out based on all the reasonable doubt presented. He was only trying to throw us off. My brother was right. He'd string Hudson up on jaywalking charges if he could get them to stick.

Instead of calling him out again on his BS, Constantine produced his phone from his pocket. An uneasy look crossed his face from whatever he read and his voice dropped to a menacing growl. "You need to go. You want to talk to one of us, do it with our lawyers present." With his free hand, he jerked his thumb toward the door.

The agent reached into his pocket and set his business card on the rolling cart. He went to take his mug, then hesitated and retracted his hand. "On second thought, you keep this. Looks like you need a little more zen than I do."

Son of a bitch. It took all my energy to keep my mouth shut and watch that man walk away without hurling his stupid mug at his arrogant head.

The second my father shut the door, Constantine shared, "The surveillance footage both inside and outside the party was corrupted. Alessandro couldn't salvage it."

"Wait, what are you saying?" *I mean, I know what you're saying, but...*

"Someone beat us to the punch, and they're covering their tracks." A worried look passed between my brother and father before Constantine added, "Someone doesn't want the Feds to know a third person was rolling with those pieces of shit last night."

Chapter 9

Isabella

"Thank you for taking them out. I just . . . when I see that many flowers together, it makes me remember . . ." I shivered, and my mother covered me with a second blanket.

"I know, I hate flowers, too. Reminds me of when Bianca died." My mother said what I couldn't. "But these flowers are to celebrate life and not mourn death." She smoothed the back of her hand across my forehead, inspecting my bruises. "I thought I lost you." Her voice wavered as she shook her head. "When I heard what happened, it was like I was reliving Bianca's death all over again."

I removed her hand from my face and squeezed it. "But you didn't lose me. Happy flowers, not sad ones, remember?" My mother had worried her way into my room every hour since I'd first arrived at the hospital, and she'd been momming me nonstop.

"Hey, up for more company?" At the sound of my sister-in-law's voice, I peeked around my mom to see Callie in the doorway. "Late for coffee, I know, but I brought some just in case."

I'd lost track of time at this point. It was Saturday, that

much I knew. "Come in." I let go of my mother's hand to wave Callie in. "Get some rest, Mom."

"I'll rest when you're no longer in a hospital bed." She kissed the top of my head, walked to the door, and gave Callie a quick forearm pat before she left.

Growing hot again, I lowered the blankets to the bottom of the bed. "This hospital gown is quite the downgrade from the ball gown I had on last night." My lame attempt to make a joke was intended to hopefully ease Callie's anxiety about all of this. The woman had been through so much this past summer, and the last thing she needed was to be dragged into hell because Alessandro had her fly up for what was supposed to be a quickie.

Callie set both cups she'd been holding on the rolling cart. That agent's coffee mug "gift" had long since been tossed into the trash.

She glanced over at my brothers talking in the hallway, most likely speaking in Italian since they were surrounded by men and women with badges. "How are you feeling?"

I leaned back against the pillow, unsure if relaxing was even possible. "I'm just—"

My words died when Hudson joined my brothers in the hall. He was dressed in jeans and a black tee but had a cane for support. His gaze slowly drifted my way before he gave the guys a nod and started for my room.

"I'll come back," Callie said quickly, dismissing herself before I could stop her, too fixated on Hudson's slow walk to my bed.

The fact he'd changed was a good sign. The cane? Not so much.

"Quit your worrying, it's just for balance. The drugs are almost out of my system, then I should be fine." He gave me an unexpected and ridiculously handsome smile. "How are you? And don't lie to me."

I was dying to reach out and touch him. Dive my fingers through his messy hair. He already had a five o'clock shadow on his jaw. His beard always had a bit more of a coppery-brown color to it than the darker hair on his head. *Such an odd thing for me to notice right now.* "I'm better now that you're next to me."

Pressing his free hand beside me on the bed, he shocked me by leaning in to kiss my forehead. Before pulling back, he murmured, "I'm so sorry I put you here." He lifted his head to find my eyes, our noses nearly touching. "I'm so fucking sorry."

While fighting back tears at the emotion in his voice, I used my good arm to reach up and hold his bicep. "I thought we established earlier you owe me no apologies. It was my fault we'd pulled over on the side of the road in the middle of nowhere. Just screams horror movie. And I was the one being avoidant, giving you attitude and acting like a total stubborn pain in the—"

"Don't do this. That's an order." He'd tried to come across as teasing, but he couldn't lose the worry in his tone any more than my brothers could whenever they'd spoken to me today. "Do you know how many things could've happened to you while I was out cold? If you'd been—"

"But they didn't happen. I mean, not to us. Two people died, but I think we can all agree they were playing for team bad guy. So, you know, their funerals." *Quite literally.*

"Isabella." He frowned and pushed away from the bed, forcing me to let go of his arm.

"Hud-*son*," I emphasized his name right back. "You kicking yourself for all the *what-could-have-beens* does just about as much good as me beating myself up for distracting you last night." At his signature scowl he seemed to enjoy reserving for me, I copied his deep exhalation with one of my own, worried I wasn't getting through to him.

"You know how hard it is for me to look at your black eye and your arm in that sling?" His voice was raw and hoarse with emotion. "Your brothers almost lost their sister."

Again. I heard the unspoken word. It'd been jostling around in my head, too.

"Was it the FBI keeping you away from me since I left your room, or did you not want to look at me?"

His forehead creased. "A little of both?" At least he was being honest.

"I want you to be angry, not sad." I held on to my sling like a safety blanket. "What I mean is that we need to focus on who put us here in the first place and why. Channel our frustrations into something useful and solve this case. I thought we were on the same page about this. Did those Feds get into your head? Did Agent Asshole visit you, too? Are you having doubts about what happened?"

"You mean Clarke? Yeah, he tried to mindfuck me and failed. Constantine told me he did the same to you. Word is I might need a defense lawyer. After the hell you gave that man, sounds like you'd be up for the job." His lips twitched, fighting a surprising smile. "Thanks for having my six."

"Always." The word came out like a breath of air, because I'd been caught off guard at how charming he'd come across discussing potential murder charges.

"But no, no one got into my head. Least of all that prick." He dropped his smile while staring at my bruised face, and his blue eyes quickly went from disarming determination to full-on devastation.

Eyes cast to the ground, I couldn't help but swing my legs over the side of the bed and stand, needing him to stop seeing me as a sick patient.

"Don't avoid looking at me just because it's hard to do." *I mean, it hurts me to look at you, too.* But I wouldn't admit that. I swallowed that last bit of space between us, my body practically flush with his. I was fully aware my brothers were in the hall, and they had to see this confrontation happening, but I didn't care. "Look at me and let these bruises motivate you to find the real shooter instead."

His nostrils flared. Mine probably were, too. But my words were working. He righted his posture, becoming a statue of intimidation again. And his eyes? They were a deep, lethal blue as the need for justice simmered there. Definitely anger over sadness and worry now.

He swung his focus to the hall a beat later. I was certain Constantine's presence there was the reason for Hudson's three backward steps away from me. "We need to find a place to lie low for a few days."

His father pretty much insisted the same thing earlier, and I was in agreement. "But where do we go? *How* do we get clear of everyone? There's so much media and police here, you'd think Taylor Swift's inside the building." I sidestepped him to go over to the window to take another look down below.

"Bella," he bit out at the same moment I felt the draft at my back.

And of course, the gown had come untied. I hadn't planned for that little tease, because this wasn't the time or the place for it, but knowing the man might be staring at my ass did manage to distract my thoughts from the darkness we'd been cloaked in all day.

I looped the strings together and whirled around while knotting the tie. "Tell me I didn't moon anyone else?"

Jaw clenched and eyes narrowing on mine in frustration suggested he hadn't turned away from the free show. "I must be blocking their view, or your brothers would already be in here lecturing you."

Good point.

"But I saw, so thank you for that," he gritted out.

"Well, at least it's one part of me not bruised. I mean, it's not, is it?" I stole a look over my shoulder, pretending to check out my own ass. "I can't even get you to crack a smile after seeing my crack. I'm losing my touch."

"Glad to see your sense of humor wasn't lost on the side of that road last night. Mine was."

"Since when did you have one?" Teasing this man was much more preferable to remembering why we were in the hospital in the first place. *Ignorance is bliss* is an expression for a reason, after all.

He fake-scowled, which was adorable until he winced, rubbing his jaw from the pain his facial expression had caused. "We were talking about something before you exposed yourself, what was it?"

"Exposed, huh? Makes me sound like a streaker running through Times Square."

And score, another smile from the man.

"We'd been talking about how to escape the hospital without having the press breathing down our necks," I finally relinquished the answer while doing a mental victory lap at the fact Hudson wasn't immune to my charms after all. At least not to my ass. The fact I was thinking about this right now meant I was probably overdue for an appointment with my therapist. "That's assuming the FBI will let us go."

"The Feds can't keep us. Seems to me you did an even better job than I did at outlining all the reasons why I'm innocent."

Minus accidentally admitting you were carrying last night to that Clarke guy.

His attention flicked to the window. "We've been ordered to remain available, though."

"So, we have to stay in New York, right? No running away to Italy, then?"

Eyes back on me, he shot out a sarcastic, "Real funny."

"I wasn't joking." I shrugged and had to clamp down on my molars to hide a grimace so he wouldn't worry. My shoulder was feeling pretty good there for a minute. "Maybe somewhere we can take a helicopter so no driving will be needed."

"We can probably make that work," he responded after quietly studying me, easily making the connection as to why I'd prefer a helo to a car.

Like almost dying in one last night.

"We should take your family's bird. My father would prefer to keep his hands as clean of this mess as possible." His tone dipped lower and borderline icy when mentioning the governor.

"Even though he's kind of why we're here." I was glad his father sought us out for help so we could save Lola's life, but he wasn't handling the aftermath of that decision so well. Not that I'd say it aloud, but from where I stood, his priority was ensuring none of this would hinder his chances at winning next year's election.

"My father's concern will always be about his job first and how to ensure he keeps it."

I really wanted to hug him right now. Make up for all the affection he'd missed out on over the years. But my brothers were still lurking in the hall, and I didn't want to cause Hudson any grief with them. Constantine would die for his best friend, but apparently, he would also kill him if Hudson ever crossed whatever lines he felt were inappropriate.

So, I got back in bed instead of wrapping this man up in my arms, denying the blanket of solace he seemed to need.

I removed the sling from my arm, discarding it on the rolling cart. "I take it Alessandro told you he couldn't access the video footage from the party?"

"Unfortunately, yes."

"And I assume you talked to Adelina?"

He nodded. "Only over the phone. The director wouldn't let her come down here yet. She'll meet up with us tomorrow."

"And was she able to shed any light on anything, or was it too risky to chat details over the phone?"

"We couldn't talk about the case. The Feds were probably listening in."

Of course they were. "We should be on the same team as the FBI, and here we are feeling like their enemy." *This sucks.*

"Your brothers filled her in about what we discussed earlier, though."

"I know the Feds won't share anything earth-shattering unless it's because they're charging us with something, but will she keep us in the loop?"

"Yeah, for sure." He shot me an uneasy look. "I did manage to learn one minor detail from one of the Feds investigating the crash earlier. The fuses to my airbag were disconnected, but they're saying it's possible the wiring system was faulty and it wasn't tampered with."

"Faulty my ass."

"It's possible they didn't screw with my airbag, though. If they needed us alive, they wouldn't want to risk killing me."

True but . . . "They could've been aiming to only kill you, assuming I'd give in easier when pressed for a location about their kidnapper friends." There was a hole with that theory, too, though. "But I suppose if that were the case, our mystery person who fled the scene wouldn't have left you alive, either."

"Unfortunately, right now, we have more questions than

answers. Regardless of the situation with my airbag, all I know is that I'm relieved yours was okay. If anything—"

"Nope, we're not doing that. If you start the blame train, I'll pick it up and run with it myself. So, if you want me to feel guilty, then by all means . . ."

The man had a black eye and bruises, but he still rolled his eyes at me.

I stole a look at my brothers in the hall talking. They were too far away to hear us, and I couldn't eavesdrop on them either. "So much for this being a quick weekend op. Enzo should go back to Maria, don't you think? We need to make him. He'll want to stay, but it's hard for him to be away from her when she's pregnant."

"I've already talked to Constantine about that, and he agrees. He'll ride Enzo hard and ensure he's on a plane tomorrow. Monday at the latest."

"What about Alessandro? Doesn't Callie need to get back to her life in Nashville?"

"She's as stubborn as your brother. Both of them are staying until this case is resolved."

I should've felt guilty about that, but I didn't exactly hate the idea of having my sister-in-law here with me.

"But what I need from you right now, is to finish that conversation we started last night."

I conjured up memories from our unfinished roadside chat and shook my head no. "Now isn't the time."

He stared at me as if I had two heads. "This is precisely the right time."

"We have too much to deal with now to worry about something so trivial." My eyes betrayed me, shooting to the window. Of course Kit was out there. No way she wouldn't chase down a story involving the two of us.

"Trivial my ass. You were upset because of something, and you mentioned feeling like you were being watched."

His worried tone triggered my gaze to rush back to him, a tired sigh falling from my lips. "It has nothing to do with what's happening now. Why don't we handle this problem first, and if there's time left over, we can handle mine." *If it's even still a problem by then.*

"I don't give a damn if your problem is unrelated to what's going on. It's important to me. I need to know." The authoritative bite in his voice nearly had me submitting to him, which wasn't my normal go-to response.

I typically tested out the dish of defiance with a side of attitude before I ultimately gave in to one of my brothers or the stubborn man before me.

"Talk." The command sailed even lower that time.

"Fine." Eyes on the blanket, I revealed, "Yesterday, someone dropped off an envelope. No address on it. No writing at all. Callie brought it to me when she'd come to my room to help zip me up." I clutched the blanket tighter to my chest. "Inside the envelope was a photo from an article—the one Kit wrote when Bianca died. Remember the photo of me standing in the rain? The one Kit used for her story?"

I worked up the courage to meet his eyes, and his shallow breaths and lack of blinking worried me. I should have waited to share.

Too late now.

"That's why I was so freaked out. Because why in the world would someone anonymously send it to me, especially *that* specific photo? And then I could've sworn someone was watching us from the fourth floor in the building across from us when we got into the Porsche. But after seeing Kit at the party, I'm sure it was her trying to screw with me."

"What?" That was all I got from him. That one shocked word. And yet, there was an entire lecture packed inside those four letters.

I know, I know. It's beyond messed up.

"It can't be a coincidence she was at the party and approached us like she did the same night I got a photo tied to her article. I don't remember her on the original guest list, which means someone tipped her off we'd be there, and she was a late addition to the press pool. I have no clue why she's messing with me, but at least we know it was her trying to get into my head, not some psycho-weirdo watching me."

Using my decent arm, I waved my hand in the air, working to wrestle his attention back to my face, hoping to calm him down. "See, I know that look. Eyes glazed over in anger. You're breathing hard without opening your mouth. You're upset."

"Of course I'm upset." He didn't grant me his eyes. Instead, his lashes fell like a curtain, jaw locked and loaded with tension, restraint barely controlled.

The man before me could easily double-tap someone in the right spot to ensure an expedient death. Not that I believed he killed Eduardo and Chris, but he wouldn't hesitate to neutralize a threat. Maybe not completely end their lives, though. He saw things a bit more black and white when it came to killing, whereas my brothers swam deep in the gray when dealing with evil.

Although Hudson had been with my brothers when they killed the man they'd thought had murdered Bianca years ago, he hadn't actively partaken in the man's death. But the guilt he'd felt for allowing it to happen weighed heavily enough on his conscience that he eventually turned in his badge.

"Did you check your home's security footage to see who dropped off the envelope?" He opened his eyes, pinning me with a worried look.

"I didn't have time. You were outside my bedroom door, and we had to go. I didn't want to distract you from the mission, so I kept my mouth shut. I planned to look after the party."

The Art of You

He peered at me for five long seconds. I knew, because I counted in my head.

"Kit's normal methods for acquiring a story may be unethical, but I can't imagine she's behind sending you the photo." He turned to the side, eyeing my brothers still hovering in the hallway.

"They don't need to know. Not now. Enzo won't leave, and he needs to." The protest was weak because I knew Hudson wouldn't listen no matter what. "They have their hands full trying to solve two murders. The last thing anyone should be doing is worrying about me."

His cane clicked against the ground as he swiveled back around. "Don't ask me to do the impossible. It'll never happen." His blue eyes thinned as his chest puffed up from a deep inhalation.

"And what's that?" I asked, letting go of that deep breath on his behalf.

"To not worry about you." His words sat heavy in the air, and I positioned my hand on my stomach at the fluttery feeling there.

He bowed his head, more than likely collecting his thoughts. Then he quietly reached for my TV remote on the rolling cart. He flipped the station to the golf channel and lowered the volume.

"What are you doing?" I asked as he set aside the remote.

"I'm going to go talk to your brothers and find out who the hell dropped that photo off at your house. And see who lives on the fourth floor across the street." He tipped his head toward the hall. "What *you're* going to do is sleep while a few of the officers hanging out by the nurses' station post outside your door to keep an eye on you."

"I don't understand." I mean, I did. He was being his typical, broody, protective self, but . . .

"Golf helps you sleep," he clarified, reading my confusion. "I know you don't play or care about the sport, so I assume those magazines by your bed are how you fall asleep at night. Plus, you've passed out in your office before with the golf channel open on your phone."

He was observant, I'd give him that. Really freaking observant. Came in handy with his previous line of work, I supposed. But then I remembered and sputtered, "The magazines. I put the photo between them before I opened my door for you. I left the envelope sitting on the desk in my room. It's a plain white one, nothing unique or special about it."

"I'll send Alessandro over for the photo when he checks your cameras."

"They're going to overreact." *The last thing I want.*

"As they should. Now go to sleep." A subtle lift of the chin accompanied his order. "In the morning, we'll get out of here. I'll have Callie pack you a bag."

Like I can sleep now. "Promise to wake me if you learn anything?"

"No." He gestured toward the TV with his cane, his balance seemingly okay now. "Sleep."

I decided to battle my way through the uncomfortable tension in the room with another joke. It'd helped before, so maybe it would now. "Only if you kiss me goodnight."

His eyes raced to my mouth as if he was actually contemplating doing it.

I wasn't about to get my hopes up, but the little crook of his lips into a semi-smile had me inhaling sharply.

"You *want* to get me into trouble, don't you?" His voice was deep and seductive, and despite everything that'd happened since yesterday, I'd swear this man was begging me with his eyes to say yes.

The air was charged. The energy in the room had changed.

I couldn't quite describe it with words—I wasn't the writer in the family—but it was a feeling. Deep down in my soul, I could reach out and touch it, the change happening. The shift between us.

The accident, photo, and two homicides hanging over our heads felt as though they were part of a Lifetime movie and irrelevant to our lives.

Pinning my tongue to the roof of my mouth, I worked hard to keep quiet and not kill the moment happening between us. I didn't want to think about how I nearly lost him last night. That we could've died.

"What are you thinking?" The murmur escaped like the fine strokes of a calligraphy pen brushing the air.

The ink barely had time to dry as his husky voice replied, "Nothing good."

There were so many ways I could interpret that, but he turned and walked out of the room without giving me a chance for a follow-up.

You felt that, too, didn't you? There is something between us. It's not one-sided.

Instead of watching golf like he wanted me to, I focused on the hall as he spoke to my brothers. I knew the second he told them about the photo because they all abruptly faced my room.

They were overbearing, and I wouldn't have it any other way. I'd do whatever they demanded for the sake of my safety, even if their overprotective measures drove me nuts.

Because the last thing in the world I wanted to put any of them through was the pain of losing another sister.

Chapter 10

Isabella

East Hampton, New York

Good vibes only, my favorite mantra, had quite literally once been written in the sand a few hundred feet away from where I quietly stood next to Hudson.

It was so peaceful there. Natural ambient noise offered a quiet companion to the sound of waves in the distance. Some were as gentle as a whisper, others more like the rolling boom of thunder. Then there was the slight whistle of the morning wind coasting along the shores beneath the sun.

I'd always loved this place while growing up. I mean, who wouldn't feel inspired here? And it was the perfect spot for us to hide out until things calmed down.

Deciding we needed to escape the city, Hudson and my brothers had figured out a way to elude the press stalking the hospital, whisking us all away to a space of relative safety.

The quintessential Hamptons residence, my parents' summer home, was a three-story, grand shingle-style cottage estate on the beach, offering stunning panoramic views of the

Atlantic. Six acres of lush green land cradled the rest of the house, with two wraparound porches to take in all of the gorgeousness.

Aside from the beach, my favorite spot was the garden and the large brick patio. It was the ideal setting to dine beneath open skies on warm summer days with my family. My *whole* family.

But without Bianca there, we weren't really whole anymore. So, as "perfect" a place as this was to escape to, even with security guards buzzing about doing perimeter checks and keeping the site secure, perfect was no longer achievable.

The good vibes were long since gone. And no amount of peaceful sounds, beautiful sights, and fresh air would stamp out the memory of what used to be compared to what was now. My sister was gone, and fourteen years later, someone was using a photo to throw her death back in my face.

At the sudden whooping of blades, I turned to see the helicopter that dropped us off back in the sky over the helipad. The pilot was returning to the city to pick up my parents, who would join us later today. My siblings and Callie had driven here a few hours ago to prepare everything for our morning arrival.

Callie had also packed a bag for me while Alessandro retrieved the photo and checked the security cameras. He'd pulled a partial image of a man slipping the envelope through the small mail slot in my door around seven on Friday night, but the image wasn't clear.

I still believed Kit was behind it. Of course she'd have someone run her errands to keep her hands clean of it.

Since our facial recognition software couldn't produce a match for the man, my brothers delivered the security footage, along with the photo and original envelope, to Adelina late last night. Hopefully her access to some high-caliber FBI tools would yield better results.

"You're awfully patient with me today," I admitted to Hudson, needing a break from my heavy thoughts. It was the first time I'd said anything since we'd boarded the helicopter at the hospital, using their helipad.

I glanced at the statue of strength at my side, wearing a backward baseball hat and Ray-Bans. Unlike me, he had no lightweight jacket to keep him warm, just a white tee for a top.

"Would you prefer I not be?" Without facing me, he hooked his thumbs in the front pockets of his jeans and continued to stare off toward the ocean.

The bruises on his face and the bandage around his right arm distracted me from answering with equal amounts of sarcasm. His injuries were a harsh reminder of why we were here. And why a sniper was perched on the roof behind a long gun.

My brothers never half-assed anything, especially not regarding my safety.

"I just need one more second before we join everyone inside."

"Take as many seconds as you need." If patience were something tangible, it would feel like a blanket of Hudson's words. His typical sarcasm was completely absent, because he knew how hard it was for me to be here.

Fidgeting with the buttons of my jean jacket, I finally got my feet to move, but in the wrong direction. Leaving the house behind me, I ventured to the garden instead.

Hudson caught up with me, matching my steps. I slowed down a bit, remembering he'd needed a cane to walk just last night, and I didn't want him feeling unnecessary pain because of me.

I did my best not to react when I felt his hand go to my back as he switched spots with me on the trail like we were by traffic instead of walking along a pond. Knowing him, he was worried I'd fall in.

I stopped once we arrived in the garden cocooned by Mother Nature. Trees, flowers, and vines crawled over every inch of the space.

"How much time do you think I have before my brothers come looking for us?" I blew out my cheeks before allowing the pent-up air to sputter free. "They'd have seen the helicopter land, and surely one of those security guards radioed to let them know we're walking the property."

"I texted them that you need a moment." He removed his Ray-Bans and hooked them at the front of his tee.

A moment was much more generous than the second I'd requested. Also more realistic. It could be an hour's worth of seconds before I found my way inside the home, where I'd probably hear the echo of Bianca's laughter ring through the hall walls.

"You're stealthy. I didn't see you with your phone." Must have speed-texted en route to the garden.

"Part of my SEAL training. I can do a lot of things fast."

"Hopefully, you slow down for some things." It took me about two and a half seconds too long to realize how that sounded.

Based on the slight smirk sitting on his lips, it took him even less.

You're great at distracting me. My heart rate was no longer at a NASCAR-worthy speed. My skin was warming up despite the crisp, cool air. That was probably partly from embarrassment at implying I hoped he wasn't quick between the sheets. But most notably, I wasn't filled with as much sadness as when we first arrived.

"Bianca would hate this," I murmured, switching from *acci-*

dental sexual innuendos back to tragedy. "She'd hate how her death changed the way I feel about this place."

"She would definitely hate that." He gestured to the beauty surrounding us. "If I remember correctly, Bianca used to sit here and write in her journal, while you—"

"Tried to capture my feelings through drawing instead of words." I sighed, my lips fighting to smile at memories because they still hurt to think about. "Bianca was often the subject of a lot of my art." I peeked over at the bench as if she were sitting there now, a pencil behind her ear and another in her hand as she scribbled her stories in a notebook.

I startled when Hudson abruptly stood before me and brushed a few wild strands of hair away from my face. When our eyes locked at the intimate gesture, he jerked his hand back as if shocked by what he'd done.

Ray-Bans back on, he hid both his black eye and his emotions. "I know you quit drawing when she died, but do you think you'll ever paint again?"

"I've tried to pick up a pencil and a paintbrush since, but my heart was never in it." I went over to a bush and plucked a flower. "I doubt I'll ever stand behind a canvas again."

"That's too bad. You were a damn good artist."

"I was young. It was more of a way to keep myself busy and out of trouble than anything else."

"Yeah, I'm not buying that, even if you were quite the rebel back in the day." With his index finger, he shifted his glasses down his nose so I could read the look in his eyes that said, *Yeah, I know about that.*

"Who told you I was such a bad girl?"

His mouth tightened, and he pushed his glasses back over his eyes, shaking his head. "Anyway."

"Nice redirect."

"I thought so," he tossed out casually while removing his

phone from his back pocket. "Constantine texted. He's worried. What do I tell him?"

"Mmm." I plucked a petal and let it go. "That we're in the garden, and you're comforting me. Dot. Dot. Dot." I pointed at his phone with the flower. "Be sure to add the ellipsis. The sentence loses its meaning without it." Holding a straight face while saying that was hard, but I managed it.

Hudson laughed, and that sound trumped all other ambient noises surrounding us.

"I'm sure that'll go over well." He typed something back to my brother, lifting his chin toward the house. "Bet that sniper on the roof will take me out the second he sees us exit the garden."

"You and I have very different ideas of comfort, I guess." I was on a roll; why stop now? "I was simply thinking about an innocent little hug. Your mind went to the gutter, sir."

He didn't give me the satisfaction of a smart-ass response to my comment. I'd consider the smirk continuing to fight for space on his face a win, though.

I freed another petal into the air, and Hudson focused on it as it drifted to the pavers between us. "How much time did you buy me before the grump finds us?"

He made a zero with his hand, then pocketed his hand. "He just sent another text. Security alerted him that Adelina just pulled up to the gate. Took a friend's car instead of her FBI-issued Chevy."

Ohh. At the news, I let go of the flower. I knew she was on her way, but I hadn't expected her quite this early. Like before-coffee early. "Well, hopefully, she has news she didn't want to share over the phone."

"If she has nothing now, she'll turn something up soon. This is her area of specialty, and—"

"You said she handles kidnapping cases. Lola's safe, and I

wasn't kidnapped . . ." I didn't catch his drift. Maybe coffee was required for drift catching.

"Many of Adelina's cases have involved women who were stalked before becoming victims of an abduction." He gestured with his good arm to start walking, and I obeyed his command, hoping he'd explain on the move.

When his words sunk in, I halted and spun around to face him. He lowered his chin to where my hands now rested on his chest. *When did that happen?*

"You think I have a stalker and someone planned to kidnap me? Just because of that photo and my overactive imagination about the fourth-floor window across from my house?"

He circled my wrist but didn't force away my touch. "Let's just hear what Adelina says, and we'll go from there." He freed his hold of my wrist, and I lowered my hands to my sides. "Someone left you a photo, crashed into the Porsche, killed two men, and we have no idea what's connected to what, but we're going to figure this out." He appeared far more confident this morning without the pain meds in his system. The SEAL was in front of me now, a fighter. "We won't let this asshole win."

"What if there's more than one asshole?" I blurted what was on the top of my mind, doubtful my photo issue was tied to the dead security guards.

"The world's full of assholes, nothing we can do about that. We just have to figure out which ones are out to get us and stop them before they do."

He was right, I supposed. "Yeah, okay." I went to turn, but Hudson stopped me, wrapping his arm around my waist. "What are you doing?"

"What I wanted to do yesterday, but didn't."

"And that is?" I stared at him, not blinking.

He drew me into his arms so our bodies were flush, and

rested his chin on my head. "That innocent hug you needed . . . well, I need it, too."

Chapter 11

Isabella

"You shouldn't even be here." I held on to Enzo near the back door, burying my face in his chest. "Maria needs you."

"*You* need me." Enzo let go of me and patted my head like I was five. Most days, I think he still saw me that way. "As long as I feel it's safe, I'll head home tomorrow. I promise. But the second we have a target, I'll be back to handle them with the team."

I didn't doubt that.

Enzo looked at Hudson, tipping his head. "Everyone's in the kitchen. Adelina is there, too. We'll join you in a second."

That was Enzo's way of telling Hudson to leave us alone, and Hudson quietly nodded and took his cue.

I'd expected Enzo to start with a lecture, not to kick things off with heartfelt words instead. "Why is being here so much harder than when we're at Mom and Dad's place on Long Island? Or the Central Park home?"

I pushed the sleeves of my jean jacket up my forearms and told him the only thing that made sense in my head. "Because it was Bianca's favorite place. Lots of happy memories here."

The Art of You

The frown came and went fast. "I think I've only been here twice since she died."

I thought back to the hug I'd desperately needed in that garden, and how Hudson had managed to calm me down so I could think more clearly. "Maybe we should come here more often because it was her favorite place, and not avoid it for that very reason."

He stepped closer, holding my arms while resting his forehead against mine. "The youngest of us is the wisest."

"About time you realized that."

"Well, it's not true when I think about the men you choose to date, though. You lose all brain cells when—"

I lifted my hand between us, silencing him with a finger over his lips. "You were on such a roll being sweet. Don't ruin it."

He let go of me as I lowered my hand to my side, and we glanced in the direction of the kitchen, both of us seemingly hesitant to get the show on the road.

"You should've told us about the photo before the op. Secrets get people killed, remember?"

Like in Bianca's case. "I didn't want to distract you from the mission."

"Your safety will always be a priority. Got it?" He narrowed his eyes, waiting for the only answer he'd accept.

So, I gave it to him. "Roger that." When he continued to regard me with a hesitant expression, I begged, "Stop worrying. I'm going to be fine when you leave. I have Hudson to protect me."

He jerked his head back as if offended. "*And* Alessandro. Constantine. Our parents." He tossed a thumb toward the front door. "Not to mention an entire team of security guards."

"Of course, I was just . . ." *No clue how to finish that.*

"Mmmhmm. I know what's going on here." At least he was smiling.

One of the main reasons why nothing may ever happen with Hudson joined us at the worst time. "And what exactly is going on?"

I faced Constantine, discreetly elbowing Enzo to keep quiet. It was never easy going up against my brothers. At three to one, they outnumbered me on everything, but at least Enzo appeared to be coming around to my side on this.

"Izzy was just telling me how eager she is to spend quality time with the family since you'll all be under the same roof for the next few days. So many people here, though, she's concerned that someone might accidentally wander into the wrong bedroom at night while she's sleeping."

The man deserved the daggers I shot along with the second elbow.

Enzo faked a wince, holding his side. "Kidding. Constantine would kill one of our guards if he accidentally slipped into your bed."

Guards, huh? Sure, sure, that's who you're referring to.

"You two planning on joining us anytime soon, or do you need another minute? You know, like that minute you took to hug Hudson outside?"

An audible gasp fell from my lips at Constantine's question. Okay, I was probably exaggerating on that part, but seriously. "You were watching us?" *And wait.* "There are cameras over there now? Since when?"

Constantine checked his watch. "Since an hour ago." Turning to the side, he gave the order to join everyone in the way of a head nod toward the kitchen. "Not you." He shot his arm in front of me the second I tried to walk. "We'll be right there," he told Enzo without looking at him.

Once it was the two of us, framed by the walls still holding on to Bianca's memory, I whispered, "Don't." My voice was so fragile and weak that I barely heard the word, so I repeated it with more punch.

"Isabella." If a sigh could ever be a word instead of a sound, it'd be a woman's name from a frustrated man's tongue.

I pouted in response. You know, more bees with honey and all that, or however the saying went.

He gently cupped my chin, urging my eyes on his. "You don't know what I planned to say."

"I do." The downturned-lip action from me in response was legit. No faking that time.

"Come here." He relinquished a deep breath, let go of my chin, and then pulled me into his arms for an unexpected hug. "What am I going to do with you?"

I angled my head so my face wasn't smashed into a wall of muscle so he could hear me. "What you're going to do is finally let me go so I can fall."

"I don't know what that means." He stepped back, arms to his sides, staring at me as if genuinely confused.

"You don't want me getting hurt."

"And why would I?" he guffawed, head jerking back.

I poked his chest with my index finger. "You've always been there for me. And with every stupid mistake I've made, you've bailed me out from both trouble and heartbreak. But I can't ever stand on my own if you're always there to catch me before I fall."

"I can't watch you get hurt if I can help prevent it. It's impossible. Not in my DNA." He drew a palm over his heart.

"You can keep me safe from criminals, sure." I twirled my finger in the air. "This mess I'm in? Yes, please. But the other stuff, no."

Based on his grimace, he'd latched on to the meaning of "other stuff" and wasn't a fan.

"You have feelings for him?" The dark undertones in his voice were as unsettling as his point-blank question. "Is that what this 'let you fall' lecture is about?"

Yes, but the timing is shit, so I should probably not let my near-death experience do the talking. "You were planning to warn me about him after seeing our *innocent* hug, right? So, I just—"

"No. We haven't had a moment alone since the accident, and I'd been planning to tell you how damn proud I am of you for being so resilient and remaining strong." His next words were rougher. "And how much I love you, but also, how fucking terrified I was that I almost lost you on Friday."

My hand went to my stomach as it squeezed in pain.

Before I could find it in me to respond, he hit me with another question, and it barreled through me, sending me back a step. "You're asking me to stand by while you fall for a man I know can't love you back?" A rattle of emotion he was probably working hard to hide managed to slip into his voice anyway.

The gut-wrenching words didn't have a chance to swallow me whole because Hudson and his horrible timing stole my attention instead.

He was standing still in the hall, a hand up on the wall next to him as if he needed the support, and it had nothing to do with his injuries. His focus wasn't on me, but on the floor.

Oh God, how much did he hear?

"Adelina doesn't have a ton of time," Hudson finally spoke, his voice low and haunted, indicating he'd heard something.

Constantine cursed under his breath in Italian, slowly swiveling around to face him. "Hudson." The apology curled up into his best friend's name. My brother was an asshole to everyone *but* the people he cared about. "I'm sorry. You shouldn't have heard that."

"You have nothing to be sorry about. *Or* anything to worry

about." Hudson slowly met his eyes. "Your sister and I will only ever be friends." His gaze cruised over to mine as he killed me with a promise. "You have my word." He pushed away from the wall, jaw strained and his solid body visibly tense. "Now, if you'll excuse me, please tell Adelina I need a minute."

Hudson brushed past us, barely grazing my shoulder, and I flinched when the screen door slammed shut.

Constantine reached for my wrist. "Izzy."

"Nothing to say. He's made himself clear." I blinked back tears. "You know Hudson, and he'd never go back on his word."

Chapter 12

Hudson

WALKING into that conversation had been like stumbling in front of a freight train, having never seen it coming.

The straw that broke the camel's back wasn't the accident. It wasn't even the fact I had an agent gunning for me, looking to slap me with cuffs on any given Sunday.

No, it was my best friend's belief about me. *"Can't love you back."* Those four words were the final nail in the coffin of whatever was left of my beating fucking heart.

Well-deserved, because what he'd said was true. And yet, hearing Constantine say what I'd spent most of my life believing hurt like a son of a bitch.

Google the definition for "can't love you back" and you'd find my face next to the résumé of reasons to not fall in love with me. He wasn't wrong about me, but Alessandro used to be—

I immediately ditched that dangerous line of thought. I couldn't latch on to the hope that if Alessandro could change, so could I. We had different stories.

I dropped my head, falling back into the past. To 2010,

when my life flipped upside down because of an email. If my father's message had come one day later, or my orders to spin up had come one day earlier...

At the sound of the back door opening, I lifted my head up. I didn't want to come across to anyone as a man on the verge of snapping. *Like I am.*

Adelina joined me on the deck beneath the unwelcomed rays of sunlight. "Isabella and Constantine said you needed a minute, but it's been five."

"Sorry. I needed—"

"Time?" She zipped up her black leather jacket and closed the space between us on the massive deck. "Are you okay?"

"No." The honest answer spilled from my mouth a bit too quickly. "I mean, yes. Confused the words."

"English is my second language, not yours." She lifted her brow, waiting for me to get my shit together. *If only.* "I'm not used to seeing you like this."

"What, bruised and banged up?"

"Wearing your emotions so plain to see." It was less of an observation and more a statement of fact.

"You saw me in the kitchen for all of five minutes," I grumbled, not looking for anyone to help walk me off the cliff of crazy right now, even if I needed it.

"I'm talking about now. You were fine in the kitchen." She narrowed her eyes, scrutinizing me. "You look like a man who just found out the love of his life is getting married to someone else."

"Stop profiling me. I'm not on your suspect list. Well, at least, I better not be." And that reminded me, we had work to do. "Aren't you short on time? Places to go and all that?" I gestured for her to walk inside, but she didn't budge.

"I can afford a few extra minutes to make sure you're good before we get to work." She ate up the remaining space between us, maintaining eye contact. The woman was trying to hypnotize me into speaking the truth. I'd seen her do it to cold-blooded killers before.

"I know what you're thinking, and you can stop. Isabella is just a friend." Did I need to wear those words on my sleeve since I didn't exactly have my heart there?

"Just friends" was becoming one of this weekend's themes, somehow sending a double homicide to the back seat.

Just. A. Friend.

Period.

Throw in some extra punctuation there, too. A fucking exclamation point if needed. Whatever would get the job done to convince everyone to drop it.

Between the bullshit from Kit at the party Friday night to Constantine serving up those tough-to-stomach words on a silver platter of kill-me-now this morning, I was done.

"Well, I wasn't questioning your relationship with Isabella Costa, but I am now. If there's something between you two, it might be relevant to the case."

Shit. I unintentionally cracked Pandora's box with that one. Now she'd try and use her heightened special powers of observation to try and lure me into opening up. Nope, not happening. Not today, at least.

"How could my *friend*ship be relevant to anything?" I hissed, not meaning to take out my frustrations on her when she'd made the trip out to the Hamptons to help.

"If Isabella has a stalker obsessed with her, and they see you as a threat, then yes, that's relevant in helping me figure out what's going on." She reached for my good arm and gave it a light squeeze. "I'm here for you. But I can't help if you're going to play hardball with me. I'm not the enemy. Looks like you have enough of them already."

Yeah, like Special Agent Clarke, who was up my ass itching

to throw bogus manslaughter charges at me. Something told me that coffee-drinking prick wouldn't stop even if Bigfoot killing those two men was a more plausible story.

"Stop Doctor Phil'ing me."

Instead of giving me the eye roll I deserved, she worried her brows together and offered me a sympathetic look.

Her sad expression hit me with just about the same effect as an ASPCA commercial about neglected and abused animals. Growing uncomfortable, I rushed out, "Did you find out something new you haven't told me that'd lead you to believe she does, in fact, have a stalker?"

"Well, there was something you never mentioned, or maybe you didn't remember, that has bothered me." She produced her phone from her pocket and a moment later offered it to me. "Someone photoshopped you out of the picture sent to Isabella on Friday."

I stared at the two side-by-side images. A photo she'd taken of the one sent to Bella along with another. "No, I wasn't in that shot . . . was I?" I didn't remember being in it, at least.

"I couldn't sleep last night, so I decided to do some digging. I pulled up the article that Kit wrote in connection to the photo, and as you can see there, you were in the background. Not close, almost like a shadow off in the distance near Bianca's apartment building, but you were there. Definitely you. So, my question is, why did this person choose to photoshop you out when sending her the picture?" She took her phone back and pocketed it.

The biting sting of chills crashed over me. Any direction she was about to run with this wasn't a good one. No road was worth traveling when it came to this. "This is your area, right? What are you thinking this means? Just tell me."

"Well, I did some checking, and I haven't been able to find a single photo of just you and Isabella online. Like ever. You've been in images with her and her brothers, but never only the two of you. *Aside* from this one."

I hated this. Hating every second of *this*.

I needed an enemy. A target package. A place to point and shoot. Instead of feeling like a sailor without orders lost at sea.

"Two possible reasons for this." She was shifting comfortably into FBI mode. "One, our suspect is obsessed with Isabella, and they see you as a threat, which is why they chose this photo to send. It was the only one they had of just the two of you, so they used it to get their message across. They want you gone from her life. It could also serve to cast suspicion on the reporter, but that would mean this person has pretty intimate access to Isabella's life to be aware you were going to the party together. High-level knowledge to also know Kit had been added at the last minute."

Stalker. Intimate access. Someone she knows? That unacceptable idea sent more unsettling chills crashing hard over my skin.

"This is often the case when it comes to women who've been abducted. It's almost always by someone who knew them, someone already in their life," she shared, her tone somber again.

I bowed my head and gritted out, "What's the other reason why I was cut out?"

"That Isabella receiving that photo could have more to do with who's *not* in it than is." She'd need to spell this out for me, the murderous mood I was in making it hard to think clearly. "Instead of this being about her, someone could've sent the photo as a message for you. They'd assume she'd tell you about it."

I felt the blood rush to my face in real time, feeling like I'd been hit by a fever. "I'm their target, and they're coming after Isabella to get to me." I abruptly turned away from her, unable

The Art of You

to handle either possibility. I stared out at the ocean in the distance, forgetting how to breathe for a moment.

"I need a lot more to go on before I can piece this together." She set her hand on my back, coming up next to me. "We don't know their motives, or if this photo has anything to do with the kidnapping case. Let's not jump ahead of ourselves, okay? It could be this reporter trying to get into your head, too."

"I've never wished so much that a reporter was looking to fuck with me more than I do now."

"Before we talk to her, I'd like to see what she does next. See who she talks to. I'm assuming your team already has her under surveillance?"

"Of course." I turned toward the house, and she let go of my back. "We should fill in the others. Get this over with."

"Wait." She reached for my arm, stopping me from heading in. "You haven't answered me yet, and I assume you'd rather do it in private."

"About what?" I raced through my memories, finally landing on what she was referring to. "No, there's nothing between us." *Only in my head and dreams.*

"If this isn't that reporter's doing, are you sure there's nothing that might trigger someone obsessed with Isabella to make their first move in scaring her?"

I flipped through months' worth of moments where I'd come close to messing up when it came to Bella, finally landing on a genuine answer. "We've flirted, but it's been harmless, and was always in private."

I knew Adelina was just doing her job and covering her bases, but these types of questions were going to give Constantine an ulcer if he had to hear them asked of Bella.

"We've been working together a lot. I pretty much see her seven days a week. But nothing has ever actually happened between us." *And it can't.* "Doubtful anyone witnessed our kiss when we were in Rome."

She lifted a brow, letting go of my arm. "Kiss, huh?"

"It wasn't like that. It was for work. We were undercover."

Damn her knowing smile. "And any other 'for work' moments happen?"

"You can put down those air quotes." At least she had me almost smiling, something I didn't think was possible after she dropped the bomb that someone had photoshopped me out of Bella's life. "Nothing. Well . . ." *Fuck.* "There was a gas leak at her place the first week in June, and she stayed in my guest room." Before she could give me shit, I offered up, "It was innocent."

"And does anyone else call her Bella aside from you? I noticed most refer to her as Izzy."

My lips slammed into a tight line. Because way to pull off a quick kill shot with that one. I also didn't know what to say. I'd never really thought about it, and I didn't remember being pressed by *any* Costa as to why I'd one day up and changed her nickname.

"I'll take that as a no." The woman before me was definitely the experienced Fed and not my friend, which was exactly what I needed. Someone objective with a new set of eyes to look over everything. "And at the party Friday night, anything happen that could be misconstrued as *more?* She went as your plus-one. Her stalker could've been there, watching you two."

"I'm sure whoever is behind that photo was on the guest list, but are they tied to the case?" That was the mindfuck I couldn't unfuck in my head right now.

"You didn't answer me."

Dammit. I relented with a deep, dramatic sigh that hurt my chest. The seat belt had abused my shoulder and upper pectoral muscle when it'd locked up to save my life. I liked the color purple, just not on my skin, and sure as hell not on Bella's.

"Still not an answer." Arms over her chest, there went her dark brow, shooting up in question.

"Constantine was watching us over cameras while we were there. So, what do you think happened between me and his sister?" In truth, if someone had a better angle of us than Constantine had, they'd have seen Bella testing my willpower. I'd wanted to take her over my knee and slap that cute ass of hers for pretty much grinding against my cock while we were dancing.

Trouble. That woman was the definition of it lately in testing my limits. But I promised myself I'd behave, because breaking her heart wasn't an option. And as of fifteen minutes ago, I'd basically written that same promise in blood by offering it to Constantine.

"I'm just trying to get a full picture so I can figure out what happened," she said when it was clear I had no plans to expand on what may or may not have happened on that dance floor. "I'm sorry to do this."

"It's why you're here." I frowned. "I assume you'll be asking her even more questions than you've asked me." God, I hated this. "This is messy, isn't it?"

"It's complex, to say the least." She patted my good arm. "But lucky for you, you have me to uncomplicate things." She forced a small smile I wished was more confident. "Let's go chat with the others, so I can get to the city and start chasing down leads."

Right. The two of us started for the back door, and I found myself hesitating before opening up.

She glanced at me. "What is it?"

"You told me on the phone Friday night you had good news, what is it?"

"Ah, you don't need to hear that now." She waved me away, lifting her chin as a directive to open the door. "We can talk about that when we've wrapped up this case. Or, well, maybe cases."

"I could use some good news." I let go of the door, facing her. "I need something to dial my anger down. It'll help me think better if I can see more than red."

"Good point." Mouth closed, she released a soft breath through her nose. "I found her. Well, actually, she found me."

It took me a second to comprehend what she was saying. "Wait." Was she serious? "Your sister's alive?"

She allowed her eyes to reflect her emotions, wearing them as prominently as I'd been wearing my pain. "Mya's been living in New York, too. She used to be a reporter—don't hold that against her—then she got into a similar line of work as you. She had no idea she'd been kidnapped when she was three. All those years . . ." She took a moment to clear her voice. "She was working a major case over the summer and stumbled upon the truth, and that's how she found me. She's with our parents now in Italy, but I, uh, finally have my sister back."

"Holy shit." I pulled her into my arms for a quick hug. "This is incredible."

"I just came back from Florence last month after having a chance to spend time with her. She's amazing, smart, and beautiful. A total badass. And hopelessly in love with an Army veteran."

I hugged her one more time, because this was the epitome of a big deal. "I'd love to meet her one day."

"You will. When things die down for her, and I ensure you don't go to prison for a crime you didn't commit, and we make sure your girl is safe here and—"

"Not my girl." She'd snuck that verbiage in pretty fast and almost pulled one over on me.

"Yeah, right, you keep saying that."

"Maybe you should believe me." I lifted a brow, and she shrugged. "Why didn't you want to tell me this in the car Friday night?"

"I didn't feel right about sharing it with Isabella listening. My sister is alive, and Bianca—"

"Bella would be happy for you, not jealous," I interrupted.

"I only spent five minutes with her in the kitchen, but you're right, I can tell she's a good person." She tugged at the sleeve of my shirt. "Come on, let's not keep them waiting."

I opened the door. "We'll celebrate when this is over. Your news and mine."

"Yours?" She shot me a funny look from over her shoulder before going inside.

"Yeah, ensuring I never have to find out if orange is my color. The Feds may not have anything to charge me with, but if I find out someone is stalking Bella, I won't hesitate to commit murder."

Chapter 13

Hudson

I'D UNDERESTIMATED my ability to act like I hadn't been kicked in the nuts. Seeing Constantine in the kitchen was bad enough, but making eye contact with Bella had me wanting to full-on retreat. It was my least favorite thing to do as a SEAL, but they never trained us for this type of defeat.

"Coffee?" Callie nudged a cup my way. I didn't have the energy to take it, but her offer at least pulled me free from my staring contest with the woman I supposedly could never love back.

It wasn't because I was broken. And I really did have a heart, so that wasn't my problem. I felt the evidence of its beats beneath my rib cage as it tried to unleash holy hell on my emotions.

"You look like shit," Alessandro's observation pierced through my thick skull, a reminder to save self-reflection for later. "I know your stubborn ass didn't take home any prescription pain meds." He tossed me a bottle of Advil, and I snatched it in time before it hit my face.

Of course I had to grab it with my dominant hand, the one

attached to my bad arm, so that was great. The quick jolt flared up the pain in my sore arm.

I cleared my throat, trying to buy some time and cover for the grimace on my face. "Sorry for the delay."

I looked back at Bella to see her stalking my way, barefoot and determined. She immediately took the Advil from me, unscrewed the lid, and placed two gel tablets in my hand, clearly worried I'd either take too many or none at all. Wordlessly, she swapped the bottle for the coffee mug and waited while I swallowed the pills.

Thanks, Mom. I half wondered if she wanted to check under my tongue to make sure I swallowed them, but I kept the sarcasm to myself. We had an audience, one of whom probably wanted to dig a ditch just in case I went back on my word and broke his sister's heart.

"You okay?" Bella mouthed, the lipreading game seeming the safest form of communication with so many people in the kitchen and up in our business right now.

I'm on top of the world, how about you? My asshole tendency to try and push people I cared about away knew no bounds sometimes. And yet, I couldn't offer the smart-ass comment to the woman before me, even if I needed to draw some new lines between us.

Adelina had seen through my BS, and it'd only taken a butter-knife approach to peel me open. Constantine would use a much different utensil on me. More like a fucking machete.

He also wouldn't have laid into her in the hallway with a warning about me if he hadn't already figured shit out. So, as much as it pained me after what we just went through together, I had to find a way to build a wall between us that consisted of more than sarcasm and attitude.

I needed to finally flip the switch to "just friends" for both our sakes. No more flirting because, apparently, it wasn't all that harmless. It may have resulted in some jealous psychopath sending her that photo and removing me from the picture because they didn't like how friendly we'd become.

"Hudson." Constantine wrangled my attention away from his sister and out of my head, which was such a bad place to be right now. "Maybe we should recap everything we know and go from there, then see how Miss Cattaneo can help going forward?" He deferred to Adelina, eyes on her. "Unless you feel the need to go first?"

"No. Sadly, nothing much on my end requires immediate action," she answered him.

I was okay with that. I wasn't ready to address the photoshopped image and face what it meant.

Callie offered Adelina coffee before settling in between Enzo and her husband at the breakfast bar. Alessandro reached for her stool and slid her closer to him.

"So, who wants to take the lead?" Adelina looked back and forth between me and Constantine as if sensing there was tension between the two of us.

That "tension" planted herself on the stool by Enzo. He offered her a frosted donut since sugar did a much better job of waking her up than caffeine.

"We can go through the details together, but maybe you should sit?" Constantine motioned for me to join the others at the breakfast bar, but I shook my head. If he was going to remain a standing, tense statue, so would I.

"I'm good." I set the coffee down, resisting the impulse to hold my back at the sudden pain there trying to betray my words.

"Fine, let's get started," Constantine said after a deep exhalation.

"We're all on the same page as far as what happened before

the op, let's try and figure out what happened after, shall we?" Adelina suggested.

"Sure." I leaned against the counter for support, crossing one ankle over the other, trying to act casual. I needed to hide not only the pain catching up with me now that the heavy meds had worn off, but also my nerves knowing that the photo had been used for a very specific reason. But *which* reason?

"I can kick things off," Enzo volunteered. "My team kept two of the kidnappers alive from the warehouse in New Rochelle where they'd been holding Lola." A dark smirk crossed his lips before he added, "And that's proof right there we can be civilized when need be."

"*Or*, proof miracles really do happen," Callie teased, enjoying busting her brother-in-law's balls. "Because how often do you leave anyone alive?"

Alessandro casually exchanged a look with Enzo, lifting his shoulders in a shrug. "My wife's right, and you know it."

A smile skirted Adelina's lips, and she tipped her chin in Callie's direction. "I'm inclined to agree with Mrs. Costa here. It's a miracle the Feds have men alive to question."

Enzo eyed Adelina that time, probably because she was the only one in the room with a badge. "We're not that bad, I swear." He cleared his throat with an obnoxious cough. "Anywayyy." He did his best to redirect, dragging out his word like Bella normally did. "What we know about the kidnappers is a whole lot of nothing. This was a quick-and-dirty, just-find-the-girl-and-ask-questions-later kind of op. But from what we could tell, and based on what Constantine saw in the van by the party, they were all in their mid-thirties or early forties. White, English-speaking males. No noticeable accents or tattoos. No IDs."

"We didn't see a need to take photos of the crime scene or the kidnappers. Or collect evidence," Alessandro added an important *if-only* detail. "Our mission was to rescue the girl. Beyond that, we always planned to turn everything over to you, and you'd have the FBI handle things from that point on."

"Well, by now, the FBI has to have the kidnappers' identities. They've probably also confirmed Chris and Eduardo were insiders. Not that they'll share shit with us," I hissed in frustration before my attention moved to Bella's downturned lip, her eyes on the donut.

"Anyway, getting back to it," Alessandro said, focusing up like I really needed to do, "after the rescue, Marc lost Eduardo and Chris at the gas station, then from there, you two were in a car crash, and we wound up with two dead Spaniards on our hands and no murder weapon. With no clue about motives or how much is connected, let alone if anything is at all."

"My question is, why run you off the road in the first place? Why not try following you first to see if you'd lead them straight to where your people were holding the others hostage?" Adelina raised a valid point.

That same thought had crossed my mind yesterday while stewing in the hospital bed, bouncing between federal agents questioning me. I'd ruled out that idea, though, making the assumption Eduardo and Chris—

"Shit," I cut off my own thoughts. "Someone must've overheard me talking over comms when I was out front waiting on the Porsche. I told Constantine I was taking Bella home." I closed my eyes, drawing up an image of the scene from outside the party. "And if they heard that, they may have overheard me tell Constantine to have the security detail tailed." *This is my fault.*

"But no one was near us when we were talking, were they? The valet was getting our Porsche and . . ." Bella's words trailed off as the pieces locked into place.

"Not that valet." I opened my eyes and exhaled in frustration. "There was a different one who parked the Porsche when we arrived. Younger guy. He could've tagged the Porsche, then when we were leaving the party, he was out of sight but listening to us." *Got the drop on me, because I'd been distracted by Kit in the doorway.*

Constantine stared at me, but there wasn't blame in his eyes. No condemnation for letting someone get the drop on me.

I owed Marc an apology. It wasn't his fault he lost track of those men, it was mine.

"We didn't vet the staff because your father's team assured us they had them covered," Constantine reminded us. "We only ran background checks on the guests. And the valet wouldn't have exposed himself to my team when he realized shit was going sideways. He'd have been outnumbered. He also may have been part of a contingency plan if things failed, which would mean they wouldn't risk having him on comms. So, I had no way of knowing they had a fourth man on the perimeter after taking down their tech guy."

Sensing Constantine and I were about to argue about who should fall on the sword of blame—and like hell would I let him do it for me—Enzo cut his hands in the air. "Don't even start with this bullshit," he said, his tone calm despite the curse. "Focus on what we know. We now have a target and a possible third suspect in the truck. We may have the shooter."

"Look at you being the voice of reason," Constantine grumbled. "Who would've thought?"

Enzo sat back down, waving him off. "I'm supposed to be the smart-ass, not you."

Constantine mumbled something in Italian under his breath before pivoting back to the case. "We already have the staff names, right?" he asked me, and I nodded. Turning to Enzo, he ordered, "Find out what you can on both valets just to be safe. Their identities had to have checked out to pass the scrutiny of the governor's people, but someone may have missed something. Get their locations."

"On it." Enzo stood again, shooting me a quick, *I got your back, don't worry* look I appreciated, then took off to get to work. It meant he'd be MIA while we filled everyone in on the photoshopped picture, but I supposed he'd find out soon enough.

"Since we don't have security footage to check, we'll need statements from guests at the party to see if anyone remembers seeing that valet there during the time of the accident," Adelina added a few quiet seconds later. "I can put my badge to use and get those for you all."

"Just don't make too many waves. We don't need you getting in trouble on our behalf," I told her.

"You really think the valet killed those two men?" Bella asked me. She was searching for my "gut" feeling in a room full of experts. A feeling she knew I trusted, which meant she also had faith in me.

Maybe you shouldn't. I messed up. "I don't know if he's our shooter, but I definitely think he was working with Eduardo and Chris." I turned to Constantine. "Let Marc know he didn't fuck up."

After a hesitant nod from Constantine, Adelina offered, "I know your father can't interfere with the investigation, and I'm not technically allowed to, either, but I'll do my best to see what the acting agent in charge knows. The walls at the Bureau talk sometimes, if you get what I mean."

I did, because I remembered. They talked a whole hell of a lot back when Bianca died. The speculation over whether I'd been involved in helping kill Bianca's alleged murderer had pretty much bled from the plaster. I still couldn't believe he'd actually been innocent in her death, but thankfully, he'd still been worthy of dying.

"We should also keep an eye on Agent Clarke, the one who gave you both a hard time yesterday, and see what his real game plan is." Adelina set down her mug and focused on me with an apologetic expression. "Clarke's a real asshole, and he's made no secret about how much he can't stand your father. He's also good friends with the AG of New York."

"Because we need more problems." *We have too many as it is.*

"Just tell me you found something after we filled you in last night? Get a match on our mystery mailman?" Alessandro asked her, switching gears.

Adelina peered at me, silently requesting permission to share the Photoshop story, and I quietly gave her the OK. She outlined the conversation we'd had on the deck, and I couldn't help but focus on Bella the whole time as she worked through her shock.

"I didn't remember. I—I should've," Bella whispered when Adelina was finished.

"None of us did. I was practically a shadow looming behind you." *Great, now I sound like I'm the stalker.*

"As for what else I learned since I spoke with you all last night, I've had no luck yet matching the face to a name in our software. It becomes too pixelated when I zoom in, so I handed it over to someone on my team I trust who's a wizard at that stuff. If anyone can get a clear image, it's him," Adelina quickly explained, bulldozing through Bella's chance to simmer in guilt she had no business swimming in. "We checked for prints as well. The only ones we found were the ones we expected. Isabella's, Callie's, and Alessandro's."

"But it's doubtful whoever dropped the envelope off is our suspect, right?" Bella asked.

"No. It'll probably lead us in a circle or wherever someone

wants us to go," Adelina answered, and we were on the same page.

Someone was more than likely an unsuspecting errand boy. "What about the fourth-floor apartment across the way?"

"A woman in her mid-thirties lives there. She was home Friday night on a date with a guy she met from a dating app. She remembers him admiring the Porsche outside, so it's possible he happened to open the curtains right when you were going to the car."

"And I was just paranoid. I'd prefer that," Bella murmured.

"You know what time her date left her place?" I asked, curious if he could've been a party crasher or secretly on the guest list, too.

"Around ten," she let me know, which placed him within a window of possibility to make it to Scarsdale and be included on my suspect list.

"I told her I would stop by later today with some questions," Adelina said what I needed to hear, that she wouldn't take shortcuts regarding Bella's safety.

When she faced Bella next, I knew what was coming. She wanted to ask her some uncomfortable questions, gather information I doubted any of us wanted to be privy to. Like her dating history and any men who might be obsessed with her after she kicked them to the curb.

Hearing about the men in her life, even in past-tense format, would make me nauseous.

"There are some things I'd like to go over with you to help me widen the suspect list so then I can actually narrow it down." Adelina had barely finished talking before Alessandro took that as his cue to leave.

He stood, urging Callie to as well while he told Bella, "We're going to give you some privacy."

Bella flattened her palms on the counter. "I have nothing to hide."

"Of course not." Alessandro scrunched his face as if unsure how to explain he didn't want to hear about his sister's sex life. "I'll help Enzo out with the valet's names, then get started with going through social media to see if there was anything posted from the party that might help."

"Good idea." Constantine gave him the all-clear to continue his escape path, then he pinned me with a hard look. "Either help him or go rest."

As much as I loved multiple-choice questions that were more like commands, I didn't answer him. I needed to get a read on Bella first.

Uneasy. Worried. Scared. All three emotions were readily displayed and gave me a solid reason to add a third option. Stay.

I released a deep sigh, deciding to put my own shit to the side so I could be there for the woman who made me crazy, even if hearing her talk about other men would make me even crazier.

I stood, walked past my best friend and around the breakfast bar, and sat next to Bella. Then, as Alessandro had done to Callie, I scooted Bella's stool closer to me, announcing multiple-choice letter C: "I'll be staying."

So much for those walls I needed to put up.

And so much for my word.

If I wasn't more careful, it was only a matter of time before I broke it.

Chapter 14

Hudson

"Hearing you talk about your past and men who broke your heart will make my trigger finger itchy." Constantine always had a way with words. Like, direct and to the point.

"You may want to go, too." Bella didn't look up at me, but she was clearly talking to me. She tried to pull off unbothered, swiping her finger along the frosting of the donut.

And I wanted to be the one to suck it off, even if I did want to go. She was right. I was uncomfortable for too many reasons.

It didn't help that I could feel my best friend staring at me as if he was considering taking the proactive route when it came to me. Kill me just in case I rolled the dice and gambled with his sister's heart, becoming the next in line to break it.

"I'm fine," I said, finally coughing up an answer. "I'll stay."

"While Hudson's time with the Bureau was brief, I'm sure his training stuck with him, so it's a good idea for him to stay." Picking up on the tension in the room, Adelina employed a firm but polished tone as though she were trying to broker a peace deal.

Constantine dragged his hand along his bearded jaw, eyes on the floor. The dude was contemplating murder.

We all breathed a sigh of relief when the thorn in our sides finally removed himself from the room.

He was like a brother to me, but what brothers always got along? The growing problem continued to be how Bella was sure as hell not like my sister.

Adelina took a seat across from us. After a subtle throat clear, she clasped her hands on the white marble counter and asked, "Shall we start?" The moment her gaze swept to my face, I felt her second unspoken question hit me: *Or is there air we still need to clear?*

"Whenever Bella is ready." Because I'd never be ready for a walk down memory lane regarding Bella's past relationships. And yet, in the back of my head, some sick and twisted part of me needed to hear what she had to say. For instance, were my lips the last she'd touched like hers were for me?

"Go ahead." Bella poked at the donut, adding more frosting to her finger, still not licking it off.

"Well, for starters, are you in a relationship now?"

I already knew the answer to Adelina's question, even if Bella never explicitly told me. First of all, when would she have time to date? She was always working.

Secondly, no way would Bella be fucking with my head every hour of every day these last few months with her just-below-the-radar flirting and all of her read-between-the-lines remarks if she was seeing someone. The woman was trustworthy and loyal. So, no, the only guy in her life was me, which was problem number one. I couldn't be her anything.

But here I am. Wanting to be her everything. To hang on to her every word. Make a list of targets to punish as needed while simultaneously growing nauseous thinking about the men who knew her body better than I did. Men who'd had the chance to wake up next to her. To see how the sunlight would catch in her hair in the morning. To brush their mouth over her smile before bed. To be the reason for her to smile in the first place.

I blinked my focus up to Bella, realizing I'd lost myself to my thoughts and didn't hear her answer. And she must have said something because Adelina was on to another question.

"When was the last time you were in a relationship?" Before Bella could answer, Adelina quickly added, "Some of these questions may seem ridiculous and too personal, but in my experience, if anyone is watching you and they sent that photo, then it's someone you've already met and know. Someone close to you. Whether that be physically in proximity, like someone living across the street, or a person you dated."

"Like a long-term thing?" Bella made a *hmmm* noise as if feigning thinking, but there I was hung up on her word choice.

I was about to skip to my own line of questions if she didn't answer soon, starting with: *Who were you with for a short-term thing? And when?*

"Nothing long-term since my ex last year. A few dates here and there since, but none that made it to a second. But it's been"—she chose that exact moment to pull her focus from the donut and glance at me—"months since even that."

I did the mental calculations, assuming those "months" were at least four since our kiss happened at the end of May.

For a woman who couldn't be mine, we'd both done a bang-up job of remaining faithful to an imaginary relationship.

Hell, I hadn't realized I'd been in one with her until this moment, but there it was. Clear as day.

The reason I turned down women's advances at my bar was sitting next to me. The *why* I gave up my normal one-night stands and chose to read, play *Call of Duty*, or hunt predators at night instead was finally licking that frosting from her finger.

Did it take getting knocked in the head and smashing my

face into a steering wheel to realize my disinterest in other women was because the only woman I wanted was my best friend's sister?

"You okay?" Adelina asked, but I couldn't acknowledge her *or* stop staring at Bella's mouth as she sucked more of the frosting free.

Well, that's it, I'm screwed. Because if Adelina wasn't in the kitchen, I wasn't sure if even Constantine being down the hall would stop me from begging this woman to let me put my face between her legs and eat her instead.

"Hudson?" Adelina mused, somehow reading my dirty thoughts. "You with us or lost in your head?"

I'm lost somewhere, all right.

I used my bruised forearm to press down on the erection in my jeans. There was something seriously wrong with me to get turned on right now. "What were we talking about again?"

"My sex life." Bella cut off my oxygen supply with those three words. "Lack thereof, I should say."

And the breath was back in my lungs. Doubtfully for long, given how much trouble I was obviously in with this woman.

"Dating apps? You ever use them? There are a lot of creeps lurking there. Any red flags?" Adelina asked Bella, reminding me of why we were here in the first place, which helped kill the bulge in my jeans a bit.

"No. No swiping left or right. No apps." Bella pushed away the plated donut and propped her elbow on the counter, setting her chin on her palm. "Honestly, I haven't encountered anyone new this year I could say would develop an unhealthy obsession with me."

"Is there such a thing as a healthy obsession?" *Where the hell did that come from?*

Bella faltered, her arm collapsing at my question. She straightened and peered at me, eyes going up and down my body as if doing a quick inventory of my appearance. "Sure. Alessandro's obsession with his wife. Enzo's for Maria."

Mine for you? No, that wasn't healthy. It was forbidden.

"Okay, so no red flags from any new guys." Adelina was the only one focused on the mission at hand, another reason she was wrong to include me in this conversation. "So, let's talk about this ex, then. Has he made contact since you two broke up? Was it an amicable split?" Adelina drew Bella's attention with those questions.

Bella brought her hands to her lap, and when I turned on my stool to get a better read on her, I didn't like what I saw.

Nerves.

What was it she didn't want to share?

My hard-on was now dead with concerns her asshole ex may be a problem, and she'd kept me in the dark about it.

"My brothers, not to mention this guy next to me, scared him off. But he only attempted to return to my life because he felt he needed me." She kept her eyes on her hands.

"What do you mean?" I asked before Adelina could.

"You remember Pablo's an artist, right? Well, when we broke up, he lost his ability to paint. He decided it was because he'd lost his muse. Me."

I didn't like where this was going, but I shut my mouth so she could continue. And so I could find out whether or not he'd be added to my shit list. The fact I didn't preemptively have that asshole on it meant I'd lost my touch.

"Pablo approached me a few times this year, begging me to take him back. To, at the least, pose for him. He thought he needed me to become inspired again. He was always high when I saw him, and he usually didn't press hard when I turned him down." She held up both palms. "To be clear, I always said no. I felt bad for him, but I wouldn't date someone simply so they could be artistically creative again."

Pose? High? *Usually?* Usually meant there'd been a time he didn't take no for an answer.

Adelina removed her phone from her pocket, presumably to take notes. "Please, continue."

Bella turned on her seat, setting her hand on my chest while locking eyes with me. And there was no chance she'd miss the thunderous beats. "He's more of a danger to himself, I promise."

"Yeah, I'd say so. Because if I find out he set a hand on you, I'll kill him." I stood so fast the stool fell back, and Bella came up with me, keeping her hand in place.

Forgetting we weren't alone, I waited for her to tell me more.

When she didn't talk, I gritted out, "Does he need to die?" I'd only planned on a very unhinged conversation with the man for asking her to be his muse, but that very well might change depending on her answer.

"Like I said, he's always been on drugs when he's approached me."

"And? Alcohol. Drugs. Neither are excuses." I swallowed, becoming increasingly tense as I waited for her to share more.

"I know." She removed her hand from my chest and looked at Adelina as if remembering she was there with us. "He's not the one who sent the photo, though. He's still in rehab. Because when he approached me the last time, he was on much heavier drugs than he'd ever used in the past, and he didn't want to take no for an answer."

My heart.

Fuck.

There it went. Out into the wild and to a lawless wasteland where rules wouldn't apply.

"He was a mess. Desperate. And, um, my refusal to be his

muse sent him over the edge. He grabbed me pretty hard." She touched her arm as if remembering.

And now so was I, finding myself back in her office the day I'd noticed the mark and asked her about it. "The bruise you had in August . . . ?"

She quietly stared at me, seemingly surprised I'd recall that moment. Of course I did. I paid attention to everything when it came to this woman.

"He shoved me to the ground, but the second he realized what he'd done, he took off. I called his mom that night to let her know I was worried about him, and she convinced him to check into rehab. So, I think we can rule him out. I didn't want to bring this up because I didn't want you to lose your mind. Or my brothers."

I stepped back, my gaze shooting to the fallen stool, and I mindlessly righted it. "What if he has someone keeping tabs on you while he's in rehab, and he discovered we'd been spending a lot of time together? He could be jealous." I highly doubted this theory, but I had to be certain of his innocence when it came to the photo. "Pablo may have chosen to have someone deliver that photo because it was the only one he could find online of us together. He wanted to remove me from the picture to make his point. To scare you."

"You don't actually believe that, do you?" Bella lifted a brow.

No. But fucking A, I hate this man.

"I'll look into him. Check who's visited him as well. Obviously ensure he's also still in rehab," Adelina said softly, speaking for the first time in what felt like hours' worth of seconds having stretched by.

"Thank you." I nodded to Adelina, trusting her to handle Pablo's innocence or guilt regarding the photo since this was her area of expertise.

The Art of You

Bella rubbed her hands up and down her denim-covered arms, keeping quiet.

"I wish you'd told me when this happened." Defeat cut through my voice. "At least, told your brothers." I slid the stool back in place beneath the marble overhang. "Things could've gone much differently with him, and—"

"I know." Tears filled her eyes, more than likely remembering Bianca now, the same as I was. "Secrets get people killed."

Chapter 15

Isabella

"I think I should let you two finish the conversation. I'm going to check in with the others." Hudson nodded at Adelina, avoiding eye contact with me. He started for the hall, only to pause in the doorway. Lifting his good arm, he set his palm inside the doorframe. "What drug was he on?"

I set a hand to my stomach at the gnawing-like pain there. "Fentanyl. His mom told me that was what he'd become addicted to."

His back muscles tightened, and he bowed his head ever so slightly, then he walked away.

It took me a few seconds to gather myself before facing Adelina. "I'm sorry about all of that. You probably feel like you third-wheeled a heated exchange between two friends. But trust me when I say Pablo isn't guilty. Not of this, at least."

Adelina motioned for me to sit. Instead of acknowledging my opinion about Pablo, she said, "That conversation couldn't have been easy."

"Easier for me to say than for him to hear. He's overprotective like my brothers."

The Art of You

"Not sure if that's all it is, but . . ." She let that "but" hang there like the echo of a bell, and she couldn't continue until it was done. "I may not work for BAU at the FBI, but I can still profile someone from a hundred feet away."

Finally planting my ass back on the stool, my legs like rubber, I pressed, "And that means?"

"That you're not just a friend to him, and he's lying to both of you if he says you are." She'd stepped right in it. No holds barred. No hesitation. "I only bring this up because, as I told him earlier, someone may be jealous of your relationship."

Well, as of thirty or forty minutes ago, Hudson made it clear there would be no relationship. He gave Constantine his word. And he'd never go back on that. But I didn't need to unburden my thoughts on her.

"I have a few more questions, and then we can wrap this up." She was waving the white flag, choosing not to push a stranger into divulging more.

Thank God.

The next thirty minutes were a blur as I went back through my history. She was thorough, wanting to know pretty much everything about my life, worried that even the least significant detail could be important. From my rebellious years in high school to the moment I found my sister murdered on her apartment floor, up until yesterday—all of it.

Once we were done, I was more exhausted mentally than physically. "I just don't think I have a stalker. And that woman's date really could've just happened to be looking out the window Friday night at that exact moment I went outside, yada yada yada, right?"

She arched her brow as if surprised I'd make light of the situation. Maybe the triple *yadas* were a bit much. "Possibly."

"This still could be Kit's doing. She'd have expected I'd tell Hudson about the picture and that someone photoshopped him from the background. Then when we bumped into her at the party, I'd assume she sent it, and she'd been trying to screw with us, then she'd get the spicy headline she wanted," I rambled, hoping it all made sense. I *needed* it to be her. "Kit would probably know my reputation, and I call shit out when I see it. I lack a filter, if you haven't noticed. She was hoping for a scene." Only it didn't come, because we were on an op.

At Adelina's second, "Possibly," I pushed at my forehead as if I could physically force the answers to our problems to surface.

I was anything but zen after this morning. More like the antithesis. My hand plummeted to the counter when my brain cells fired up, circumventing the exhaustion. "Zen as fuck."

"Excuse me?" A slight smile of confusion tugged at her lips.

"That agent, Clarke, right?" At her nod, I continued, "He's itching to throw charges at Hudson for something, even if he has to make up a crime." Well, at least it felt that way based on our conversation. "He's in league with the AG, who's planning to run for governor against Hudson's dad."

Adelina's brows shot together, and I could see the wheels turning.

"Could Clarke be working with this reporter to help create problems for Governor Ashford?" Was that too much of a stretch, or just the right amount of leaning into the idea? *Please say yes.*

"He could be Kit's inside source about the guest list, as well as the one to get her included in the press pool at the last minute." Good. She was saying what I'd hoped to hear.

"Hudson never goes to these things, so when Clarke saw him on the list, he may have seen this as an opportunity to take a shot at him to get to his father." I stood as more and more came together.

"The reporter may not know about the photo sent to you. Clarke could've arranged for it to be sent to keep everyone's hands clean. He just planted her at the party knowing she'd make waves," she suggested.

"And while they were both clueless about why we were really there, we gave them a headline they never saw coming."

That night felt like such a blur. I had to untangle the web of memories before landing on one important "point" of the overall picture.

"Kit seemed genuinely surprised when I confronted her about the photo. Well, I didn't outright mention it, but she was taken aback when I accused her of targeting me. As much as I don't like her, she may be a pawn in a bigger game, and you're right, she didn't know about the photo." The lengths people would go to for a campaign was sickening. "Of course, it may not even be Clarke, and I just want it to be because he's an easy target to pin this on after how he treated us yesterday."

"These are all theories," she reminded me but kept her tone optimistic. "Good ones, but I still have to do my due diligence and bark up every tree and see what I can turn up. From Pablo to my colleagues."

"I *need* it to be this theory, okay?" I wasn't above begging for her to pull some magic out of her FBI hat and prove my hypothesis correct.

"The game of politics is ugly, so it's possible," she said in a somber tone as I took a seat. "But for now, I think we stick to the plan to keep an eye on this reporter's next moves before we question her. See who she talks to and what she does. Probably a good idea to tail Clarke, too." She stood and circled the counter, then sat next to me.

"What does your gut say?" Was hers right like Hudson's often was?

She peered up at the ceiling before dropping words I didn't want to hear. "If all evidence points to this theory, it's because someone wants us looking one way when we really should be looking another."

Chapter 16

Isabella

"A LITTLE EARLY FOR DRINKIN', don't you think?"

I loved when Hudson's Texas drawl made an appearance. Setting down the unopened bottle on the bar counter, I slowly turned around to find him doing that sexy lean thing in the doorway of my father's game room. Arms folded. Attention locked on me with concern.

"*Or*, hear me out, we could pretend we're at the airport. Rules don't apply there. Well, at least not judgment of prenoon drinking."

He didn't budge an inch at my joke. His brows remained tight, and so did every line of his body. Rigid and tense.

"Adelina's gone," he cut straight to business. "Constantine went with her. Enzo, too. They don't want her running around the city without backup, especially since the questions she's asking could get her killed."

Good idea.

He pushed away from the doorway and came into the room, sweeping his hand along the felt pool table before stopping to pick up the eight ball. "She insisted she'd be fine. Her job is dangerous after all, but we outvoted her on the safety thing. It was five to one. Callie ruled in our favor as well."

His tone was almost eerily distant and detached, and I couldn't stand it. Was he mad about Pablo, or knowing I'd be opposed to some medieval idea he'd probably conjured up? Like putting Pablo's head in a guillotine.

"Will my brothers fly back here later with my parents?" My words were stiff and had me wondering whether I required a drink to get through this talk.

Hudson kept his eyes on the sphere in his hand, perhaps hoping it was one of those Magic 8 Balls, and if he shook it, all of the answers to our ever-growing list of questions would be revealed. "Constantine decided it'd be best for your parents to stay in the city for now. Your mom objected. She was also outnumbered."

"So democratic of you all in your decision-making processes." Despite my sarcasm—which was so second nature I just couldn't help it—I probably would've voted the same as my brothers on that one. Having my nervous mother here would only increase my anxiety. "Where are Alessandro and Callie?"

"Unpacking in the suite on the second floor of the pool house. He'll follow up on some leads from there." He set the ball down and rolled it, sinking it in the corner pocket. "I guess your brother wants privacy while we're all staying here."

Yeah, so no one hears his wife screaming his name during sex. At least one of us here is getting lucky. What a thing for me to be thinking about considering everything going on around me.

"So, it's just us in the house right now?" I lowered my voice like that was a dirty little secret.

"Us and a few of the security detail rotating in and out of the home, yeah." *Still* no eye contact.

"Adelina tell you our theory about Clarke possibly working with Kit?" I asked after stifling a frustrated sigh.

"She did." He set his back to the pool table, bracing his hands on the wood on each side of him. "As much as I hate the idea you're being dragged into the political limelight for the sake of a headline because of my father, I'd sure as hell prefer that to the alternative."

"You." I pointed to him when he *finally* looked up at me. "Me." My finger briefly landed on my chest. "Same boat." I tried a smile to see if that'd do the trick to loosen this man up. "In your case, submarine."

He closed one eye and faked a shuddery reaction. "I fucking hated those things. Leave it to me to discover I'm claustrophobic a day too late."

"And here I thought you opted to go out for the Teams because it sounded cooler. All this time, it was because you were afraid of going down under."

A light, genuine laugh fell from his lips, and I was relieved to see I could crack through his defenses without too much effort.

"So, um, what do we do now?" I asked when silence replaced the sounds of his laughter.

"We have orders to rest and recover and let everyone else handle things for today." He stroked his jaw, his facial hair coming in even more since he'd last shaved on Friday.

I searched for something to lean against so I didn't prove my family right, that I was too tired to stand without support. My gaze flicked to the camera in the room. Constantine had a security app on his phone and was probably checking it regularly. No sound in the room, at least.

"We're not actually doing that, are we?" Before he could answer, I lifted my hand. "Let me guess, they voted and won."

"Prettttty much."

"Did you just drag out a word? Copying me now, huh?" I went over to the poker table and set my palms on the felt.

"You're a horrible influence, what can I say?" Even-toned voice despite the tease. Were his walls already back up?

"Oh, the worst." I did my best to soften him once again. "But um, what do we do with our time, then? I'm incapable of twiddling my thumbs or sitting on my hands. I need a distraction."

His eyes narrowed on my mouth, and now I couldn't help but imagine the perfect distraction—his lips on mine.

If Bianca was writing my story, she'd surely add in a stolen moment. Probably in a library instead of the game room, but I'd take it anywhere.

The second Hudson locked on to the bruise at my temple and the purple beneath my right eye, his jaw strained and the brood was back.

Bianca, cut me some slack here. I almost looked up at the ceiling, as if she could hear me and really was authoring this moment. *I think we've had enough tension. I'm ready for him to give in to desire. For some fireworks.* I had to give it a shot just in case. God had a sense of humor when it came to me, so anything was possible.

If only Bianca really could pen my life to paper. She'd give me a perfect happily ever after. I just wished her story had turned out with one as well.

"Are you going to keep staring at me like I'm a broken piece of pottery you have no clue how to fix?"

"You're not broken. No fixin' needed." The husky sincerity in his tone and the way he peered at me almost had me believing that.

If only. "Are you going to tell my brothers about Pablo?" I hadn't intended to pivot to another uncomfortable topic, but the second I'd thought it, out it came.

The Art of You

He shook his head, not taking any time to consider my question. "Your story to tell, not mine. That's up to you if you share."

Phew. "Thank you." The blue felt of the poker table beneath my palms stole my attention and I remembered the first time I'd ever sat here. Felt like yesterday, not decades ago.

"What are you thinking about?" Brave of him to ask considering when it came to me, you never knew what kind of answer you'd get.

"My dad taught me to play poker when I was only seven," I shared. "All of us kids, actually. We used to sit together at this table in the summers and play endless games. Instead of poker chips, or even dollars, he had us play with pennies and nickels." I smiled at the memory, doing my best to hang on to the happy ones. It was hard never knowing when the sadness would try and steal them away. And inevitably, it always did.

He came around the poker table, standing opposite of me. "You're in front of Bianca's seat."

I kept my eyes on the chair as he gripped the back of it, the slight veins in his hands popping from the tension.

"Pigtails and a missing front tooth. That was me. Permed hair and boys on the brain was Bianca." I almost laughed at the image. God, I missed her.

Shit, I was losing the plot. Why was I sharing this story?

I blinked my attention up to him, finding him quietly waiting for me to continue.

"One thing I struggled with when it came to poker, and still do to this day, is I never played hands I didn't think I could truly win. It's not that I couldn't bluff, I didn't want to."

"Being honest isn't the worst trait to have." He semi-smiled and shrugged.

"But I did lie to you. In August." I resisted the impulse to close my eyes while I shared how I'd been dishonest with him, even though he was now well aware of that fact after my interview with Adelina. "Pablo walked uninvited into my house. I never got around to changing the locks. He had a key, and I completely forgot about that. Any time he'd come by before, he'd always rung the bell."

He let go of the chair and took a step away from the table as if it were made of fire not hardwood.

"I've changed the locks since." I quickly extinguished the flames before the man lost the plot, too. "Anyway—"

"Don't 'anyway' me." He swiped his palm across his eyes as if wishing he could unsee something, his broad shoulders losing some slack in their typical tense state. "You can't brush off the fact you were so casual about your safety and expect me to not freak out. You let this man have a key to your place, and you forgot to change the locks after you split?" He was shaking his head now.

Consider his control broken in half.

Not the story I'd wanted Bianca to write.

Where was a firefighter when I needed one to put out this new inferno I'd inadvertently caused?

"God, you stress me out." He tore his hand through his hair, then winced at the movement, accidentally using his injured arm. "I should've taken more pills," he added under his breath.

"Not good for you. Two was enough."

The eye roll wasn't lost on me. I about dropped another *anyway* on him to try and swing back to the point I'd been trying to make, but I didn't want to be a total brat. He was right, after all. I shouldn't have been careless with my safety.

"So." Was that better than a sarcastic *anyway*? I hoped. "As I was saying, you already know what happened with Pablo, but the reason I'm rehashing this is because of what happened in the office the next day. You asked me about my arm, and I knew if I didn't remember everything my dad taught me about bluffing and having a poker face . . . well, I knew what would happen. So I lied to you. I was trying to protect you, not Pablo. I didn't want you getting in trouble by going after him."

"The last thing you need to do is protect me." He circled the table, dragging his knuckles along the felt with each step closer. When he stopped before me, he slowly guided his eyes up. "When I'm not running a bar, I hunt predators for a living. I'm well aware of the consequences of my actions and what would happen if law enforcement discovered how I took justice into my own hands."

What if that asshole Fed looked into Hudson's past, and he found out about his extracurricular activities and actually did come up with charges to throw at him?

"I don't regret my actions with the men we've hunted. They were pure evil. Demons, as far as I'm concerned." His hard gaze softened as his shoulders relaxed. "But I would've regretted the way I handled Pablo had you not lied to me. The rage would have consumed me. I don't know if I'd have been able to stop. I'd remember what happened to Bianca, and I'd have lost it." He closed his eyes, his chest rising and falling as he worked to control his breathing. His anger stoked even now.

Memories of finding my sister in a pool of her own blood catapulted to my mind. And there it was. Proof of how fast the happy times could be stolen and replaced with the ugly.

"I would have been wrong, though." Hudson's words as he opened his eyes abruptly snatched me back to the present. "No mistake about it, he deserved to be punished for ever setting a hand on you, but Pablo's not evil. Those drugs he took are. That drug *is* the devil. It steals lives." His long pause, and the sad hitch to his tone, forced my eyes to open. "It killed a teammate of mine."

Oh God. "I'm so sorry."

He was staring at the floor between us, and when he lifted his head, his blue eyes were glossy.

Somehow, I'd blinked, and in the space of that time, he'd gone from fuming mad at Pablo to the verge of showing an emotion I rarely saw from him.

"You never told me." I set my hand on his arm, but he immediately backed free of my touch.

He huffed out a deep, seemingly taxing breath. "I don't want to talk about this." He turned away, his back muscles drawing together. "Distraction." The word came out low and gritty. "I need one." He slowly faced me again while drawing his hands to his hips.

I did my best to keep my emotions in check. To not sob on his behalf, knowing he was hurting on the inside and I'd been unaware of his struggles. He had a much better poker face than me. How long had he been hiding his pain? *What happened to you that you don't want to talk about?*

"Please, Bella." His jaw clenched, but I spotted the slightest wobble of his chin. The fissure in the solid wall of strength he was doing his damndest to maintain. "I need a distraction."

I thought back to Friday when I'd asked for his help to distract me at the party. "The eighties," I blurted. "Movies, I mean. Bet my parents still have all of our DVDs in the theater room. We could watch some classics. You know, like *Ghost. Dirty Dancing.*"

"Swayze," he said under his breath, which I took to mean, *yes.*

I offered him my hand, a little worried he wouldn't take it.

He looked up toward the ceiling, and when I followed his eyes to the camera there, my shoulders slumped.

Constantine.

I flinched the second I felt his skin touch mine. "Feel like

The Art of You

having a stiff drink with our candy?" he asked, taking me by surprise.

It took me a second to lift my gaze from our clasped palms to find his face.

"Who said anything about candy?" I bit the inside of my cheek, still trying to get over the fact Hudson was holding my hand knowing my brother might see this moment.

"That sweet tooth of yours did."

The weight of what he'd been holding seemed to slip away like a magician performing a trick. Poof. Gone. He'd successfully hidden his pain under the rug, exactly the way I'd stowed the photo away between the magazines on Friday. *Now look where we are.* Secrets always came out one way or another.

"You're right about that." I forced a smile.

"So, are we pretending to be at an airport where the rules don't apply, or what?" His sexy tone was nothing more than a bandage.

Now wasn't the time to force him to unearth his secrets. He'd begged for a distraction, and I would put every one of my father's poker tips to use, bluffing my way to acting okay. Just like he was.

"Only if you promise to show me whether or not you can dirty dance."

Chapter 17

Hudson

BELLA WAS CURLED UP ASLEEP on the couch, her head on my lap. I couldn't help but stare at the bruise around her eye and feel guilty we'd even been in an accident in the first place. I should've never let that happen.

I went for my scotch to work the lump down my throat, careful not to disturb her as I reached for it on the table next to me. The drink did nothing to ease my guilt, so I forced my attention back to the screen.

After watching her two favorite Swayze movies, she let me watch one of my favorites of his—*Road House*. But we were now on film four, and she'd switched the vibe up quite a bit to *The Shining*. Apparently, much like golf, horror helped her fall asleep.

It also could've been the food we overindulged in that knocked her out. We'd chased down our Cantonese dim sum, dumplings, and sweet and sour pork with alcohol. Not to mention the woman had to be in a sugar coma from all the candy she'd eaten.

The Art of You

But aside from bathroom breaks, we hadn't budged from this spot on the couch in about seven hours.

Maybe we were ignoring a whole host of problems that kept building up to what I felt would be the point of no return, but spending this time with her had to be the best seven hours I'd experienced in a long damn time. Though, I'd have to admit, I may have been more focused on her than the movies.

While sipping my drink, I mindlessly ran my fingers through her thick hair, watching the kid in the movie ride his tricycle down an empty hallway at the Overlook Hotel.

My hand went still as I realized we were no longer alone. Alessandro was in the doorway, staring at us. He quietly gestured for me to join him, and I set aside my drink, contemplating how to extricate myself without waking Sleeping Beauty.

After stealthily maneuvering her into a new position so I could stand, I went into the hall and immediately addressed the elephant in the room. "About what you saw."

"Relax. I'm not Constantine." He folded his arms, propping his shoulder against the wall at his side.

Works for me.

"I appreciate you looking after her today."

Not really a hardship to spend the day cozied up with her.

"How's she doing now?"

Despite her bruises, which killed me to look at, she didn't seem in pain. Well, from what she'd told me. "She's fine, I guess." Maybe he should've been asking her this, though.

"What about you?" He angled his head, eyes narrowing, likely preparing for me to lie to him.

So, I went ahead and gave him the truth. No sense in hiding it. "Feel like someone played whack-a-mole with my chest, face, and back."

"Sounds pleasant." He smirked. "You should be taking something stronger than Advil."

"Says the guy who can't even handle cold medicine without acting drunk."

He rolled his eyes before glancing at the open door. I started to close it, assuming he wanted more privacy, but then opted to leave it slightly cracked.

The idea of leaving Bella asleep and alone with Jack from The *Shining*, even if he was on screen, didn't sit well with me. As crazy as our weekend had been, I was prepared for the impossible to happen. For fictional characters to come to life. The dead to start walking. Pigs to actually fly. And Constantine to tell me he'd love having me as a brother-in-law.

I rubbed my eyes at the last thought. That one definitely snuck up on me. It had no business being in my head. Time to switch gears. Kind of. "You hear from your brothers?"

"Constantine texted that he'd rather go over everything with us in person. He and Enzo should be here in an hour or two." He pushed away from the wall. "Not sure if that makes me feel better or worse."

Same.

"Anything from your dad?"

After unleashing a disgruntled sigh, the mere thought of my father souring my mood, I shared, "If the Feds learned anything helpful from their interview of the two suspects, they've yet to talk to my father about it. So, unfortunately, nothing on my end to share." My gaze flicked to the bandage still on my arm, the memory of the car accident and the fact I could have lost Bella still far too fresh. "Where are you at with looking into that valet? Enzo turned that job over to you, right?"

"I'm still looking into the both of them, especially the one that first parked the Porsche when you arrived. Nothing conclusive yet."

It's probably a waste of time.

"Eduardo and Chris knew you were coming to the party, but they didn't know the real reason why since the ambo kept them in the dark. They thought you fell for the trap to draw you away from where the real ransom drop would take place. Sounds like they had a contingency plan set in place in case things went south like they did."

"The truck at the gas station and that valet for an assist, you mean?"

"They could have easily recruited that valet. Told him they had concerns about a potential threat to the ambassador and tasked him with tagging your vehicle."

No one should've been able to get any kind of drop on me. I'd been unfocused. Not only with Bella at my side, but with the ghost of an old friend in the back of my mind.

"The kid may have even thought he was helping protect the ambo from you."

"The kid?" I arched my brow.

"Now that I'm forty, anyone under twenty-five feels like a kid to me."

"Fucking same, which is why I didn't even check out Bella—"

Alessandro's arms fell at the same time I realized what I'd almost confessed, fortunately cutting myself off and finishing that thought in my head.

And where the hell did that come from, anyway? I did the math in my head. Shit. She was twenty-five when I started calling her Bella. Seven years ago. It should've been hard to pinpoint an exact date, but it'd been a memorable evening. She'd come home from London for her birthday, and since our travel schedules never seemed to align, it'd been the first time I'd seen her in two years.

Her family threw her a party worthy of royalty, and I'd

never forget the moment I set eyes on her walking into the hotel ballroom. She was suddenly all grown up. The way her fitted black gown clung to her golden-tan skin, it appeared to have been glued to her body. Her hair had been pinned up instead of wild and down like normal.

After I'd picked my jaw up off the floor, the name Bella rolled from my tongue when I'd told her happy birthday.

I hadn't looked back since, or thought about why I'd used that name, until Adelina mentioned it this morning.

I blinked, remembering where I was. I hauled my ass from the past to the present. "So . . ." I cleared my throat. *Focus.* "Even if that valet tagged the Porsche, he's still more than likely not our shooter, which brings us back to square one."

Alessandro stole a look at the theater room, and I wasn't sure if he was about to press me on my earlier unfinished thought. He wound up going in a completely different direction than I expected and said, "I'm guessing Izzy hasn't been on her phone in the last thirty minutes. I know you rarely use social media, but she does all the time." His gray eyes slipped down between us and to the floor. Shoulders breaking forward yet again from the weight of whatever he planned to share.

"No, her phone is in her bedroom. Why?"

"Since Callie and I have spent all afternoon in the depths of social media hell poring over posts connected to the party . . ."

I'd never get Bella's remark about ellipses and their emphasis out of my head. I swore I could visibly see the three dots rolling between us as I waited for Alessandro to continue. "What is it that'll make me want to actually commit murder?" My nerves were toast at this point.

He reached into his pocket and unlocked his phone. "Your name is already a trending hashtag on X. Videos are spreading like wildfire across all apps. You're going to want to punch a few people. I did. I may have spent more than a few minutes swinging at the heavy bag in the gym." He kept his hand curled around the phone. "I'm sure your father will be blowing you up with calls the second his campaign manager lowers his blood pressure. Probably throw a glass instead of a punch like I did."

My stomach was already doing motherfucking cartwheels, why not turn them into rings of fire? "Just hand it over."

He finally set his phone on my open palm. "Start with X. It's where Kit published her story. And it's the origin of this mess."

I stared at the image Kit had posted of me. It was the photo she'd taken of us outside the party when I'd been distracted. "Twenty-seven million views in thirty minutes? Is that even possible?"

Alessandro shrugged. "The internet is a strange beast."

I forced myself to open Kit's article, and it took me less than two seconds to understand why Alessandro expected me to snap.

Kit severed my arteries with her words, and I'd bleed out in no time.

I had to breathe as steadily as possible through my nose as I read her article, doing my best to remember to keep control. *Who the hell told Kit this? And why now?*

Kit claimed to have a reliable source who shared the real reason I left the Navy. Her source claimed my father had lied about why I truly left, choosing to use my mother's cancer as a way to garner sympathy and support for his campaign rather than acknowledging my career as a SEAL ended in 2010 because of a disastrous op the government covered up as a training exercise gone wrong.

Everyone on my team had been ordered by Command to keep our mouths shut about what went down that day. That op had been fifty shades of motherfucking classified by orders of

Joint Special Operations Command. And JSOC had taken their orders from Congress.

"It gets a bit more . . . gross. The accusations," Alessandro warned after recognizing I'd paused only a few lines into reading.

Because there I was, right back in Afghanistan, surrounded by both gunfire and buildings ablaze.

"Hudson?" He gently set a hand on my shoulder, pulling me from my past hell and into this new nightmare.

I forced myself to continue reading, and my stomach dropped even more. "I did *not* sleep with your sister," I hissed. "You believe me, right?" My eyes burned as I fumed at the accusation that I'd slept with Bianca Costa and had moved on to my next target: *"The last female darling of one of New York's wealthiest families."*

My hand holding the phone shook as I read someone's comment to her vile story.

"Son of the governor is trying to manwhore his way into becoming a billionaire."

"Of course I know you didn't sleep with Bianca." Alessandro's words had me peering up at him, and he slowly removed his hand from my shoulder. "What about Izzy?"

"I didn't sleep with either of them, dammit." The deep drop in my voice did me dirty. While it was the truth, I felt guilty how desperately I wished that I could sleep with Bella.

He cleared his throat, not even close to being subtle about it. "I meant, does Izzy know you never . . . with Bianca? You and Bianca were close back then, and if she reads this article, she might wonder."

Jesus. "It never really came up in conversation," I drawled, unsure if I meant that sarcastically or in anger at this entire situation. We already had too much to deal with, and we didn't need more. But the fact Kit published the story had me more inclined to believe she was connected to everything, just as Bella had first assumed. "Maybe the photo really was from Kit."

"I guess we'll know more when the guys get back."

I handed him the phone. "I can't look at this any longer. It's all bullshit."

"So, you don't have a thing for my sister?" He lifted a brow as he pocketed his phone. No humor there, just an honest question. One I couldn't answer.

I tightened my mouth into a hard line, unable to bluff my way out of this. I was too unhinged. He'd see right through me. "I would've left the Navy to take care of my mother, that's true," I said instead, finding myself wrestling with guilt, my least favorite emotion. "But what you don't know is I also handed in my trident and didn't re-up because of what happened on that last op." My stomach roiled as I stared at the floor between us. "Kit's anonymous source either came from Command or someone in Congress. That, or someone from my old team talked."

He paused. Processed. Took it all in, then surrendered a quick, "Fuck." Another long pause. "I'm sorry. But, uh, assuming it's not someone from JSOC or Congress, any idea who from your old team may have a grudge against you?"

My body locked up, the tension mounting. I hung my head, giving in to that wicked emotion of guilt again, and admitted, "Yeah, probably everyone." *At least those still alive.*

Chapter 18

Hudson

TAKING my phone from my pocket, I gave Alessandro the six-digit code, which was my mother's birthdate, then held it out. "Call Adelina for me. Tell her to look into a man named Alfred Anthony Andrews. See where he's living now and what he's up to. Find out if he's been in New York recently."

"His parents must've had a sense of humor," Alessandro remarked while accepting my phone.

"We used to refer to Alfie as Triple A whenever we were Stateside. He was the man you called when you got yourself into trouble. He always came in for an assist."

"Sounds like a good guy. Why am I looking him up? You don't really think he's this reporter's source, do you?"

"I could've sworn I saw him at the party Friday night. It was just for a second, but it's hard to miss a six-foot, redheaded, bearded man in a tux. I thought I'd hallucinated him. He wasn't on the list, and I haven't seen or heard from him in years. So why would he be there, you know?" I set my hands on my hips, trying to wrap my head around everything. "Given Kit's viral story today, and the fact I was photoshopped out of that photo sent to Bella, maybe he was there." *Or maybe it was Pablo who sent the photo, hell if I know.*

"If Alfie made it through security without being a guest, then someone helped get him in," he said as if it were a fact. "As a Teamguy, he'd know how to avoid the security cameras. Probably could kill the footage after to hide the fact he was there, too."

I wasn't even close to being ready to believe Alfie was connected to any of this, but I had to rule out every possibility, especially since it meant keeping Bella safe.

When I kept quiet, stewing in my thoughts, Alessandro suggested, "I'll get some up-to-date photos of him as well. See if I can find him in the background of anyone's posts from the party."

"You won't find him in any," I said after an exhausted sigh. "He'd never make that mistake."

"But you saw him. Well, *if* it was him there."

I swallowed. "Then he wanted me to see him. Probably screwing with my head, the same way someone screwed with Bella's by sending her that photo."

"I guess my question is why would he be coming after you now? Why not a long time ago? You think Kit found out who was on your team? Sought some of the guys out looking for a story, and he gave her one? Or someone reached out to her, and you were the target all along?"

"Why send *that* photo to Bella, though? What's the point other than hoping to stir up trouble with Kit before we bumped into her? It doesn't add up. Why not send something to me instead?"

"Because messing with her, especially with something tied to such a sensitive topic, would piss you off a hell of a lot more."

He tapped at his chest with my phone. "People can come after me all day long, but they go near my wife, they've issued themselves a death wish."

"Well, Bella's not mine." *So I have to keep telling myself.*

"But whoever did it knows she's like family, and you'd do anything for family."

When I didn't reply to that, he killed me with his next words. "I won't suggest the possibility your SEAL brother was working with the kidnappers, but we can't exactly *not* throw the idea at the wall to see if it sticks."

"No." I shook my head. "He'd never. If Alfie's involved in this, I think it was just his bad luck he and Kit picked this weekend to screw with me." I blew out a deep breath, and with it the pain in my chest from the accident resurfaced. "I don't know what to think. Nothing makes sense anymore," I admitted, trying not to let my voice break. "My head's all over the place." I stole a look at the theater room, assuming she'd be waking anytime. "I gotta get out of here for a second. Go for a walk on the beach. That's why I need you to handle the call to Adelina for me. And when my father gets wind of this—"

"I'll handle him, too."

One thing I could rely on with the Costas was they'd never ask me questions about my service time. I knew Alessandro wouldn't press to learn why my old team may hate me. He'd let me share if, and only if, I wanted to.

"Take it easy on the walk. You were just in a car accident."

The pain would be worth the fresh air and the chance to clear my head. "Copy that. Just get me when the guys are here."

He continued to study me. "You sure you're going to be okay?"

I gave him the only answer that made sense to me. "If

Bella's good, I'm good." I started past him, then hesitated and shot a backward glance. "We won't be able to protect her from those headlines and reading that garbage, will we?"

"No." He frowned. "Best we can do is damage control."

Chapter 19

Isabella

An hour had gone by since I'd woken in the theater room, discovering Alessandro working on his laptop instead of Hudson next to me.

After I'd rubbed the sleep from my eyes, he'd sucker-punched me with the news. He ripped the Band-Aid off quick and dirty, letting me know I'd need a bottle of antacids the second I went online.

Apparently curiosity didn't only kill the cat, it killed me. I wasted no time in demanding my phone he'd taken from my room and was holding hostage.

I'd skipped over my mother's worried texts and voicemails, since she clearly was privy to the news, and I embarked on a journey down the rabbit hole of social media. Let's just say it was no Wonderland.

Keyboard warriors on steroids were rampant, spreading lies and filth about Hudson and my family. Now I understood why Hudson was MIA. Alessandro told me he'd needed air, and he didn't want to share that air with anyone.

My first reaction—aside from wanting to test if a cell phone was flushable—was to head to the beach. Not to take a casual stroll, but to dive into the cold Atlantic, hoping to stop myself from responding to the comments and slanderous accusations.

Alessandro seized my phone again and forbade any cold-water plunges. He even went as far as assigning one of the guys protecting us here to follow me everywhere while he continued chasing leads.

Malik, one of Constantine's most trusted operators, was currently hovering in the hallway outside my bedroom like another overprotective brother. And what was I doing? Standing by the window, marinating in my emotions, waiting for Hudson's return.

Wanting to forget the horridness I'd read, I decided to fill my mind with memories of my time in the theater room with Hudson. I still couldn't believe I passed out watching *The Shining* with my head on his lap. Somehow, our afternoon together had been perfect. And perfect wasn't something I'd expected to get out of today considering why we were at this house in the first place.

"My God, Izzy."

My shoulders startled back as Callie's voice abruptly cut through my thoughts.

I turned to see her in my bedroom doorway, staring at the easel that hadn't budged from its current position in over fourteen years.

"Did you draw that?" She came into the room, her cowgirl boots clicking across the hardwoods on her way to the canvas that'd been parked on the easel for nearly half my life. The only reason it hadn't collected dust was because my mom made sure it didn't.

I swallowed the lump in my throat. "Guilty."

"I had no idea you were an artist. You're incredibly talented."

I let the compliment roll off my shoulders. I didn't feel talented, I felt like a failure. "It's unfinished." I joined her by the very object I'd avoided looking at since we'd stepped foot in this house. "Just like her life."

"That's Bianca?" she whispered. "I thought it was a self-portrait."

"Me? Don't be silly. Look at her. She's gorgeous." I faked a laugh, and Callie playfully swatted the side of my arm.

"Girl." I interpreted her polite remark as Southern code for *Bullshit*.

"Well, beauty is in the eye of the beholder." I touched the drawing as if I could reach through the canvas. Dip my hand into the past and actually feel my sister's face. Be with her while she was still alive. "One person's masterpiece might be used as another person's dart board. So, there's that, too."

A gentle nudge of affection in the form of an elbow caught me in the ribs.

"She was always reading or writing in the garden when we were here, and I followed her around like a lost puppy," I said somberly. "I was her shadow. I thought she was the coolest."

"From what Alessandro has shared about her, she was pretty incredible. Just like you. She'd be proud of the woman you've become." Callie held my arm, then leaned over, resting her head on my shoulder as we both stared at the partially finished sketch. "Do you still draw? Paint? I'm surprised Alessandro never mentioned it."

"It's one of those things my family doesn't bring up at the dinner table, with anyone. You know, an off-limits topic. Like politics. Religion. They avoid conversations about our failures." *This is one of mine. Giving up my passion because I became passionless.*

"Hardly call this talent a failure." She lifted her head, searching for my eyes.

The Art of You

Sometimes I felt guilty about how much I loved having Callie as a sister. And Maria, too, of course. I was scared Bianca would think I was replacing her. It was hard to keep a wall up between them, though. They were experts at knocking them down. After all, Maria cracked Enzo's, and Callie blew down Alessandro's.

"I quit because she died, and Bianca would hate that. She'd hate it with every fiber of her being."

Well, damn. Now I was getting emotional all over again. I'd prefer being pissed off at faceless strangers on the internet to coping with this type of pain. This type didn't go away with any passage of time. You never truly got over losing someone you loved. *And why would I want to?*

"I have this fear that if I try to draw again, it'll be of the crime scene. I'll see her dead on that floor, resting in her own blood and . . ."

At some point, as I lost myself to my thoughts, Callie had pulled me in for a hug.

"I'm scared I'll only be able to depict death and sadness. And I've had enough sadness fill up my cup to last a lifetime. Why overflow it with the bad, you know?" That was the first time I admitted that. Heck, I'd never even told that to my therapist when she'd pressed me about taking up art again.

Callie gave me time to pull myself together. To work through what I'd admitted, quietly holding me the entire time.

When I finally pulled back, she gestured toward the canvas. "As beautiful as this drawing is, what I think you might need is a blank canvas to start with. You can always come back to this one. And when the time is right, you'll know." She met my eyes, and I had to fight back the tears.

"A clean slate?" I murmured more like a question.

"And no rules holding you hostage. Give yourself some grace. If what you create is sad, then it's sad. Maybe you have to work through your emotions to get to the place you were before." She let go of me, her tone soft as she added, "And maybe you'll find yourself somewhere different. Better, even. But you'll never know if you don't try."

I turned toward the window, catching sight of Hudson back on the property. "Thank you," I finally managed to get out. He was back, and I wanted—no, *needed* to get to him. "I, um." I faced her.

"It's okay. Go to him. I'll handle Malik so you two can be alone. I've got your back."

"Thank you." I pulled her in for another hug, forging past the remnants of pain lingering in my limbs. "If I do draw again, you've gotta let me sketch you one day. Cowgirl boots. Guitar in hand. My brother would pay good money for that."

She chuckled, then waved her hand, reminding me I had places to be and all that.

I looked over at my sister on the easel, then to Callie. "Maybe it's possible I can help Hudson the way you helped my brother."

"What do you mean?" she asked softly.

"Revive his heart so he can love again."

"Not possible." Callie shook her head, then held up her hand between us. "Hudson's heart isn't dead. You can tell in the way that man looks at you. You're the definition of a masterpiece in his eyes. You're like livin' art to him." Her soft Southern accent flowed through her words. "I mean, really. The man has it bad for you."

"Really?"

"Easy to discern as an objective outsider."

"Well, you're no longer an outsider. You're family. You're my . . ." I'd said this before, but standing in front of the drawing of Bianca made it feel that much *more*. "My sister."

She flicked a tear from the corner of her eye, trying not to get choked up, same as me. "You better go. You're ruining my mascara," she laugh-cried. "Go help that man understand he's allowed to feel what he does and that you both deserve happiness."

"I'll do my best, but he's stubborn."

"Your brother was also a serious pain in the ass, but I didn't give up on him. And you're a fighter like me. I have faith you'll knock some sense into him eventually. Then you can draw me, and I'll write a song about you two. A fair trade from where I stand."

"Got a title?" I teased. And then the reality of what happened sank in. Callie had managed to do the impossible. She'd helped me take that polar plunge, washing away my anger without ever having to get cold and wet in the freezing Atlantic.

"Work in progress." She winked. "But aren't we all?"

"Touché."

A devious smile crossed her lips a beat later. "It's close enough to bedtime, right?"

Barely seven. "For a toddler," I said with a laugh.

"Maybe you should change for the night before talking with Hudson." She lifted her brows up and down suggestively, waiting for me to get her drift.

I went to the doorway and stole a look at Malik in the hall. His back was to the wall, one booted foot propped up as he read something on his phone. *Hopefully not the rumors about my family.*

I quietly shut the door. "You want me to put on PJs before I talk to him? Hudson will lose his mind with me walking around like that in a house full of security."

She slapped her hands together, then focused on my dresser. "Precisely."

"It didn't work before," I said as she opened up a dresser

drawer. "I wore a bikini around him at his apartment in June, and he didn't so much as give me a passing glance."

Callie continued to rummage through the drawers filled with clothes she'd packed for me, seemingly unsatisfied. Tossing me a look from over her shoulder, she shared, "And did you know he spent almost all of his time at the office or hunting assholes with Alessandro because he couldn't handle being near you that weekend? At least, that's what Alessandro told me." She punctuated that bit of info with a devious wink.

"Wait, really? I *was* driving him nuts? Like in a good way, I mean?"

"So nuts he had to release his tension by chasing down jerks with my husband. And for a man who is allegedly a one-night, non-committal kind of guy, you'd think he'd have handled his pent-up energy in a different way."

And he didn't. Shit. She was right. Hudson could've easily spent those two nights I was at his place with another woman. Instead, he came back every single night, moody and scowly, but he always returned. "You're giving me too much hope." My stomach knotted, nerves returning for a different reason than before.

"Well, as Dolly Parton likes to say, '*We can't just **hope** for a brighter day, we have to **work** for a brighter day.*'"

"Seize the moment. *C'est la vie*, huh?"

"Absolutely." She settled on something from the dresser and tossed it at me. "Now, go fight for what you want."

Chapter 20

Isabella

BEYOND OFFERING A STELLAR PEP TALK, Callie ran a wicked game of interference. As I got dressed, she left my room and told Malik she twisted her ankle and needed help walking back to the pool house. It was the perfect opportunity to escape my shadow and head to Hudson's bedroom.

Callie's beautiful words replayed in my head, serving as the ammunition I needed to propel me down the back stairs and to the other end of the house, where Constantine had strategically placed Hudson's room.

With my heart in my throat, I stopped outside his door, surprised to find it cracked open. I took that as an invitation to intrude before I lost my edge and remembered why we were at the house in the first place.

Hudson was sitting on the bed, seemingly in a daze. Shirtless and in sweatpants, barefoot and hunched over, his tee dangled from one hand. His strong back muscles were flexed, and with the bandage from his arm lying on the comforter next to him, the marks the accident left on his skin were starkly visible. I shuddered inwardly at the evidence of what he'd been through. His wounds were worse than mine.

He slowly lifted his head, locating me. He was an elite operator, so I knew he'd sensed me coming before I'd even opened the door.

"You okay?" I asked while closing and locking up behind me.

"Isabella." I ignored his use of my name as a reprimand, opting to stay bold in my determination to communicate with him.

We had to start somewhere, and I didn't want his statement to Constantine this morning to be the end of things between us before they ever had a chance to begin.

"There aren't cameras in the bedrooms." My reminder only had him standing.

"And that means what exactly?" He tossed his shirt on the bed, then planted his hands on his hips while scowling.

My eyes skated to the visible waistline of his briefs that had the Lululemon logo on them.

"I'd meant that gift as a joke, you know. I honestly didn't think you'd wear them."

"Can't waste a perfectly good pair of underwear, now can I?" He followed my line of sight to the view I was very much enjoying. "Better question is, did you tell your brothers you bought me these briefs for my birthday to get a rise out of me?"

This man was a masterclass in rolling with it and giving it back to me as good as I gave it to him. God help me, I was in trouble. And it was the only kind of trouble I wanted to be in.

Unable to stop gaping at him, I mumbled, "Mmm. Nope." I never expected to see him in the briefs, even if it was a partial view. I'd bought them one night after two martinis, and it took a half a bottle of wine to actually gift them. My nerves weren't always made of steel.

And on that note, internet trolls be damned. They were officially banished from my head, right along with that bullshit story Kit wrote. I'd deal with that woman later. Well, soon-ish. Someone had to go after her for her egregious words about my sister, as well as her lies in regard to Hudson's service time.

But right now, hello distraction in the form of gray sweatpants, perfect abdominal muscles, and the delicious V-line disappearing into his briefs.

My hand had a mind of its own, and my finger ran along the seam of my mouth. "Are you okay?" I asked again when realizing he'd avoided answering me the first time.

"I'll answer that if you stop staring at me like you're starving." His tone alone had me almost going feral. I was borderline there before, and his words, so deep and masculine, hit every pleasure sensor in my brain and body.

And God help me, some men really did age like fine wine. Hudson was proof of that. He'd become even sexier over the years. Considering he'd already started out hot as fuck in his twenties, it was no wonder I had trouble maintaining my self-control ever since he'd crossed over to the forties.

He had a hard-as-granite body, jawline sculpted from concrete, and eyes that could burn a hole through my panties with the intensity of his stare. And yet, it was his intelligence, big heart, the way he made me laugh, not to mention how he dealt with my attitude in his own special way, that had me falling all over myself far more than just his physical appearance.

"So help me, Bella. You have to stop looking at me like that."

Boom goes the dynamite. I was acting no different than a character from an *American Pie* film. *Jeez.*

Attempting to act my age, I met his eyes and said, "I came to check you out."

"Obviously," he bit out.

Shit. Thanks, Freud. "Are my cheeks as red as I feel?"

"You *feel* color?" His mouth stole my attention, it was quite the showstopper.

"Hot, I mean." I slowly walked over to him, and he couldn't hide the appreciation in his eyes as he studied me from head to toe with each step I took.

I'd been so laser-focused on his body, it was possible this wasn't his first time taking in my tiny pink shorts and loose, off-the-shoulder Metallica tee, *sans* bra. Callie had opted for fun and sexy without running the risk of giving him a heart attack by wearing a negligee for any of our security team to see.

"I'm not sure how many different ways I can say your name right now to get you to understand me, but I'm going to try again."

I could hear Metallica's "Enter Sandman" playing in my head the moment our gazes connected. The hard, intense beats. The banging drums. The vibrations from the music thrummed between us as he locked his arms at his sides.

"Izzy." That name was enough to snap my spine fully straight. He narrowed his eyes like a challenge while slamming his lips into a tight line.

I hadn't heard him call me Izzy in years. In the past, he usually just said my full name, but a time or two he'd call me by what everyone else did. Then, one day, I suddenly became Bella. I never asked why, worried if I pointed it out, he'd stop. I loved how it sounded far too much for him to do that.

"Alessandro said he tasked Malik with watching you. Where is he?" He lifted a brow, eyes going to my shoulder, keying in on the same purple mark I spied on his body. Evidence of our seat belts saving our lives.

We'd shared that horrible moment together, and maybe it was time we share some good ones, too. *No time like the present*. Why not ignore the heaping pile of dog shit in the form of bad media online, a potential stalker, and a mysterious murderer, surrounding us?

"Malik's walking Callie to the pool house so I could come here and see you."

He grimaced as he focused on the purple by my eye and at my temple. Maybe I should've put some concealer over the bruise before coming. It hurt him to see my injuries just as much as it pained me to see the ones on his skin.

The moment his attention went to my shirt and his nostrils flared, I lost all thoughts about the accident. I clocked the exact moment he zeroed in on the fact my breasts weren't hidden by the world's most uncomfortable invention, high heels coming in at a close second. "So, he didn't see you like this? Did anyone else?"

"On the hall cams, I suppose." I shrugged, forgetting I was a shitty bluffer around people I cared about. "Does it matter? I'm in shorts and a tee in my own house."

His hard body engulfed all of the space between us in one quick stride. We were so close, he had to lower his chin to find my eyes. "Why are you doing this to me? Alessandro is down the hall, and Enzo and Constantine will be here any second." His chest rose on a deep inhalation, and when he released it, his bare skin touched my body. "Are you looking for a distraction like I was this morning?"

He was giving me a way out with that question, one I didn't want to take.

"I'm assuming your brother filled you in?"

I nodded, unable to speak as his hand lazily skimmed my outer thigh, just skirting the line of my ass cheek. Was he even aware he was doing it?

"The mood I'm in . . . this is a bad time." His warning

would've been more effective if he stepped back or stopped heating my skin with his touch. "Dangerous, even."

"Dangerous to what?" A shaky exhale followed as his hand skipped over my ass and skimmed up my back, finally stopping on my one bare shoulder.

"To my control." And just like that, he'd dropped the words. Set them there between us for the taking. And I was about to run with them, all the way home, but then he sent me a curveball instead. "You have something you need to ask me, I suppose."

He was trying so hard to use his words as a wedge between us, but I didn't budge. *Not today, sailor. Not this time.* "I know you didn't sleep with Bianca." But Kit deserved my mother's famous soap in her mouth to wash the filth from it for writing such a thing about my sister.

"You never thought that?" His hand on my shoulder went to the back of my head, and he tangled his hand in my messy hair, never losing hold of my eyes. Nostrils flaring. Jaw clenched, bladed and sharp.

The man was wound tight. The beach stroll did nothing for him. Maybe I'd been wrong, and this wasn't the perfect *no time like the present* moment for us. But here I was, stuck between a rock and a hard body.

"Not for a second," I admitted. "Never crossed my mind." There was another beautiful Italian I was curious about, though. "Maybe Adelina? I'll admit, Friday night in the car, I wondered."

"And do you wonder about that now?" His hand traveled to the nape of my neck before landing once again on my shoulder. He swept his thumb in small circles there.

"Yes," I confessed. "I can't imagine you working side by side with a woman that stunning and never..."

"I haven't made a move on you, and we're colleagues, have

I? You're smart and witty. Downright hilarious." I'd take those compliments every day of the week. "And . . . beautiful," he surrendered. "And I have to be around you seven days a week. Look at you all the fucking time." He'd pretty much snarled his words, such a sharp contrast to how he'd first spoken.

He abruptly removed his hand from my shoulder as if realizing what he'd said and was only now paying attention to where he was touching me. *How* he was touching me. His hand on my heated skin had branded me. I was his now. The way I wanted to be.

"That wasn't an answer," I protested. "It was deflection."

"Guess my old man taught me well." He mumbled something incoherent under his breath before relenting, "No. The answer is no."

Because I was a masochist sometimes, I asked, "Is she single? Maybe there's still hope." My lack of filter was both a blessing and a curse. In this moment, it was definitely my enemy. Those words materialized from that ugly pit of hell known as jealousy. The idea of him being with her or anyone made me, well, crazy. "I'm sorry. This isn't the time. I—I shouldn't have said that."

An expletive dropped from his mouth as I went to turn away, only for him to stop me, encircling my good wrist, drawing me around to face him. "No, Bella, I don't want her. Isn't it obvious who I want?"

I swallowed, shock managing to do the unimaginable—keep my mouth shut.

"But if this weekend has reminded me of anything, it's that life isn't fair, and you can't always have what you want." He let go of me.

I wasn't ready to call it quits and stamp out hope. Not when this was the closest he'd come to admitting his feelings.

"Why can't you?" I whispered. "Am I not worth the risk?

To see if there might be something more between us? My brothers will—"

"Constantine is right about me. What he said to you is why I can't take the risk, because I have too much respect for you. It's not about him." He drew the back of his hand along the contour of my cheekbone while closing his eyes. "I know myself, and I know my limits. I would hurt you. At the end of the day, I know it'd happen. Because that's what I'm good at." Emotion butchered his words right along with my heart. "I'm too fucked in the head, and I won't take a chance with your happiness just because I'm desperate for one night." His eyes flicked open as he left me with that cliffhanger.

"To be yours for one night would be worth the risk. I'd accept the consequences of what that'd mean and what might come next."

He dragged his knuckles along my jawline, staring at his own hand as it moved as if in a daze.

"I don't mean here and now, given what's going on, but promise me one day you'll consider giving us a chance, even if it's for one night."

He stopped grazing his hand over my skin and met my eyes. "I'll never make you a one-night stand."

His matter-of-fact words felt like rejection, and I was too stubborn to roll over and give up. "Then let it be two. Or we could be naughty and give each other a whole weekend."

"Your poker face isn't holding up, darlin'. You couldn't handle being with me, then walking away as if it never happened."

If he called me darlin' one more time, I'd lose my last vestiges of control and demand that night right now. "How do you know?"

He brought his nose to mine, hand in my hair again, gently fisting it. "Because *I* couldn't."

I wet my lips, searching for the breath in my lungs he kept stealing. I wasn't ready to cave and walk away from a conversation I felt had barely begun. But I also knew we were pressed for time. Fighting for what I wanted, and getting him to see beyond his stubborn ideas, would have to wait for another day. I'd have to one-step-at-a-time my way through this, starting with a touch of hope to get us moving forward.

"Airport rules, then," I sputtered, the idea seemingly silly, but maybe it was a creative loophole to our problem.

He freed my hair and dragged his knuckles along my exposed collarbone. This was the most action I'd ever experienced from this man, and I wasn't ready to back away. "Why, you feel like drinking?"

"No, I mean . . . what happens there is like being out in the wild, right? What if we take a moment to let whatever happens happen?" At his brows slamming together with concern, I quickly explained, "Not sex. Just sixty seconds of indulging without judgment. In this case, from ourselves." I shrugged. "We can even set a timer."

His hand wandered along the side of my neck.

"Since you enjoy having your hands on me so much, what if we steal one minute together? We've had a horrible weekend, and things seem to be getting worse, not better. I could use sixty seconds of bliss, even if it's an artificial construct. Don't make me walk away from you feeling"—I pouted—"so unsatisfied."

He eased back to find my eyes, a hint of amusement glinting in those beautiful blues. "Well, we wouldn't want that." He dipped closer, and I shuddered when he tenderly pressed his lips to the bruise at my temple before bringing his mouth to my ear. "But there'd be nothing artificial about what happened between us, sixty seconds or not."

His rich, deep tone had carried his words with such power and authority, I could've come on command if he ordered.

The subsequent sigh that followed, echoed that of a man repenting his sins in one hasty breath. "I'm afraid I'm going to have to say no, though."

No, no, no. Dammit.

He rolled his bottom lip inward for a brief moment. Mouth back to my ear, he confessed, "Our kiss in Rome was only a few seconds, and it's been haunting me for months." His breath at my ear gave me chills as he added huskily, "But one minute with you, and I'll carry that with me for a lifetime."

Chapter 21

Hudson

THIS WASN'T THE PLAN. Walk on the beach to calm down and cool off, followed by a shower—*that* had been the plan. Instead, I was a moment away from giving in to Bella.

But if I did, I'd be a selfish prick. I wouldn't deserve her friendship or her brothers'. I'd inevitably lose her. And for that reason, I allowed the responsible part of my brain to take over.

I set my finger under her chin, urging her adorably parted lips to close. She'd either been stunned into silence at my words or the fact I admitted I had feelings for her.

Backing away from temptation, I grabbed my shirt from the bed, deciding to wait on the shower.

"Need help?" I was surprised she didn't dig her heels in and push me to change my mind about the kiss. It wouldn't take much to get me to bend to her will, and she had to know that.

"I'm fine." I tried to put on the shirt and failed. "I don't need this." My frustration flared and I flung it on the bed. When Bella sidestepped me and bent forward for it, I didn't stop myself from staring at her ass in those short shorts. It wasn't the distraction I should have been looking for, but it definitely took my mind off my arm.

"Probably not the best idea to remain shirtless." She bunched the fabric between her hands, holding it between us like a security blanket.

"Right. Constantine." I'd nearly shattered the promise I made to him just this morning—remaining only friends with his sister.

"You're not worried about Enzo or Alessandro, are you?"

Her question was so innocent and soft that it took me a moment to realize she was right.

I'm not. "Constantine's the one that thinks he's your dad. Means I have two to deal with if I want . . ." Shit, where was I going with that? More importantly, why the hell did I just say that?

Her shocked brown eyes hit my face in record time. The little *hmmm* noise from her was a delayed reaction before she busied herself with fixing my shirt, adjusting it from the inside out. I hadn't even noticed it'd been like that. "Surprised you got this off."

"I was highly motivated. Needed that shower." *Still do. With you in it. Fuck.* Time for one more step back.

"I don't blame you after that filth I read online. I actually wanted to jump into the Atlantic, hoping the waves might wash it off me as well." She gestured for me to come closer—such a bad idea—and bend my head forward.

With the shirt hanging around my neck, she shifted around to my side, helping my arms through the sleeves. I wasn't *that* incapable, but part of me didn't mind letting her take care of me.

"Mission success. How's the pain level?" She smoothed the fabric down over my abs, taking her time to allow her fingers to roam there. She definitely enjoyed torturing me.

"Tolerable," I lied as our gazes connected, and I found myself walking forward.

She backed up against the wall.

Unable to stop myself, I nailed my forearm flat alongside her, drawing my body nearly flush to hers.

"Hmmm. And now your arm really has to be hurting up in that position."

"Consider me highly motivated again to not care about the pain." *What am I doing, dammit?* And yet, my other hand went to the wall, locking her between my arms. "You came here full of piss and vinegar, strutting around in those tiny shorts, looking to start trouble with me. You need a distraction. A little bit of tension relief in the form of an argument." I left off the fact she wanted me to adjust both her attitude *and* her hips by holding on to them while she rode my cock.

The immediate scrunch of her forehead was a definite yes.

I knew how much biting my head off for the silliest things helped relax her, and I'd always been willing to take one for the team.

"I'm tense and upset from what I read. I'm as angry as I assume you are. Hence your walk and need for a shower. *But* I wasn't looking for a fight, and you know it. I was looking for . . . a different kind of tension relief."

She lowered her hands from my chest, and I quickly dropped my good arm to reach for her wrist, planting her palm back where it belonged. Right over my heart.

"I didn't expect"—I dropped my gaze between us to where I held her—"you to want that tonight. Not with what you've learned about my past. I thought I'd find you wearing your go-to faded gray hoodie, holding a bottle of scotch, prepared to offer me your favorite teddy bear to try and talk me off the cliff."

"What cliff?" She sounded both exasperated and scared.

"A metaphorical one." I frowned, once again peering at her. "Because I'm not just angry." *I'm slowly dying on the inside.*

"And what are you?" she whispered. "What would make me want to wear my hoodie and give you Rugby?"

I didn't give her an answer, unsure how or where to start.

"Rugby is back in the city, or I'd go get him for you."

I let go of her since I had no business holding her. Her arm fell slowly between us as my hand went the opposite speed to the wall.

"And I sleep with him because I have no one else to sleep with." She pouted, knowing what buttons to press with both her comment and that little downturned lip.

It's working. You're distracting me. But it was also becoming clear Alessandro hadn't told Bella that the story Kit wrote about my op was, in part, true.

Of course he didn't spill my secrets. Unless he was talking to his wife, the man was a steel trap. Callie could get information from him as easily as Bella could from me. We were both . . .

No, I wasn't love-drunk. Not possible. Or was it? Just because I'd spent every day with this woman for months straight, and I'd wanted to kill every man who dated her since she'd turned twenty-five, didn't mean I was in love. I loved Bella as a friend, of course, but fuck, I didn't even know what the other kind of love felt like. Never experienced it before.

Shit, now I did need to get drunk-drunk with some of the Costas' expensive scotch.

"What'd my brother keep from me that'd have me wanting to cuddle instead of what I, um, offered?"

I still wanted her original offer, which was a reminder of the position we were currently in. I stood tall, allowing my hands to return to my sides, giving her space to breathe. *And* for me to calm down before I begged for those sixty airport seconds.

The way she was making me feel, I'd even go so far as to kill for them. But not hurting her was more important than what I wanted.

It was now or never. I hesitantly revealed, "Friday night, I was off my game because I could have sworn I saw a guy from my old team there. My former SEAL team. Alfie wasn't on the list, and I haven't seen him in twelve years. Not since the funeral we both went to for our team leader, Matt." I paused to search for the words to continue. "Kit's story wasn't total bullshit," I confessed. "That last mission I was on in Afghanistan was a failure at every level. I may have left the Navy because of my mom, but I . . ."

She sacrificed the space I just gave her, coming right back at me. She reached around and cupped the back of my neck, urging my head down, wrapping her other arm around me for a hug.

I couldn't resist and returned the gesture, arms encircling her, accepting whatever safety and comfort she'd give me while trying not to take more.

"Oh, Hudson." The way she said my name, was that the sound of forgiveness?

Forgiveness for what happened in 2010 wasn't hers to give, but if she could, I'd take it. Which was exactly why I needed to untangle myself from her embrace.

But I'd give it five more seconds. You know, airport rules or something like that.

I buried my face into her hair, breathing in the smell of her shampoo.

"Matt, he was the friend who died from fentanyl, wasn't he?" she asked, hugging me even tighter.

I wasn't sure how we'd gone from sexual tension to this, but there we were. "Yeah, he did. He blamed himself for his decisions the day of our op, the same way I've been blaming myself for defying his orders." I pulled back and looked her in the eyes while unloading my guilt aloud for her to hear. "I stayed behind at base while my teammates walked right into an ambush and everything went to hell."

Chapter 22

Hudson

THE KNOCK at the door stopped me from sharing the story I'd kept buried for years. *Anyone but Constantine.*

"We're back. You good?" Because God had it out to get me, of course it was him. "Alessandro updated me."

Bella brought a finger to her lips, which was comical. Did she think I'd planned to tell her brother she was in here with me?

And yet, somehow her cute gesture killed the bad vibes. The woman had the magic touch. That, or I was even more fucked than I thought and straight up putty in this woman's hands.

"Hudson? You in there?"

Bella mouthed, "Talk," as if I'd forgotten how.

"I was in the bathroom, sorry," I finally said, still staring at her in some kind of daze. "I was gonna take a shower, but I'll meet you in the kitchen instead. Give me five."

"I'd like to talk to you alone before we meet with everyone else."

Of course you would. Before I had a chance to come up

with an exfil plan, Bella was already en route to the bathroom. She gently closed the door, and I felt like I was a teenager trying to hide a girl I'd snuck into my room.

After opening up for Constantine, I did my best not to act like he was my mother about to clear the room to ensure it was only me in there. Thinking back to my past, my father never would've given a damn if I had a girl in my room. The only wisdom he ever imparted was to always wrap it up. Surprised that wasn't part of his campaign slogans with the number of times he'd probably had to follow his own advice.

"Alessandro told me about Alfie." Constantine's statement jarred me free of the past, reminding me of two things: he was in my bedroom, and so was his little sister. "You okay?" He set his back to the wall by the door and locked his arms over his chest.

I closed my eyes, taking a minute. Taking the sixty seconds Bella had offered me in a much different way. To pull myself together before opening up.

"I'm struggling to believe Alfie could be behind any of this," I finally said, opening my eyes to acknowledge what I hoped was the truth. "It's not who he is. But after Kit's story today, it's hard for me to deny it was him at the party. I saw what I saw." *Him.* "He was a good guy. I should've reached out over the years, but I didn't think he'd want to hear from me. Maybe if I had, he wouldn't have gone down whatever this path is that he may be on now." I wasn't ready to fully convict Alfie. Not that I knew what he was guilty of yet.

"I think we should follow up on the whereabouts of everyone on your team from that last op. See where they are and what they're up to." He casually glanced at the bathroom door before swinging his attention my way.

"It's a short list." My hands tightened into fists at my sides as I thought back to that day. "Only a few of us are still alive."

The Art of You

Constantine dropped his head. "I know one SEAL on Echo lost their life that day. And two were severely injured. And your team leader, Matthew Shaker, died of an overdose two years after he left the Navy." The information he was sharing was about as close to my heart as it could get. "You went to his funeral, and you wouldn't let me come with you," he added after the recap of my hell.

I had no idea if he was looking at me again, because I couldn't rip my eyes from the floor, but I nodded. That was also my cue to him to keep going. The less I had to say, the better.

"I thought your team was on a routine training exercise outside the wire, and their Humvee rolled right over an IED." There it was. The lie I'd been living with for fifteen years. "I'll never forget the moment I learned it was your team. I thought we'd lost you." His accent slipped through deeper that time. "When I found out you weren't with them that day . . ."

The man was a hard-ass, but he had another side he rarely showed. I didn't deserve sympathy, though. I didn't deserve a damn thing.

"I wasn't on the mission, no." I tensed up all over again thinking back to that day fifteen years ago.

The burns that destroyed half my brother's body. The blast that took another brother's arm. The sniper that killed Devon, the new guy who'd taken my spot. The damage a blast had done to Matt, both physically and mentally, getting him addicted to pain pills afterward. And so on, and so on.

"Mission." He announced the word like it was reinforced with steel. "Not a training exercise, then. There was a cover-up."

"Yeah, you could say that." This was the conversation I'd been on the verge of having with Bella, and now she was still hearing it, but through a door.

"The question I don't want to ask, but now I need to is—"

"You don't have to. I'll tell you," I cut him off, saving him the trouble. I looked up and over at the bathroom door, practically confessing we weren't alone. "I chose not to join Echo on that mission. Defied orders, in fact. I stayed behind." I set my hand on my chest while pivoting back to him. "I should've died that day instead of that kid fresh out of Sniper School. Or, at least, maybe if I'd been there as Matt wanted me to be, I could've helped somehow." My eyes burned as I resisted and fought the emotion trying to unleash in the form of tears. "The CIA intel was dead wrong. The orders from Command to spin up came from suits in Washington, sitting on their asses and pushing for a victory. Echo should never have been on that mission."

I let each fragmented thought of classified information hang in the air.

"But nothing will change the fact that it was my team out there who got butchered without me. I thought staying behind was the right thing to do. I was trying to protect them. I'd just found out my mother was going to die. I was worried my head was off and I'd make a bad judgment call and get someone killed." I'd been wrong. So, so fucking wrong. "I didn't know they were going into an ambush. They needed me, and I wasn't there for them. So yeah, I'm sure they hate me for not being there. Blame me for staying back." How could they not, Alfie included?

Constantine quietly stared at me, probably unsure what to say.

"You know what's really fucked up? They tried to give me the Navy Cross." I slammed my hand over my heart as if the medal was pinned there now, and I was itching to rip it off. "I refused it." Like hell did I deserve that. "I showed up too late with the QRF team. All I did was help get everyone out."

Guilt about took me to my knees, but Constantine caught

me before I hit the ground. The man never let anyone fall, not even when they may have deserved it.

Once I was steady on my feet, he threw his arm around me, hugging me like a father would a son. "You made the right choice."

Like hell I did.

I straightened and stepped back, tearing a hand through my hair.

"You put your brothers first by staying back," he reassured me. "Their blood is *not* on your hands." He pointed at my chest. "It's on the Taliban's and on those who pushed for an op that shouldn't have been greenlit in the first place." He'd make one hell of a father, and had he stayed in the Navy, one hell of an admiral one day.

He cupped his mouth, eyes flicking to the bathroom door again.

Oh, he for sure knew she was there.

"My saying this won't change how you feel. I get that. Being spared when your brothers are lost is a fate worse than death." He faced me again. "But you did the right thing."

"Echo Team was my family, and our family was ripped apart that day. If I didn't have my mother and you all to come home to, I don't know that I wouldn't have gone down the same dark path Matt did."

Matt wouldn't let me help him. I tried. Really hard. But he wanted nothing to do with me. With anyone, for that matter.

"I wish you'd told me this years ago. I could've helped. You've been carrying this a long fucking time."

"We were under orders to keep our mouths shut. The families knew the truth, of course. We'd never tolerate them being lied to. But Command believed if the media was aware our SEALs walked into a trap, it'd look like too much of a win for the Taliban. Help boost their morale and recruitment numbers." *Partially true, maybe, but still.* "Politicians were doing what they do, just trying to save their asses."

"A hundred percent." He squared up his stance again, locking his arms across his chest. "They ever get the men responsible for what happened?"

"Yeah, it took them about five months to track them down, but they did. I was already out, taking care of my mom. Shortly after, she died, and—"

"My sister was murdered." His words fell flat right between us.

"It was a bad twelve months." *Understatement of the year.* I'd been carrying those months with me every day like a nightmare that wouldn't quit.

"I knew you were upset back then, and rightfully so, but guilt is a whole other animal." His forehead tightened, eyes flashing to the bathroom door before meeting mine again. "I understand now. I get why you haven't been able to—"

"Everything okay?" Enzo interrupted us, drawing our attention to where he stood in the doorway now.

"Yeah, it's fine." I clamped down on my back teeth. "We'll be right there." My eyes were probably bloodshot. But somehow, I did feel better getting this off my chest.

Constantine nodded at him, letting him know it was okay to leave.

"Take a few minutes, then meet us in the kitchen," Constantine said once it was just us again. He added in a low, unwavering voice, "I'm sure my sister is dying to hug you right now." He angled his head toward the bathroom. "Don't let me stand in the way."

Chapter 23

Isabella

I ASSUMED the silence in the bedroom was my cue to open the door.

Hudson was quietly standing there waiting for me—quite literally a heartbeat away—his good arm up, hand braced against the doorframe, his other hidden inside the pocket of his sweatpants.

"How much did you hear?"

I stepped forward and wrapped my arms around his waist as my answer. *All of it. Every painful word.* I waited for him to hug me back. And when he finally did, I cried out between sniffles, "I'm so sorry. I had no idea."

One hand lazily stroked up and down my back as he tried to soothe me. It should've been the other way around. But he was always taking care of me, protecting me, making sure I was comforted.

"I'm okay, I promise." With his other hand, he reached between us for my chin, commanding my eyes up. "I'm tough. Don't you worry about me."

"Don't ask me to do the impossible." I whispered the same words he'd said to me in the hospital.

His eyes were red but not glossy from unshed tears. "And what's that?" he asked, turning my question back on me.

"To not worry about you," I murmured.

He brought my face back to his chest, both strong arms firmly snug around my body. The human version of my Rugby bear.

He cupped my head, shushing me. Calming me. That was supposed to be my job. I had to stop ugly crying. My tears wouldn't help ease his pain any more than they'd solve world peace.

Giving myself only a minute to let go, I forced myself to zip up my emotions. I'd save them for tonight, when I was alone in bed. "I never would've come to your room like this had I known there was so much weighing on your mind."

He pulled away, searching for my face again. His hands rested comfortably on my hips as we stood in the doorway. "Remind me what your intentions were again."

Oh, he remembered, but for some reason he wanted me to repeat them. My gaze fell to the barrier between the two rooms. His feet were on the other side, mine still in the bathroom. The wood threshold between us felt like a fragile barrier I refused to examine. "To tease you," I relented. "I'm sorry."

Cradling my chin again, his silent demand for my eyes overwhelmed me, and I submitted. The shivering from my sadness morphed into a different kind. His hard jaw strained like a blade of steel covered in sexy scruff. "No apology needed."

Why'd I feel like that wasn't what he'd planned to say, but he'd chosen the safer route?

"We should probably go. Your brothers have news."

The Art of You

"Right." The whisper floated between us like a secret. "He knows." *That I was in here*, I finished my words in my head.

"He does." The firm grit of his tone signaled he wasn't sure what to make of that.

Same. I wanted to believe Constantine would stop acting like my dad and let me date who I wanted, but I also believed in Santa until I was in the sixth grade, so I didn't quite trust my judgment when it came to men. "So, um, we're going out there now?"

He was still holding me captive. Blocking my path with his muscular frame. Cupping my chin with his big hand. Blue eyes laying siege to my heart. I was met with a nod and a terse look, but he didn't budge.

We remained quietly staring at each other for a little longer before I stated what I hoped he already knew, "I'm here for you. Always."

He released my chin, dragging his knuckles along my jawline and up the side of my face, simply staring at me as he dropped a husky "Ditto" on me.

That word sent me back to the theater room, to cuddling with him as we watched *Ghost*. *Ditto . . . if you know, you know.*

His hand blazed a new trail, his eyes following the path down the column of my throat before sweeping to my shoulder. His touch became gentler when moving to the purple welt the seat belt had left there.

He frowned as he shifted the sleeve farther down my arm, then bent forward, kissing the bruise. His lips pressed gently against the tender spot, keeping hold of my hip with the other hand.

He slowly lifted his head, adjusted my sleeve back in place, and found my eyes. "Better?"

"Mmmhmm," was the best I could manage. I wasn't sure how I'd gone from crying to turned on so fast. I searched for that wicked emotion known as guilt, recognizing I shouldn't be feeling like this now of all times, but that contrition escaped me.

He guided me around so my back pressed against the doorframe, and he set his hand over my head. There was something so masculine and sexy about a man standing in such a dominant position. He was leaning so close our noses nearly touched. Close enough our breaths tangled as one.

"I don't think I want to face reality yet." The gruff underlying quality of his tone had my nipples hardening. Thankfully, my dark shirt probably concealed the desire I had no business having.

He'd told me he couldn't be with me before Constantine interrupted us. And now I better understood those demons he'd been fighting for so long. He'd been to hell and back, and he'd chosen to take that walk alone instead of letting any of us support him.

Then his past came hurtling back in the form of ugly words on the internet. A ruthless attempt to try and knock him down again.

Yet, there I was, the mental chaos of his confession still swirling like the debris from a building implosion, wondering if this man might say, *Fuck it*, and kiss me.

"Airport rules."

Those two words from him blocked the train wreck happening in my head and pried my lips open. "A distraction you need before we go out there? Or is this something more?"

He closed his eyes.

Thinking

Considering.

Shredding my sanity with the longest pause of my life.

Blues back on me, his voice hoarse, he finally shared, "It'll always be something more with you."

The Art of You

The "flutters," as my sister used to call them, erupted in my stomach, and I silently thanked the doorframe for continuing to do its job of keeping me upright.

"What's changed?" A better question: *What's wrong with me?* The answer: *I'm unable to shut up and take what I asked for.*

He glanced at the closed bedroom door before returning those bold blues to my face. "I don't know if it has changed. I truly don't know yet."

Too soon. Too fast. I got that. He'd only just shared the truths he'd kept bottled up for fifteen years. He'd been tethered to one way of thinking for so long, change would take time. I supposed I could relate.

"I probably have decades of bad habits I have to see if I can undo first." That was one of the most honest things I'd ever heard a man say to me. "But I don't know if I'll survive leaving this room if I don't feel your lips on mine."

He nailed me to the floor with those words. With those hooded eyes. That clenched jaw of what was left of his restraint.

"There are much worse things I can think of to be haunted by," I admitted, remembering what he'd said. "If this is the last time, or merely one of many, I'm willing to risk it if you are."

He frowned. Not the most encouraging sign. I should've just fisted his shirt and kissed him, never giving him a chance to doubt anything.

"I can't guarantee I'll be able to change, but—"

"There are no guarantees in life, I know that." I reached between us and set both hands on his chest. His heart was flying even faster than mine.

"Five seconds," he offered through barely parted teeth.

"Five Mississippi seconds?" I arched my brow.

"I reckon that's the only way to count, isn't it?"

His raspy tease had me bunching his shirt. I was on the verge of losing it if he didn't kiss me soon. I was trying to be ladylike and let this man take the lead, but so help me . . .

Remaining in the doorway as we held each other's eyes felt like we were caught between two directions of where things may go with us.

This image burned into my head like a sketch happening in real time. I could see my hand racing over the canvas. His body. Mine. The two of us existing here as living art, neither talking nor moving, just existing.

This was my blank canvas coming to life. My fresh start. I just had to take it.

"Ready for me?" Those three words had been a lifetime in the making.

I nodded, and he took his sweet, Southern time. Mouth hovering before mine. And then he did it. Claimed me.

The second our lips touched, the picture in my mind of us in the doorway went from black and white to full-blown color. And when his tongue licked at the seam of my lips, seeking permission to further send me over the edge, I gave it to him.

He groaned as I parted for him, and he swallowed my breathy cry.

Arching into him, I let go of his shirt to slide my hands under the material. Desperate, achy need had me running my fingers over the ridges of muscle, and his abdomen flexed beneath my touch.

Deepening the kiss, turning it from gentlemanly to fucking my mouth with his tongue, he rolled his hips forward. His hard-on strained against his sweatpants. His free hand went to my side, thumbing down the waistband of my shorts, simply smoothing his fingers over my skin there.

The kiss had taken on a life of its own. His hand wandered up my silhouette beneath my loose tee, and he cupped my breast. When he rolled my nipple between his finger and thumb, I tipped my chin back, gasping for air.

"Oh, God," I whispered before he dropped his mouth over mine, as if already missing it.

I was greedy for more. For his hands and lips to explore every inch of my body.

He removed his hand from my shirt and trailed his fingers along my collarbone. When his mouth left mine, I opened my eyes to find him locking his hand around the column of my throat. He was gently holding me, both of us breathing hard while staring into each other's eyes.

Holy hell.

He growled out a curse or two and hissed, "I need five more seconds."

I opted not to share we'd definitely already sailed beyond those first five at least thirty seconds ago.

He let go of my neck and set his mouth along my jaw. Trailing kisses in a path to the shell of my ear as he squeezed my ass. His other hand was no longer on the doorframe but on my other ass cheek. He sunk his fingertips into my flesh, drawing me flush against his cock, and I rotated my hips, grinding against him.

"Tell me to stop," he demanded in my ear.

"Don't stop," I begged instead, grasping the back of his neck, desperate for the barriers of our clothes to be gone.

"You're killing me." He seized hold of my wrist and guided me to the vanity, lifting me up onto the counter. Scooting me closer to the edge, he hooked my legs around his waist, and growled, "Five more seconds," before slanting his mouth over mine.

I dug my fingertips into his back as I continued to rock against his crotch, ignoring the fabric between us. I could come from his expert tongue guiding mine and the friction between us alone.

He thrusted right back, as if his cock was already inside me, holding my face hostage between his big hands. As he devoured me, the colors continued to explode all around us.

He let go of my face and dragged his lips over to my ear. "If you don't stop me," he pleaded in a low, guttural tone, "I will fuck you right here on this counter. I don't want that happening."

Oh, I do. But he was right, maybe not for our first time. "Oh-okay," I whispered—more like whimpered—as I fought to catch my breath and return to reality.

My legs remained locked around him as he straightened to find my eyes. "What the hell was that?" His brows tightened as he eyed me with apprehension, both of us breathing hard.

"I think it was art."

I was about to explain what I meant, but he distracted me by tracing the pad of his thumb along the line of my lips, and I caught his flesh with my tongue.

"Such a bad girl." He unwrapped my legs from his waist and stepped back.

I set my feet against the cabinet doors for support while studying him. He had no idea how naughty I could be for him. How long I'd waited for this, never thinking it'd happen. But the images I'd conjured up to keep me warm at night were explicit and erotic.

The wicked gleam in his eyes as he stared at me had me parting my knees and drawing a hand between my thighs. I wasn't wearing panties, and I was ready to show him just how bad I'd truly been prepared to be when coming to his room tonight.

His gaze shot between my thighs, his hands going to his

The Art of You

hips as if working to restrain himself. Chest puffing out. Nostrils flaring.

Leaning back on my elbows to remain in this position with my knees open, I nearly lost my balance.

He swooped in and bent forward, drawing his good arm behind my back. "You want me to touch you, do you?" It was more like a promise than a question falling between us, and I could only nod my affirmative. "You want me to feel how wet and ready you are? How swollen with need your beautiful cunt is for me?"

I let go of my shorts, needing both hands to brace at my sides now.

"Tell me, Bella. Tell me you want me to put my hand between your thighs and make you come. To slide my fingers inside your slick pussy and fuck you while you wish it's my cock instead."

Oh my God. Dirty talk from Hudson sent me over the edge. To the Land of Fairy Tales (not the Grimm ones), where I'd happily live every day. A place of miracles and unicorns. And even Santa Claus. Anything was possible with this man.

"Tell me. Use your words, darlin'." He set his mouth against mine and demanded, "What. Do. You. Want. Me. To. Do?" How a man could punctuate each word and turn syllables into erotic harmonies was beyond me, but it was a thing, and he just did it.

I inhaled as his hand went to the inside of my thigh and traveled beneath my shorts, and I lifted my hips in expectation.

"Touch me, please." It was one thing to think dirty things while getting myself off with my vibrator every night, it was quite another for me to stare into the eyes of a man I'd always considered off-limits and say them.

"I need more than that." He started to pull his hand away, and I panicked.

"Fuck me with your hand while I imagine it's your tongue on my clit," I rushed out, not wanting to lose him. "And yes, I'll be wishing it's your cock inside me."

A dark smile cut across his lips. It was one I'd never witnessed in my life and was grateful he'd saved it, gifting it to me during a moment like this.

With his other arm still around my back, keeping me in an arched position, he finally gave me what I wanted. He guided my shorts down to my thighs to give him better access, and he palmed my bare pussy like he was taking ownership of it. Staking his claim that it'd be his forever and no one else's.

He captured my moan of relief at the contact and kissed me hard while dragging his knuckles along my wet sex.

He stroked me with his fingers. Then, moving them in and out, dragging my arousal over my sensitive flesh, he brought his mouth to my ear. "Do you know how badly I wanted to do this while you were at my apartment that weekend? I wanted to rip your bikini off with my teeth." He stopped touching me, and it was pure torture waiting for more.

"What else did you want to do to me?"

"Pull your pussy to my face and feast on you all day long." His fingers went to work again. Stroking. Soft and slow. In and out.

And I lost control. My stomach muscles nearly spasmed from trying to resist before I came hard, unable to contain my cries. "Oh, God. Yes, yes, yes." I trembled against the heel of his hand as I climaxed, and he caught my last "Yes" with his lips as I about collapsed onto the counter.

I would've whacked my head against the glass if it wasn't for Mr. Stealthy coming to my rescue. His hand flew up to cradle my skull, keeping me safe.

A few quiet, sated moments later, a devilish smile crossed his lips and he helped me off the counter before righting my shorts in place. He cocked a brow, eyeing me up and down, then went to the sink to wash the smell of sex from his hands. Good idea, because I just remembered where we were supposed to be.

We were no longer safe in the land of Make-Believe, but had returned to my parents' house, thrust back to the reality of dealing with an unknown number of enemies with unknown motives.

He dried his hands, then faced me, resting his hip against the counter. And just like that, a mask of indifference moved over his face at lightning speed. The bulge in his sweatpants and my swollen lips were the only proof we'd taken a hell of a lot longer than five seconds of "airport" time.

"What now?"

"We talk to your brothers, and I think I need a word with Kit about her source."

Not what I'd meant, but I supposed that was my fault for not being specific. I went ahead and rolled with it. *Kit.* A thorn in our sides. "Oh."

"As for what happens between us, though . . ." He let his physical guard down, his arms dropping to his sides. "I don't know."

That was better than avoidance or rejection. "This just happened. It wasn't planned, so we, um—"

"Wasn't planned, hmm?" A smile tugged at the edges of his lips. "Little Miss No Panties."

"Right, well." I fidgeted with the hem of my Metallica tee. I probably needed to change before heading to the kitchen, also put on some underwear and wash the smell of sex from between my legs.

He stepped forward and swept the pad of his thumb along the curve of my cheek. "We'll talk about this at some point, okay?" His voice had switched from playful to serious.

I did my best to fasten my lips with some imaginary tape so I wouldn't stumble into word-vomit territory like I was so good at.

"Are you okay?" His gaze worried its way up and down my body as if calculating whether or not he fucked up and did hurt me.

"I don't regret what happened, if that's what you're asking." I kept my tone as steady as possible once he met my eyes. "I only regret not doing more."

Chapter 24

Hudson

THERE WERE ONLY a few things in life I truly feared anymore. As I stood there outside the kitchen door, bracing against the frame, mentally preparing myself to go in, I realized facing off with Bella's brothers was one of them. Not *walking before a firing squad to my own execution* kind of fear. The much uglier kind. *Rejection.*

By now, all three Costas surely knew I'd been alone with their sister in my bedroom. And no doubt Constantine would assume I'd broken my word to him.

That five seconds of airport time with Bella had blurred into five minutes of *I'd lost my damn mind.* I didn't know what to think, or how to feel about what happened. Not yet, at least. But I did know not even my fear of her brothers rejecting the possibility of us would actually stop me if I made up my mind about what I wanted.

The question was, could I change? Was it even possible for me to start over at forty-two?

I lifted my chin, searching the ceiling as if Bianca might be watching over us and could tell me what to do. Preferably in the form of orders. Those were easier to follow than my heart.

When the door abruptly swung inward, my forward lean nearly sent me colliding with Constantine.

"I was just coming to find you. We were getting worried." He scrutinized me like a human lie detector, waiting for me to trip up. Nothing got by this man.

Constantine may have been overprotective with his sister, like a dad to her, but the man had also stepped in as one for me. Despite being the same age, he'd always been there for me, recognizing my old man was severely lacking in the fatherly department and picked up the slack when I needed it most.

I'd never forget my first year in New York. My father, a senator-hopeful at the time, had landed me a scholarship at a too-rich-for-my-blood private school. At sixteen, I'd been a classic nerd, more interested in video games, *Star Wars*, and reading than sports. Without money to buy myself protection, you could say I was getting my ass kicked on a regular basis.

Then one day, Constantine stepped in. He'd seen enough, and he'd laid the ground rules for the whole school with one simple statement: *"You have a problem with Hudson, you have a problem with me."*

No one ever bothered me again. He'd taken me under his wing, and while my inner nerd was still very much part of me, I'd changed from that point on. Became stronger and more resilient. Toughened up both mentally and physically. Joined the Navy and became a frogman.

And now I've made out with your little sister.

Guilt clutched me by the throat, closing off my oxygen. After everything he'd done for me, always having my six no matter what, I'd let him down. Crossed the line with Bella I promised I'd never go over.

"Hudson?" Constantine slapped a hand over my shoulder,

careful to avoid the bad one where the seat belt had dug in during the accident. "You with me or somewhere else?"

Keeping the door open with his shoulder, he waited for me to answer, but I continued to quietly stand there, my mind going numb.

"Why don't you come in and sit?" he offered, recognizing I was lost to my thoughts.

"I'll stand." I pushed away from the doorframe, and he dropped his hand.

"Then do the standing thing in the kitchen?" A smile ghosted his lips.

That smile gave me a bit of life. Only psychopaths smiled when they wanted to commit murder, right? And he was far from that.

He propped the door open with a stopper, and I finally followed him into the kitchen.

Enzo nodded in greeting, keeping quiet as he stood leaning against the counter with his hand in a bag of chips. Alessandro wasted no time chucking a bottle of Advil at me. This time, I remembered to catch it with the hand attached to my non-jacked-up arm.

"Guessing you went against my recommendation and didn't take anything stronger." Alessandro smirked.

Nope. I twisted the top and paused, staring down at my hand, remembering where it'd been five minutes ago. Between Bella's legs. Guilt, that ugly fucking beast, came back to haunt me all over again.

"It's childproof. Need an assist?" The wise-ass, Enzo, with the jokes, sucked me free from the vortex of remorse.

"I'm good." I stole a look at him, and shocked myself by actually sporting a smile. "You can continue eating like you're the pregnant one, not your wife."

Enzo volleyed something back in Italian, probably a well-deserved jab. The fact they were acting so casually meant Constantine filled them in on the full story of my past, and they were trying to mask their pity with humor. They knew the last thing I'd want was sympathy.

So, that's why no third-degree about what happened with your sister? Because you feel bad for me?

When Alessandro's attention flew somewhere in the general direction behind me, I assumed it meant Bella had joined us.

"There you are, Little Miss. I was wondering what you were up to."

Little Miss No Panties should not have been my first thought upon hearing Alessandro's greeting, probably not even my second. And yet, there it was. Right along with the memory of Bella's walls tightening around my fingers while climaxing.

"Malik escorted me from the pool house. Don't worry. No walking around outside unsupervised."

Relief coasted over me hearing Callie's voice. The shit-eating grin on Alessandro's face, as if he hadn't seen his wife in a year, should've clued me in, even if his nickname for her hadn't.

Callie gently patted my back before walking by me. I took that to mean she was also aware of the truth about my last operation.

I was board-certified in the ability to bury my past six feet deep when needed, and I had a feeling I'd need to tap into that honed skill to get through this conversation.

"Where's Izzy?" Callie asked as her husband drew her to his side.

"Yeah, where's my sister?" Enzo asked me around a mouthful, brushing crumbs off his shirt. I had a feeling Maria didn't let him binge on junk back at home, so he was taking the chance to misbehave while away.

"How should I know?" I dumped four tablets onto my palm, set aside the bottle, and retrieved a Smartwater from the fridge, opting not to check Constantine's reaction to Enzo's question. I wasn't sure how long his grace would last.

"Ah, speak of the she-devil." Enzo's words had me quickly swallowing the evidence of one-too-many. Well, by Bella's standards anyway. She had no idea how much of this I'd taken to Band-Aid the pain while serving. It was a miracle I had both kidneys and a fully functioning liver.

"Hi." Bella sounded awfully close behind me as I guzzled down the whole bottle before slowly lowering it to my side.

Facing her, my back now to the others, I breathed a sigh of relief that she was fully covered. Maybe my brain wouldn't glitch like it had when we'd been alone.

She stared at me, her eyes holding mine as she raced her thumb along the collar of her pink monogrammed top, a matched set with her pajama bottoms. When her attention shot to my hand, I followed the movement to find I'd squeezed the plastic bottle, my knuckles whitening from my grip.

When the hell did I do that? Eyes up, they landed on her mouth. Her lips were a little swollen from our make-out session, and now I was wondering if another part of her was still sensitive. She'd said what happened between us had been art, and yeah, that was one way of putting it.

When she hit me with her sexy, teasing smile, my efforts to send her a warning glare to behave were wasted. Because she was no longer eyeing my face, but had tuned in to the problem south of my waistband—my growing erection.

The little vixen was loving every second of this, too. She really was the only one who had the ability to distract me from everything, whether it was an op—case in point Friday—or a possible inquisition by her brothers.

I hadn't been self-aware enough last week while prepping

for the mission to realize that having her go as my plus-one may throw me off my game. She could've been killed in that crash, kidnapped, or shot. All the bad *ors* imaginable could've happened. But I was fully aware now, and that meant no more undercover assignments together.

I knew Alessandro wouldn't be able to operate with a clear head if Callie were with him. Same was true with Enzo and Maria. I'd thought it'd be different for me, but that was before I fully accepted the truth staring me in the face. *I have feelings for you.* Nothing like almost losing the woman you care about to wake you up.

"Think you two can finish up your telepathic conversation so we can fill you in?" Alessandro asked, his tone still surprisingly relaxed given our current state of all-the-fucking things.

Bella broke our connection but kept her beautiful smile in place as she walked around me and over to the counter. She went straight for the dark chocolate candy bars. I *may* have texted one of our security guys a grocery list of must-haves earlier, worried we'd run out of her favorite things and fast. Now I regretted not asking her brothers to bring her favorite teddy bear and hoodie back from the city.

Now she'd have to sleep alone . . .

No, don't go there. I can't join her in bed.

"What'd that water ever do to you?" Enzo tossed another flippant comment at me, but he was right.

When I looked down, the bottle was mangled between my palms.

"Yeah, yeah," I grumbled, turning to the side to see Bella swapping the chocolate for the Advil.

"How many did you take?" Her accusing tone wasn't lost on me, nor the fact of how much I rather enjoyed how much she cared about me.

"The normal amount." I decided to take this moment to

locate the recycling bin. I left the kitchen before she called me on my BS, hoping to down-boy my cock in my environmentally friendly pursuit.

The laundry room was around the corner from the kitchen, and I took a second longer than necessary to toss the bottle in the appropriate bin as I listened to the indistinct chatter from the Costas in the other room.

Everyone in the kitchen shared that last name, and now I was standing there wondering if Bella's first name would sound better paired with mine.

Isabella Ashford. Bella Ashford. Mrs. Ashford.

"You okay?" If anything or anyone was going to kill the throbbing pain of unrelieved tension in my sweatpants, it was Constantine getting the drop on me as I stared at the recycling bin.

I cleared my throat and faced him. "I'm as to be expected," was the best I could give him. At least I was finally able to speak directly to him, a marked improvement from before. "Tell me you all have something, and that's why your brothers are so relaxed."

"Truth?" He lifted a dark brow, doing the scrutinizing thing again. But now I understood it was from a place of worry not anger.

I folded my arms. "Ideally."

"They're just good actors. Although, they're probably overdoing it. I ordered them to zip their mouths about Kit's story and the truth about your op. Told them to behave normally. Thought you'd prefer that after the day you've had."

Figured. "So, no leads? Alessandro said you had news to share once we were together."

"We do have some stuff, and the conversation Alessandro had on your behalf with your father while you were on a walk earlier was enlightening. I just wish we had more to go on." He motioned for me to leave the laundry room.

"You assign someone to keep an eye on Adelina? I assume she's still chasing leads, and I don't like her doing that alone," I said as we reentered the kitchen.

While I'd been gone, Bella had parked herself next to Callie at the kitchen table in front of the bay window.

"Yeah, I pulled two guys from here to stay with her," Constantine confirmed, settling in front of his laptop again. "And Marc is now in Arlington."

"Why's he in Virginia?" I asked. "I thought Marc was keeping tabs on Agent Clarke? Or was that Kit?" I was losing track.

Enzo's mask fell when our eyes met, and his apologetic, sad look of regret hit me hard. I was having enough trouble concentrating, and I definitely wouldn't have survived this conversation had Constantine not done me a solid and told them to remain quiet about what they'd learned.

"Marc's watching Clarke, which is why he's in Arlington," Constantine affirmed.

"You told Marc he didn't F up on Friday, that one of the valets probably eavesdropped on me, right?" I wasn't sure why Alessandro was smiling until I rewound my words and replayed them. "Fuck up. I meant, *fuck* up."

"I was getting worried that knock to your head may have crisscrossed your wires. Made you start watching your mouth like Enzo's been trying to do," Alessandro joked.

"I'm in agreement with Maria. They have a daughter and twins on the way," Callie said, defending her sister-in-law. "One day, I'll be asking the same of you."

"Good fucking luck with my brother on that one." Enzo shook his head, then shrugged. "What? My family isn't here."

"Anyway, we were talking about the case, weren't we?"

Constantine, always the dad of us all. "And yeah, Marc's aware but still feels bad. Teamguy mentality, nothing to do about that. Not going to change him as much as I can't change you."

True.

Alessandro removed my phone from his pocket and walked over and set it on the counter next to me. "Your father's going scorched-earth on his whole staff. I'm sure he'll be calling again. I had to silence the ringer before I threw your phone in the Atlantic. He's not happy."

I wasn't in the mood to talk to anyone about what I'd read online today, least of all my father. I'd be getting the governor on the other end of that line, not a man worried about his son. "Is he just pissed about the news cycle or about the homicide case?" The pendulum could swing both ways as to why my father was blowing up at his staff.

"It turns out Kit was blackmailing your father's favorite assistant." Alessandro joined his wife at the table. "She forced him to add her name to the guest list at the last minute on Friday. She didn't tell him why she wanted to go, just demanded he get her an invite. Explains why we didn't know she'd be there. His main assistant has been trading Kit favors for her silence for about a year now."

"What kind of blackmail? What other favors?" I positioned my back to the counter, using it for support.

"Kit discovered he was cheating, and she used that to extort him in exchange for not exposing him online," Enzo shared, rolling his eyes in disgust.

"Your dad is now questioning all of his staff, worried he has more 'problems' in his inner circle." Alessandro's use of air quotes was a sign his wife was rubbing off on him.

"Your father was talking as if the story Kit wrote about the government cover-up was a lie. Sounded pretty convincing, too." Enzo had to step right into that topic despite Constantine's orders. "Does he not know the truth? And if not, then no reason to believe someone on his staff knows. Puts doubt on them being Kit's source, right?"

"Your dad was still a senator back then," Alessandro picked up with more questions before I could answer Enzo, "but I'm guessing he wasn't one of the ones pressing JSOC and the Agency to rush that op in order to offer the public a victory, right?"

"No, he wasn't in on that decision to send my team." *He wouldn't have risked emailing me about my mom that day.* "I didn't tell him or my mom the truth about what happened. It sounds like he never looked into it or found out, but I'm sure he'll be calling his friends at the Pentagon and CIA to see if they'll help him kill the story regardless of whether he believes it's true."

"Aside from that conversation with your father," Constantine continued, redirecting us, "we have a few other things to share." He looked back down at his laptop. "Adelina let us know the Feds picked up that one valet for questioning."

"The one who parked the Porsche?" I asked, standing taller at the news.

Constantine nodded. "Yeah. Adelina had no choice but to offer the Bureau that lead while we were in the city. They must've found something from his texts or emails that suggested he was tied to the kidnappers."

That's something.

"As for the photo dropped off at your place, Adelina's tech guy"—Constantine turned to the side on his stool to look at Bella—"cleaned up the image and got a hit while we were in the city. His name is Deacon Jones. He's bounced around between shelters for the last two years. Lost his job and home. We tracked him down, but he was on something."

The Art of You

My stomach tightened, preparing myself for the punch I felt coming. Anything but *that* drug, dammit.

"Deacon used the hundred bucks someone gave him to drop off the envelope to buy fentanyl." Constantine delivered the bad news quickly. "His description of who paid him off made it sound like—"

"The Tooth Fairy made him do it," Enzo remarked dryly.

"So, he wasn't helpful." He flicked away the bag of chips on the counter. "We also showed Deacon photos of Kit and Agent Clarke to see if he recognized them. Also, the photo of the guy who'd been on a date with the woman across the street Friday night. Struck out on all three."

"But he wasn't all that coherent, so we should try again," Constantine suggested, eyes on me. "Maybe we need to force him to get clean so we can talk to him."

"Like help him pay for rehab, or force him to get clean in other ways?" Callie spoke up, putting her teacher voice into play.

"The second way would be much more expedient, but . . ." Alessandro let his wife fill in the blanks, and I'd take her shake of the head as a firm no to kidnapping the man. "Fine, we'll help him sober up in a more ethical way." His shrug was aimed at Enzo. "Happy wife, man, happy life. Don't act like you're not guilty of the same."

I stopped paying attention to them when I realized Bella was staring at me with her sad, puppy-dog eyes. Who was she thinking about now? Pablo? Matt?

I really hated that drug and the people who trafficked it. But it also reminded me of something important. "No way Alfie would ask him to deliver the photo." A touch of welcoming relief hit me at that. "He'd recognize the signs of addiction and assume how the money would be used. He might be Kit's source, and maybe was even at that party, but no chance in hell would he risk someone ODing on his dime." He may have changed over the years, but not *that* much.

No one questioned me. No one offered a plausible explanation as to why Alfie might be responsible. They trusted me the way I trusted my instincts.

Bella nodded, offering her support in my confidence about Alfie. "Did, um, Adelina mention . . ."

"Pablo-Not-Picasso?" Enzo swiveled on his stool to face her, tossing out the nickname he'd used for her ex last year. "She mentioned he's in rehab. Coincidentally, because of the same drug we were just discussing." His shoulders fell. "Two visitors in the last month. His mom and sister. She doesn't think he, or any of your exes, are tied to anything, but she's not ready to cross Pablo off her list yet."

"And that has me worried." Constantine twisted around to peer at her. "Is there something else I need to know about the artist? Another reason why Adelina wants to keep him on the potential suspect list?"

Bella's gaze abruptly flew to me, a plea to help rescue her from this without her brothers feeling the need to murder her ex.

Was I really going to help save Pablo? *Christ.*

Realizing I now had eyes on me, I did my best to think of a distraction, and then a legitimate question wound up saving me. "Wait, did you say you have a photo of the woman's date from across the street?" They said they showed it to Deacon, and I'd missed that detail, too focused on the mention of the drug.

"What'd you find out about the woman's date?" Bella abruptly ran with that distraction. "Was he really just admiring the Porsche?"

Constantine turned around, narrowing his eyes my way, letting me know he wouldn't be letting the subject of Pablo go forever. "Yeah, we spoke to her, as well as her date. His background checks out. They met through a dating app. He's an accountant for one of the major firms. Nothing in his story that's a red flag." He stood, resting the laptop on his palm before placing it on the table in front of Bella. "You recognize him?"

I joined them so I could check him out and ensure he hadn't faked his background, that he wasn't one of the other guys from my old Team suddenly deciding to take revenge on me fifteen years later. It felt absurd to consider, but I couldn't dismiss any possibility.

"I don't think I've seen him before," Bella said as I looked over her shoulder. "You?" She turned, catching my eyes, but I'd been leaning in to view the screen from just over her shoulder, so now our faces were too damn close.

Her lashes fluttered as she stared at me, and I had to swallow and order myself to stand upright so her mouth wasn't so close to my own.

"No." I cleared my throat, not as subtly as I'd have liked. "He's not familiar." I glanced at Constantine at my side. I had no clue what he was thinking, and honestly, I didn't want to know.

Regrouping, I studied the screen again, but from a distance. The man was an average-looking thirty-two-year-old white guy with brown hair and eyes.

"No serial killer or stalker vibes from what I can tell," Bella said softly. "But pictures can be deceiving."

"Well, he stays on our suspect list the same as Pablo. Just in case," Constantine said as if only now making up his mind on that.

"Our suspect list feels as long as it does short," Bella murmured, resting her elbows on the table before lowering her forehead on top of her hands.

I had to resist the urge to stroke her back and offer her comfort. It was already taking all my energy to resist brushing my mouth over her bruises, as if somehow I could heal her with my lips.

"Anything else?" I turned toward Constantine as he returned to the breakfast bar.

"Unfortunately not," he answered.

"This accountant wasn't on the party list, right?" I asked.

Alessandro shook his head no. "Not unless he used an alias. I've been scouring social media for pictures and videos from the party to see if Alfie, or anyone who wasn't supposed to be at the party, was there. Haven't found anything that's stood out yet."

"People were too busy reposting and resharing the video of us dancing, as if that was newsworthy," Bella said after an exasperated sigh, lifting her head. She swiped away the wild strands of her hair clinging to her face. "I should call Mom back at some point since she clearly got wind of the stories and is worried."

"You should phone your dad, too." Alessandro lifted his chin at me like a directive.

"Right. That'll be the highlight of my night." I reached around to my lower back, the achy pain there not yet suppressed by the medicine. "I also think I should speak with Kit, preferably in person."

"That's exactly what she's expecting, and why I think you should hold off until we know more," Constantine responded, shutting his laptop.

"I can get her to tell me her source. To see if she's connected to any of this mess." And that was precisely what this was—a disastrous and confusing mess. I may have been exhausted and in pain, but it felt like we were chasing our tails. And that chase was intentional and purposeful.

"Someone may be watching her, waiting for you to confront

her," Alessandro said, seemingly in agreement with Constantine. "That headline may have been a carrot being dangled for you. Maybe for your old man, too."

Shit. They were both right. But still. "We're missing something. Like the main point," I shared my thoughts aloud, bringing my hand around from my back to my stomach to emphasize this was a gut feeling. "I think everything is connected somehow."

"What could it be?" Bella stood and faced me while Callie and the others quietly joined her on their feet, too.

All eyes were on me as if I could pluck the answers from the universe and offer them up on a silver platter. I wasn't even close to being able to come through for them right now.

"Why don't you call your father, then get some rest? We can regroup tomorrow. See if our guys following Kit and Clarke turn up anything by the morning. Adelina's still trying to get the Feds to share details of the case, too." Enzo was offering up a reprieve, but I wasn't sure if I was ready to take it.

I covered my mouth, eyes on the ceiling as I tried to rally and think through this as if our lives depended on it. *Because they very well might.* What was I missing?

"If the kidnapping is connected to the photo, to Kit's headline story, even to Alfie being at the party—and my gut says I didn't imagine him—then I have to believe Ambassador Aldana's daughter wasn't taken for money. And whatever reason she was abducted might somehow be what ties everything together." That was the best I could manage right now given my state of mind, but it was a start.

"Your dad and the ambassador seemed pretty close in the library," Bella noted. And in the chaos of the weekend, I'd nearly forgotten that. "Maybe they're more than friends."

"Those men could've abducted any number of rich people for money, but they chose a diplomat. And what do ambassadors generally do? They make deals and have access to a lot of high-level shit, right?" Callie pointed out, and Alessandro nodded at her.

"The ambassador said diplomacy doesn't always work. Maybe Hudson's right." Bella continued running with the theory I'd let loose. "Maybe those men wanted something from her that she couldn't risk giving up. Not even for her daughter's life."

"And it was a classified something she couldn't share, so she lied about what the kidnappers wanted?" Callie proposed.

I'd happily let Bella and Callie go back and forth on this. They were doing a damn good job.

"It could also explain why the ambassador is holed up at the embassy and not talking," Bella said with a nod, her eyes lighting up at the possibility we were finally onto something.

And if that something meant Bella didn't have a stalker, I was on-fucking-board.

"Maybe the ambo can't tell us the real story about why Lola was taken, *but* she might have told my father. A bedside chat. He could've even been there when the call came about Lola's abduction," I finally interjected my two cents.

"The better question is, why isn't he telling us?" Bella looked at me, and I knew the answer to that.

My father was either trying to save his own ass, or someone else's he cared about. In this case, that someone wasn't me, it was the ambassador.

I turned toward where I set my phone on the counter and wasted no time, not caring I had an audience for the call. I had no secrets to hide, but it sure as hell seemed like my old man did.

He answered on the second ring and I placed him on speakerphone. "I've been trying to reach you," he rushed out.

"The reporter, I know," I gritted out.

"Not about that." A low hiss fell over the line. "Well, not only about that. But we do need to talk."

"Yeah, no shit." I had no patience for whatever BS he was about to try and run me over with in his effort to turn the conversation the way he wanted it to go.

I faced everyone in the kitchen, finding them staring at my phone.

"We have to talk in person. Send me your address. I can't meet tonight, but I'll come to you first thing in the morning. Just sit tight. Don't do anything stupid before then. Do *not* contact that reporter, you hear me?"

Nothing like taking orders from him at forty-two. *Jesus.*

At the feel of Bella's eyes on me, I glanced her way. She was worrying her lip between her teeth while studying me, probably curious if I'd blow up or keep a lid on my emotions. I was still on the fence.

Time was ticking, and my father's patience would soon expire if I didn't give him a "roger that."

"I have something I need to talk to you about, too," I finally managed out instead of offering my obedience like he wanted. "And it can't wait."

"It's going to damn well have to. This discussion can't happen over the phone. Things have changed. You're going to have to trust me and wait until tomorrow for our talk."

Of course he'd steamroll over me and ignore what I needed. Nothing would ever change when it came to him. "Just give me something. What's changed?"

I overheard chatter in the background, then a door slam shut. "The FBI is no longer in charge of the investigation. That's what's changed. That's all I can tell you. I'll see you in the morning. Seven sharp." He hung up before I could get another word out.

"What the hell does he mean the FBI aren't in charge?

They wouldn't turn the case over to the local PD. Not when the bodies were diplomatic security," Alessandro pointed out, and I released a deep breath that did nothing to help the pain settling in my chest.

"No, not them." I met Constantine's eyes, knowing his thoughts more than likely just landed on the same agency mine did. "And if it's who I think it is, then we were right about the ambassador's daughter. It was never about money."

"The Company? You think they took control from the Feds on the FBI's own stomping ground?" Enzo asked. But was he really surprised they wouldn't play by the rules?

The CIA wasn't supposed to operate on American soil. But Enzo and his brothers weren't exactly supposed to run off-the-books ops for the government—mostly for the CIA—in exchange for not serving prison time, either.

"Of course they would," Enzo answered his own question when no one spoke up. "Looks like I'm not going home tomorrow after all."

Chapter 25

Hudson

At the sound of a text, I rolled over to my side on the bed and went for my phone on the nightstand. *Bella* . . .

> Bella: You awake?

> Me: No.

> Bella: Real funny.

> Bella: I can't sleep.

I switched to my back, propped my head up with my good arm, and used voice-to-text to continue what I assumed would be a lengthy conversation with her.

We'd had a few of these late-night talks in the last few months. I'd never thought much of it before. Just two friends chatting about anything and everything until three in the morning. Totally normal. So, I'd thought. Now I knew better. This was part of the "more" that'd been happening between us, I just hadn't forced myself to accept it until this weekend.

> Bella: I've tried everything to fall asleep and nothing is working.

> Me: I'm sure you haven't tried everything-everything. Golf channel? A nice horror flick?

> Bella: Neither helped. I did try.

> Me: Hmmm.

> Bella: I think the problem is that, well . . .

> Bella: I don't want to be alone.

And there it was. I'd been expecting that, but it was something she'd never texted me on our previous late-night chats.

> Me: I'll be sure someone gets your bear from the city tomorrow so you don't have to sleep alone.

Not what I wanted to say, but I was trying to be good. Brothers in the house and all.

> Bella: What about tonight, though?

> Me: You didn't need him the weekend you stayed at my place . . . I think you can go one night here.

> Bella: I wonder why I didn't bring him. Maybe I was hoping someone else would cuddle with me instead?

> Bella: (Like I'm asking you now.)

> Me: You want me to fill in for Rugby? <teddy bear emoji>

> Bella: If I promise I'll behave, will you?

> Me: Expand on your definition of "behave," please. We may not share the same one.

> Bella: Hands to myself. No accidental "bumping" of any kind. Sassy mouth in check (since I know that turns you on, and don't lie and say it doesn't). Fully clothed (in the PJs I had on in the kitchen, at least). Panties on.

> Bella: Don't ask me to wear a bra, though. That'd be cruel and unusual torture. (It's not like I have big boobs anyway. I mean, your hand played abracadabra with my breast and made it disappear tonight. Covered the whole thing.)

Was she trying to kill me? I sent her three back-to-back emojis. The same little guy with a cocked brow.

> Bella: And that means?

> Me: You're not selling me on the whole behaving thing. Talking about your sassy mouth, panties, and tits. Try again, miss.

I was hard. *Great.*

> Bella: My brothers are down the hall and asleep. I know your head is as off as mine, if not more. I really do plan to be good.

"Sure you will be, sweetheart. Such a good girl." I trashed

the voice message I almost sent. How the hell would I share a bed with her?

> Bella: Also, I think you're safe from ACE. They didn't try to kill you earlier for being alone with me. So, if we're just sharing your bed (because mine is lonely and lumpy) and they were to find out, I have to believe you won't face Judgment Day.

> Me: Do your brothers know you refer to them as ACE? <laughing emoji> I like it, though.

> Bella: Came up with it on the fly just now. <winking emoji>

> Bella: Sooo . . . what do you say? Will you put me out of my misery and sleep with me?

The bubbles on her side seemed to bounce like they were on steroids as I spoke into the phone, this time for a voice memo.

"You have no idea how desperately I want to put us both out of our misery and sleep with you. No. Fucking. Idea." I stared at the blue arrow, unsure if I should commit to sending her an actual voice message. Against my better judgment, I didn't X out of it, and let it fly. I also sent a quick follow-up text.

> Me: I just proved why you can't sleep next to me. You know it. I know it. The whole house probably does now, too.

When she kept quiet, I brought my arm from behind my head, sliding it beneath the covers to remove my briefs. My cock was ridiculously stiff already. Like hell would I survive this woman sleeping next to me, but the idea of her alone and sad in her bed was too brutal of an image.

> Me: It's impossible for me to say no to you. You know that, right?

> Bella: You did earlier.

> Me: Yeah, how long did that "no" last?

The only way I could behave was if she told me to. Because if she gave me the green light, I had zero fight left in me when it came to turning her down.

> Me: If you come to my room to sleep (the actual definition of that word), you have to promise not to let me have you tonight. No touching, teasing, kissing. Not with your brothers in the house. Bad enough I already fucked you with my fingers under your parents' roof. <face palm emoji>

> Bella: You're not going to Hell for what we did earlier, just so you know.

> Me: I know. I'm now extremely aware Hell is real and the place I've been living in before this weekend.

> Bella: That makes my heart hurt. <sad emoji>

> Me: No sad eyes. Not allowed. Send me some heart eyes instead. <winking emoji>

> Bella: Give me a reason to.

Fucking A, she had me there. Before I could come up with anything to say, she sent another message.

> Bella: You have my word for tonight. I'll behave. If you're not ready to see if this "thing" between us can be more, especially while under this particular roof, I'll respect that.

> Me: I gave your brother my word this morning. <screwy eyeball emoji> Look how that turned out.

My surrender came in the form of a text a second later.

> Me: Just give me five minutes. <Melting emoji>

> Bella: A big, tough SEAL being so adorable and honest is just sexy as all hell.

> Bella: And why not right now? (Patience isn't my virtue, and you know that.)

I stroked my cock from root to tip, wishing it was her hand or mouth there instead. Yeah, I was in trouble.

> Me: I definitely recall, but I've gotta ... take care of something ... so I'm not quite as tense before you show up. (Increases my chances of surviving alone with you to 5%.)

> Bella: I literally just thought the letters LOL in my head. I think I've been spending too much time texting instead of speaking. (Side note: thank you for the mental image. Now I'm horny.)

> Me: Like you weren't already before? <devil emoji>

I just couldn't stop myself anymore. The line in the sand. The steel barrier. The whatever we wanted to call it that'd

The Art of You

been between us for years? It was gone. We didn't skip over it. We buried it six fucking feet deep. But buried things didn't always stay buried, so . . .

> Bella: Are you already touching yourself? <fire emoji>

> Me: What do you think?

I continued to fist my cock, thankful for that Advil so I could use my dominant hand without my forearm hurting. I thought back to the bathroom, when she'd spread her knees and boldly showed me her cunt.

> Bella: I'm touching myself, too.

"Of course you are. Such a bad girl." I sent it as a voice message, my words a damn near growl. I pushed the covers back so when I was ready to come, it'd be on my bare chest instead of on the bedding.

She replied with a voice memo. *Finally.*

I pressed play, and her breathy words had me clenching my jaw. "Make up your mind, sailor. Want me to be your good girl or your bad one?"

I responded immediately, gritting out, "I just want you to be mine."

I hit send before I realized what I'd said, my abs contracting and my body tensing as I came, then finally relaxed for the first time since the accident.

I closed my eyes, my left hand hanging lazily at my side still clutching the phone. The chime from her message woke up my brain, and I lifted up the phone to read it.

> Bella: Does that mean you've decided I'm worth the risk?

She was worth it all. Living. Dying. And everything in between. That wasn't the issue.

> Me: I don't want to hurt you. You get that, right? If it was just my feelings to consider, I'd have made you mine a long time ago.

> Bella: Well, maybe almost dying will finally wake you up. Help you see your feelings matter, too. And to understand that taking a chance on us being "more" is much better than living our lives always wondering if we should've . . .

> Me: I did the "almost dying" thing for a living in the Navy. That never woke me up. But almost losing you this weekend has.

> Me: I'm trying, I promise.

> Bella: That's all I want.

> Me: Now, are you coming to my bed . . . or what? <winking emoji>

Chapter 26

Isabella

"WHAT ARE you doing roaming the halls in the middle of the night?"

Enzo's voice froze me in place, and I hung my head, trying to come up with an excuse. The hall was only lit up by a motion light near the baseboards. "Midnight snack?" *Why'd I say that like a question?*

"Sure you were." He didn't wait for me to turn. Nope, Enzo went around and cock-blocked me. He even went so far as to open his inked arms and set each hand on the opposite walls to really prove his apparent opinion on the matter. Standing before me all edgy and tense, he may as well have been playing a twisted game of Monopoly. I didn't need to see his eyes to read, *Do not pass Go and do not collect any orgasms.*

For his information, I had no plans to "collect" anything but a decent sleep. I'd already had two O's this evening, one by Hudson's hand earlier and one by my own a minute ago.

But perhaps I needed to give Enzo a chance to explain instead of putting words in his mouth.

"I don't want to be alone." My defense felt as floppy as

post-rain hair. It sounded pathetic even if it was true. "We were just going to sleep together."

The barrier of his arms fell like a bridge being lowered—slow suspension and controlled movement. "I may be laid-back lately, but I don't want to hear about my little sister having sex."

I swatted his chest with the back of my hand. "Sleep as in sleep. That's all we planned to do. He's not going to bang me under our parents' roof, especially not with you guys in the house. Jeez." *Gone Baby Gone*. It wasn't just a movie name, but seemingly the appropriate title for my mouth. *Ugh*.

"It's a damn good thing you bumped into me, not the others," he grumble-growled. It was apparently a thing when it came to my brothers, and they did it well. Could've taught a masterclass in how to make words leave their mouths in the form of wild animal-like sounds.

"I didn't *bump* into you. You stopped me." Semantics, but it was the best I could do right now.

"Do we need to have *the birds and the bees talk?*"

Okay, the humor in his tone that time was not only unexpected, it was such a dramatic change that I had to wonder if I was sleepwalking.

"No, Bianca did in fourth grade. And Mom gave me the 'Men are from Mars, and Women are from Venus' speech half a dozen times more than necessary, too."

"Relax. I was fuckin' with you. I know he wouldn't do something like that in our parents' house." I couldn't see his mouth, but there was a smirk there for sure.

Bullshit. You know we already did something. Just not sex-sex.

"If sleeping next to Hudson makes you feel better, then go. I won't stop you. Just remain in a parallel position."

I couldn't help but laugh that time, then cupped my mouth,

worried I'd wake up Constantine. "You sound ridiculous," I teased in a low voice, lowering my hand.

"You mean as ridiculous as you only wanting to join Hudson so you're not alone does?"

You have me there. "Why are you roaming the halls anyway?" *I'll take deflection for $400, please.*

"Maria's struggling to sleep, too. If she's up, I'm up. It's only fair. I'm going to the living room to FaceTime her. Constantine's room is right next to mine, and you know how he is if he doesn't get his beauty sleep. Don't want to keep him up."

"Well, tell Maria hi, and I'm sorry you won't be going home tomorrow."

"Yeah, yeah." He shooed me away. "Now go. Don't stay up too late."

I smiled. "Roger that."

Maneuvering around him in a hurry, I rushed to Hudson's room. The door was unlocked, and the room was pitch black when I opened up.

"Don't trip." His husky voice was like a little beacon of light, helping guide me to him after I'd shut the door.

I knelt on the end of the bed, feeling around in the dark, finally locating his leg. He was on top of the covers. Bare legs. No sweatpants.

"I came in my good-girl PJs, and are you only wearing briefs?" I wasted an arched brow since he couldn't see me as I crawled up the bed, continuing to glide my hand along his leg.

He reached for my wrist. "What happened to your word, miss?"

"I was just trying to find my way to you."

"Sure you were."

He pulled me over so I was snug against his side. He was on his back, so I shimmied around and faced him, hooking my leg over his, stretching my arm across his hard chest to hold on to him.

"I can't sleep in clothes, but you'll be sleeping in yours. That's an order." He lazily ran his fingers under the sleeve of my top and along my arm, up and down in soft strokes. At least he hadn't pushed me off him. Drawing his other arm around to my shoulder, he completed the puzzle of our perfect hug.

"How am I doing as a substitute for Rugby?" he asked a few quiet moments later.

I lifted my chin to peer up at him, but my eyes had yet to adjust to the darkness. "I think it's safe to say you're doing such a good job, I may just have to keep you forever."

* * *

While gargling mouthwash the next morning, I stared at the vanity in a daze, remembering all the deliciously wonderful things that happened in here the night before. After that, I returned to the bedroom just in time.

In the short minutes I'd been gone, Hudson had gone from asleep to having a night terror.

I rushed back into bed, doing my best not to startle him.

"It's a trap," he repeated under his breath.

Oh God, was he back in the past and reliving that operation?

It was 6:20 a.m., and while it wasn't quite light enough outside to illuminate the whole room, it was enough to see him clearly.

The strain in his jaw from grinding down on his teeth. The tight draw of his brows as if in pain.

"Shhh. It's okay. You're dreaming." I swept my hand back and forth over his forehead in calming strokes. "You're okay. It's just a bad dream."

The Art of You

Hudson's body jerked. His muscles locked up. And before I knew it, he flipped me over, anchoring himself on top of me. I shot my hands up to cradle his face, hoping to snap him from the past and back to me.

"It's me," I cried as he blinked a few times, then finally set his eyes on me.

"Bella?" My name came out like it'd pained him to say it. He didn't move, just remained staring at me.

I brought my hands down along his arms and over the flexed, rigid muscles. "It's okay," I said softly. "You're okay."

He angled his head, brows slowly knitting as he finally pieced together where he was and why. "We slept?"

"Passed out pretty fast actually." We really did just need each other. No sex. Just warmth and safety. "I kept my promise. I behaved."

"Did I make a promise?" That deep morning voice. Holy hell.

I swallowed. "No."

He kept himself over me but dipped his chin, dropping his gaze between us. When he slowly rolled his hips forward, and I felt his hard length press against me, I forgot all about his bad dream. And I was pretty sure that nightmare was long gone for him, too.

His briefs weren't the best barrier. Nor my silk PJ pants. Because as he nudged himself between my legs, it felt like we were naked, and I could truly feel him.

Palms to his slightly damp chest, I felt his heart race wildly beneath my touch. He moved his hips again, forward and back.

I wasn't sure how he was keeping himself in this position with his beat-up arm, but I also couldn't focus on much more than the friction he was creating with his movements. Hitting me in the perfect spot with each thrust. Missionary sex without the sex, but . . .

The next time he rubbed his cock against my silk-covered center, I shivered. He must've thought I was cold, because he reached back and pulled the covers over us.

Sheltered in place beneath this man, his hips kept a steady rhythm on top of me, moving as if he were inside of me instead.

"Unbutton your top. I want to see your tits."

The rough order sent my fingers flying from his body to mine. I fumbled with the buttons, and with the heavy weight of his cock resting against me, my breath hitched with anticipation. It was quite possible he was going to get me off without ever physically touching my skin.

The second my buttons were free and the top was open, he pushed upright a bit and briefly shifted the comforter to the side so he could better see me.

He licked his lips, eyes pinned to my breasts. "Perfect. So fucking perfect." He moved to his forearms, bringing the comforter back over us as his chest met my heated body. His hard muscles to my soft skin. And then he did what I hoped. He slammed his mouth over mine.

I worked my arms outside the cage of his position so I could touch him. We were both bruised and still injured, so I wanted to be gentle, but it was hard to restrain from running my hands all over him. To his back muscles. Rigid abs. Broad shoulders. Tight triceps.

My hand wandered beneath his briefs next, and he went still the second I wrapped my hand around his shaft. I swept the pad of my thumb over his crown, catching his precum.

"What are we doing?" I asked between kisses.

"Acting like teenagers." He licked my lips open, commanding control and owning my mouth the way he already owned my body. "Being reckless."

Reckless just became my favorite word if it meant having our limbs tangled together and his tongue in my mouth.

It was also too hard to jerk him off from this angle, and since he wouldn't free me from the prison of his arms, I wasn't sure how to make it work.

"You're not going anywhere until you come, sweetheart," he ordered between kisses. "So move your hand so you can rub that pussy against my cock. Just keep your panties on so I don't wind up inside you."

"Oh, but wouldn't that be a happy accident? You pushing your cock inside me instead of just playing pretend."

"Want me to stop this, miss?"

His threat was empty; he knew I'd never say yes to that.

I'd take dry humping over nothing every day that started with T. You know, today and tomorrow. And there was always one of those.

"Right now this is the only way I can . . ."

His cliffhanger hurt my heart. It scared me he still wasn't quite on board despite the overwhelming evidence there was "more" between us.

"Don't stop." I decided to get out of my head and enjoy this moment. "But I'd very much like to get you off, too."

"Not right now." He nudged his nose against mine and kissed me. "Now, do what I said and move your hand." He locked eyes with me, waiting for me to nod yes to his command.

I did as he requested, then arched my back to shift my PJ bottoms down to my thighs, creating less of a barrier between us.

"That's my girl." He brought his mouth over mine, and I moved my hips in circles while holding on to his arms, chasing relief only he could give me.

I neared my orgasm, desperate to feel this man inside me.

"One day. Just not now," he gritted out, reading my thoughts, giving me hope with his promise there'd be another time.

And those words sent me over the edge.

Breathing hard, my stomach muscles clenched, and I let myself go and came.

I barely registered the sound of the door flying open, but Hudson went dead still on top of me.

"Wake up, we—"

Constantine.

Because of course of all people to come in, never expecting for me to be here, it'd be him. Why didn't I lock the freaking door?

"Fuck." Constantine cursed again but in Italian, slamming the door shut.

At least we were mostly concealed by the comforter, but Hudson hung his head and swore as well before rolling off me.

"I'm so sorry," I whispered.

"Not your fault." He lowered his legs to the floor and stood. The bulge in his briefs wasn't close to being killed as he went for his sweatpants. "I chose to be reckless." He'd kept his voice so low I barely heard him as I buttoned up my top.

Constantine knocked. "You decent?"

Still here? Really? I sat taller, clutching the bedding to my chest.

Hudson adjusted the waistband of his sweats, then faced the door, tearing a hand through his messy hair. He was still shirtless, but called out, "Yeah, you can come in."

The hall was lit up behind my brother. His broad, muscular frame filled the doorway where he remained. He didn't look at me and kept his attention on Hudson.

"It's not what it looked like," I stated quickly. "I didn't want to be alone last night, and he was having a nightmare, and I—"

My brother lifted his palm, a plea for me to stop talking as he swerved his gaze my way. "You're both adults. I'm"—he scowled—"sorry I didn't knock first."

Okay, not the reaction I'd expected from the grump.

Constantine focused on Hudson, clearly not wanting to see his little sister in his best friend's bed. "We have some possible news from Marc."

"Something happen in Arlington?" Hudson picked up his shirt and held it at his side.

"Yeah, Clarke met with someone in a park at zero five hundred. Come down to the kitchen so we can fill you in before your dad arrives."

Right. The governor would be showing up at seven a.m.

Constantine quietly left and closed the door without saying another word.

Hopping out of the bed, I went over to Hudson and offered to help him with his tee, but he stopped me from assisting.

"That didn't really happen, did it?" he asked, brows drawn tight.

"Which part? Him walking in on us while I was getting off, or the fact he didn't kill you?"

"Both." He dropped his forehead as if fearing that despite what just went down, he'd lost his best friend. "Fucking both."

Chapter 27

Isabella

Deciding it'd be better to show up in something other than PJs after my big brother embarrassingly walked in on us, I went ahead and changed.

I switched into jeans and the one hoodie Callie did pack for me. A simple Lululemon white one. Now, of course, I'd never look at Lululemon the same after seeing Hudson in those briefs.

Once in the kitchen, the anxiety of facing my big brother kicked up a notch.

I tugged at the hoodie drawstrings as I laid eyes on Constantine. He was standing in front of the bay window with his back to me, dressed more casually than normal in jeans and a black tee.

Enzo and Alessandro were also there, sitting behind the breakfast bar, focused on a laptop. They didn't shoot me any knowing looks or lopsided grins. Or scowls, for that matter. Just quick good mornings.

"Callie still asleep?" I asked, making a beeline for the Nespresso machine.

The Art of You

"Yeah, I didn't want to wake her." Alessandro peered over the screen at me. "Malik's outside the pool house, though."

I popped the hazelnut-flavored pod into the machine and set one of the bigger mugs in place, then covered my nervous stomach with a shaky palm.

"So, what's the news?" At Hudson's deep voice, I spun around to face him. "What'd Marc find out in Arlington?"

He went straight to the laptop, not meeting my eyes, locked into operator mode. He was probably assuming that'd be the best way to cut through the awkwardness.

Enzo slid the laptop to his right so Hudson could have a look while bringing us up to speed. "Marc took a video of what he saw. We waited to wake you until we could get an ID on the man at the park with Clarke."

When the coffee was ready, I decided to give it to Hudson instead, along with Advil. Only when I held out a single gel tablet for him did he look up. He accepted the coffee but didn't touch the Advil until I upped it to two. He grumbled under his breath, then nodded his thanks before returning his attention to the laptop.

It was a miracle I didn't need anything myself. My arm and shoulder weren't even sore anymore. The poor guy seemed to have taken the brunt of the accident.

"The man Clarke met with is Seth Maverick. He works for the DOD at the Pentagon," Alessandro explained after Hudson tossed back the pills.

Constantine faced the room, brows drawn, gaze tight on me. I couldn't get the best read on him, not when I was pre-caffeinated.

On that note, I went to the machine to make myself a cup. Or better yet, a peace offering for Constantine in the form of java.

"Their conversation could have been related to the investigation, right? Or maybe he's trying to find out why the case was taken from the FBI and handed over to the Agency," Hudson suggested.

"Could be what he told his boss, at least." Enzo pointed at something on the screen. "But look at this exchange here. Seth's pissed. Shoves Clarke. Pointing back and forth between them. He's angry about something."

I abandoned my coffee endeavor and headed toward the viewing party. "I take it Marc couldn't get close enough to overhear them?" Standing alongside Hudson, I pointed at the screen. "Can you zoom in so we can try and read his lips?"

"You're always mouthing words, how about you give it a go?" Enzo teased.

He probably forgot I'd learned American Sign Language in college and could read speech damn well. Either way, he slowed down the video speed and hit play.

I watched the heated back-and-forth between Agent Clarke and this Seth guy. When I leaned forward in front of Hudson, he straightened his posture to give me a bit more space, keeping our bodies from colliding in front of Constantine. *Good thinking.*

"I'm almost sure he said the letters AAR," I interpreted. "Rewind and replay again." Hands to the counter, I brought my face closer to the screen. "Then after he pushes him, I think he says the word girlfriend. And that's all I can make out." I stood upright, drawing my hands to my waist.

"AAR." Hudson's eyes moved to his coffee mug. "What if Seth somehow got his hands on the real version of the after-action report for the operation in 2010 and gave it to Clarke?"

"And what, Clarke gave it to his girlfriend?" Enzo picked up with the line of thought.

Then I ran all the way home with it. "So, Kit and Clarke are dating, and he gave Kit the AAR. And now Seth's reaming Clarke out at five in the morning, which says to me she wasn't supposed to publish that. Maybe not yet, at least." *And the plot of this madness thickens.* "Does that mean Kit, Clarke, and this DOD guy are working together to try and take down your father? Or did Clarke lie to Seth Maverick about his plans for the AAR?"

"Maybe this helps rule out the idea you have a stalker, at least," Alessandro commented, letting go of a relieved sigh.

"I mean, a girl can hope, right?" I went over to the Nespresso machine, trying to pull off nonchalant in all of this when I was still, in fact, very "chalant." That was definitely a word, right? "What if Clarke's been keeping tabs on your father for a while, looking to nail him on something?" I faced Hudson again. "He could've gotten wind of Lola's roommate reporting her missing, and that the ambassador denied she'd been taken days before the party."

"Then he found out I was suddenly attending an event with the ambassador, and since it seems he's privy to our extracurricular activities, he assumed I was going to rescue her daughter." Hudson set down his coffee, hands going on each side of the mug.

"Clarke was probably planning to expose our side gig whether we failed or not," Constantine said in a low voice. "But things didn't go as he expected, so he had Kit run with that story."

"Because the CIA hijacked the case from the FBI yesterday," Alessandro added. "And now Seth's pissed at Clarke, worried the headline will fall back on him as the source of the leak."

"I didn't think it was Alfie behind the photo and story." Hudson shook his head. "But the fact Clarke had access to the AAR involving that op, not to mention I could've sworn I saw

Alfie at the party, still doesn't sit well with me. I think we're missing something. There has to be more to the story."

"You think Clarke reached out to Alfie after reading the AAR? Maybe he got Alfie on his side, encouraging him to help take you down?" Alessandro's accusation had Hudson reaching for his coffee again.

"I don't know what to think anymore." Hudson looked over at me, frowning.

"What we need to do is talk to this homeless guy again. Get him clean. See if he can pinpoint any of our suspects as the one who paid him to be the delivery man," Alessandro said.

"We're still going to help sober him up in a non-kidnappy way, right?" Enzo asked him.

Alessandro looked over his shoulder as if checking for Callie. "Do what you have to do for expediency's sake. But you know, the safe way." He scratched his stubbled jawline. "Civil, I suppose." He was turning a leaf, so it would seem.

And if my brothers could change and be slightly less morally gray to make their wives happy, then Hudson could be . . . well, I just wanted him to be happy. Happy and with me, preferably.

"Yeah, okay. As soon as the governor shows up and shares his news, I'll hop on his helo back with him to the city. Whether he wants me to or not," Enzo remarked.

"I also woke up Adelina an hour ago and asked her to see what she could find out about this Seth Maverick guy." Constantine finally joined in on the conversation, but he didn't budge from his place by the window.

"You two are getting quite comfortable, huh?" Alessandro's joke earned him Constantine's scowl. Better him getting that look than me.

Forgetting I'd started the coffee machine, I blinked in realization the cup was full. Talk about a metaphor I could use in my life right now. Not even half full. Just brimming with goodness. *Please, please let that happen soon. For all of us.*

I rounded the counter and brought my brother the peace offering.

Constantine stared down at the mug, and I hadn't realized I'd chosen one that said **Disney Princess** on it. The corner of his lip hitched. Watching him fight that smile gave me hope.

He went to accept the mug, then stopped himself when his phone rang. "It's Adelina, she must have something," he announced.

I set the cup in front of him and went back to the machine to finally get my own drink.

"Hey, we're all here," Constantine told her. "Putting you on speaker. What'd you learn?"

"Morning," Adelina greeted. "Well, I've discovered it's a really small world."

"Why do you say that?" I asked, going for a mug from the shelf. I chose the one that had **NAVY** on the side. If Constantine was going to be a princess, I could be the sailor today. At least I never lost my sense of humor, even in the face of all of our problems.

"Seth Maverick's ex-wife is Sydney Archer-Hawkins, and Sydney works for Falcon Falls Security, which is where my twin sister, Mya, works."

The mug fell from my hand at Adelina's words, crashing to my bare feet and shattering.

"Don't cut yourself, dammit." Hudson to the rescue without missing a beat. He rounded the breakfast bar, skipping right by Constantine to bend down before me and pick up the broken pieces.

I squatted in front of him, our eyes meeting. "Did she say Falcon? And, um, sister? I thought her twin was missing." It took me a second to notice I'd mouthed my words to him.

Hudson nodded, continuing to pick up all the pieces of my reaction. I assumed that was a yes to both my questions. "She's alive. I just found out yesterday morning. I meant to tell you."

"You lost your twin sister?" Enzo's voice was low-pitched and grave. I forgot he was more than likely not-in-the-know on Adelina's past.

"I did. She was taken when we were three, but she's alive. I only recently found out. She's in Italy right now, but she works with an American security company in a similar line of work as you do. So, that's what I meant by small world."

"It's about to get even smaller." Enzo's deep voice cut through the room, and he had to be lost to the past now, thinking about Bianca. Wishing so much his twin, *our* sister, could be found, too. But she'd been murdered, not taken.

With his free hand, Hudson reached for my elbow and guided me to stand, probably worried I'd lose my balance given the weight of the conversation.

"What do you mean by smaller?" Adelina asked as Constantine swapped the phone for the Disney mug.

"Your sister works with a friend of mine, Jesse McAdams." Enzo stood and tore his hands through his hair. "Jesse's the one who broke the news to me that I didn't kill the right person fourteen years ago for my sister's murder."

Really small world.

"Falcon, they, uh, well, we worked with them to figure out who really killed our sister," Alessandro continued for Enzo, his accent growing thicker.

"I had no idea you did that. Or that you . . ." Adelina audibly cleared her throat over the line. "You were with them, weren't you?" she whispered, as if now connecting the dots. "That's why you really left the FBI, isn't it?"

Hudson stared at the broken pieces of the Navy cup in his

hand. More symbolism to complete the morning's chaos. *No, no, no. Where was my full cup of hope?*

"Yeah, that's why I eventually turned in my badge," Hudson answered in a low voice.

"And this Agent Asshole knows about the deal our father cut with the AG to avoid prison time," Alessandro let her know. "So, Clarke's got an ax to grind with Hudson. Hell, with all of us. He's not a fan of us playing outside the rules, but he sure is okay with doing it to try and fuck with us."

"Hmm." Adelina paused. "You'd think Clarke would also be pissed at his AG friend since he helped make the deal happen."

"Dean, the AG, who I'll now be referring to as Dean the Dickhead, probably manipulated Clarke the way he's working over Kit and any other number of people to ensure he becomes governor next year." I regretted part of my words the second I locked on to Hudson. He had to be thinking about Alfie now, wondering if Clarke or the Dickhead got to his old teammate, too.

"You should know, though, that the man we killed wasn't a saint," Constantine said, and I assumed he was speaking to Adelina now. He lowered his mug back to the counter. "He may not have been Bianca's killer, but I don't feel bad about taking his life, so let's not start thinking about that now."

And *that* comment was meant for Enzo. I knew by the way Enzo was raking his hands through his hair, he was spiraling a bit. Was he thinking about Bianca? Or still feeling bad about killing the wrong man?

My brothers and Hudson took responsibility for that guy's death, but I also knew Enzo took that man's last breath.

"Constantine's right," Alessandro said with a nod. "We have enough to worry about than to focus on some sick fuck who also deserved to die fourteen years ago. May that prick *not* rest in peace as far as I'm concerned."

Enzo slowly faced the room, dragging his hand across his mouth before moving it down the column of this throat. "We can't bring Bianca back," he said while peering at me, "but we can ensure nothing ever happens to Izzy. So, I'm not leaving New York until I know with absolute-fucking-certainty that she's not in danger."

"Of course," Adelina said almost immediately, and I was relieved she seemed fine with dropping the discussion about what had happened all those years ago. "I'll call my sister and ask her to talk to Sydney for me. If it's okay with you, I'll explain what's going on, and see what Falcon might know."

I looked to Constantine next, curious if he'd object. He had a beef with one of the owners of Falcon Falls, Carter Dominick. Although, I supposed they kind of buried the hatchet when they operated together last year in Upstate New York. That partnership ultimately led to Enzo killing Bianca's *real* murderer in our parents' home on Long Island last fall.

"Yeah, that's fine," Constantine agreed as Hudson tossed the broken pieces of the mug in the trash.

Hudson then checked his watch, noting, "My father will be here soon, so let's touch base later today. Swap notes."

After the call ended with Adelina, Enzo announced, "I need air." He scanned the room, looking at us all one by one, finally resting his gaze on Hudson. "I'll be back once your father's helo touches down." He left before anyone could object, and I hated that he was reliving the nightmare of his past all over again.

"Why do I feel like none of this is a coincidence?" I spoke my thoughts aloud while mindlessly wandering back to the cabinet, prepared to get a new mug. "Like *any* of it."

Constantine came over and reached up into the cabinet for me, offering me an orange mug that said *Happiness is one cup away* as he confirmed, "Because I don't think it is."

Chapter 28

Hudson

I WAS DONE with walks back into the past. I just wanted to go forward for once. Enzo had the right idea—I needed air.

I parked my ass outside on a bench that had a view of the helipad while waiting for my old man. My inability to sit alone with my thoughts led me to scrolling the internet. Probably not the best idea given my current state of mind.

One minute of "just checking" what else had been posted since yesterday turned into "oops, I-lost-track-of-time."

Where was he, anyway? *Late, like always.*

Swipe after swipe. Image after image. I finally settled on one video that didn't piss me off. No headline or caption. Just our names beneath the two of us dancing at the party to "Unchained Melody." I had to admit, we looked good together.

Screw it. I decided to screen record the video so I could keep it. While it saved, I watched again, realizing I'd missed something important the first time.

The downward angle of the shot meant the camera had to have recorded us from above, so the footage had to have been pulled from the CCTV cameras from within the house.

The Art of You

I opened up the profile of the person who'd posted the video on X. No name. No description. A random string of numbers and letters for a user name. And the only content was this one video.

There was an Instagram username listed, so I switched to that app. I only had an account for my bar for promo and shit, so I had to use that profile to check it out. I typed in the account name, but it was private. No profile picture either. Zero followers. Not following anyone. And yet, 363 posts.

On the off chance someone wanted me to see this and follow them, I went ahead and made the request. I copied the profile link and sent a text to the Costa brothers, explaining what I'd stumbled upon.

> Alessandro: Well, that's creepy as fuck. I'll look into it.

> Me: My thoughts exactly. Thanks.

I looked up to see my father's helicopter in the distance on approach.

> Me: The governor is here. Be in soon.

> Alessandro: Copy that.

Figuring it'd take my father a few minutes to land and make his way over to me, I used my time to scroll through Instagram with one target in mind. I ignored my notifications for my bar profile and went to one of the few names I followed.

Bella's last two posts were from Nashville. One was of her with Alessandro and Callie at their wedding, and the other was from the next day when she'd gone on her first horseback ride.

Of course, I had no choice but to join her on that little adventure. Contrary to popular stereotypes, even though I'd grown up in Texas, I wasn't exactly a cowboy. But I knew my way around horses, and I'd been worried about her safety.

Bella had bought cowgirl boots while in Nashville and had proudly worn them to ride. Saddled alongside her, it'd taken all of my restraint not to steal her away and make love to her in a field while she wore those boots, and nothing but those boots.

I'd managed to behave that day. But as of this weekend, I'd officially shot that "good behavior" to hell. I'd snapped in the bathroom last night and lost my control in bed this morning.

I closed out the app and bowed my head at the memory of Constantine walking in on us, clearly assuming I'd been having sex with her. Damn close to it. The only reason I'd held back was because of that nagging fear in the back of my head I'd one day lose her forever.

More concerns, along with decades' worth of mistakes, filled my mind as I waited for my father. I was almost relieved when he approached, needing a reprieve from my guilt.

My father was without his entourage, so I had to assume they were back in the helo waiting for him. "I don't have much time," were his first words to me.

I stood and stowed my phone, ready to get this conversation over with. "Fine." I motioned to the house and started walking, in no mood for small talk on the way.

"I'm sorry."

He dropped the apology so quickly, it took me a few seconds to stop moving. I was on the steps leading to the back deck, and I remained there while turning to confront him.

Standing down below, he cupped his mouth and met my eyes, shaking his head. Was he throwing up in his mouth at having to utter those two words?

"For?" I prompted, resting my palm on the railing at my side.

His hand fell and he copied my move, reaching for the rail-

The Art of You

ing. "For withholding information from you. That decision could've cost you your life on Friday."

"What kind of information?" My body tensed as I waited for answers.

My father looked around. First, up toward the roof where a sniper sat on a long gun. Then off to the garden where another security guard walked.

"The kidnappers never wanted money, did they?" I went ahead and made it easier for him to spit out the truth.

He shook his head. "Do you remember the attack at our embassy in Algeria last October?"

I nodded, unsure where he was going with this. "Two Marines were killed while protecting a diplomat there," I answered. "What does that have to do with Spain and Ambassador Aldana?" I went down the three steps to join him on even ground. I'd wanted to have this conversation with the others, but if my father would be more candid if it was just the two of us, then so be it.

"What you don't know is the CIA heard chatter about an attack beforehand, but decided the intel wasn't reliable and opted not to act in advance. Turns out, they were wrong. It was a credible threat."

"They could've been saved," I seethed, drawing my hands to my hips, still uncertain how this news connected to the ambassador's daughter. Or to Clarke. To anyone for that matter.

"Unlike what happened to us, Spanish Intelligence, CNI, did take preemptive action when they had a similar threat from the same group back in April. They not only saved their embassy from an attack, they caught the head of the terrorist cell responsible. They were able to tie him directly to the attack on the U.S. embassy in Algeria as well."

Fuck. Now I knew where this was going.

"The Spanish have him in one of their black sites and refused a request to transfer him to U.S. custody," he went on. "The kidnappers demanded Ambassador Aldana provide the location of the black site in exchange for her daughter. They knew she couldn't negotiate his release, so this was the next best thing. They'd planned to hold on to Lola until after they'd successfully rescued their boss from the black site, worried she'd give the military a heads-up they were coming for him otherwise."

And there it is. I pinched the bridge of my nose, closing my eyes.

"I was with the ambassador when the call came in, which is how I know things even I shouldn't."

Yeah, the public sure as hell didn't know those lives at our embassy could've been saved that day, just like they didn't know the truth about Afghanistan. "You convinced the ambo to let me try and help first before giving up the location?"

"You and I both know they'd never have turned Lola back over, even if she played along. I offered her an alternative. *You.* She'd get her daughter back and not lose her job by giving those assholes what they wanted."

My hand slowly fell to my side. "If she gave up that location, she'd have been responsible for the deaths of everyone at that black site, not to mention having the blood of those Marines on her hands, too. And every future death that terrorist would cause," I hissed.

"And if it was Isabella's life on the line, what would you have done? Don't act like you wouldn't put that woman ahead of your country."

"I'd find a way to save her no matter what." I leveled him with a hard look. "But I wouldn't negotiate with savages who kill innocent people." I remained locked in a staring contest with him, forced to squint with the morning sunlight in my

The Art of You

eyes. "You should've told me I was dealing with terrorists Friday. I brought Bella to that party, dammit."

"Apparently, we now know you were dealing with mercenaries hired by the terrorists to kidnap Lola."

As if that fact made a goddamn difference to me. Facts were fucking facts. "This is why the CIA took control even though we're on U.S. soil," I tossed out a moment later, remembering that important detail from our call last night.

"The CIA intercepted chatter about the kidnapping after the fact. When they learned the FBI had two detainees, POTUS put in a call and allowed the Agency to take those men and the valet off their hands for questioning. From what I know, they're useless. The terrorists outsourced to these men to keep themselves out of the equation in case things went sideways, which they did. The valet also claimed he was only paid to tag your vehicle and eavesdrop on you when possible."

I figured as much about the valet. "I'm sure the terrorists have a backup plan since the kidnapping attempt failed."

My father's jaw shifted, a clear tell he knew more, and I was also right.

It clicked a moment later, and the blood drained from my face. "The Agency isn't going to tell the Spanish about this, and the ambassador won't tell her government the truth about what they were really after, am I right?" I didn't wait for an answer. "She's protecting her own ass. And the CIA is going to set a trap to see if the terrorists make a play for their boss again. If our government tells the Spanish, they'll preemptively move the target and put their site on high alert. The Agency will not only miss their chance to locate the whole terrorist cell, but lose the opportunity to get their hands on the boss like they originally wanted." I turned away from him, cupping my jaw in anger.

This was the kind of shit that got my men killed on the op

that day. Playing politics with lives on the line. Decisions being made by suits instead of the uniforms on the ground who actually knew what was going on firsthand.

I spun back around when another thought hit me. "Who told you this? The ambassador wouldn't have this kind of insider knowledge when it comes to the CIA."

"I still have friends in Congress and at the Pentagon. Don't forget, I was a senator before, and in the military before that."

"Yeah, well, these friends of yours are now sharing classified intelligence with someone who lacks the proper clearance. Not exactly legal," I reminded him.

"Do I need to remind you about your side gig? No badge, last time I checked. You turned yours in, throwing away the chance to become a director one day. You know how much that could've helped me to have you inside the Bureau?"

"Always about you and what helps your career," I said bitterly.

He ignored my words and spit out, "The good news is you're now in the clear. The Feds have orders to leave you and the Costas alone. That call came from the President himself. He knows what you did Friday—not only saving Lola, but also keeping the ambassador from giving up their black site." He looked back over his shoulder toward the helo, an indication he had no plans to stay and talk with my team. "As for the third shooter on the side of the road, just forget about it. It's no longer your concern."

I faked a laugh. The borderline losing-it kind. *No longer my concern, huh?* Had he lost his damn mind? Apparently. "Let me ask you, is the President privy to this plan of the Agency's to sidestep the Spanish to get their hands on these terrorists themselves, risking innocent lives lost as collateral damage?"

My father's jaw shifted again. "If you so much as open your mouth about what I told you, so help me . . ." He stabbed the air, his finger narrowly missing my chest as I stepped back in disgust. "Go back home and put this behind you. That's all you need to do right now. I'm still working on damage control from the press, but you need to keep a low profile with Clarke so hell-bent on finding something on you to get to me."

I couldn't believe this. And at the same time, I could. This was the governor, not a father I was talking to, after all. "The case isn't closed. Not for me."

"I said to drop it."

I was about to lose my head, and had I not heard the sound of the door opening and shutting behind me, I would've.

My father looked up and I pivoted, following his gaze to see Bella and her brothers on the deck.

"What's going on?" Constantine called down as I faced forward again, determined to get through to my father one way or another.

"Let me be very clear, I won't sit by and let the CIA play a game of fuck around and find out resulting in the loss of more lives the way their bogus intel did back in 2010."

"What are you talking about?" His jaw didn't hitch that time. He really didn't know the truth about the op that day, did he?

"Maybe Kit wouldn't be so hell-bent on taking me down to get to you if you hadn't broken her heart."

"Like you're any fucking better when it comes to women. Look at your own reputation." That low blow from him as he lifted his gaze, presumably peering at Bella, had me locking my hands at my sides. "Now tell me, do I have to do more damage control with the press than I thought I did?" He skipped right back to the point before I could, concerns for his campaign hanging in the balance after all.

My news would send him over the edge I'd already jumped off.

"Maybe ask your friends in Intelligence or in Congress instead, why don't you? Let them tell you what really happened that day in 2010. Have them share how bad intel the CIA forced my team to follow resulted in catastrophe. Congress and the CIA covered up their mess back then like they're now trying to hide why those two Marines really died." I was the one stabbing the air between us this time. "There was no training exercise that day. I wasn't on the op because of your email about Mom. Men lost their lives, and I've been dead on the inside ever since."

He abruptly stared at the pavers between us, and I decided not to wait for him to process what I'd said. Because a burning question was now sitting in the back of my head, and I had to ask. My gut said I was right and already knew the answer, though.

I dropped my head forward and rasped, "Just tell me one of your pals in D.C. isn't Seth Maverick." *Because so help me.*

"How do you know that name?"

I took my time to look up, my stomach in knots. "Maverick's playing both sides," I revealed, determining I was right. "He leaked the truth about my operation to Clarke, yet he never told you. Then Clarke shared the after-action report with his girlfriend, Kit." I tore my hand through my hair, shaking my head.

He stared at me, rubbing his hand back and forth over his mouth. "Seth wouldn't have access to that kind of intelligence," he said dismissively, acknowledging he was one of his contacts. "And no, he didn't tell me about the CIA's plans. I don't know how you got his name, but—"

"Maybe it's you who should learn to keep your mouth shut and stop talking to your pals in D.C." I was too pissed to let him continue. I'd heard enough.

A low hiss left his mouth as he brought himself closer. "I'll tell you what, it's obvious someone sure as hell woke a sleeping giant"—he looked up at the deck before facing me again—"but it for damn sure wasn't me." He turned, preparing to retreat to the safety of his yes-men waiting back by the helo, but I shot out my arm, stopping him.

    He stole a look over his shoulder at where my hand rested on his arm. I leaned in closer so he could hear me *lima charlie*, loud and clear in a way I'd never once spoken to him before. "Go. Fuck. Yourself."

Chapter 29

Hudson

"I'm good. Just need a second." I threw my hand up in the air without looking back, waving Constantine away so he'd get off my ass and stop following me.

"You'll have to take that second with me, then." Constantine came up alongside me, easily outpacing me on the beach since my body was still not 100% from the accident. Ray-Bans back on, he asked, "Me or Izzy? Take your pick."

"You're not my type, man," I tossed out. "And I'm not in the mood to talk to anyone."

Boiling point officially reached. That heart-to-heart with my old man—in front of everyone else, no less—had sent me over the edge.

Nothing quite like Bella hearing my father call me a fuckboy mere hours after Constantine found me in bed with her under their parents' roof to really kick off my Monday morning. Throw in the fact we'd now have to find a way to intervene with a CIA operation while not winding up a casualty or behind bars.

So, yeah, I needed to cool off. Alone.

The Art of You

"Izzy was going to chase after you."

I ignored him, walking as if I had places to be. And I did. *Anywhere but here.*

"I figured you'd be in a foul mood, and I didn't want you yelling at her," he went on, and I abruptly stopped and faced him. We were only inches away from where the Atlantic ate away at the sand.

"So, you volunteered as tribute, huh?" I may have been angry, but not with him. "I'd never raise my voice to her, and you know that. Insulted you'd even think such a thing."

"You're right." Despite the sun glaring in his eyes, he removed the shades he'd only just put on. His shoulders, which always seemed to be holding the weight of the world, dropped. "Your father's wrong about you. About his accusations against us, too."

I grunted. "I can't do this now."

"Which is precisely why it's the exact time you need to have this conversation." He pointed off in the direction of *anywhere-but-here* I'd been planning to escape to. "I know you. You're going to get lost in that big fucking head of yours. Overthink shit. Because that's what you do. You'll come up with a hundred reasons why you don't deserve X, Y, or fucking Z." He hooked his shades at the front of his black shirt, continuing with his mission to get in my head only to pull me from it. "You're not like your father. Are we clear?"

I dove my hands into the pockets of my sweatpants, listening to him without really allowing myself to absorb his message. I wasn't ready yet. Maybe I never would be.

"I hate your father. Always have. And based on what I just overheard back there, I always will." That was the first time he'd told me point-blank what I'd assumed he'd always felt about my old man. "He was MIA most of your life. Right up until he needed you for his own gain. He forced your mom to leave her home in Texas and move you two up to New York, even though they weren't married anymore, just so he didn't look like the absentee father he was while running for political office. He abandoned his family, and—"

"I abandoned mine, too," I damn near snarled at him, lifting my hand from my pocket and setting a fist over my heart. "Echo Team was my family. They were my brothers, and I wasn't there for them. And I'm not just talking about the op, I'm talking about the aftermath."

And just like that, I was back in the sandbox of Afghanistan instead of on the beach in the States.

"I should've fought harder to stay in their lives. I tried to, but clearly not hard enough." I leaned closer to him. "I walked away. Just like my father did. And then I thought joining the Bureau would somehow make amends, but no . . ."

My words trailed off, picked up in the morning breeze and carried to the place where dreams and hopes died.

"Maybe my father is right," I finally went on. "And that sleeping giant is the past I've never really put behind me. Because that operation is clearly connected to this somehow, and Alfie might be involved, too."

"I can't tell you what to think or how to feel about what happened that day in Afghanistan, but I'd have done the same thing as you. I'd have sat that mission out. So, go ahead, call me a coward, too."

My eyes fell between us to the sand. "Bullshit. You'd have compartmentalized and focused on the three feet in front of you. You'd have gone out on the op, and you know it."

"You ever stop and think maybe you weren't there that day because you weren't meant to die? That your father's email came at the right time, because without it you'd have been on the long gun and a sniper would've killed you instead?" His words hushed the chaos in my mind, drawing my attention

The Art of You

back to him. "Does your life matter more than his? No, of course not. He was someone's son, too. But maybe it just wasn't your time, brother. Maybe you didn't die because you're needed here."

I opened my mouth to object, but when he narrowed his eyes on me, it was clear he wasn't done with his lecture.

"You have another family aside from Echo Team. Don't you dare act like we're not also yours. You've always had our backs. Suited up and had our six at every fucking turn, right down to taking out Bianca's killer. Both times. I don't want to hear this bullshit that you're someone who retreats in the face of danger. You are not like your father." He tossed a hand toward his parents' house. "You have a woman in there who is so crazy in love with you, it's now obvious to me she's been dating all these assholes to waste time until the right one figures his shit out."

The hand still hovering over my chest fell to my side as I stared at him, trying to calculate what sounded like two plus two equating to five. Because no way did he say that.

"And in case I'm not making myself clear, you're him."

Shock hit me across the face again when he spelled it out for me.

"Listen." He dialed down his tone a bit while lifting his eyes to the cloudless sky. "We all have a past. Mistakes we've made. I have to look at myself in the mirror every day and know one of my sisters didn't feel comfortable enough to tell me about the man she loved. And if she had, maybe it wouldn't have cost Bianca her life." He slowly lowered his face to meet my eyes, pupils dilating. "I've been making the same mistakes with Izzy. She's afraid to be honest with me, and that's on me. But I refuse to lose another sister."

"What the hell are you trying to say?"

"I'm saying don't let me stand in the way of you being with Izzy."

His tone was as clear as his words, and yet, I still wasn't sure if I'd heard him correctly.

"There are no guarantees it'll work out between you two. But I know if it doesn't, it'd never be because you cheated. Or because you put hands on my sister. So, if you split, I won't have to kill you, and it won't fuck up our friendship. I'm telling you this now because I didn't realize I've been making the same mistakes I did with Bianca with Izzy. Not until this weekend." He closed his eyes, letting go of a deep breath. "I also didn't know the shit you've been carrying for fifteen years, which is undoubtedly the real reason you've stayed single all this time. That changes things." Eyes open again, he stated, "Knowing what I do now, do you really think there's anyone else I'd rather have as my brother-in-law than my best friend?"

I was grateful when he held up his hand as a request not to answer. I wasn't even sure what the hell to say.

"Don't use me, or your past, and especially not your father's fuckery, as an excuse to keep you from being with the woman you clearly love."

From *"can't love you back"* yesterday to *"clearly love"* today. Was he right? Was that what this aching pain in my chest was? Love?

"Figure it out, and do it quickly. Looks like we'll have a new mission to handle with these terrorists, and I don't need your head out of the game because you're worried about losing what's right in front of you." He removed his shades from his shirt and put them on, then turned toward the house. "And do me one more favor," he added, shooting me a quick look over his shoulder, "lock the fucking door next time."

Chapter 30

Isabella

TWICE THIS MORNING, Constantine had stopped me from both running my mouth and running off. He'd literally swept me into the air and held me up to prevent me from telling off the governor for being a selfish bastard.

Constantine had refused to let me go while he'd told Ashford, *"You better get the hell off our property before I change my mind and let my sister have the word she so desperately wants to."*

Hudson had shifted to the side, looking up at me on the deck while Constantine had prevented me from losing my control.

Standing alongside us, Enzo had issued a quick, *"I'll catch another ride to the city,"* to the governor. Then he'd muttered, *"Not a good idea for us to be in such a small space together. I want to hit the fucker, too."*

Once Governor Ashford had left, Hudson quietly killed me, abruptly walking off alone toward the beach.

I'd struggled in my brother's hold trying to go after Hudson, but he wouldn't let me go, telling me to give Hudson space. The man didn't need space, he needed a hug.

It'd been fifteen minutes since Hudson and his father had taken off in two different directions, and while I was glad the governor was gone, I was losing my patience waiting for Hudson's return.

Thankfully, Constantine had finally let go of me, but only to go after Hudson himself. He'd assigned Alessandro and Enzo to babysit me. The only time one of my overprotective bodyguards left the deck was to get me a blanket, noticing me shivering from the cold.

"He'll be fine." Enzo came up next to me where I was hunched over the railing, eyeing the beach. "He needs a minute."

"It's been over fifteen," I sputtered, shaking beneath the blanket even though I was no longer cold. These were anxiety-induced chills, which were the worst.

"If I were him, I'd need all day," Alessandro said from behind me, and I turned to glare at him as he looked up from his phone. "What'd I say?" He shrugged, not realizing his words didn't help.

"He's back." Enzo guided me around to face the steps, but the only "he" I could see was Constantine.

"Where's Hudson?" I lost hold of the blanket, rushing toward my brother as he slowly ascended the deck steps.

Constantine turned toward the beach, but Hudson was nowhere in sight. "He's working the problem."

"And that means?" I asked as he bent down and picked up the fallen blanket, offering it to me.

When I didn't accept it, he lifted his chin as a simple request to take it or else. That "or else" meant he would keep his information to himself and order me inside. "So stubborn. You two are a pair, I swear," he grumbled when I'd yet to relent.

The Art of You

"He needs time to think. To confront his demons. He knows we have his back, working the problem here with what we've learned this morning, while he does that." He walked behind me and set the blanket over my shoulders.

"I don't want him doing that alone." I didn't attempt to make a run for it. Not yet, at least. I had to be smart. Three to one right now. Odds weren't in my favor.

"You have to let him." Enzo had Constantine's back on this, dang it.

I frowned and faced the three of them while keeping myself bundled inside the warmth of the blanket. "He's a *Team*guy, not a lone wolf, remember?"

"He has us, and he knows that." Constantine stood tall, like the tower of strength he truly was for our family. "But shit is about to hit the fan. We're going to have to get involved in the affairs of the CIA whether they like it or not, and that means we'll need help from Falcon Falls. I don't like this, trust me, but it has to be done."

"Wait, what are you talking about?"

The blanket started to slip, and Constantine didn't miss a beat, righting it back in place as he reminded me, "Falcon Falls has an in with POTUS and the director of the CIA. Whoever is spearheading this operation against this terrorist cell must be using a back door to do it. Information isn't being shared between agencies, that much is obvious, and I have to believe it's on purpose to prevent both the President and director from thwarting their efforts. That tells me this is personal."

His words flew over my head, and I blamed the slow processing rate of my brain squarely on the fact I never had coffee. "Translate, please. Remember, I speak Italian, not Greek."

Constantine angled his head and let go of a deep breath. "My guess is at some point those terrorists are the ones who inadvertently"—he narrowed his eyes as if hating what he was about to say next—"woke the sleeping giant. And somehow that connects to the governor or us. Maybe both."

My shoulders dropped dramatically when my brother's words clicked in place.

"We need Hudson at the top of his game before we figure out our next steps on how to proceed. All I know is we have to get ahead of the storm here before it swallows us whole." Those bone-chilling words from my brother gutted me. "If something goes wrong, Hudson will blame himself for it, and you know that. Right or wrong, he will. Just like he feels responsible for what happened fifteen years ago."

The last thing in the world I wanted was for Hudson to bear the burden of more guilt he didn't deserve.

"So, give him time. We have plenty to do in the meantime." Constantine gestured in the direction of the helipad and turned toward Enzo. "I've got our pilot heading here now. He'll take you to the city so you can help sober up our delivery guy. Show him photos of every possible suspect again when he's clean. From the woman across the street's date to the governor himself. Leave no one out."

Enzo nodded at the orders.

"I'll keep working on hacking that Insta profile that posted the video footage that must have come from the CCTV cameras at the party, as well," Alessandro remarked.

I forgot he'd mentioned that to me before the governor had arrived.

"I'll update Adelina on what we know over a secure line and have her be our liaison with Falcon if she's up for it," Constantine offered. "If not, Enzo will need to call Jesse McAdams for an assist."

I pivoted around toward the beach, hating Hudson was out there by himself. "Is it safe for him to be alone and unarmed?

What if someone's watching us?" I looked up at the sky, searching for a drone that wasn't there, because it sure as heck felt like we were under a microscope.

"I already texted two of our guys to follow him."

Thank God. I clutched the blanket tighter, shivering again, but grateful Constantine had provided me with the right answer.

My brothers put their silent communication skills to work. Before I knew it, Alessandro was heading inside with Enzo following behind him.

So, you want a word with me alone, huh?

Once it was just the two of us, and the sniper on the roof of course, Constantine closed the space between us.

I scrunched my nose with displeasure. "Another lecture coming?"

"No, but will you accept an apology?"

The blanket fell from my shoulders, but he had fast hands, quickly reaching out to fix it.

"You want to do this now, even with everything going on?" I was fine with postponing talking about him walking in on us in bed until February 30th.

"I do. I need your head clear, same as Hudson's."

I supposed he had a point. "What do you want to apologize for?"

"Well, a lot of things, but let's start with this morning." His jaw shifted to the side, clearly uncomfortable with bringing up the fact Hudson had been on top of me. "Then rewind to what I said to you yesterday. I didn't know all the facts, and I gave you bad advice." He exhaled heavily, stalling. "I'm not sorry for running off all the dickheads you dated in the past, though." He shrugged. "They weren't right for you, and you know it."

Okay, what are you getting at? My heart was flying. Like

right up into my ears now. I could barely hear the sounds of the waves in the distance anymore.

"Bianca never felt comfortable confiding in me about who she loved and—"

"She didn't tell any of us." I had to stop him right there. I'd had the same guilty thoughts, and I wasn't going to let him go to that dark place. Nope. No way. "I know where you're going with this, but the choice she made to keep us in the dark is not on you. Or me."

It took me a long time and tons of therapy to accept that after learning that Bianca had been in love with someone forbidden. I hadn't realized Constantine had been simmering in the same thoughts, but without an outlet to help him face the truth.

"Look at me." My turn to play the parent between us siblings. I reached for his forearm, letting the blanket fall as I took a lesson from Hudson's book on punctuating words for maximum effect. "Not. Your. Fault."

"I don't want to push you away like I did her. I was overprotective with the men in her life, too. You know it, don't argue with me. I'm sure she vented to you a time or two about me, even if you were only a teenager." He refused to meet my eyes, his accent thickening more than normal as he continued. "And I've unintentionally been pushing you away by not letting you fall and get back up on your own."

I sighed while fighting back tears. "You and Alessandro. Just big teddy bears. Terrifying ones when it comes to bad guys, but..."

I pulled my brother in for a hug, since he'd never admit he needed one. He was always the giver of advice and hugs, never asking for anything in return. I was beginning to wonder if he truly didn't know how to ask. "You're not pushing me away, I promise."

"Well, I'm going to try and do better. And if Hudson is who you want to be with, I won't stand in the way. In fact," he said while pulling back to look at me, "I'd happily support you two if you were to ever do the whole, uh, thing."

I blinked back tears. "The thing, huh?"

He scowled, and it was adorable. "The *wedding* thing. I forgot English for a second."

"Sure you did," I said with a chuckle, unable to hold it in. "You tell Hudson this?"

He let go of me and stepped back, a hand resting on the nape of his neck. "I did."

This was the definition of leaf turning. Who'd have thought our case would result in something good. "You threaten him with bodily harm if he breaks my heart?" I challenged, checking to see if he really was prepared to flip the page.

The side of his lip lifted. "No need." His mouth became a hard flat line a moment later, though. "But do I need to have a word with your ex? Don't think I forgot about that."

I hung my head. "No words needed. Or arms broken. Or anything, okay?"

"Then look me in the eyes and tell me he never laid a hand on you." There was the other bear, the non-cuddly one. The one that would rip a man apart for hurting me.

"I can't do that," I whispered. "But I will ask you to trust me when I say Pablo needs help, not an ass kicking, and he's getting it now in rehab."

My brother was eerily quiet, which forced me to search out his eyes again.

"You're much more forgiving than me," he said in a low voice. "I'll *think* about showing mercy. Best I can offer right now."

"I'll take it," I agreed, following his gaze toward the steps to see my guy there.

Hudson slowly finished walking up to us, never losing hold of my eyes in the process.

"I'll, uh, give you two a chance to talk," Constantine offered.

"No, stay." Hudson's brows drew together, and he pulled his phone from his pocket.

"What's wrong?" I let go of the blanket and started for him.

"Alfie messaged," he shared, staring at his phone. "He says we need to talk. In person."

I reached for his arm. "He say why?"

His blue eyes landed on mine as he revealed in a surprisingly steady voice, "Yeah. He said he has my Glock if I'd like it back."

"I'm sorry, what?" My thoughts were officially scattered all over the place, and I wasn't sure how to assemble them and draw a conclusion.

"I'm thinking that means he was the third guy there the night of the accident." Hudson turned his attention to Constantine, his shoulders collapsing. "He's our shooter."

Chapter 31

Isabella

"I know I locked that door." Hudson stood in the doorway of his bathroom, strong hands parked above the navy-blue towel where it hung dangerously low on his hips.

Hudson in that towel with sexy, mussed-up wet hair and beads of water rolling down to his happy trail was the prime example of how one's brain could truly short-circuit. And it took me a second to regroup, to remember why I'd picked the lock to his bedroom in the first place.

In my defense, I hadn't expected to break into his room and find him so *sans*-clothes-like. I guess he'd opted to take a quick shower in hopes it'd wake him up from what had to feel like a living and breathing nightmare. It did to me, at least.

He'd left us on the deck after declaring he'd be meeting Alfie alone, tossing out the order, *"I'm going to pack. Don't follow me, or try to stop me."*

I was pretty sure that command was mainly for me, and Constantine had told me to let him cool off yet again, but I'd given up on waiting. *And* taking orders. I'd been too overheated to sit around and wait. The only way for me to rein in my temperature was to talk to Hudson myself. After a bit more pushing, Constantine relented.

"Plan on talking? Or are you here to slow me down from what I plan to do whether you like it or not?" His jaw ticced so hard I'd swear it had a heartbeat.

His grumpy tone reeled me back to the problem—him trying to leave us to lone-wolf a meeting that could very well be a trap. "I plan on talking you out of going. At least, going alone."

I glanced at the bed off to my left. No clothes in sight. Just weapons he must've retrieved from our small armory here. Was he planning to go to war? What the hell?

When he didn't speak, I did it for him. "Did Alfie say where you're meeting? What time? You think this has to do with what your father told you about the kidnappers? The terrorists? Did he demand you come by yourself or are you just going solo to try and protect us?"

Nada. Zilch. Zero.

His jaw tightened as his only response.

So, I continued. "Please, enlighten me on all the red flags you're going to try and turn green. I'm listening."

Arms folded across his chest now, he leaned into the doorway and casually crossed his ankle over the other. He was buying himself time. Stalling from the inevitable—a fight between us. And yeah, I'd fight like hell to prevent him from marching off to his death. He wanted war? He could have one with me right now.

"With Alfie officially involved, this whole thing is really starting to point to me as the problem. My father may have been right, which means it's my responsibility to clean up the mess." There was less grit to his tone than I'd expected, more so somberness.

"We're in this together. All of us. And like hell is your dad right." I crossed the room and stood directly before him, but his gaze remained pointed down, now at my black-painted toenails.

"It's possible there's another explanation as to why Alfie was out there that night of the accident. I need to find out." Ever so slowly, he gave in and looked at me. "But if he's in any way responsible for you nearly dying..."

Then what? Nope, he couldn't finish that, and I knew why. "You won't hurt him," I whispered, emotion choking me up. "Alfie was your brother. A Teamguy. You won't be able to pull the trigger if you have to, and you know it. Not even if he's trying to draw you out and kill you."

He didn't answer, and he couldn't. Because I was right.

"How do you know it's really him who texted? Someone could've hacked his phone. Or used a burner. What if this is Clarke's doing? Or that Seth Maverick guy?"

"Alfie didn't text from his personal line. It was an encrypted message from an unknown number, but he referred to himself as something that'd let me know it's really him. Triple A. Only those on our team called him that. No one else would know. And before you ask, no, that name wouldn't have been in the after-action report Maverick or Clarke read."

Unable to stop myself, I reached for his face. His jawline flexed beneath my touch as he went for my wrist, removing my hand, but keeping hold of me. "Maybe we didn't die Friday night because Alfie couldn't bring himself to pull the trigger like he was supposed to."

His thumb swept along the inside of my wrist as he kept hold of my arm between us.

"You don't really believe he was working with the kidnappers or the terrorists, do you?" I could see the doubt in his eyes as clear as freaking day.

"I don't want to, but fuck. It sure as hell looks like he's guilty of something."

He freed my wrist and sidestepped me, forcing me to turn toward him. To study his strong back as he walked to the bed. The corded muscles in his bruised arm tightened as he brought his hands to his hips.

"Alfie could have easily hacked the CCTV footage at the party, too. And it's probably him screwing with me on social media, posting the video of us dancing online."

Shit, that was a lot to take in. But then I remembered something Adelina had said yesterday. "If all signs point in one direction, it's because we're looking the wrong way."

"Or, maybe, if it looks like a duck, it's just a duck." He swung around to face me, nostrils flaring. "Or in this case, a frogman."

"Then why now? Why, after so long, is he doing this now? Answer that for me, and I'll let you leave this room and won't try to stop you."

"Sleeping giant. Someone woke it up," was all he gave me, and I was done with that analogy, especially since it'd been started by his father.

"Well, screw it. We'll be Jack and climb the beanstalk and take out the giant, then. How about that?" I pushed back, losing my cool anytime I thought about the governor.

Hudson rotated his neck side to side, eyes shooting to the ceiling as if searching for words he'd never find there.

When he remained quiet, I went to the bedroom door and set my back to it, becoming a human barrier to his escape. "I'm right about you not leaving..."

"Those dots I can feel hanging in the air, are they for extra emphasis? As in you being a pain in my ass?"

Three long strides brought him over to stand before me. I held up my hand between us as if I could pulverize steel with my touch, knowing it really was the other way around. The

The Art of You

dark, hooded look from him could obliterate every one of my defenses *if* I let him. "I'm going to save you time here."

"Oh, yeah? By helping me pack or by moving out of my way?" His left hand went to the door over my shoulder, and he leaned in like a challenge. "You know I can lift you, don't you? A sore arm won't stop me."

I was very much aware this man could set me aside like a fragile doll inside a glass case. I also knew he would never treat me like some empty-minded porcelain doll, because he always treated me like his equal.

"I'm going with you. We all are. Wherever you go, we'll have your back." I finally unleashed the speech I'd struggled to scrape together beneath his heated stare. "End of story. Not up for discussion."

"I disagree." His words slid across my skin, his rejection caressing my lips like silk. "You may have me wrapped around your finger, but we both know when it comes to two things, I have the control."

There it was again. That dark look in his eyes coupled with the rich depth to his tone that had me inhaling and wanting to whisper, *Yes, sir, whatever you say, sir.*

I was aware of the fact he was trying to distract me from my mission, knowing exactly how to twist me into a pretzel and make me forget the sky was blue and that I hated being told what to do. He was successful, too. The sky was now painted a seductive crimson, and I was ready to fall to my knees and obey the sailor's orders.

"What are those two things?" My voice betrayed me, the stuttery hitch letting him know exactly who was in charge. And it wasn't me.

He stood tall, backed two steps away and held two fingers out, folding back the others. Staring deep into my eyes, he slowly gestured for me to come to him in the sexiest way I'd ever witnessed anyone do in my life.

I followed his command, and a slow smirk crossed his lips before he spun me around, placing himself in front of the door instead of me. And just like that, he'd removed the obstacle in his way of leaving.

His hand flew around my body, and he hauled me against him, my hands landing on his chest. "I'll be in control of your safety, for one, which means you won't be coming with me." With his other hand he brushed my hair behind my ear, only to drop his mouth over it and let his breath fan across my heated skin.

"And the second?" I waited for him to continue, knowing his distraction efforts were masterfully done and I was running on autopilot.

"Who makes you come from now on is most definitely the second. And in case I'm not being clear . . ."

That cliffhanger was delivered brilliantly. The man was a quick study. Forget shivers rolling only down my spine, they encompassed every square inch of my body. "Only you?" Was that his way of letting me know without directly saying it that he wanted us to move forward?

Instead of his hand, which I'd have preferred, fear clutched the front of my throat. This was his version of an *In case something happens to me* speech before riding off to battle. No, no, no. There would be no leaving me. No operating solo.

"You're good. You—you had me there," I sputtered, then pushed away from his chest to try and break the spell he'd put me under. "But, no."

One brow lifted in question. "No, what?"

I spun away from him, clawing at my hair as I tried to convert the mush he'd made of my brain into something solid and usable. He was a damn good interrogator. But unlike my brothers who preferred to play with knives in getting people to open up, Hudson definitely took the bees-with-honey approach to get people to bend to his will.

"You're not leaving me." I moved the gun box for the 9mm to the side and sat down with a *harumph* of frustration falling from my lips.

"I'll come back for you." He'd said those words so innocently, and I latched on to that "for you" in hopes it meant what I wanted it to. That we'd be together one day. Not riding off into war, but into the sunset.

Just maybe not on a horse. My ass had a long memory, and it'd yet to forget the literal pain riding one had caused me.

That thought helped me move past the darkness so I could remind him this was a two-way street. "I'm sorry, but if you get control over my safety, and my orgasms, I get control over yours. Works both ways. Fair is fair." I stared at the floor in a daze, chewing the side of my lip.

"You do, huh? Is that how this works?" The touch of humor there had my attention, and he reached for my arm and urged me to stand before him.

"If by 'how this works,' you mean a relationship, then yes."

I had to stick to my guns so he didn't take off by himself with actual ones. Worried he'd melt me with one look and have my nerves folding out from under me lightning quick again, I hurriedly added, "I won't let you become a damsel, or whatever the dude version is, in distress."

Watching him fight a smile gave me hope. Perhaps I was managing to gain strategic ground in our little war, edging closer to claiming a victory. It was time to swoop in and remind him he wasn't alone.

"You'll go, get yourself in trouble, then we'll have to swoop in and save your ass at the last minute. It'll be soooo much easier if we just have your back from the beginning, don't you think?"

He hung his head at that.

"You know I'm right. This isn't like the books you read. This is real life. And if you take off like some stubborn lone wolf, there's no guarantee it ends well. Do you really want to be responsible for single-handedly ruining my life?" I'd gone from a teasing tone to about to cry in the space of a second. "Because if something happens to you, I'm done." Breathing hard, tears pricked the corners of my eyes as I considered that horrific possibility. "You're not just Constantine's best friend. You're mine. And maybe love comes and goes for people, but a friendship like ours is forever, and I—"

"Fuck." Hands flying to my face, he matched my deep breaths and rasped, "I'm trying so hard not to love you, and you're making it so goddamn difficult for me."

His mouth fell over mine, and my lips parted like a sea for him, allowing him safe passage right to the kingdom of my heart.

His hands went from my face down to my arms as he ravished me with his hungry kisses, letting me taste the word *love* he'd dropped.

Pressed up against him, gathered in his arms, the towel dropped from the friction between us, and he stole his lips away from mine and stared at my eyes as he stood naked before me.

"Stop trying so hard not to do something you so clearly want to do," I whispered, my voice nevertheless still breaking. I wasn't sure why he was fighting it so much, especially now that he'd cleared the air around his past and Constantine gave his blessing, but the fight was still there. Right in the way he was staring at me now, and it scared me. "Just love me instead."

His forehead tightened as he thumbed away a tear. He

opened his mouth, but shut it when the sound of a text from somewhere in the room chimed.

He bowed his forehead to mine at the interruption. "That could be Alfie with a location." His low, guttural voice ripped through me.

"You should check it, then," I said between sniffles as he skated his hands down to my wrists, then let me go and moved backward with hesitant steps.

As much as I wanted to remain tethered to this moment, that fear in his eyes pulled me in with the same impact. So much so, I couldn't even shamelessly check him out when he knelt to pick up the towel.

He tightened it around his hips and went for his phone. "It's him. He sent me coordinates."

I turned to see him typing, probably checking for where Alfie planned to try and steal him away from me.

"Looks like I'm going to Spain today." His words gave me whiplash, jerking my head up in shock.

"Doesn't that sound problematic? Trappy-like given that we now know the terrorists are probably going to a backup plan to free their boss. And that the CIA may let them so they can try and swoop in and grab them all?" My hand flew to my chest and over my heart. "Probably in Spaaain." I put as much emphasis as possible on that word in case my guy wasn't thinking clearly. His head still misplaced in the guilt-blame gutter. Plus, my sassy mouth usually did better at getting through to him than my rational one did.

Instead of answering me, he simply said my name like it had a question mark both before and after it.

"Yes?" The word caught in my throat, barely coming out. The idea of him resisting help and flying to Spain alone had me feeling like that broken coffee cup from earlier. I was in pieces. Fragments of busted-up pottery.

His brows pinched as he stared at me while he lowered the phone to his side. "Just so you know, you're more than a best friend to me." Not what I'd expected him to say, but I sure as hell hoped this wasn't him trying to distract me again. I had to admit, he'd done a hell of a job with the smolder and brood moments ago.

Then another thought hit me, forcing the breath in my lungs to slip out in the form of a somber sigh. I was now not only worried about a distraction, but that he may follow up his sweet comment with a "but" and break my heart.

"Well, who am I, then?" I asked when he'd yet to elaborate, my anxiety taking over for my mouth.

He tossed the phone on the bed, then ate up what was left of the space between us. Reaching for my hand, he locked our fingers together and swiftly drew me against him. "The woman I'd bring home to my mother."

It took me a dizzying moment to put two and two together. Because of course I'd already met his mom, but—

He interrupted my internal rambling by covering my mouth with his.

Instead of the rejection I'd expected from him, soft kisses of surrender followed. And between them, he told me what I needed to hear. "Pack a bag. Looks like you're coming to Spain with me."

Chapter 32

Isabella

Manhattan, New York

WE'D BEEN at our security office in Chelsea for about an hour, waiting to meet Adelina before heading to JFK, and I'd managed to keep myself busy with chasing a few leads while wondering where in the world Hudson had gone off to after we'd arrived.

Thankfully, our security office wasn't known to the public the way our other family business was, so when we arrived at four o'clock, we hadn't been greeted by the media or paparazzi. They'd definitely tried reaching out to us on every single phone line and email address they'd been able to track down. All calls and messages ignored.

I pushed away from my desk, set aside my blue-light glasses, then decided to search out Alessandro and see if he'd had any luck gathering information while we awaited our flight to Spain.

And damn. Our entire family needed to learn to knock (and lock doors). Myself included. Because when I swung open his office door, I had to cover my eyes. "Oops, sorry," I blurted, catching him in the middle of something, and it wasn't research.

Callie was on his desk, legs wrapped around him, her cowgirl boots at his back, and yup . . . not the sight I needed to see. Now I knew how Constantine felt.

With his back to me, and thankfully his shirt was on and covering his ass since his pants were around his ankles, he tossed his hand in the air, waving me away.

Don't have to tell me twice. I reached around and twisted the lock before closing the door so no one else accidentally walked in on whatever was about to happen on that desk.

Guess my brother wanted a quickie with his wife before we left for Spain. I knew it killed him to leave her, but he wouldn't risk taking her on an operation out of the country. Too many unknown variables. She'd be staying with my parents on Long Island and would be heavily protected.

Callie wasn't part of the security team, but dammit, *I* was. Despite some pushback from my brothers in the Hamptons after Hudson shared the Spain news, I won four to one in a vote to join them.

Enzo had been the adamant "no," which had taken me by surprise. I'd thought it'd be Constantine, but he was the one to remind everyone I was an asset with my tech and comms skills.

"Hey, you, hang on." *Speak of the devil.*

I stopped walking to track down where Enzo was, finally walking back a step and hanging a right to find him in Hudson's office. Sadly, Hudson was notably absent.

"What's up?" I remained in the doorway, wondering if I could pull off the casual lean as well as the guys could. Arms folded, I gave it a try.

Enzo had his back to Hudson's desk, hands on each side of

it as he shot me a worried look. "I hate that I'm not joining you all. I don't like this."

"You can't leave the country with Maria potentially delivering your twins early. If you were in Spain, and she wound up in the hospital, you'd never forgive yourself." We'd already gone over this about five times today, but maybe the sixth time was the charm. "Besides, you need to follow up with our delivery guy here. Get him clean. See if he can ID anyone. You're still helping even if you're not boarding that jet."

He stood to his full height and pushed his sleeves to his elbows, exposing his numerous tattoos. "I have a bad feeling about this trip."

No longer feeling relaxed, the casual-lean thing lost its luster and I pushed away from the doorway to join him in the office. I looked around at the three overstuffed bookcases to my left, and I'd bet money on the fact Hudson had devoured every single book packed tightly onto each shelf. A man who was well-read was so incredibly sexy.

"You're not rejecting the fact I'm telling you I have a bad feeling, so does that mean you feel the same?" Enzo roped my attention back his way.

"It's more like I have this annoying itch beneath my skin, and scratching it doesn't help. It's like a phantom itch. Or too deep to get at it or something. That's the feeling I have. Not bad. Just . . . *unsettling*." Made sense to me, at least. Based on the look in his eyes, he was about to drug test me.

"You're not making me feel any better. In fact, I feel ten times worse." He ran his knuckles up and down his jawline as if in a trance, eyes on the floor. "I know C is bringing two of our other guys with you all just in case, but I think we need more than that to replace me."

C, huh? First time I'd heard my brother abbreviate Constantine's name down to a single letter outside of texting.

"Well, you're irreplaceable, we all know that." I tried to keep my smile and voice casual, hoping to calm his nerves and distract his mind.

"Yeah, well, Adelina will be here soon to give us an update before you fly out, but I went ahead and reached out to Falcon Falls myself. I just got off the phone with Jesse. I haven't filled in the others yet, but I shared our situation with him."

"And?" My smile evaporated at the dark tone in his voice.

"He can't step in for me like I hoped. His team's not operating right now. He couldn't tell me the details, but they're handling the fallout of another case."

"Well, Jesse may be a badass in his own right, but he's not you. So don't worry about someone covering for—"

"He made a recommendation, though. He has a SEAL friend he trusts, and he's in New York now. He rolled with us on that op in Upstate last year."

The op that led to us discovering Bianca's murderer wasn't really dead. That memory was at every turn lately.

"His wife's former CIA. She helped us with some tech stuff this summer. Jesse trusts him, and my brother-in-law, Ryan, vouched for him from their SEAL days, too." Was he trying to convince me, or sell himself on this idea? "It helps that he has contacts in Spain and a place for you all to stay when you're in Barcelona, too."

"So, if this turns into an operation, and not just a casual meet and greet with Alfie, we'll be better prepared?" I rubbed my arms up and down, trying to chase away the chills.

"Yeah, and he's got us covered flying into the airport. That'll come in handy so we're not detained because of the weapons we're bringing, too." He checked his watch. "He'll be arriving any minute, should be just behind Adelina. And Jesse said Adelina has some news for us."

My brother's gaze flicked from his watch to something over

The Art of You

my shoulder, and I turned to see Hudson filling the doorway, holding a duffel bag. He locked eyes with me, and as if on cue, announced, "Adelina's downstairs."

I bit the inside of my lip as I stared at this powerhouse of a man before me in all black. Despite the bruises on his face, you'd never know he'd been in an accident. His posture was perfect, head held up, and his impressive arms were on display in his well-fitted T-shirt. The black backward ball cap topped off the imposing look.

"We'll meet you downstairs. I need a minute with your sister first." Hudson stepped to the side of the door, letting Enzo know he could, and should, leave.

I turned to see Enzo's gaze bouncing back and forth between us before he took off from the room.

Hudson shut *and* locked the door behind him, then quietly dropped the duffel bag on the couch. "I swung over to your place to get a few things to take with us."

"You didn't tell me why you were leaving. Was it safe to be walking around alone given what's going on?"

He shot me a funny look. "I can handle myself, don't you worry."

That you can. "I take it you borrowed a key from one of my brothers?"

"I did. I'm thinking I'll be keeping it, too."

I liked the way that sounded.

"Anyone else have one I should know about?" he asked almost casually, refacing the couch.

I did my best not to stare at his back muscles and glutes in those black jeans as he bent forward, digging into the bag. "No need to change my locks, no," I reassured him as he turned around with Rugby.

I walked over to him, feeling my heart sigh as loud as my mouth did.

He handed me the worn-out bear, and I clutched him to my chest and said the first thing that came to mind, which wasn't a thank-you. "Does this mean I'll be sleeping alone in Spain?"

"No, ma'am, it doesn't." His husky tone rattled something free in my chest.

Desire. *Phew.* This man could ma'am me all day long, too.

"I thought you'd like to have him with you on the flight, along with your favorite sweatshirt."

I peeked around him to see what else he'd packed in that magic bag. My preferred brand of dark chocolate candy. Two golf magazines, but not the same ones I'd hid the photo between. *Good call on that.* "My sketchpad, too, huh?"

He shrugged. "I saw it on your desk. Untouched from the looks of it. Thought you might want to—"

"Touch it?" I licked my lips, eyes on those strong hands of his, remembering the way he'd touched me with them, craving for him to do that now.

When he didn't respond, I forced my gaze up to his face, and the heated look pointed my way sent me another step closer to my very own Man of Steel.

"I may have checked your dresser, too." He smiled. A wicked, dark one, and he nailed the landing with it.

Heat flooded my stomach, coursing down to kindle an achy need between my legs. "What'd you find there?"

"A vibrator you won't need anymore."

Oh. My. Damn.

"You feeling color again?" His smile traveled to his eyes, forming crinkles at the edges.

"Yes. Red-hot, in fact." My tongue raced along the seam of my mouth as images and possibilities infiltrated my imagination.

"So, what did you take from my dresser?"

He removed the bear from my hands and set him aside

The Art of You

before hooking his arm behind my back, surprising me by drawing me against him. "Now, I don't remember saying I actually took anything." Lifting his fist between us, he urged my chin up, pinning me with those gorgeous Mediterranean-blue eyes.

"No sexy lingerie, then?" I teased.

His hand at the small of my back flew up to my neck. "I couldn't take the chance you've ever worn anything there for someone else." The possessive bite to his tone as he gently fisted and tugged my hair woke up some primal need in me to be controlled by this man.

"So, you want me naked, then?" I pushed up on my toes, anxious for his mouth to claim mine.

"Oh, I want a lot of things. To not have waited seven years to wake up and get my shit together for one."

Seven years? What are you talk—

He silenced my thoughts by giving me what I wanted. The kiss of all kisses. Hot and passionate. *Dominating.* He let me know I was his and only his.

I latched on to him, desperate for more, then trailed my lips down to the side of his neck.

"Mmm," he groaned before guiding my face to his. "You kiss my neck like that again, and I won't be responsible for what happens next."

"Like christening your desk?" I'd be his first in this office. While I wasn't in denial about his old reputation, I also knew he'd never bring a woman here.

He brought his hands to my face and met my eyes. "Like getting you pregnant."

Welp, there went my ovaries. But did he really mean that, or was it one of those in-the-heat-of-the-moment things? The man kept giving me hope we had a future, and I was still engulfed in the fear that hope would be snatched away from me the way my sister's life was stolen. Good things always came to an end at one point or another.

Deflecting from my dark thoughts, hating they were spoiling a sexy moment, I offered, "Guess you checked my medicine cabinet and correctly assumed I haven't taken the pill since before the accident."

I'd somehow forgotten to have Callie pack my pills and Rugby when she'd thrown my things together over the weekend.

I narrowed my eyes. "The fact I'm turned on by this violation of my privacy would suggest I may have issues."

He nipped my lip with his teeth. "Don't we all?"

Fair enough. "So, is my birth control in the bag, or . . .?" Why did this feel like one of the most important questions I'd ever asked him?

His brows tightened, and he quietly stared at me for a long moment. "Of course it is." Eyes racing to my mouth, he murmured what I assumed to be a tease, "Up to you if you take it."

Chapter 33

Hudson

FOCUS UP. I sent the message to myself, hoping it'd download and compute as a directive. But the order didn't seem to be registering as Bella and I made our way down the stairs to meet up with everyone.

Because did I really just tell Bella I wouldn't mind her carrying my child? The words had fallen so fast from my mouth, it appeared her lack of filter was rubbing off on me. She'd probably thought I'd meant my last comment to her as a joke, but I had a feeling she'd be wrong.

Christ, we hadn't even had sex yet, and I was already mentally building us a house and constructing a crib for our child.

No. *Children.* Plural. And whenever my ticket was punched, Bella would have our kids in her life to love and protect her.

She reached for my hand, locking our palms together, and I went dead still on the bottom step. Had she overheard my thoughts somehow? Did she know I was imagining our dream house together? Me, the guy who didn't do relationships, who fucked just to fuck. Well, at least until this woman kissed me in Rome.

"You okay?" Her soft tone implored me to look her in the eyes and hide the fact I was un-fucking-raveling. I'd vaulted right over a few relationship steps up in my office. Went straight for what I really wanted deep down and didn't truly understand. Not until recently. Not until I'd almost lost her. Not until I'd almost lost everything.

A family. With her.

"I'm sorry for . . ." *What I said?* I left those last three words in my head, because wouldn't they be a lie? I wasn't sorry for my words. Maybe for the timing, but that was about it.

"Ready?" Enzo's simple question was a backhand over a bruise, stealing my attention back to reality.

Maybe that was for the better. I didn't trust myself not to go ahead and skip another step. Drop to my knee right there and ask her to marry me. Make it as official in real life as it was in my head.

Yeah, consider me awake now. Eyes wide open. All I saw was her and our future. Fuck everyone and anything that tried to get in our way. *Especially* my own damn *what-if* fears.

"Yeah, we're ready," I finally spat out, taking that last step down, which felt entirely too symbolic of something much bigger.

Bella let go of my hand only once we were in the former living room we'd converted to a war room a few months back.

Alessandro and Callie joined us a minute later. He was in the process of tucking his shirt into his pants, not giving a damn everyone knew what he'd just been up to in his office.

The second Alessandro's foot passed the threshold, Adelina cut right to it. "Seth Maverick delivered the classified files to Agent Clarke because he was threatened."

"Start from the beginning of what you told me," Constantine prompted, arms folded with his back to the wall opposite me.

Adelina had my undivided attention as she brought us up to speed. "Sydney spoke with her ex-husband for us, and when he wasn't cooperative, she took a less traditional approach to get him to share the information we needed."

"Moves fast. I like it," Alessandro remarked, looping his arm around his wife.

"She waterboard him?" Enzo asked. "I would've loved to have done that and then some to Maria's ex."

The fact he'd shown mercy to Maria's ex-husband still went down in my book as one of the greatest shocks of my lifetime. It was also proof people could evolve.

"No, but she got fairly agitated with him and may have lost her temper at one point. I can't say I blame her." Adelina opened her phone and motioned to Constantine to turn on the TV, and she screenshared the video to it. "She filmed a message for you."

In the video, Seth was seated in a dark room with his hands behind his back, ankles taped to the chair. A blonde version of Lara Croft, with a bow at her back, stalked behind him, grabbed his hair, then forced his head up so he was staring at the camera.

"I like her," Callie commented, and Alessandro kissed the top of his wife's head.

I focused back on the screen as Sydney said, "Say word for word what you told me. Don't leave out anything."

Seth hissed a curse or two before speaking. "Three weeks ago I received a zip file from an unknown address. Just a string of numbers and letters. I sent it to trash, assuming it was spam. Next day, the same email. This time the subject line read: Urgent, and the subject line included my son's name, so I opened it." He paused to catch his breath, but Sydney kept hold of his hair, ensuring his eyes remained on the camera. "I was ordered to download the files and wait for instructions. I would've reported the email to the Pentagon, but there was a photo inside the email that didn't require downloading. It was of my son outside his school. I opened the image and checked the location and time. It'd been taken a minute before the email was sent."

"*Our* son," Sydney rasped.

Now I understood why she was pissed. Seth had kept her in the dark on something involving their child. I'd have gone ahead and tortured him. Forget waterboarding. I'd use a scalpel to get the answers from him.

"Go on," Sydney prompted, and Seth gritted out something about his pain level, which she ignored.

"Another email came a second later. They must've tracked the email and knew it'd been opened. They informed me our son had eyes on him, and a sniper could easily take a head shot. If I were to report the email or tell anyone, especially my *lovely* ex-wife here," he said while forcibly twisting his head to try and look up at her, "they'd take the shot."

Sydney peered at the screen. "There were twenty classified documents in the folder. I had a look at them an hour ago. Only one file pertained to the 2010 SEAL op. The rest were all other examples of how bad intel *or* the CIA's lack of action led to military deaths."

"What?" Caught up in my fury over the information, I forgot I was watching a recording, so she couldn't answer me back.

"The embassy attack last October was in there as well," Sydney added before ordering her ex-husband to continue talking.

This was getting worse by the second.

Bella reached for my hand, not caring we were in front of anyone. The feel of her palm with mine steadied my pulse.

"The next day, the sender demanded I personally share the files with a Special Agent Clarke at New York's FBI field office. They wanted Clarke's girlfriend to publish an exposé story about what I gave him when the time came. The sender said any deviation from the plan would result in *our* son being killed. If I tried to pull Levi from school, or do anything different than normal . . ." He let his words trail off as he tried to turn his head toward his ex-wife. "I should've told you, I regret that now. I was trying to protect our son, and I made a mistake. The man was forcing me to be a whistleblower, and I knew the blowback would wind up on me, but I was willing to go to jail and risk my job to keep Levi safe."

"I could've protected him. You know that." Sydney shoved his head forward, letting go of his hair. Eyes on the screen now, she walked around Seth's chair, coming closer to the camera to talk to us herself. "As you're well aware, Clarke's girlfriend jumped the gun and published a story she wasn't supposed to, using the intel in a way the blackmailer more than likely wouldn't approve of, which is why Seth panicked and called the emergency meeting in Arlington. Clarke apologized to him, letting him know he only gave Kit the one report so far, and he'd wait for further instructions when to release all the documents to her."

"I picked up Levi right after that meeting," Seth continued for his ex-wife, "worried we were screwed, and he might suffer the consequences of Kit's story. I was planning to make a run for it, leaving Virginia with my son, but Sydney stopped me."

"You're damn lucky I was contacted to have a word with you," Sydney seethed. "And it was me who found you and Levi first."

Adelina paused the video and went in front of the TV,

facing us. "So far, Seth hasn't heard from the blackmailer, and no attempts have been made against him or his son, but Sydney will keep them both safe. If contact is made, I'll be the first to know."

I wasn't sure what this still meant regarding Alfie, but we were right about something. "This is personal for someone. Someone died from bad intel, and our mystery emailer blames our government for it and wants the world to know it. My guess is it's someone tied to my operation in Afghanistan, which means they also blame me." I pulled free from Bella's touch and dragged my hands through my hair. "They've done their homework. Using people with ties to me in one way or another to execute their plan."

"You think they know we have a connection to Seth Maverick through Falcon, or . . . ?" Enzo left his question hanging.

"I don't know, since my father's friends with him, it may just be about that, not Falcon." I shook my head, agitated my father was actually kind of right since Seth wasn't supposed to have access to those files. "Given the shit Kit's already written about my family, it's also possible she was selected because of that. Not to mention the fact she used to date my father. This person has been studying me, and he knew Clarke was now dating her. That has to be why Seth was tasked to approach Clarke with the files." I cradled the back of my neck, ignoring the lingering pain in my forearm as I stared down at the floor trying to put this together.

"He may also be aware of Clarke's beef with us over our extracurricular activities, and how it would play into Clarke's friendship with the AG running for governor, too," Enzo pointed out. "Depends on how long he's been tracking you. Probably all of us."

"It's possible our mystery person sent the photo as a way to throw us off." Something told me we were still missing something, but one thing was damn clear to me now. "Someone's been playing me, and for God knows how long. This is about that op, though. How can it not be?"

"Does that narrow our suspect list to your old teammates and their families?" Enzo asked, not beating around the bush with an option I didn't want to consider. "Everything points to Alfie being connected, though, and now he wants you in Spain."

Before I could respond to that, a thought hit me. "What's the email address the files came from? I'm guessing both Seth and Sydney tried tracing the origin without any luck."

Adelina unlocked her phone, swiped to something, then handed her cell to me.

I stared at the email name, which was a familiar string of numbers and phrases. "It's a match to the Instagram and X account that posted the video from the party," I said to Alessandro before tossing him the phone. "We need to get access to that account somehow." My hands fisted at my sides as I tried to calm the hell down, angry at myself for missing all of the signs that were right in front of me.

"You're not still planning to go to Spain after all of this, right?" Callie asked softly, tugging Alessandro's arm so he'd face her.

My shoulders slumped as I answered for him. "I have to go and see what Alfie has to say."

"And if Alfie's setting a trap?" Callie asked.

"We have no choice," Bella said, having my six on this. "We'll keep Alessandro safe, I promise."

"Since I'm staying behind, I'll get my hands on every name I can that's connected to that 2010 operation," Enzo offered.

"And I'll add their faces to the list I'll show our delivery man once I get him clean."

"Falcon is looking into things on the cyber end as well. Let's just say this person poked the wrong mama bear by going after Sydney's son." Adelina nodded. "Sydney's not going to rest until she finds who's behind this. Between the cyber experts on Falcon, and the contacts they trust at the CIA, they'll have our backs on this."

"We may want to make another call to Falcon. They have a direct line to the President," Constantine suggested. "We need to find out what the Agency's really planning to do about these terrorists. Make sure Alfie's not drawing us into a trap."

"There's one other reason Alfie may have been on the road that night, and why he's asking me to meet him in Spain." That idea only just poked its way into my awareness. "And you know exactly what I'm talking about."

I didn't need to spell out that reason for him, Constantine would catch my drift.

"You willing to stake your life on that theory?" Constantine asked, catching on as quickly as I'd hoped he would.

Smoothing my hand along my jawline, eyes on the floor, I finally conceded, "Yeah, I am."

Before Constantine could say more, Enzo shared, "My replacement is here. I'll let him in."

My mind was racing faster than my heart as the reality of what we were up against slammed into me. "You shouldn't come," I told Bella.

"That sounded like a statement, not a question." She reached for my hand. "I'm going to pretend you were asking me, though, and my answer hasn't changed. If you're going to Spain, so am I."

I closed my eyes, feeling like I was being pulled in two

different directions. And for the first time, my gut wasn't talking to me. I didn't know what to do.

"We didn't formally meet last time." A deep voice pulled my attention to the man in the doorway. He walked farther into the room and offered his hand to Alessandro first since he was the closest. "Roman Riviera." He looked to me next, as if sensing I was a fellow Teamguy. "How can I help?"

Chapter 34

Isabella

In the Air

Now I KNEW why Bianca used to say she'd rather edit the "garbage" she wrote the day before than have to stare at nothingness the next morning. Blank pages were the worst.

If I eyeballed the sketchpad any longer, maybe I'd hallucinate something to appear on paper. I wasn't sure what made me think that after fourteen years of being unable to draw, I'd magically be able to start up on a semi-bumpy flight aboard our family's plane.

The jet was a commercial airliner before my father purchased it and outfitted it into a motorhome for the skies. The space and luxury it provided definitely had its perks. Maybe a nap in the bedroom was a better idea than the staring contest I was having with the blank page.

I set the sketchpad on the empty seat next to me and went to unbuckle, but the order, "Don't," from a deep voice off to my side, stopped my attempt, freezing my hands in place. "Turbulence. Stay seated."

The Art of You

From my peripheral view, I spied Hudson in the aisle next to me. I lifted my chin, allowing my gaze to take a nice, slow journey up his body before landing on the blue sapphires pinning me with a hard, broody look.

I let go of the belt, obeying, but couldn't stop myself from pointing out, "And yet, you're standing."

"I'm twice your weight." He parked a palm on the top of my seat and dipped his head to meet my eyes. "Don't you worry about me."

"Oh, but I will anyway, and you know it." I wasn't sure if I'd mouthed those words or they got lost in the ambient airplane noise.

A quick smile dusted across his lips, one that managed to hit his eyes. I'd consider that a win. He'd been living in broody central since we'd left New York.

The man was a deep thinker, probably even more than I was, and it was clear there was a lot wreaking havoc in his mind.

As he continued to quietly study me like I was an abstract painting that didn't make sense, I mentally went through the list of *whys* he'd become a grump since leaving our office, checking off each one.

For starters, he was stressed about this whole mess, particularly after hearing Seth Maverick's confession. *Totally reasonable.*

Secondly, I was on the plane with him heading into an unknown situation that could be full of metaphorical or even real minefields. Still a coin toss if his old teammate was on our side or not. Hudson had one hopeful theory he'd asked Falcon Falls to look into—about Alfie being a spy—and sadly, it didn't pan out.

Thirdly, we received two semi-disturbing phone calls en route to JFK.

And finally, I couldn't help but wonder if he regretted his joke about my birth control, realizing how forever-like that sounded.

The next bump in the sky knocked my head back to the present, and provided evidence that Hudson being over two hundred pounds didn't stop gravity from doing its thing. The jolt knocked him sideways, his momentum propelling him around in front of me as his hands scrambled for purchase on the back of my seat. His legs settled on each side of mine as he stood there, anchoring himself in place and forcing me to pin my knees together.

If my brothers weren't somewhere on board, I'd tease him to have a seat on my lap so I could keep him safe from the forces of physics he'd tried to deny. *Who am I kidding?* The man was all muscle and would crush me.

The next few little dips down in the sky sent my stomach right along with them. And yet, Hudson remained a statue of stubbornness in front of me. Definitely not a bad view. I tracked the veins in his arm up to his bicep before following along the strong curve of muscle to his broad shoulder.

"Are you okay?" he asked, stealing the line I'd planned to toss his way.

"You mean, am I concerned that, according to Jesse—who learned from the freaking President himself—that our Central Intelligence Agency has been compromised from the inside?" The aforementioned phone call number one. "*Or* disappointed your father blames us for him winding up in Splitsville with the ambassador, deciding to go for round two of being a jerk to you all in the same day?" And that had been the second call we were graced with en route to JFK.

That snark in my tone was meant for all the assholes causing us these headaches, not for the man before me, who only deserved my attitude when I was hoping he'd fix it with his tongue in my mouth. Or between my legs.

His jaw locked tight, straining beneath the facial hair coming in since he hadn't shaved since last week.

The turbulence seemed to stop, as if someone had hit the snooze button, but Hudson remained in the same position.

He quickly scanned the cabin before returning his eyes to mine, which had me believing we were still alone in the area I'd carved out for some me-time.

My brothers were more than likely still in the main cabin, chasing down leads with Roman and the two other operators who'd come along for the ride.

So, it's just us here, nestled between two walls and the clouds.

"This whole thing got a lot more complicated with that call from Jesse, and the fact I let you on the flight after learning that news has me questioning my judgment." Narrowing his eyes, he punctuated his words, snapping them out one by one as he seethed, "You. Should. Not. Be. Here."

I didn't blame him for worrying about me joining him on a mission that still didn't have a target package. Hard to go into a fight when you're not sure who you're actually up against. But I was here and he needed to accept that.

Okay, here we go. I went for the buckle, and no warning from him was going to stop me this time. I needed to stand to confront his doubts. Plus, I knew he had to be uncomfortable with his head bowed and his beat-up arm in that position. Broody and uncomfortable would not make this conversation any easier.

"Did I tell you that you could get up?" His deep, authoritative tone caught me off guard, and I *almost* tossed whatever was left of my Miss Independent ass out the window.

Apparently, I enjoyed having him boss me around. Not only did I remain parked in place, I slammed my lips shut as it all clicked—the *why* he was being a bossy alpha. He was itching for a good fight.

Forget uncomfortable and broody, he was stressed and in his head. And he needed tension relief in the only way possible considering our location. Message received. In the past, arguing with him about the silliest things always helped snap me free of my sad or bad mood. Maybe it was time to return the favor.

"No turbulence right now." I made an O-shape with my fingers, then started for the buckle to piss him off the way I was certain he wanted me to do.

Unbuckling, I tried to stand, but he refused to move, hovering in front of me like a sexy blockade.

He angled his head, eyes piercing mine as he issued the challenge he knew I'd accept. "I won't tell you again."

Defiance was my specialty, and he was about to get the max if that would help him. I used my smaller size to my advantage and played a game of limbo with his arm, trying to duck under to get free of my muscular trap.

"Not so fast," he rasped, hooking his arm around my waist in one fast movement. He drew my back to his chest as we stood in the aisle.

He surprised me when he gently set his hand at the column of my throat, then slid his palm higher, allowing his thumb to sweep back and forth at my jawline.

If he held me like that any longer, he'd have my permission to bend me over the couch opposite us and take me right there. No man had ever made me so, well, whatever *this* was.

"You really shouldn't be here." His breath danced over the sensitive part of my ear before he dropped his mouth and nipped my lobe.

"So you said. Want me to jump from the plane? Would that

make you feel better?" There it was. Sarcasm. For a minute, I'd forgotten how to apply it like a pressure point. Minute over.

"Do you know how badly I want you?" Okay, not an answer, but at the same time, better than one. "How much I want to take you into the bedroom right now. And it has nothing to do with tension relief." The dark edge of his voice as he kept his hold of me had my skin breaking out into chills.

"So do it." I arched my back so my ass would press against the thick bulge I felt behind me. "Do all the things you've ever wanted to me. I just need something to bite down on so no one hears me screaming your name." I kept my voice low, knowing what I'd said was as realistic as me actually drawing while on this flight. I highly doubted he'd make a move here.

His hand remained at my throat while his other wandered beneath the waistband of my leggings.

Okay, so we are doing this? We were out in the open and exposed to anyone who happened to walk into the cabin. Curtains for dividers were all that separated us from being caught.

The moment his fingers shifted my panties to the side, I trapped the moan inside my mouth by clamping down on my back teeth.

"Why are you soaking wet?" he drawled.

Looping my arm back to cradle his neck and draw myself even closer to him, my thighs tightened around his big hand as he pushed two fingers inside me. "You're a smart man, I think you can figure it out." I closed my eyes as he continued touching me.

"Such a bad girl." Another nip at the shell of my ear as he continued to finger me.

"Only for you." My promise had him stopping the strum of his fingers over my clit.

"You really are dangerous." He withdrew his hand and

spun me around before I had a chance to know what was coming. "Going to get me in trouble."

"But Constantine approves, so . . .?" I whispered as he took hold of my face.

His pupils dilated as he stared at me as if drunk on love. "Your parents will murder me if I get their daughter pregnant before we're married." He laid the words out fast, then slanted his mouth over mine and kissed me.

I lost track of my ability to Freud my way through this. I'd expected a fake fight, not for him to tongue me so deeply we might become one.

"Enzo call—" Alessandro with his lovely timing had Hudson's lips freezing against mine. "Sorry to, ahem, interrupt. Can you join us in the main cabin?"

"Be right there." Hudson's ability to talk with his lips still up against mine was impressive.

The fact he didn't back away with my intimidating brother present was also sexy as hell.

"Copy that," Alessandro said, and I assumed his lack of a lecture meant he was on the same page of approval as Constantine.

I didn't check to see if we were alone as Hudson reset his attention on my mouth. He sucked my bottom lip, lightly tugging it between his teeth. Latching on to his forearms, he had me growing dizzy with desire all over again.

"Killing me, Smalls." He moved his hands to my wrists. "Your pulse is racing." He locked eyes with me.

"Gee, I wonder why." Angling my head toward the main cabin, I added, "Now to face everyone and not look like I was just good and properly fucked will be a challenge."

"They won't think that." I'd never known a smile could be so erotic, but the one before me now had me getting red-hot all over again.

"No?" I shot back in challenge, waiting for an explanation.

Still holding me, he dropped his tone even lower, and I felt that fluttering pulse take root between my legs when he murmured, "Because if I were to *good-and-properly-fuck-you*, you wouldn't be able to walk afterward."

Chapter 35

Hudson

My control had evaporated, the remnants shattered on the floor as I prepared myself to face everyone and get an update from Enzo.

My rebellious girl led the way, her hips swaying in a hypnotic cadence, creating a perfect visual in my mind. My hands parked on each glorious swell, her palms on my chest, her hair down over her shoulders as she rode me, moaning and coming all over my cock.

Apparently, fucking, not fighting, would be my only hope to adjust my foul mood. But it would wait. It had to.

From listening to Seth Maverick's confession to learning from Jesse on behalf of the President that the Central Damn Intelligence Agency had been compromised, my head was completely messed up.

And to top it off, everyone overheard my father going for round two on the phone before we'd boarded the plane. Yelling at me about the consequences of "opening my mouth" to someone (Jesse) who'd then "opened their mouth" to the President himself, leading to his girlfriend getting in trouble for withholding the truth from her superiors about the real reason for her daughter's abduction.

Yeah, well, fuck my old man. We weren't going to let innocent people die to protect the ambassador's job. There had to be another way to stop this storm from making landfall, we just had to focus up and figure it out. But with all roads leading to the middle of no-fucking-where, I was losing both my patience and my hope I'd problem-solve us out of this disaster.

With every passing second since we left New York, I couldn't help but question how Bella managed to rope us into letting her come. We'd changed our minds at the airport, deciding it was too risky for her to join us. But Bella, in all her stubborn glory, had pulled out some BS executive order card, playing it like an ace up her sleeve. So much for not being a great poker player. She vetoed our decision to stay behind with Enzo after we'd outvoted her. She'd refused to accept no for an answer. Then, she walked her fine ass up the steps of the plane, and hid out in the middle cabin the whole flight.

After wasting time following dead ends with the others and stewing in negativity, I'd searched her out. Next thing I knew, I wound up wanting to spread her legs open and drive my cock inside her.

Fuck. I still had her sweet scent on my fingers as we joined everyone, and I had to stop myself from drawing my hand beneath my nose and inhaling.

Bella quickly wrestled my attention her way, spinning around to stand by Alessandro. She ran the pad of her thumb along the underside of her lip, staring at me like she was mentally mapping out how she'd get me off with that sexy mouth of hers.

Locking my hand over the top of the seat next to me, I was one bad decision away from throwing everyone from the plane so I could have the sixty seconds of airport time she'd promised me yesterday.

I scanned the cabin, looking around at everyone gathered there. Why the hell were they studying me as if I had a live grenade in hand?

Jesus, I had no business being any type of tactical leader right now. Consider me just body number five on an arrest warrant, no different from the New Guy I'd once been at the Bureau. Don't give me the keys to the kingdom and expect me to call any shots. I wasn't in the right state of mind. It was the same feeling I'd had fifteen years ago and why I sat the op out, but for very different reasons this time.

Constantine peered at his sister, shaking his head. He probably assumed she was to blame for the fact I'd returned looking so unhinged.

Bella erased the space between us, and talk about perfect timing. Turbulence struck again, sending her into my arms. Keeping my legs wide and my stance firm, I kept us both upright and held on to her. "Easy there."

Her lashes fluttered as she quietly stared up at me. And there we were, having another moment in front of everyone as if we didn't have a mission to focus on instead.

"Here, sit," Roman offered, vacating the seat I had been balancing against.

I continued to remain fixed in the aisle. I wasn't sure how she was managing to do it, but she slowed down my racing heart with her soft, brown eyes pointed at me.

I could see the three feet in front of me again, which stopped me from concerning myself with the six-feet-deep hole I might fall into later.

Classic Teamguy mentality. One step and day at a time so you don't dig yourself an earlier grave than necessary.

Clearly, getting roped back into the past this weekend had

done a motherfucking number on my head. I needed to level back up.

"Remember, you're an elite operator. One of the Navy's best. Don't forget it. Got it?" my team leader's words from forever ago shot through my head.

Why the hell didn't you let me help you with your addiction? I closed my eyes, exhaling a breath of frustration.

"You need more time?" Constantine was being far more patient than I deserved.

I swallowed and opened my eyes, realizing the turbulence had stopped, but I was still hanging on to this woman like she might be taken from me here and now. *Please, God, anything but that. I can't lose her.* "I'm good."

The reminder of why I had to slip back into operator mode was peering at me with her big worried eyes.

"Sit." I gestured with my head to Roman's empty seat, guiding her there so she understood I wasn't taking no for an answer.

Once she fastened her belt, I dropped down next to her, not wanting to be far. And screw it, I reached for her hand on top of the armrest and laced our fingers.

From the corner of my eye, I caught a flicker of a smile from her, which helped steady my pulse even more.

"What'd Enzo say?" I finally asked, shifting my attention to the others.

"The delivery man was able to identify who gave him the envelope," Alessandro shared, taking a seat opposite us. "He was, uh, somehow expedient in his methods."

"Who is it?" I tightened my grip on her hand.

"The woman's date from across the street. The accountant." Alessandro dropped his head as if regretting the fact we hadn't seen this coming. But how could we have? "His name wasn't on the party list, we checked before this news. He could've still been at the party under a different one since he left his date's house at ten that night. That's enough time to get to Scarsdale. He may have hacked the security feeds, making him our mystery Instagram poster, too."

"Assuming you already double-checked his background again, I'm guessing no red flags?" At least I was capable of thinking about the case again.

"None." Alessandro shook his head. "But he could be damn good at altering his identity. If he has the skills to corrupt CCTV footage and is somehow behind the classified files being sent to Maverick, as well as this mess now happening at the CIA, he'd be able to spoof our systems when looking into his identity."

"Or, this guy is just another Seth Maverick. One more pawn to throw us off the real trail," Constantine suggested.

"I can't imagine this guy running the risk of showing his face to the delivery man if he's the magician behind the curtain to our chaos." Bella had echoed my own thoughts. "Unless, of course, he *wanted* us to find him, just like he planted that video online because he hoped we'd find it on X, leading us to his Instagram account." She looked over her shoulder at me. "If he's been following you, or all of us, for some time, he knows we'd dig deep. He's planting clues he wants us to unearth for a reason."

That *reason* kept sending me back to the 2010 operation. In my head, this case had to somehow tie to that failed mission. Well, unless we were too close to this thing and missing the bigger picture somehow.

"Enzo and Adelina are almost to the address for him on file now. Single-family home on Long Island. They were already at our parents' place with Callie, so it's a short drive," Constantine shared. "Malik's with them for backup."

"I'm assuming you've already looked into any possible

connections between some of the classified cases that were sent to Maverick that he wanted turned over to Clarke?" Roman asked, taking a seat alongside Constantine on the couch off to our left.

From what I knew about Roman, he was not only married to a former CIA officer, he was a certified genius. Between the two of them, they had a lot of experience with cases like the one we were dealing with.

"We have, but no notable connections yet," Constantine answered.

"Something had to have set them off on this vendetta now," Roman said, and I had to believe that was true as well. "I think that's the one missing piece to understand the motive. Until we can lock on to that, we'll remain three steps behind."

Right. I let go of a frustrated sigh.

"The answer must be in those twenty files about instances of bad intel leading to servicemen and women dying." Roman pointed to the nearby laptop on the table at his side. "This has to be an inside job, which most likely rules out this guy Enzo's going to talk to. They were able to get their hands on classified files and nearly launched their own unsanctioned CIA operation all with the touch of a button."

When Jesse had shared our concerns with POTUS, it prompted President Bennett to speak with the CIA director. After untangling a mess of encryption, it was discovered operational orders had been sent with the CIA director's signature from the director's server.

Assuming the terrorists had a backup plan if their kidnapping scheme with the ambo's daughter failed, a small U.S. military assault team was already on the ground in Spain, prepared to wait for the terrorists to hit the Spaniard's black site.

The problem? The head of the CIA swore up and down he never gave such a command. Considering the director had been in the Situation Room with the President at the time the email had been sent, it was safe to say someone with damn good skills from inside the Pentagon had set up the director. That same person set up Seth Maverick, too.

The President ordered the assault team to stand down. Doing what was morally right, he alerted the Spanish authorities that their black site was probably compromised. Hence the call from my old man afterward about his girlfriend getting in trouble because of the calls we'd made.

"Someone went to a lot of trouble to ensure the head of this terrorist cell doesn't—" I dropped my words as it finally fucking clicked. I let go of my hold of Bella's hand and stood. There was the big-picture moment we'd been missing. "It's about the last of the twenty files. Two Marines died in the embassy bombing last October. Good intel—intel that was ignored—could've saved them." I checked the date on my watch. "The one-year anniversary of that attack is in a day and a half." I shook my head, remembering something else. "The Instagram account has 363 posts up."

Bella abruptly unbuckled and stood. "What if that's some sick countdown to whatever they have planned?"

"That means someone has been plotting their revenge for almost a year," Alessandro said as a call came over his phone. "How the hell are any of us tied to that bombing, though?"

"This asshole pulled us in for a reason, but maybe it's not for the reasons we originally thought." I planted a hand on the wall at my side for support as Alessandro accepted the call, placing it on speakerphone.

"Tell me you have something," Alessandro remarked quickly.

It sounded like Enzo was hacking up half his lungs from coughing so hard. Sirens blared in the background.

"What is it?" Bella asked, beating me to the punch.

The Art of You

"There was an explosion," Enzo choked out, still coughing. "We're fine. The house blew before we got to the front door."

"What the fuck?" I looked around at the others, trying to grapple with the news and the fact Enzo, Adelina, and Malik could've died.

"I'm so glad you're okay." Bella's voice broke as the reality of *what-could-have-been* slammed her back into her seat.

"If someone is after us, why not wait until you were on the doorstep? Or inside?" I hated raising that point, but it had to be said. They could have easily been killed. So, why were they alive?

"Well, we were saved alongside that road, too," Bella murmured, and I dropped my gaze down to peer at her. Her quivering lip nearly did me in.

I wanted to wrap her up in my arms and comfort her, but right now wasn't the time. Turning to one of the two operators who were on board with us, I requested, "Nick, can you get the bear from the duffel bag in the middle cabin?"

"Thank you," she mouthed, and I wasn't trying to treat her like a baby. But she was mine to take care of. *Mine to protect.*

The reality of the situation slammed into me again. I could've lost her Friday. And Enzo today.

I dropped down next to her as Constantine muttered, "Whoever is behind this whole damn thing is no guardian angel."

My hands tensed in my lap, and Bella reached over the armrest and uncurled my flexed fingers to clasp my palm.

"He's the grim reaper," Alessandro said in a deep voice, drawing my eyes, "and we're all still alive because he wants us to die on his own timeline."

We had a day and a half to get ahead of this fucker before he checkmated us.

"I need to call my wife," Enzo said, his words barely audible. "Be in touch when I know more." He ended the call before we had a chance to check if he was truly okay, mentally and physically.

I didn't blame him for wanting to get on the phone with Maria ASAP. The only person I'd wanted to talk to or see after the accident Friday night had been the woman currently holding my hand.

"Whoever is behind this is looking to end things on the anniversary of the day someone they cared about died, right?" Alessandro's question had my attention flying back to him. "What in God's name do any of us have to do with that attack in Algeria?"

"The photo," Bella whispered as if that was the answer. "Somehow, in some crazy way, I think everything ties to Bianca's death. Right down to that embassy bombing."

Chapter 36

Isabella

Barcelona, Spain

"I was expecting a creepy old bomb shelter or something, not a five-star hotel for a safe house." I looked around the fancy suite, my eyes finally settling on Roman. "Since your name is on the building, I'm guessing you have strong ties to the place?"

He casually lifted a shoulder. "It's a long story. But this place is safe. We have the entire top floor to ourselves. No one will breach this property, trust me."

Somehow, even in my tired and shocked state, I did trust him. It was now after nine in the morning Barcelona time, and so much had happened since we'd taken off from New York. My brother nearly being killed in an explosion none of us saw coming had certainly heightened all of our emotions and our wariness.

An hour before our plane had landed, I'd spent some time talking to Maria, trying to calm her down. I couldn't imagine being pregnant with twins and learning the father of her babies almost died.

Right now, Enzo was en route to Charlotte, deciding he needed to be with his family and protect them in case someone was targeting all of us. And my father doubled the security at his place where Callie was staying. I knew it killed Alessandro not to personally protect her.

We had to leave the rest of the investigation Stateside up to Adelina for now, and she was working remotely with Sydney to try and help piece together what was going on.

"Anything from Alfie yet?" Constantine asked Hudson, drawing my focus back to the hotel suite.

I went over to the kitchen area, needing to keep myself busy so I didn't relive that call with Enzo. It would be too easy to drown in the fear of *what-ifs*. I could've lost another sibling . . .

"No, but I let Alfie know I'm local. Hopefully he makes contact soon," Hudson answered.

I lifted a Nespresso pod in a silent question to the room to see if there were any takers. Everyone nodded but Hudson, his eyes still trained on the floor.

He stroked his jaw, continuing his staring contest with the carpet, probably working through his own *what-ifs*. "I'd really hoped Jesse was going to tell me Alfie worked for the Agency, and he'd been at the party undercover."

Yeah, me, too. Him being our hero alongside that road Friday, and on our side in this whole mess, would move mountains in making me feel better, even in the midst of so much uncertainty.

"Since we ruled out Alfie being Agency, that could mean our mystery person pulled him into their revenge plot," Alessandro commented while setting a weapons bag on the couch in the living room.

"To fuck with Hudson?" Roman asked.

"Probably." Hudson finally looked up, catching my eyes.

The Art of You

"The asshole behind this has done such a bang-up job leading us in so many different directions, I don't know what to think anymore."

"But they must all lead to one place somehow, I'm sure of it," I offered, sharing my thoughts as I waited for the machine to warm up.

"And it's brought you to those two Marines. To Rose and John," Roman reminded us.

Rose and John. Two innocent people who should've been alive. I still had no clue how they were tied to us, though.

The guys quietly began unpacking, turning the suite into our command center, and I went back to work on making everyone coffee.

A few quiet moments later, Hudson joined me in the kitchen. He rested his hand on my forearm, stopping me from reaching for the next finished cup of joe. "Can we talk?"

Not the best words on the planet to hear. I slowly shifted around to face him. "Okay."

He looked off toward one of the two bedrooms, then took my hand and guided me from the kitchen. We walked past my brothers and Roman as if it were no big thing Hudson was taking me to a bedroom. And maybe it wasn't anymore.

The second we were alone and the door was shut and locked, Hudson had my back up against the wall, one hand planted alongside my head. "Are you okay? We haven't been alone since Enzo..."

"Just shaken up. Talking to Maria wasn't easy," I admitted. "I'll feel better when he's back in Charlotte to watch over her and their daughter." I set my hand on his chest. His heart was thumping hard and fast. "The work you guys do is dangerous, but this is three levels above what you normally do, and it's just"—I swallowed—"overwhelming. And to be honest, I'm scared."

He bowed his forehead against mine and smoothed the back of his free hand over my cheek.

"I can't lose anyone again. I just can't." A few tears I'd fought back while on the call with Maria finally escaped. "I'm terrified I'm going to lose you for other reasons, too. Like you're going to change your mind because of all this and push me away."

"Understandable on the first part. I get it, I do." He lifted his head and gently swiped away the tears beneath my bruised eye. "But I'm going to need you to get out of your head about the second thing." His husky tone wrenched my attention from his mouth and to those bold blues of his. "You're overthinking, and I don't want you doing it. Not about us, at least, got it?"

About us?

"I'm not changing my mind. I won't push you away because of this case or any other reason." His hand moved under my sweatshirt and around to the arch in my back. His touch was a silent command to shift closer. "I'm a man of my word, and you have it."

You gave my brother your word, too. I applauded myself for keeping that thought under lock and key.

"That was different." His smug smile was all too knowing. The man really could read my mind. "You can't blame me for breaking that one. Your fault, really."

I wasn't sure what just happened, but he shifted the energy between us with three quick words. Sad and worried to something soothing in the space of a moment. This was also a different version of the man who'd fingered me on the plane.

I'd expected Enzo's near-death experience to send Hudson running away from me, and here I was in his arms instead.

Muscle memory took over for my hands, and they roamed over every edge of the hard planes of his body. "How so?" I finally asked.

The slow drag of his eyes down to my hands, then back up to my face was about as erotic as if it'd been his palm between my thighs instead. "I'm trying to understand how I held back for as long as I did. Seven years of lying to myself. Seven years of having to watch you with other men when I knew deep down you were mine."

His words were beautiful strokes of heaven coating every inch of my skin like paint. Filling in the blank space, especially in my heart. A living and breathing canvas. "Tell me more." My hands found a new home at the side of his neck. "Tell me everything."

I needed a distraction from all the darkness. From the fear. The worry. And all the unknowns. I needed his love. I needed *this*.

Somehow, he recognized that without me having to ask him. We really did know each other well. Built a foundation through our friendship brick-by-brick for what we could now have. A future.

He removed his hand from beneath my shirt, allowing it to wander between our bodies. Cupping my chin and smoothing the pad of his thumb along the line of where he held me, he rasped, "That kiss in Rome woke me up. I hadn't even known I was sleeping."

*So, you're Sleeping Beauty, and I'm the prin*cess *who kissed you?*

Forehead tight, eyes pointed on me, he revealed, "There's been no one else since. I'm sure you've wondered." He lightly shook his head, drawing me even closer. "After that night in Rome, I've been faithful to a dream I never thought I could have but refused to let go of."

I closed my eyes, tears on the verge of falling again, but for a better reason. "I'm glad you held on."

"And I'm damn thankful you didn't give up on me." He

stopped stroking the line of my jaw. "So, please, no overthinking about us."

His hoarse tone and words rattled something loose from inside me. That ugly four-letter word. Fear. "But . . ." *What an original cliffhanger.*

"I told you last night I wasn't sure if I could change, I remember." He released my chin and set his forehead to mine once again. "But I can, and I will. I think I already have, I just didn't realize it before."

Our bodies were now flush, so I could feel his heart beating as if it were the soundtrack to my soul.

He shifted back to locate my eyes. "I originally thought I couldn't be with you because of my past. Because of your brothers. But it was more than that. I was afraid that if I were to ever have a chance with you, I'd lose you. The way I lost my mom. My brothers on Echo." His words were like sandpaper, rough over my skin as they came across. He was hurting, and it killed me. "I thought staying away from you kept both of us safe from experiencing that kind of pain."

I brought my hands from the sides of his neck to his face, working hard not to cry as I waited for him to continue.

His voice was husky and deep as he admitted, "Then I almost lost you Friday anyway. All that effort to protect your heart. To protect my mind. It was all bullshit. Because if your life ended, mine would've been over, too." A sheen covered his eyes. "Fuck labels." He shook his head. "Because you've been mine for a long time." His brows tightened as he stared deep into my eyes. "I'm ready to admit to you, and to myself, that I'm already so deeply and madly in love with you, my heart is incapable of beating unless yours is. So, if anything were to ever happen to you, it happens to me, too."

Chapter 37

Hudson

BELLA STARED at me in shock, chasing away tears with the back of her hand as her wobbly bottom lip caught a few, too. I had to admit that wasn't the reaction I'd expected after telling her my truth. That I not only now knew I loved her but felt it deep in my bones. Breathed it like air. Was starved for it, too.

I pushed away from the wall, arms falling dead at my sides. Did I just fuck everything up? Speak too soon?

Sure, I'd pushed the envelope a bit with my not-really-a-joke comment about her birth control yesterday. But this was different. It was serious and honest and as unplanned as the heart attack I was about to have if she didn't speak.

"Say something, please." I caught her wrist, preventing her hand from erasing the evidence of her emotions.

Blinking her way from my lips to my eyes, I locked our fingers together, on the verge of shedding my emotions in liquid form, too. "I, um—"

"Hey, we need you." Goddamn Alessandro and his motherfucking knock cutting her off. "It can't wait."

No, but the words I wanted to hear more than anything in the world would now have to.

Bella's shoulders collapsed, and I brought our clasped hands between us and brushed my lips over her knuckles while meeting her eyes. "Later," I mouthed.

She lightly nodded, brows drawing together.

"We're coming," I called out as she used her free hand to discard her tears.

Her brothers would probably think I was in here breaking their sister's heart once they set eyes on her.

Freeing her hand, she turned to face the door. But before she opened it, she peeked back at me and whispered, "Remember what Patrick Swayze liked to say to Demi Moore in *Ghost*?"

Ditto for love. I nodded in understanding.

"Well, *that*." She'd said it so damn softly and sweetly I about fell the fuck over at what she was telling me.

You love me, too.

When she faced forward, my palm landed on the door like a knee-jerk reaction, keeping it closed.

I encircled her waist with my other hand, and she relaxed her back against my chest and angled her head to the side. Leaning over her shoulder, I bent forward and kissed her, needing to taste her love on her lips.

And I felt it in that kiss.

She'd done what I'd never thought possible. She freed me from my past. Regardless of who was behind this mess we were in, I didn't care. Not about their reason or motivation. Fuck it all. Everything that mattered from that moment on was right there in that room with me.

I knew I was finally ready to find a way to forgive myself and let go of the guilt that'd been weighing me down for a third of my life. Now that I had her, I'd do everything in my power to never lose her. And I meant every word. If there was ever a day when her heart wasn't beating, mine would officially stop.

It took all of my energy to free her from where we stood, hating to walk away from the sanctuary and serenity the space had provided, even for that brief moment. But it was time to once again focus up and switch gears. Find a way to put all of this chaos to bed, so we could all move forward.

Once we were back in the living room, Alessandro wasted no time chucking a phone at me. Thankful my arm was finally healing, I caught it mid-air. Bella and I looked down at what was displayed on the screen as he announced, "We know who's behind this."

"The accountant?" Bella asked. "That woman's date from across the street?"

"Yeah, but the name we had was an alias," Constantine told us. "Facial recognition software provided his real identity. He's Rose's husband. His wife was one of the Marines who died in the embassy attack."

And just like that, my world flipped upside down. For a split fucking second, I felt sympathy for this guy. Because I'd kill every last son of a bitch I believed responsible if anything happened to the woman standing next to me.

"He works at the Pentagon. The house on Long Island was a diversion to throw us off. He lives in Virginia. And he's not a spy or an analyst," Alessandro rasped, drawing my eyes, "just an unassuming IT guy."

Constantine crossed the room, exchanging a quick look with Roman at his three o'clock in the process, prompting Roman to speak.

"My people are looking into Rose's background, as well as his. If there's a connection between you and them, they'll find it, I promise," Roman shared.

Before I could offer my two cents, my phone in my pocket buzzed from a text.

I handed Alessandro's cell over to him and decrypted the message on mine. My eyes shot straight to the window as I revealed, "Alfie's here. In the lobby."

"You told him where we're staying?" Constantine asked in surprise.

"Of course not." *He must have tracked us from JFK to here.* "He wants to come up." I went over to the weapons bag on the couch and retrieved a Glock, tucking it at the back of my jeans.

"Mind taking Izzy to one of the other suites down the hall?" Constantine asked Roman. "I don't want her in here when we talk to him. Have our two operators out in the hall go with you."

"You sure you don't want some backup here, too?" Roman asked, looking back and forth between us.

Constantine went for a weapon as well. "The three of us are good." In a steady voice he added what I sure as hell hoped to be true, "Just having a conversation."

Roman eyed Constantine's rifle, shaking his head. "Yeah, well, those are the only kind of conversations I usually have."

Chapter 38

Hudson

THE ELEVATOR DOORS opened and Alfie stood between two of the hotel's security officers Roman had requested to escort him to our floor.

Alfie's green eyes immediately locked with mine. He'd aged, same as me, since I'd last seen him in his twenties. God, that was forever ago. "I'm armed. Knife at my ankle. A nine mil at my side. Another at my back."

"One of those mine?" I stepped to the side, gesturing to the two security officers to let him out into the hall.

A hesitant look crossed Alfie's face before he joined me. "The one at my back, yeah."

"Love to know how you wound up with my Glock." I did my best to keep my shit together, and instead of waiting for an answer, I turned and went to our suite.

I ordered the hotel security to hang back in the hall and ushered Alfie inside, closing the door behind us.

"He's carrying," I let Constantine and Alessandro know, not taking my eyes off my current target. "My nine mil?"

Alfie showed me his palm while reaching around his back with his other hand.

From the corner of my eye, I noticed Constantine coming closer with the short-barrel rifle meant for close-quarter combat.

"We're on the same side," Alfie said while returning my Glock. "I'm hoping we are, at least." I released the magazine to check it as Alfie added, "Missing one."

I side-eyed him while returning the magazine in place. I arched my brow, waiting for him to continue. It was hard for me to believe Triple A was really in front of me and not a figment of my imagination.

Alfie scanned the room, saying, "Just removing my phone from my pocket. Easy with your trigger finger."

That was more than likely meant for Constantine. The man could intimidate even the most skilled operators on the planet.

"How'd you even find us?" Alessandro asked.

"My teammate tracked you. Should be more careful." Yeah, that kind of remark wouldn't win any of us over, even if he was right. Although, I'd thought we'd covered our asses leaving the airport.

"Just tell us what's going on," Constantine hissed. "Talk." He let the word hang low and flat in the air.

Alfie turned his phone around and showed us two images of Chris and Eduardo—the ambassador's security detail—from before they were killed. "These two men were turned by terrorists who are responsible for multiple attacks around the world. I now know that Chris and Eduardo were tasked with getting information from the ambassador. Specifically, the location for a black site here in Spain where their boss was being held," he cut to it. "My team's working with the theory that the terrorists realized the only way to get the ambo to give up the address was

The Art of You

by having her daughter taken. They must've concluded torturing Ambassador Aldana wouldn't be a viable option to get her to talk. The terrorist cell outsourced and hired American mercenaries to take her daughter, keeping themselves clean of the hit."

"How in the hell do you know this? You're not CIA. Where do you fit in?" I asked, stumbling my way through shock as he casually pocketed his phone.

"I'm in the private security business now. My guess is you are as well, and that's how our paths crossed Friday."

I wanted to believe him, fuck did I ever. But I'd need more to go on before I felt comfortable enough for Alessandro and Constantine to lower their weapons.

"I was hired last week to take down the assholes responsible for a terrorist attack at a U.S. embassy in Algeria last year that killed a man's wife."

Alfie's words were both a punch in the face and a gut shot. "I'm sorry, but what? *He's* the one who hired you? Green?" *Rose Green's husband?*

"You know about Peter Green?" He scrutinized me for a long moment, attempting to put two fucked-up pieces together.

All I could do was nod.

He stroked his red beard. "Yeah, well, Green hired my team. Works at the Pentagon. He had access to a ton of intel to help expedite our search, leading us to the ambassador. We discovered too late the ambo's daughter had been taken. We used aliases to get into the party, and—"

"Green was with you at the party?" So, my gut feeling we had other eyes on us that night had been spot-fucking-on.

"He came late, but yeah, he was there," he confirmed.

"What happened next?" I didn't need to fill in the details. Not yet. But I did have to find a way to calm my racing heart pumping up into my ears so I could better hear him.

He cleared his throat, coughing into a closed fist, and I caught the gold band on his wedding finger.

I wasn't sure why, but knowing he was married somehow made me feel, well, better. Like maybe his life didn't suck after leaving the Navy.

"My team was hoping to help find the ambo's daughter, as well as figure out who was corrupt on her team to interrogate them. We wanted a location for the terrorist cell, as well as to determine their plans to free their boss."

I tore my free hand through my hair, trying to wrap my head around how disgustingly but *expertly* we'd all been played.

"Your name wasn't on the party list when my team checked it, and although it was your old man's event," Alfie continued, "I didn't expect to see you there. I was actually shocked to see you, to say the least. I did my best to keep out of sight after we made eye contact."

No damn way was it a coincidence my former teammate was hired for an assist by the man causing chaos in our lives. We really had been playing a game of Clue all this time with Mr. Green of all fucking people like some sick joke.

"My team was already tracking everyone connected to the ambassador. We had their vehicles tagged, including Chris's truck, which had been parked at the gas station," he resumed his explanation. "We saw your pal here," he added while eyeing Constantine, "take out multiple men outside the party, including the one down the street in the van. That's when I realized you were probably there for the ambo's daughter."

I was a second away from revealing the truth, but I opted to keep my mouth shut and let him continue. I needed to know how he ended up with my Glock and why I was down a round.

"Go on." Constantine's command cut over my shoulder to Alfie.

"We still had concerns that someone on the ambo's team was an insider, so when I saw Chris's truck on the move, going the opposite direction of the city, we followed him. I didn't expect they'd lead me to you," Alfie shared. "Realizing the tracker had stopped moving before we had visual contact, we parked on another road and made an on-foot approach with night vision. Eduardo was in the middle of removing a tracker from the Porsche while Chris took the gun from your hand. You were unconscious. Realizing too late they had company, Chris fired off a round, and it caught my teammate, Keith, in the arm. We'd wanted Chris and Eduardo alive to question, but I couldn't run the risk they'd hurt you. Sirens were in the distance. We were short on time." He'd whipped out the play-by-play so fast, I had to slow down his words in my head to really absorb them.

I closed my eyes, bowing my head. *You saved Bella.* He really did deserve the name Triple A. He'd been my insurance that night. Come to my rescue.

"We took Chris's and Eduardo's phones, your Glock, and the tracker Eduardo removed from your Porsche. I also made sure you and Isabella had a pulse. We had to take off after that, covering our tracks."

That also made me look guilty of murder. I let that slide and kept my thoughts to myself as I looked up at him. "So, what are we doing in Spain? Why'd you ask me to come here? Clarity could've come over a secure line."

"Because the terrorists had a backup plan. They already hit the black site yesterday," he revealed. "Based on that wide-eyed look of yours, you're not aware their boss is now free?"

I turned to put eyes on the Costas. "The Spanish government must've lied to POTUS. Didn't want him to know they'd been compromised and lost the terrorist." I could see that happening. Lie after lie in a big game of CYA. *Cover your asses.* The resounding theme to our problems.

"We have a fix on the terrorists' current safe house, and we're going after them ourselves. The chatter suggests they're moving during daylight today, presumably because no one would suspect them to roll out in the afternoon," he let us know. "Since we're after the same people, I thought it'd be best to join forces rather than get in one another's way. Prevent any unintended casualties and provide each other an assist."

I swiveled around, facing him. Was he really asking me to go on a mission with him?

"We were hired by the ambo to save her daughter," I finally admitted, cluing him in to how we were involved. "My guess is you were hired for two reasons." I lowered my eyes to the Glock still in my hand, everything finally clicking together. Everything except why Green was after us for the death of his wife.

"And those reasons are?" Alfie asked.

"I don't doubt that Green wants revenge against his wife's killers, which also means he more than likely masterminded this whole plan to get the terrorist leader free from the black site. He *wanted* him to escape. He probably spoon-fed the terrorists the intel they needed when he was ready, knowing what they'd do."

"Green couldn't kill the boss as easily if he was behind bars," Alfie said, not questioning me, but seemingly following along.

I set aside the Glock, deciding I believed Alfie, and he was no longer a threat. He'd saved the woman I loved after all.

"What's the second reason my team was hired?"

"Your connection to me," I said bluntly. "Green's out for my blood, too." I gestured toward the Costas. "Maybe theirs as well."

The Art of You

Alfie jerked his head back. "What the hell did you do to him? You weren't responsible for his wife's death."

I squeezed the back of my neck where pain lingered. "That's the question we still don't have an answer to."

"Something seemed off with this, and then with that reporter leaking the intel about our operation from fifteen years ago . . . it felt too coincidental," Alfie acknowledged. "I should've dug deeper. But we were short on time, and since he worked for the Pentagon, and all that checked out, I just thought—"

"We were all played," I cut him off. "He's been pulling the strings for a long time. Orchestrating everything. You couldn't have known. I sure as hell didn't understand much of anything until five minutes ago," I admitted. "Green wants the truth exposed about what happened to his wife, but he can't make it just about her. It alone won't garner attention from the media, and it will pull scrutiny of who leaked it solely his way as well."

"Which is why there were twenty files he'd planned to have that reporter share when the time was right," Alessandro tacked on. "Including the one he discovered about your op to really screw with our heads, too."

But Kit and Clarke pulled the trigger early, just targeting me.

"One problem at a time." Constantine lowered his rifle. "Even if Green maneuvered us like chess pieces to get us here to do his bidding, we still need to stop these terrorists from escaping before they kill more people."

"I also don't think we can turn this over to the government here to let them step in," Alfie said. "We run the risk they'll sit on the intel too long and get caught behind more red tape. They may miss the chance to get them."

I was in agreement with him on that. The Spanish hadn't

even fessed up to POTUS that their black site was already hit when President Bennett called them.

"Green didn't just bring us here to be his tool against his enemy. He sees us as one, too," Constantine remarked before setting his sights on Alfie. "But we can't let these terrorists get away with murder. So, we're in."

I checked my watch. Fucking daylight op, not ideal. "When do we spin up?"

An uneasy look crossed Alfie's face, and yeah, we were all in the same confused-as-fuck boat. "We need to hit their safe house once they try to roll out. Based on the intel we have, they plan to advance in ninety minutes, give or take. They're fifteen kilometers outside the city on the border of a park. My team still has them in their sights."

Alessandro came up alongside me. "How many tangos are we up against?"

"Thermal heat imaging suggests nine inside the safe house. A few on the perimeter. Overwatch tower with two snipers. Four SUVs parked there."

At least he'd done his homework. Decent start for the op.

"So, as they're loading up the vehicles, we take out their guys in the tower and disable their front and back SUVs to box the other two in. Then we move in on the target," I said in agreement, and he nodded. "How's the terrain around the safe house? You said they're near a park. I assume they're not in a civilian-populated area?"

"No other buildings or homes nearby. Isolated and wooded area. Only one dirt road in and out. Gated and fenced property sitting on two acres. There's a shed on the edge of the property, about five hundred meters away from their parked vehicles, that has a decent vantage point for overwatch if we can breach the property without being caught. A skilled sniper could handle that location as overwatch."

I didn't miss how Alfie's eyes narrowed on me, as if curious if I still had my magic touch on the long gun.

Yeah, yeah I fucking do.

"We can't let them drive away from their property, or we run the risk of civilian casualties or getting detained by the police ourselves," he went on. "But it's doable. We have an infil plan mapped out we'll go over with you all."

"Still out in the open, but they will be, too, I suppose," Constantine said, inserting himself into the conversation again.

"We're down to only three on my team aside from me. Keith's our best sniper, but he's the one who was shot Friday night. He'll sit on comms for us. He'll be our eyes with the drone we have up, and our ears as well."

I let go of a deep breath. "Yeah, okay." I'd still need my people to check into Alfie and his team before we rolled out, and he had to know we'd be doing that.

"We'll communicate the plans over a secure line. I don't want to risk us being together until it's go time." Emotion caught in his tone for the first time since he'd arrived. "I'll call in about thirty. We'll map everything out then and meet up a mike out from our infil spot."

All I could do was nod, still trying to wrap my head around the turn of events.

"And, uh, just so you know, you made the right call fifteen years ago. No one on our team blamed you for what happened, or for . . . Matt." He locked eyes with me. "I have a wife and two kids. A good life. The others do, too. We're better. I mean . . ." He paused for a moment and cleared his throat. "I won't lie and say I don't suffer from PTSD here and there, but that has nothing to do with that one op. You know how it goes, dodging trash on the road while driving, worried about a hidden IED. But, uh, that's standard shit most of us will always deal with after serving."

Another pull of emotion from him, was followed by a heavy sigh that didn't sound entirely defeated.

"All in all, man, I'm good," he continued, clearly needing to get this off his chest. "Just thought you should know that before we head out."

I bowed my head, accepting just how much I did need to hear that.

"Alfie," I called out without looking up. "Thank you for saving our lives on Friday. I owe you one."

"Just have my back out there today," he responded in a firm tone, "and consider us even."

Chapter 39

Isabella

"Yes, of course I'll be safe. Love you, too. Talk soon." Roman ended the call with his wife, catching my eyes as I entered the living room of the suite. "Are you doing okay?"

"I'll be better when I know what's going on," I said as someone knocked.

"It's me," Hudson called out.

Wasting no time, I ran over and flung the door open, my breath catching at the sight of him.

He offered me a semi-smile, which set off a stone of hope skipping into my stomach. He then peeked around me, eyes on our third wheel. "We're rolling out soon. Alfie claims he's on our side, but we should verify the backstory he just gave us and check out his team, too."

I did a little fist pump in my head at the news and let go of the door and lunged for him.

Without missing a beat, he slapped his palm to the door to keep it from whacking into me, and I looped my arms around his waist.

"My team will fill you in," he told Roman. "They're waiting

for you next door. We'll join you soon." He moved his free hand up and down my back and whispered, "We need to move so he can exit."

I blinked back tears and pulled away, nearly colliding with Roman, who was patiently waiting behind me to leave.

Once it was just the two of us, Hudson deadbolted the door and pulled me against him, quickly relaying what Alfie had told him and my brothers.

I took a few quiet moments to process it all. *Daylight op?* That meant an on-foot approach without cover.

"We'll be fine," he said, reading my mind as I turned away from him and faced the window.

My stomach twisted, and I banded my forearm across it, trying to work through all the *what-ifs* that could happen on an op that'd be taking place soon.

"Rose's husband is using us to take out his enemy, but it doesn't sit well with me that we're operating before we know the full story," he continued, likely recognizing I was uncomfortable and concerned about the op. "But one step at a time. We'll figure out why he hates us, and what his plans are after, and stop him."

I faced him, rubbing my hands up and down my arms, suddenly freezing cold.

"But since there are still so many unknowns, you need to stay here with security rather than joining us on comms."

That got me moving, and I quickly erased the space between us. "Oh, hell no. I'm coming. I've proved myself to be a valuable resource and asset. I'll stay a safe distance away, but I will be there to support you."

He laid the whole broody-scowly look he did so well on me. "We back to this again? When it comes to your safety, I will veto any decisions that put you in harm's way."

My hand skated along the ridges of his muscular arm

before I slowly walked my fingers up and over to his chest. "Oh yeah? How'd that work out for you when trying to stop me from getting on the plane?" I used my sexy "radio" voice, as I liked to call it, knowing it always made him glitch and give in to me. "What if while you're on the mission, Green comes after me here? What if that's what he wants? For you all to be distracted so he can get to me?"

His nostrils flared, and I lifted my gaze, trying not to focus on the bruises still marring his skin.

"Wouldn't you rather have me within arm's reach so you can get to me if need be? Within a mile of the op?"

He continued to stare at me. Processing. The simmer of rage percolating behind those blues as he marinated in the *what-ifs* himself.

"I can't handle someone coming into this hotel and killing innocent people just to get to me." It was a very real possibility, and one I knew we both wouldn't be able to live with.

He lifted his chin, eyes on the ceiling while stretching his neck so his Adam's apple was visible as he swallowed.

"Put me on comms with this teammate of Alfie's you mentioned. And if you can spare them, post our two operators with me. But either way, I'm going." I removed my hand from his chest and turned, prepared to go change into something more mission appropriate.

He seized hold of my wrist and spun me around, gathering me in his embrace in one fast motion. "You're a stubborn pain in my ass."

"And you love me, don't even pretend you—"

He cut off my words, crashing his mouth down over mine. He was using his special power over me now. Turning *me* into putty in his hands when that was supposed to be my job.

Freeing my wrist when he felt my arms go limp, he palmed my ass with both hands and squeezed, drawing me tight against his erection. This conversation had taken quite the turn.

"Tell me what I want to hear," he rasped between kisses.

"That I'll behave?" I murmured. "Not on your life, mister."

"No, the other thing."

Before I could answer, he caught me off guard, lifting me into the air, and my legs wrapped around his body like they'd been made to fit there.

Holding me, he walked forward until I was up against the wall. I kept my ankles linked at his back, and he held my ass with one hand and rested his other against the wall over my shoulder.

"I need to hear the words before I go out." His plea had me pulling back, nearly slipping free from his hold as I began to panic, but he wouldn't let me go.

"Don't act like you may not come back." With our lips broken apart, and my eyes on his, I whispered, "Don't you dare ask me for those words as if they may be the only time you'll hear them."

He allowed my feet to find the ground, but he kept my back to the wall, leaning forward to maintain our connection. "There are no guarantees in life."

Well, I had a lot to say about that. Like, screw that entire sentence and then some. "No, this is one thing I need you to guarantee."

He uttered a few choice words in frustration, more than likely at this whole situation.

"Tell me, please. Promise me you'll be okay. And you'll hear those words over and over when you return. And when you come back to me, I'll give you everything, including my body and my heart."

"You and I both know damn well I already have your heart." The edges of his lips lifted into a dark, unexpected smile. "And, darlin', you do realize I'm already highly motivated to survive, don't you? Knowing you want me, and feel *ditto* for me, has me wanting to live. Forever, actually."

Well, that was incredibly beautiful and romantic. "Sixty seconds of airport time, then," I relented. "Use it wisely."

He shot me a cute lopsided grin, reading me perfectly. He knew I wanted a hell of a lot more than a minute, and he'd be getting it. We both deserved it.

"Yes, ma'am." He scooped me into his arms and wasted no time carrying me into the bedroom.

"Careful with your arm."

"I don't give a damn about my arm," he said while walking with me.

He set me down in front of the bed, then he immediately knelt before me, taking both my sweatpants and panties along with him.

"And what are you doing?" I asked teasingly.

"You know exactly what I'm doing. What I've been thinking about doing for damn near forever." He buried his fingertips into the sides of my hips and lifted his blues up to my face. "And you know what I'm waiting to hear." Eyes returning between my legs, he demanded, "Use your words. Tell me what you want."

"Oh, God."

"I'd prefer my name instead." He smirked. "Now, tell me you want me to slide my tongue over your cunt. Lick your pussy for *just* sixty seconds. Tell me. I need to hear you say it. Do you want me to eat you out?"

This man and his mouth would do me in. "I want you to go down on me," I murmured, bringing my hands to his shoulders, bracing for the impact of his tongue. I felt his warm breath skate across my heated skin.

He leaned closer, eyes locked on mine, then slowly dragged

his tongue along my slit. After only one expert stroke of his tongue, I saw the other side. It was pretty and colorful. Radiating light. It was art in its purest form.

"Be more explicit," he commanded.

My thighs tensed and tightened with need. I was soaking wet. "Fuck my pussy with your mouth," I finally admitted, feeling shy but also empowered.

"Attagirl," he remarked in a deep, sensual voice before lowering back between my legs.

With every flick of his tongue, and groan of pleasure from him, I lost my control, unable to hold back anymore. "Do you have a condom?" I cried out, digging my fingernails into his shoulders when he sent me even higher, brushing against the pinnacle of orgasm heaven.

He swirled his tongue at my most sensitive spot before stopping. "Maybe." The word rolled from his lips, teasing my clit.

Oh jeez. He was massaging my center with his tongue again, and I wasn't going to last. Chills swept over my skin and I held on to him even tighter.

He kept going, not missing a beat. His hungry moans as he licked and sucked matched my cries of ecstasy.

My nipples hardened, and the muscles in my legs tensed as my toes curled. I threw my head back as a feral scream ripped from deep within my lungs as he made me come harder than I ever had. Releasing his shoulders, falling onto my forearms on the bed, I writhed against his face, riding out the orgasm even longer.

"That's my girl," he said huskily, not stopping until I was totally spent. He dragged his finger down the inside of my thigh to my knee before standing.

I slowly sat upright, finding his cock strained against his jeans as he stared at me. The man was sin in the most beautiful form. And all mine.

The Art of You

I left the bed, kicking my sweats and panties free from where they sat around my ankles as I eliminated the space between us.

"And what do you think you're doing?"

I reached for his button and zipper. "I'm getting you off, too."

He took hold of my chin, urging my eyes up to meet his. I'd bow to this man every day of the week. Happily be his own personal canvas to create beauty from if he'd be mine.

"Don't want your cock in my mouth?" I arched my brow, then licked my lips, and he growled out something too low for me to hear. Maybe it was only a string of sounds.

"Fuck yes, I do." He nodded. "But you're not getting me off that way."

I swallowed, continuing to work down his zipper even as he held me captive with his eyes. I didn't need to see what I was doing to make it happen. "No?"

He shook his head, gaze flying to my mouth as I licked my lips again. "You have my word, by the way. Before we do this . . ." He cleared his throat. "I promise you I'll come back."

My hand went still, and my heart jumped at what he was saying. Tears of relief snuck in, as if his word really could cement his invincibility in battle in stone.

He held my chin a bit tighter and bent forward to brush his lips over mine. "Now, may I make love to you, sweetheart?"

"After I get a taste, yes, please."

"May I take more than sixty seconds with you?" His lips stretched into a sexy, knowing smile, and I gave him an eager nod.

My chest tightened, trapping the breath in my lungs before he kissed me and freed it. Letting go of my chin, he stood tall, towering over me like a masculine block of rigid muscles.

This is happening. And now of all times. But I didn't care, I needed him, and he needed me. I was so anxiously excited I was actually shaking as I worked down his jeans and briefs.

His cock was big, thick and veiny, and I circled both hands around his shaft. He reached down and tangled his hand in my hair and held on as I circled my tongue around his crown, tasting a drop of precum. "Tell me what you want me to do." I sent his words back at him and lifted my chin to find his eyes piercing mine.

"Use that naughty mouth of yours to fuck my cock," he ordered. "Take it all."

I shivered in reaction to his delicious demand as I dropped my mouth over him like a good girl and deep-throated the hell out of him.

"Fuccccck," he hissed as I swallowed as much of him as I could, trying not to choke as tears pricked my eyes. "Breathe, darlin'." Pulling my hair, he gently tugged. "Breathe."

Still caring about me while I had him in this position.

I pulled up to breathe as he'd instructed before sliding my mouth up and down over his length. Taking my time. Torturing him the way he'd done to me.

"I'm gonna come. You have to stop," he commanded a minute later, then gently yanked my hair. "I need to be inside you."

It took me a few more seconds to heed his words, then I finally lifted my mouth and dragged my hand across my swollen lips.

"So fucking bad, I swear," he remarked in a strained tone before taking me by surprise, dropping to his knees in front of me. He snatched my face between his palms and kissed me hard. Tongues dueling with overwhelming intensity. He pulled away, eyes closed, seeming to live in the same land of ecstasy as I was. "I need to feel you."

And at that, he had me naked on the bed so fast I barely realized it'd happened. He produced a condom from his wallet and rid himself of every article of clothing he had on.

I rested on my forearms as he stared at me while he stroked his cock. "If only you hadn't missed a few days of your pill. I want to feel you bare so goddamn bad it hurts." His voice was rough and raw, and it made me want to throw logic out the window. I'd give anything to carry this man's child, but I also didn't want my traditional parents hating him for getting me pregnant prior to marriage.

"Get over here," I pleaded as he rolled the condom over his shaft.

He climbed on top of me, holding the weight of his body on his good arm. "So beautiful. God, I love you so much," he said before kissing me.

He'd given me his word, and I couldn't hold back any longer.

"Hudson," I cried while he nudged himself between my thighs. He pushed inside me, and I gave him my truth. "I love you, too."

He lifted his head, going still as he kept our bodies deeply connected.

He smoothed the back of his hand across my cheek as his eyes glossed over. "I could die a happy man." His lip briefly caught between his teeth, probably sensing my panic at his words. "But I'm not going anywhere, I promise. You have me for as long as you want me."

A few tears escaped my eyes as I held on to his arms and demanded, "Stay with me forever and ever and ever." I sniffled. "That's an order."

"Roger that, ma'am." An adorable smile cut across his lips.

As he slowly began moving inside me, opening my tight

walls, I also felt myself moving on. Moving *forward*. Becoming free of the cage of my past, certain I could finally even learn to love myself again.

Chapter 40

Isabella

S*HIT, shit.* I jumped up from my seat as hot coffee managed to burn right through my jeans.

"Damn, I'm sorry." My new comms partner, Keith, could pass for a younger Luke Perry, but not quite *Beverly Hills 90210* young. Probably my age. Give or take a year. "Not a klutz, I swear." He offered me paper as a napkin to try and dab the wet spot.

That's not going to work. Since removing my jeans wasn't currently an option, I applied the paper to my lap, keeping my head bowed forward so I didn't whack it on the ceiling of the van that'd been outfitted as our temporary command center. "You like your coffee scorched-earth hot, huh?"

"That I do." Keith gave me an awkward smile before returning the lid of the Yeti thermos, positioning the coffee on the other side of our work station.

Good call.

Dropping back in my seat, I ignored the uncomfortable peed-in-my-pants feeling and focused on what I'd been doing before I was shocked to my feet. We finally had eyes on the terrorists' safe house via the drone footage, and I wanted to ensure we'd have multiple angles of the property covered before they rolled out.

I did a quick radio check with the guys standing outside the van as they prepared for the op. "You hear me okay?" My voice was meek from nerves, and it pissed me off.

"I hear you. *Lima charlie*," Alessandro responded. "Loud and clear."

He must've kept his finger on the button, because I heard Hudson ask someone, "What's your call sign?"

My stomach squeezed at the *Echo Four* as a response from who I was pretty sure was Roman.

"That, uh, was mine back on the Teams," Hudson answered, obvious hesitation in his voice that even I could detect over the radio.

The connection ended a second later, and I sat back in my seat, worried about Hudson all over again. Would Roman's call sign draw Hudson back to the past? Working alongside Alfie already had to be doing a number on him as it was.

Keith shifted on his seat. "What made a billionaire get into this line of work, if you don't mind my asking?"

Keith was the new guy on Alfie's team, tasked with staying back with me because he'd been shot on Friday.

I was too in my head for small talk, but I also didn't want to be rude. Especially since he was shot with Hudson's gun essentially while his team saved our lives. "I'm not a billionaire just because my parents are. Not really." I shrugged, hoping he wouldn't prod. "What about you, why are you in private security?"

"I come from a long line of people who serve and protect. Only natural for me to do the same. Right the wrongs in life. Seek justice for those who can't do it themselves." His tone was almost somber, and I had a feeling he'd lost someone, too. Maybe he would understand after all.

"Military background?" I asked him.

"Army, yeah," he answered as the back doors opened.

We both twisted around to see Hudson standing there.

"We're about to leave," Hudson informed us, his eyes locked in on Keith. I could tell he didn't feel comfortable leaving me in a van with a man he didn't know, even if we had two of our operators standing guard outside as another layer of protection.

The last thing I wanted was Hudson to be worried about me and get distracted while being shot at. I'd need to ease his concerns before he left to guarantee he'd keep his word and come back to me safe and sound.

Keith stood. "I'll go talk to Alfie and the others."

Hudson stepped aside so he could exit, then he climbed in and shut the two doors behind him.

Dropping into Keith's seat, Hudson turned to face me, shifting my chair around so my knees went between his open legs. The man didn't miss a thing, noticing the stain on my jeans. "You wet your pants, darlin'?"

The light chuckle escaping my lips was a welcome change to the constant hard beats of concern occupying my chest, drumming up into my ears. "Coffee accident."

"You get burned? You okay?" He arched his brow. "Maybe I should lower your jeans and kiss you. Make you feel better." He raced his tongue along the line of his mouth, effectively kicking to the curb any last lingering worry.

So, so good at distracting me. People could take a masterclass from this man on how to get your target comfortable. Then again, I was pretty sure I had the same effect on him.

I smiled, sliding into my sexy, feminine-husky voice as I assured him, "As much as I'd enjoy your mouth between my legs again, I think you have a world to save from bad guys. Rain check?"

Holding the arms of my chair, he scooted me even closer and bent forward. "Absolutely," he said before kissing me with a soft open-mouthed caress that managed to make me dizzy.

And when his tongue met mine, I officially forgot where we were and why. One hand cupped my face, shifting up into my hair, as he deepened the connection and swallowed my achy moan of need.

"I'll come back to you, I promise," he rasped again.

I slowly blinked my eyes open, battling the lightheaded feeling he'd given me. We went from making love to fighting terrorists, and I was struggling to wrap my head around it all. So much had happened since Friday. How was it only Tuesday?

"I know you will," I said after nervously swallowing my lingering fears.

"I don't like leaving you." He sat tall again, lowering his hand from my face to the top of his tactical camo pants. He had a 9mm strapped to the outside of his upper right thigh, and surely more weapons hidden elsewhere.

"I'll never enjoy these moments. The dangerous part of our work." Since I couldn't pull off a poker face with him, why bother lying? "But it's who you are, and what you do is important. I'll put my big-girl panties on and wait for you every time."

"I suppose that's better than you sitting in here pantyless since you love to be the death of me when going without them," he teased, his voice almost hoarse.

Oh, shit.

His poker face was failing him right now. *He* was worried.

"What's wrong?" I reached for his hand, his gloves not on yet. "You have a bad gut feeling, don't you?" Worry lodged in my throat and found a spot back in my stomach yet again, ramping up into a sense of dread and nausea.

The wince from him didn't sell me on his confidence. "Something feels off. What if this is what Green wants? Us to be apart?"

"We have no choice. Not unless you want me rolling with you?" We were boxed into this decision now and I was determined to make sure his head was on straight before he went out there. "He wants the terrorists dead, and I'm fairly certain he won't make a move on us until tomorrow."

Tomorrow was day 365, the anniversary of his wife's death.

"So, one problem at a time. Remember?" I kept my voice as soft and convincing as possible so he didn't get in his head and then wind up losing it out there. Not a freaking option.

"Maybe I should stay here with you?" he suggested, frowning while closing his eyes. "Roman's an excellent sniper. He could take my place."

As much as I liked the idea of being next to him instead of a stranger, I also knew he'd never forgive himself if something happened to my brothers or the team because he hadn't been with them. "I have three people here to watch over me. No one knows where we're at. Alfie said he didn't tell Green our current location, and Constantine swept every square inch of this van and surrounding property for trackers. He's paranoid like you."

He stretched his neck out, chin pointed to the ceiling.

"You didn't spin up with your team in 2010, and you've never been able to let that go. I think you need to do this. I feel like this might truly be what helps you let go of what happened and move forward." I kept my voice as calm as possible, hoping I got through to him, believing in my heart I was right.

He finally gave me his beautiful blues and laced his fingers with mine, bringing our clasped hands between us, kissing my knuckles.

I dug deep into my stubbornness and went on. "I don't want any obstacles standing in our way of being together after this. I don't want you picking me over the mission, either. I have your six, and I need you to have theirs. Got it?"

"God, I love you so fucking much." He lowered our hands and kissed me again, even more passionately this time than before, stealing my breath and my worries along with it.

I just had to trust everything would be okay, and that his bad gut feeling was nerves. It was hard not to be worried when we still didn't know how we fit into Green's vengeance equation.

After our kiss, Hudson reached around his back and produced a Glock.

"For protection." He handed it to me. "Put it at your back beneath your jacket."

I held the heavy piece of metal in my hand, recalling the lessons given to me. "If this makes you feel better, then okay."

"It does." He nodded, waiting for me to follow his order, so I positioned it at my back and hid it with my jacket as instructed. "I also need to hear your voice every two minutes while we're gone. I need reassurance you're okay if you want me to stay focused. Can you do that for me?"

"Keith and I will be relaying information from the drone. But I don't want to pop over the radio if I have nothing to share just so you hear my voice. That might distract you."

"Not knowing you're okay will be much more distracting. I'll also turn my ass around and sprint the mile back here if I don't hear from you." He took hold of my chin in his big hand, commanding my attention.

The guys would be sneaking up on the safe house on foot from here, and I didn't doubt for a second Hudson wouldn't act like an Olympic runner to get back to me if he didn't hear my voice.

"I'm waiting for confirmation, sweetheart. If you want me to leave you, I need you to say you understand. Your safety is in my hands, remember?" A dark smile cut across his lips as if remembering the other thing he controlled—my orgasms.

Distracting me again. "Yes, sir," I finally surrendered.

The side of his lip lifted and he set his mouth to mine for one more kiss before we joined the others outside.

My brothers were decked out in military gear and Constantine handed Hudson his skeleton-looking mask before offering him his rifle.

They all looked lethal and intimidating as fuck. Just the way I wanted them to be.

"You've got this," I promised before hugging Alessandro first, then moved on to Constantine. "Bring him back to me, okay?" I whispered. "I can't live without him."

Constantine pulled back, only his eyes visible with the mask on. "You have my word, sis."

Chapter 41

Isabella

"THERE." Keith pointed to the screen, and I flinched as his arm flew forward, brushing against me. "Alpha Team, we have multiple tangos exiting the house now."

"This is Alpha One," Constantine radioed back. "That's a good copy." He paused. "Alpha Three, advance to your position," he told Hudson, and I kept my eyes glued to the screen providing our aerial view.

"This is Three, roger that." Hudson scaled the wall and quickly maneuvered to the shed that sat over five hundred meters away from the safe house. Once he was in position on the roof, he went prone, lying flat on his stomach as he set his sights on the house and confirmed he was in place.

I switched over to the second aerial view we had, which was of the safe house. "This is TOC," I began, keeping my word to communicate every two minutes so my guy wouldn't worry. "The men are moving in groups of four to the SUVs. No sign of the boss yet." I had the leader's photo taped to the wall alongside my screen so I could recognize him. "Zooming in for a closer look. Hold."

"Roger that," Hudson responded. And maybe I needed to hear his voice as much as he did mine, because every time he spoke since he'd left, the knots loosened a touch in my stomach.

"That's him," Keith said, pointing to the screen after I'd zoomed in on the second group of men huddled around a man.

"This is TOC, we have eyes on the HVT," I shared quickly. "He's getting in the third Range Rover. Back seat."

"Delta One here, that's a good copy," Alfie's team leader replied. "Delta is holding in place, ready to advance when the word is given."

And those knots in my stomach intensified once again now that the mission was unfolding in real time.

I still couldn't believe the terrorists had freed their leader from an intelligence black site. Then again, they had the magician behind the curtain—an IT guy at the Pentagon, no less—pulling magical strings for them to lead him right to his death.

"TOC, come in. This is Alpha Three," Hudson transmitted. "Tell me I'm not seeing what I think I see." He'd have a decent view of the scene from his overwatch position, and shit, he was definitely not imagining anything.

No, no, no. I zoomed in closer at the third grouping moving to the front SUV. "There's a kid. Maybe ten or twelve." Alfie's intel didn't include anything about a child being here. *Shit.* "Not sure who he is or why they're not putting him in the same SUV as our HVT, but he's being shielded like royalty."

"This is Alpha One," Constantine said. "Did you say they're placing him in the front SUV?"

My shoulders fell as I responded, "Yes." They'd have to change their plans. They couldn't launch an RPG and take out the front vehicle to blockade the others now, not with a kid in there.

"We're not turning their leader into a martyr in front of his kid and creating a new terrorist today," Constantine said in a steady voice.

That was another element my nerves hadn't given me time to consider. "Does that mean you're not shooting to kill?"

"Affirmative. We'll need to take the boss alive. I don't want him dying in front of his son," Constantine responded.

"We can't let that asshole live." At Keith's words, I pivoted to catch his eyes, finding his nostrils flared and free hand balled into a fist on the desk.

You lost someone to terrorists, didn't you? Well, maybe a lot of *someones* since he'd been Army. That made my heart hurt for him, too.

"We'll do what needs to be done," was all Constantine said, foregoing his call sign that time. "Switching to the backup plan now," my brother continued. "Alpha Three," he continued, "on my command, take out the watchtower. Once they're down, pick off as many as you can from your position on the property, then we'll need you on the ground for support."

"This is Alpha Three, roger that," he answered, then Constantine gave orders to Echo Four next.

I keyed in on the location where Roman was hiding in the woods. I couldn't see him since he was in camo, but he was using a sling up in a tree to give him a better vantage point as a sniper. Not ideal, but it was the best we could work with for our second sniper position.

"This is TOC. Looks like the house is empty. Everyone is now in the vehicles," I shared. "Two still on the perimeter and two in the tower. The front SUV is about to roll out."

From the corner of my eye, I spied Keith's balled hand move to his lap, disappearing beneath the makeshift desk.

An uneasy feeling snuck up on me, and I leaned back in my seat, the Glock butting against the chair, a solid reminder of Hudson's concerns.

The Art of You

Before I could ask Keith if he was okay, or check in with the team, Hudson's phone began ringing. I'd forgotten he'd left it in the van in case Adelina or Enzo called with news.

"Don't answer that now." Unlike how he'd spoken to me before, Keith's voice was sharp and abrasive.

Hello, concerns times ten. Something was definitely off.

While I didn't want to follow Keith's orders, I was currently too focused on what was going down on the screen to answer Adelina. Constantine gave the go-ahead to Hudson and Roman, and they didn't miss.

They nailed their marks in perfect and impressive timing. Four tangos down. Two each.

"Good work," I whispered, remembering Hudson needed to hear me so he wouldn't worry.

"This is Alpha Three. Snipers in the tower are down."

"Echo Four here. The perimeter is also secure. You're clear to move in."

"Roger that. Alpha and Delta, you're a go," Constantine directed, and now all I could do was sit back and watch the scene unfold like a movie.

My brothers and the others moved into view now, breaching the property and shooting only at the second and fourth SUVs, leaving the ones with the child and the boss alone for now. The nonstop ringing from Hudson's phone served as a soundtrack to everything playing out, but I also knew the radio wasn't live, so the rings wouldn't transmit and distract the teams.

"Silence that fucking thing, or I will." Keith's bone-chilling words were as unsettling as his tone. He'd gone from the semi-charming guy who'd spilled his coffee on me earlier to creepy phone-caller guy in a horror flick.

The calls stopped before I could act on his command, and with Keith deeply focused on the action on the screen as if his

355

own life depended on the outcome, I took the opportunity to reach for the phone.

Before I could grab it, he caught me off guard, securing a strong grip of my wrist.

"Remove your hand from my body, or so help me, when they come back, they'll sever it from your arm," I ordered, trying not to let fear take over.

Keith swiveled his head to meet my eyes, and they were as dark as coal and downright terrifying. The mask had been lifted, and whoever he'd been pretending to be before was gone. He'd pulled off the poker face of all poker faces, and Hudson's bad feeling was staring back at me instead.

I went to open my mouth and scream for help from our guys outside, but sealed my lips together when I realized he had something pointed at me.

His right arm still seemed to work just fine despite the injury carefully concealed by a bandage, and he was gripping a 9mm.

I calculated my options and what to do. He'd shoot me before the van doors ever opened if I did yell for help, and I had no clue how to access the gun at my back and defend myself with a trained operator holding on to me. *I'm screwed.*

He kept his dark eyes pinned on me as I searched for strength and resilience to think through this massive problem. "How do you fit into this? Who's Rose Green to you?"

"TOC, come in, this is Alpha Three. Are you good?" Hudson asked over the radio.

"Tell him you're fine," Keith ordered. "And you better sell it, or I'll remove you from the equation. Then your death will distract them. Get them killed."

I closed my eyes as fear officially hijacked my thoughts. My brothers and Hudson couldn't lose me. They'd never . . . just no. *I have to live. I have to.*

"Bella, come in." Hudson chucked protocol out the window and went right for it, worry taking over.

"Answer him, goddammit," Keith ordered. "They have a mission to complete."

I opened my eyes, and with my free hand, reached for the controls. "This is TOC, we lost connection for a moment, but we're back. I'm here."

"Roger that. Good copy," Hudson responded immediately, and I bought myself two more minutes before he'd panic again.

Keith was right; they had a mission to focus on. I couldn't let anything happen to them because of me.

"What do you want? Who are you?" I asked him once my hand was off the controls, needing to buy myself time.

"This is Delta Two. The kid escaped. He's taken off, and he's armed." Alfie's words temporarily distracted me from the man who had my life in his hands, and I peered at the screen.

"This is Alpha Three," Hudson remarked, "I'm going after him."

"Rose was your sister, wasn't she?" I asked him, because that was the only thing that made sense to me. The lengths my brothers would go to protect me. The revenge they took in the past when Bianca died. All of it.

But according to our research, Rose didn't have any family, just her husband.

"Rose was a good person. The best fucking person on this planet. She gave her life in service to this country, hoping to redeem our family name, the same as I did. And it was for nothing." He showed his teeth, snarling as he leaned closer, drawing the 9mm right beneath my chin, pushing it up so my eyes were on the ceiling.

The guys outside would open up and check on us soon, I was sure of it. Hudson's orders. But if they did, this maniac would probably go ahead and shoot me.

"But our brother wasn't even a killer. All that time we believed he was. All those years of shame. Court acquittal or not, everyone thought he took your sister's life. We were treated as lowlifes. Our family was destroyed." Anger curled around his words. "We had to change our names. Escape from the stain of what we *believed* our brother did."

Shock pulled my head forward as it all connected.

"When my sister was murdered by these terrorist pieces of shit, and her husband came to me and let me know she never should've died . . ." He shook his head, letting his words trail off. "That opened Pandora's box. I told him our real names, and we went down a rabbit hole that led us to more lies and treachery. Those lies brought us to your fucking family. To the fact they killed my brother and the government covered for them. Then last year, your family took out your sister's *real* killer." Spit hit my face as he continued. "Your family took everything from us." The gun pressed harder into my throat, and on instinct, I reached around with my free hand to try and push him away. He didn't move an inch. "And now, I'm going to take everything from your brothers and Hudson the way they took it from me."

The embassy bombing really did wake the sleeping giant. It was too much to process.

I jolted when the doors abruptly flew open, and I thought he'd put one in my head. I'd see the bright light soon. The other side would steal me away to where Bianca was.

"Boss, it's time to go. Pilot says we need to take off." An unfamiliar voice drew my eyes, and where were our guys?

"What'd you do to them?" I whispered, trying to see beyond the stranger outside the van to locate our operators. That's why they didn't do their regular check. *Please be alive.*

"Relax," Keith said, reading my thoughts. "I wouldn't kill *innocent* veterans. They're just taking a nap." He didn't budge from his position, keeping his back to the door, which meant I couldn't try and make a move for my gun with my free hand. "We can't go until the mission is over."

I could faintly hear the sounds of helo blades off in the distance. He was going to make an escape, and since today was only day 364, that meant he was probably taking me with him, still intent on punishing my family on the anniversary of Rose's death.

"We have maybe two minutes. They're bound to find out about what happened in New York soon. We need to get ahead of them," the stranger said.

My stomach somersaulted yet again, because what the hell happened in New York?

Chapter 42

Hudson

"TOC, DO YOU COME IN?" I hadn't heard from Bella in two minutes, and I needed her voice in my ear to calm my heart rate down. Leaving her had been one of the hardest decisions I'd had to make, and I'd yet to shake the bad feeling since I'd left.

"This is TOC, that's a good copy." It was Keith, not Bella, and my gut twisted uncomfortably again, throwing my focus.

I nearly missed a tango playing peek-a-boo from a tree off to my nine o'clock. I dropped to my knee and swiveled in one fast movement. Head shot. He was down. Hopefully the last of the tangos out there.

"This is Three, I've locked on to the package," I confirmed the moment I laid eyes on the kid heading for the back fence.

"The HVT is down," Alessandro shared the good news. "Alive, but just barely. All tangos, aside from the kid, have been immobilized."

"TOC, can you confirm?" Constantine asked. "Any movement from your vantage point?"

"Nothing," Keith said. "You're clear."

"Bella." Her name popped from my mouth like a reflex.

The Art of You

The silence was deafening, and it stopped me in place. "Something's wrong."

"Get down, the kid's coming at you with his shotgun." Bella's words had me taking cover, narrowly missing a round to the face that would've ended my promise to make it back to her.

Now that I knew Bella was okay, I continued on mission. *I am not shooting a kid.* On my knees, I located the boy boldly advancing closer, his face partially wrapped by a bandana.

"This is Delta Two," Alfie announced, "I'm coming up behind him. Distract him for me."

Yeah, easy enough. Not getting taken out by a ten-year-old in the process, not so much. "Don't shoot, and I won't," I yelled to him, hoping he spoke English.

The boy slowed down but didn't lower his weapon. At least he didn't fire again. I'd call that a win.

I shifted from low carry to rear sling, not wanting my rifle in front of me when he approached. Even a kid could ragdoll me if he grabbed hold of my weapon and went dead weight to the ground.

He stalked closer, and I slowly raised one hand to lower my mask, needing to add a little humanity for him. The skeleton face might have him thinking he was just playing a game of *Fortnite* or *Call of Duty*.

"On my count," Alfie said over comms, and I spied him army-crawling up behind the boy.

I will not kill a kid. Please, please don't make me hurt him. I wasn't sure who I was sending that request to, but when he started to lower his weapon, I fell back onto the heels of my boots in relief.

Alfie pinned him down and I stood to gently disarm him. As he cuffed him, I transmitted, "He's been detained."

Constantine responded by requesting everyone sound off with their call signs, looking to confirm we were all safe.

No casualties or injuries on our side.

I turned toward the safe house, prepared to exfil, but Keith's words over the radio shocked me back down to my knees.

"Kill the HVT or I kill Bella. Your choice. She's currently incapacitated, as are your friends here."

Without hesitation, I turned toward the safe house while yelling to Constantine over comms, "Do it. Do what he says."

"I already did," Constantine responded immediately as I started for the house, hoping one of the SUVs was still drivable. "If you touch my sister, if you set a hand on her—"

"You don't get it," Keith cut him off. "You can't hurt me. There's only one thing you can try and steal from me now, and I won't let you."

"And what's that?" I asked as my world spun upside down but my legs kept moving on autopilot.

"My revenge," Keith answered. "Tomorrow is day 365. If you want to see Isabella again, meet me back in New York. Delta Five. Out."

* * *

No blood in sight, but Bella's vanilla-scented shampoo I'd inhaled while we'd made love lingered, mixing in with the smell of the bastard's coffee.

She was really gone, and I failed her. Failed everyone.

Rage burned through me hard, hot, and fast before it took me down to my knees in front of her empty chair inside the van.

My knees slammed onto the hard floor as I bowed my head, trying to pull it together to work through the problem.

"This doesn't make any sense. We vetted Keith when he joined in June. Army Ranger. Excellent service record." Alfie was somewhere behind me, but I couldn't look back to search him out. "He's the one who tracked you to your hotel, though. I should've fucking asked how, he, uh... Christ, I'm so sorry."

I barely heard what he said, too busy bouncing between red-hot anger and terror, struggling to think straight since I'd learned she'd been taken.

"I've alerted everyone I know at the airport to stop them if they show up. They'll more than likely not leave out of Spain, though," Roman said from behind.

"We need to get back home." I tried to stand but my legs failed me. "He wants this thing to end there on our turf. Mission accomplished here, and now—"

"I have a dozen missed calls from Adelina," Constantine interrupted me. "She must know something."

I lifted my head at his strained voice, catching sight of my phone on the desk alongside the Glock I'd left with Bella. *This is my fault. I should've stayed back in the van.*

"She'll be okay. We have to believe it," Alessandro said, his voice breaking right along with all of our hearts. "He wants us in New York to finish this, which means we have time to get to her."

"Adelina's not answering, but she left three messages," Constantine said. I had no idea how he was keeping it together, but I was glad one of us was. "Come on. Get up."

He urged me to my feet. I'd never felt so fucked in the head in all my life. On one hand, I was ready to kill anyone who stood in my way of finding Bella. The other part of me already felt dead.

Constantine helped me outside the van, and we joined the others. Well, the few who were there. The rest of Alfie's team was back at the safe house dealing with the mess to cover our tracks. They also had to get the leader's son to safety.

When I set my back to the side of the van for support,

Constantine let go of my arm and played Adelina's first voicemail over speaker.

"I have new information," she rushed out. "Rose legally changed her name when she was eighteen. My guess is her husband managed to bury her real identity under a million pounds of layered encryption so we wouldn't make the connection. It took one of the best hackers at Falcon to finally find the truth. But, um, Rose had two brothers." Her pause screwed with my already damaged mental state. "Her older brother was the man you, um, killed, after Bianca died. Her other brother is on Alfie's team. Keith."

Constantine fumbled the phone and Alessandro moved fast and caught it. "What the fuck did she just say?" Alessandro asked as shock tore a hole through my already beaten-up heart.

Bella was right. She'd thought this was about Bianca, but I never imagined *this* was the missing piece.

"There are more messages." Constantine cut off my thoughts, and my arms went lax even more when his composure failed. I hadn't seen his tan skin this pale since learning Bianca had died.

"Malik and I are about to pull up to your parents' house, but . . ." There was an unnaturally long pause before she yelled, "Something's wrong." The call died, and so did my heart.

Alessandro dropped the phone. "Calliope."

I stared at Constantine as he picked up the cell, remembering we still had another message. I wasn't sure how much more we could tolerate and keep it together.

"We were too late," Adelina began, her voice trembling over her final voicemail. "Your family couldn't get to the safe room in time. Your dad is being airlifted to the hospital. Your mom is okay and she's with him. He's alive, but he was shot twice trying to stop them from . . ." Adelina paused, then whispered, "They took Callie. They came for her."

Chapter 43

Hudson

Long Island, New York

WITH THE SIX-HOUR TIME DIFFERENCE, we managed to make it to the Costas' family home in Oyster Bay around midnight Eastern, which officially put us at day 365—the anniversary of Rose's death. There wasn't a chance in hell we'd let it be the day Bella and Callie died.

We fought hard with everything we had in us to remain mission-focused and to think like operators en route back, not like men who'd had our hearts ripped from our chests. It hadn't been easy, though. I'd be lying if I denied I'd thrown up twice on the flight home. Alessandro hadn't bothered to hide that he'd done the same. We'd both cycled through the stages of grief, landing on anger more often than not.

Resting my elbows on the desk, I bowed my head into my palms, unable to watch his parents' security footage anymore.

Alessandro had replayed it a dozen times, watching the men fast-rope in and knock out most of the security with gas as his father had tried to get his mother and Callie to their safe room.

Eyes remaining closed, I listened to Alessandro's repeated mouse clicks as Constantine conversed in Italian from somewhere in the office. He was getting another update about his father from his mom. His dad was out of surgery but still in ICU, and not yet awake.

"I promise, I'm bringing them home," Constantine finished in English before ending the call, and I lifted my head and swiveled the chair around to look back and forth between him and Alessandro.

Feds were still there and swarming the property, combing through the evidence of our failure. We should've seen this coming. These assholes had been ahead of us at every turn.

"She was in the bathroom when my father tried to get to her and pull her to safety," Alessandro said in a daze. "I'm going to retrace her steps."

"That won't bring her back." Constantine shook his head. "Never mind. Do what you need to do," he added as his phone rang. "It's Enzo."

Alessandro remained seated as Constantine placed the call on speaker.

"I'm taking Maria to the hospital," Enzo rushed out. "She's in labor. The stress . . ." He let his words trail off before picking up in a new direction. "This is my fault. Actions have consequences, and I killed that man, setting off the chain reaction. And now everything is fucked, and I'm just . . ." He switched to Italian, and Constantine hit him right back with something in his native tongue.

We needed a target. A fix on their location so we could stop feeling so damn helpless sitting around. My worst fears of losing Bella were happening in real time, and if we didn't get actionable intelligence soon, I'd officially lose my goddamn mind.

Frustrated with their Italian back-and-forth blame game I was sure was happening, I finally spoke up. "Be with your wife and daughter. Just focus on protecting your family."

"I'm so sorry," Maria whispered over the line between deep breaths. From the sounds of it, her contractions were getting closer. "You'll get them both back. And Dad will be okay, too. No one is dying today. It's going to be a celebration of life, you hear me?" she added between her labored breathing. "My babies are going to be born on the day we finally put the past behind us once and for all. There will be only happy moments to look forward to."

Alessandro slowly stood, holding the top of his chair, catching my eyes.

"I need you to confirm you heard me loud and clear," Maria remarked. "Do not piss off a woman in labor. Tell me everything will be fine."

"You have my word." Constantine spoke for all of us while I grappled with trying to not lose it all over again.

I squeezed my eyes closed, and memories of my time with Bella over the years flipped through my mind. *We're meant to be together, and so help me . . . Bianca, please watch over your sister. Keep her safe until we can get to her.*

"I'm so sorry." Enzo's broken voice hauled me back to their father's office, and I opened my eyes. "This is my fault. Green must've found the statement I gave to the CIA when we signed the deal, right down to where we tortured Keith's brother and how I took his life. If I hadn't opened my mouth, Keith wouldn't know what really happened."

"You should never have tried to sacrifice yourself in the first place, throwing yourself on the sword like that," Alessandro said in a somber tone. "Because we were all there. All complicit. But regardless, Keith would've found out about this some other way. Don't you dare blame yourself."

"He's right. I need you to compartmentalize and focus on your family. We have it covered here." Constantine continued to remain in command of his emotions, trying to keep us all focused and in line. "Keith's brother was a killer, just not Bianca's. If we didn't take his life, he'd have hurt more women. So, this conversation is over. Guilt won't bring Izzy and Callie back. End of story, you hear me?" He looked at me, then to Alessandro, for confirmation. "The only assholes to blame for what happened are the men we're going to kill today when we save our family."

Alessandro stroked his jaw, eyes on me, the rage once again simmering behind his grays. He was ready to go. The beast was back, and we needed him. Now I needed to wake the fuck up, too.

"Just . . . keep me updated." Enzo sounded as lost as I felt. "I'll have my phone on me. Let me know when Dad wakes up."

"We will." Constantine swapped a few more words with him and Maria before ending the call, turning his attention to a new problem standing in the doorway.

Special Agent Clarke, of-fucking-course.

Clarke lifted his hand as a request to hear him out, then locked his arms over his blue-and-gold FBI raid jacket. "Dean's house was broken into an hour ago while he was asleep. He was stabbed before his security detail could get to him. He's in surgery. A different hospital from your father since he was in Manhattan."

"What?" The word barreled fast from my mouth, but honestly, I shouldn't have been surprised by this. Dean was the AG who'd helped arrange immunity for the Costas after killing Keith's brother, orchestrating the deal between their father and the CIA.

Clarke pushed away from the doorframe. "Listen, Maverick told me what happened, and why I was really given those files. I shouldn't have handed Kit the AAR from your op, and she won't be getting the other nineteen reports. I also didn't know Maverick's kid was at risk, or I'd never have . . ." He cleared his throat. "Now I know what's really going on. Well, some of the story. I can draw a conclusion as to why this house was hit, at least."

"No," I said, shaking my head. "We're not doing this now." If he planned to try and stop our rescue mission, he'd wind up in the hospital, too. No fucks or regrets given.

Clarke met my eyes, and I saw something there that had been noticeably absent in the hospital. Compassion?

"Look, while we may not see eye to eye on how you conduct your, uh, side business, it's clear to me who our enemies are, and they're not in this room." He turned to the side, patting the doorframe. "I won't be stopping you from doing what needs to be done, but if you can keep those fuckers alive so the FBI can have a go at them, it'd be appreciated. And if not . . . just be sure Adelina's nearby, and leave before more badges show up."

Yeah, I didn't expect that. "One less obstacle to deal with is fine by me," I said after Clarke left.

"Same." Alessandro turned toward his brother. "Holler the second Echo Team and the others are here and we have a location." He started for the door, presumably resuming his time-killing mission until we could save Bella and Callie.

Constantine checked his watch. "Roman and his team are en route. Adelina picked up Sydney from the airport twenty minutes ago. They're on their way. All we need is a location, and we're spinning up."

At least we had a team of SEALs prepared to step up, along with a real-life Lara Croft wanting her own vengeance against these assholes for threatening her son. And while Alfie's team had to hang back in Spain to wrap things up, he'd flown with us to have our six here. Since Rose's brother—Keith *Oberland*, not Keith Jenkins—and her husband clearly had an arsenal and their own militia at their disposal, we'd take all the help and resources we could get.

As Alessandro left the room, I removed my phone from my pocket, hating playing the waiting game as much as he did. Opening Instagram, I checked to see if there were 365 posts yet. The friend request hadn't been accepted, and we'd yet to convince anyone to unlock the account for us because of privacy laws. But what was more concerning was the fact Falcon Falls and Echo Team, who had some of the world's best cyber experts, couldn't crack the account.

"Follow him, will you?" Constantine tilted his head toward the hallway. "I have a hunch I want to check out."

I stowed my phone instead of chucking it at the wall like I wanted to do. "What kind of hunch?"

"Something Enzo said got me thinking. If Keith read Enzo's statement from the CIA and knew where we killed his brother . . ."

I walked back a step as it clicked. A possible location. Thank fuck.

"That factory is still owned by my family. That whole row of properties down by that port, actually. All still abandoned because of what we did. My father decided not to sell off the properties, so they're sitting there desolate and empty."

"And you think he took them back to where this all began for him, where we killed his brother?"

"Gut feeling." He unlocked his phone, preparing to make another call. "I'm going to divert Echo Team there to do some recon. I'd suggest we jump on a helo now and head over, but I don't want us going the wrong way if we need to be elsewhere."

The Art of You

I nodded, feeling like that was all I was capable of doing, still stuck between two modes: extreme worry and rabid rage. "I'll let Alessandro know."

I left the office, walking fast, fueled by adrenaline at the possibility we might finally get one step ahead of the architects of this madness.

Upstairs, I found Alessandro on his knees in one of the hall bathrooms, holding on to something.

"What is it?" I asked him, barely registering the notification sounding from my pocket.

"It's positive," he said in a strained voice while unfurling his hand. "My wife's pregnant. She was taking a test when those assholes . . ." He lifted his chin to the ceiling, breathing hard and fast.

I wasn't sure what the hell to say or do. The only thing that'd help this man was to save his family. That was the only way I'd survive this, too.

"We're getting them back today. I swear to God we are," I said while reaching for my phone.

Slapping a hand to the counter, my breath froze in my lungs when I saw my friend request had finally been accepted.

I clicked on the notification, and at the sight of all 364 images there, I collapsed to my knees in front of Alessandro. Blistering heat shot through my body as I processed what I was seeing.

"They've been watching all of us," he rasped. "My wife and I in Nashville. Maria and Enzo in Charlotte. You at the bar. And Izzy . . . fuck, they must have cameras inside her house."

The blood drained from my face. I had to swallow back the bile rising up in my throat.

Images of Bella in a towel inside her bedroom. Several of her in only her underwear and bra. One of just her bear on the bed, and why in the hell . . .

I let my thoughts go as it dawned on me. "The gas leak. That's when he planted the cameras to take these photos." *Fuck.* "I guarantee he planted a tracker in her bear. Hell, any number of things at her place could have trackers or listening devices."

"She had the bear in Spain." He muttered something in Italian, then bit out, "Alfie said Keith was the one to track us to the hotel. That's probably how."

"Keith couldn't take the chance he'd lose track of us if we didn't play ball and meet Alfie. He'd have contingencies in place." *The post of the bear is to fuck with us.* Consider him successful. This guy had been five steps ahead of us at every turn.

"I'm going to kill them," Alessandro said steadily in a dark voice, echoing my thoughts as a new image was posted.

It was of Bella and Callie, tied up in chairs, eyes closed, heads hanging forward.

My stomach dropped all over again as I stared at them.

"He has them at our factory." Alessandro abruptly stood, becoming mission-focused, while pocketing the pregnancy test.

I forced myself to stand as well. "Constantine was right."

Alessandro's pupils were dilated, the darkness smothering whatever humanity was inside him. He didn't have to say anything else, I was already on the same ready-to-commit-murder page.

"They want us there where it all started."

Alessandro snarled, "Then that's where this ends for good."

* * *

"Pull him back," Echo's team leader ordered, eyes on the small screen on Echo Three's wrist. "They'll bloody kill him if they see him," he remarked, his British accent pushing through. "And we're not losing anyone today."

Echo Three gave the order, and his canine about-faced and immediately left his current position. He'd sniffed out explosives and confirmed our fears. Enough C4 to take out the entire building was rigged to blow inside the garage, directly below the room where Bella and Callie were tied up.

We only knew they were alive, as well as their exact location, thanks to impressive tech Echo Team came equipped with, including a drone the size of a bee that gave us an inside view of the factory. All that intel boiled down to deactivating a weapon while engaging with twenty armed tangos without letting Keith or Green turn this into a suicide mission. I had to believe they were fine with going down as long as we went with them, and that was our biggest obstacle—fighting an enemy willing to die.

"You clear the room for me, and I can defuse the bomb. I'll have my wife in my ear walking me through it," Roman said.

Echo One turned his attention to me. While killing the power and jamming the cell signals was a good start, the assholes inside still had the advantage. They had the women we loved in direct danger. One wrong move, and we'd lose them.

"I say we have a mad minute," Echo Two, the Teamguy with the deep Southern drawl, offered, standing alongside his leader. "We go in quick and dirty in those first sixty seconds. Shoot every threat possible in the kill zone."

As their Belgian Malinois padded up to us, Echo One nodded. "I agree. My guys will provide cover for Roman so he can defuse the explosives. That means you'll need to deal with the tangos on every other floor."

Constantine shifted my way, adding, "Delta Team will

handle the breaching points for a quick entry for Alpha and Echo."

Alfie, Adelina, Malik, Marc, and a few of our other operators were on Delta, while Alessandro, Constantine, Sydney, and I were Alpha tonight.

"I can mount the 249 and set the rest of the line for the ambush," Alfie offered since he had the M249 SAW at his side. It wasn't as heavy duty as the 240, but it'd serve its purpose. The belt-fed machine gun could quickly and easily take out a large number of tangos, clearing a path to get us to Bella and Callie within that mad minute.

And we really only had one fucking minute. Any more than that, and these assholes might shoot to kill before we could get there, or set off the charge and take down the whole building.

"What's our ROE?" someone on Echo asked, deferring to his team leader.

Echo One and Constantine swapped a quick look before the Brit answered. "They shoot first, then defend your position and open up on them. Neutralize every threat without killing them if you can, but use your best judgment."

"Once Echo Four confirms the bomb has been defused," Constantine said, knocking his night-vision goggles in place, "we move in for the rescue."

"Roger that." Echo Three patted his dog's head, then resecured his brain bucket on him. "We'll get them back. Don't worry. We run these kinds of ops all the time."

"We need to step on it," Echo One announced, showing me the small screen on his wrist that gave him a view of Bella and Callie from our small drone.

I leaned over to look just as Keith stretched his arm out, a 9mm in hand. My body locked tight, and I went for my M4, tipping my head so my NVGs fell into place. "Move out. Now."

Chapter 44

Isabella

Five Minutes Before

I was stuck in limbo. Lost somewhere between reality and my past with no idea how long I'd been gone. The drugs were heavy, and I kept skipping back and forth between the bleak here and now and the happy but diaphanous walks down memory lane the drugs lulled me to.

I wasn't here. No, I couldn't be.

I was walking in Central Park, the crunch of leaves beneath my boots on a fall day.

Or texting Hudson while sipping coffee as the sun peeked over the buildings before work.

In the Hamptons in our garden with Bianca as she laughed at something funny I'd said.

Attempting to resist the drugs again and face hell, I opened my eyes, hoping Callie wasn't there with me, and that the last time I glimpsed her during these sandman-like hours was a hallucination.

My eyes dropped closed the moment I laid eyes on her tied

The Art of You

to a chair, the same as me. *No, no, no. Why are you here? Alessandro will lose his mind even more, and...*

The tears that should've come still didn't spill.

What drugs did he dope me up with? Instead of fear and despair, I felt oddly numb.

Chancing one more look, I parted my eyes to catch Keith setting a camera up on a tripod inside the desolate, cold space.

"You're awake." Keith's voice effectively snapped me free from the safe haven of my mind I'd been living in.

I now had to face what was happening, and the drugs lost their ability to dull my senses with every step he took my way.

He squatted before me so we were eye level. There was something dark and sinister in his eyes that had me choking back the words I wanted to hiss.

Keith cupped my chin, and a shiver bolted down my spine, winding into my arms to where my hands were cuffed behind my back. "If we had more time, I'd make you mine. Maybe you could even learn to love me."

What. The. Fuck? My stomach protested and my words died on my tongue. I still couldn't seem to find my voice. It was lost somewhere between that fall day in the park and summering in the Hamptons. The safe space of my past before my world had become dark when Bianca died.

"I've been watching you since June. I've been in your house a few times, actually. There was never a gas leak." He spelled it out for me, the dark edge of his voice cutting me in half right along with the truth. He lowered his hand from my chin to my throat but didn't squeeze. "You sleep with that bear every night, so I got a little worried when Calliope over here didn't pack him for you when you were at the hospital." He licked his lips slowly and deliberately while staring at me as I blinked, stunned and speechless.

He'd watched me? Been in my home? What did he do to

my freaking bear? How had I not sensed this? My stomach roiled, realizing what else he'd have seen, then. Thank God I always covered myself in bed when I touched . . .

Now the tears broke through the haze of the drugs, encouraging a smile from the sick bastard.

"You could say I've developed a bit of an obsession with you. I guess that's what happens when you watch someone as beautiful as you all the time." With his free hand, he reached around and fisted my hair, tugging the strands and demanding my attention.

His eyes dipped to my mouth before ravaging a slow, sick path of destruction down my body to my lap.

"Let her go." Callie's throaty rasp had me trying to twist to look at her, but his hold of me was too strong, and my efforts were wasted. "Don't touch her."

"I'll get to you in a moment, Miss . . . what does your husband like to call you again? Right, right." He kept hold of me, smiling, while turning his head her way. "Little Miss Tennessee Whiskey."

"You son of a bitch." At least her voice was working, unlike mine, and her chair legs made thud-like noises against the concrete as if she were trying to physically hop her way to him.

I was as stuck in place as were the words behind my lips, though. Feeling trapped inside one of the world's most disturbing paintings. Like a Francisco Goya mural. Not so much afraid right now, but sick to my stomach.

"Now, what was I saying?" He dismissed Callie's continued pleas to leave me alone and found my eyes again while pulling my hair harder. "I thought I lost you Friday night in that crash, and I felt something I hadn't in a long time." He angled his head. "Fear." A slow smile slipped across his lips. "Because you're only allowed to die by *my* hand." He narrowed his gaze on my mouth like it was his next target.

I jerked my head back when I realized what he was about to do. He covered my mouth with his in a sloppy, disgusting kiss, and I did the first thing that came to mind as Callie yelled for him to stop.

I sank my teeth into his bottom lip, hoping to draw blood.

He finally let go of my hair and throat to break free from the strong grip my teeth had. With his face hovering only inches from mine, he ran his tongue over his bloody lip, dragging it across his white teeth and following it up with a creepy-as-fuck smile.

And then the fear hit. My body had yet to catch up with my head, because I was still lacking the anxiety-driven chills I'd expected to have.

"They're going to kill you for that. For all of this." Callie's words broke me free of my frozen-in-shock state.

"I'm certainly hoping they'll try, or I'd be very disappointed," the asshole said nonchalantly.

I was a second away from finally getting my voice to work when I clamped my teeth shut at the loud sound of a door banging closed and an angry voice echoing through the space. "What the hell is going on? I just saw your last Instagram post."

Keith dragged his thumb along the line of his lips, catching more blood before standing tall to face off with whoever was there.

I looked over at Callie sitting next to me, only five or so feet away. No tears, just a look of defiance and anger simmering in her eyes. The drugs had to be losing their grip on her, too.

"Green," Callie mouthed, and I followed her gaze to see Rose's husband rounding our chairs to confront Keith.

"What in the hell is going on?" Green demanded as Keith went to the tripod. "You said the Instagram account was just to throw them off. That the cameras were to keep an eye on them. That photo you had me deliver, and the explosion . . . all of it was just to fuck with them and ensure we set them on the path we wanted, and . . ." Green's voice trailed off and he tore both hands through his hair. "You promised no one innocent would get hurt. So, why are they here in the same factory your brother died, and why in God's name did you post the location to Instagram? Why are there over twenty armed men here?"

"You forgot to ask about the C4 in the garage. You miss that when you came in?" Keith played the role of psychopath rather well. His voice may have displayed a casual arrogance, but he seemed even more unhinged than his brother—the man Enzo had killed *here* apparently.

I hadn't recognized where we were before because of the drugs, but now it all made sense. Keith brought us back to where, in his mind, it all started.

"No one innocent gets hurt. You promised me." Green stabbed the air in my direction.

"I didn't take the pregnant one." Standing behind the tripod, focused on the screen of the camera as if watching me through the lens, Keith shrugged. "That's me being a good boy." He lifted his chin and winked at Green.

Oh, the sick bastard. But that meant . . . *Maria's okay, thank God.*

"You never told me you planned to kidnap these women." Green's voice cracked. "Do you have the AG tied up here somewhere, too?"

Jesus, was this really happening?

"No, I sent someone to his house to kill him." Keith stepped around the camera, his hand going to the sidearm strapped to his outer thigh.

"Fuck. This is . . ." Green winced, shaking his head. "I can't be involved in this. The plan was to use them to kill the terrorists for us. Share the results and consequences of the bad intel with the world that led to Rose dying." He gripped his hair, pulling at it. "Then, and only then, we'd expose the truth that they killed your brother. But at no point, did we discuss *murdering* these women in the name of revenge."

He was spiraling, and this could be good for us.

Green lifted his chin to the ceiling, breathing hard as his hands went to his hips. "I got you the money. The intel. I did everything you needed. Hid your real identities so deep not even God himself could find the truth until I wanted anyone to."

"There is no God, or my family would be alive." Keith shot an angry look at Green while removing his 9mm from the holster. "What'd you really expect me to do once you told me the truth about what you found out about my brother?" He gestured back and forth between me and Callie with his gun. "I read Lorenzo Costa's statement he gave the CIA. He murdered my brother right here. Payback is a motherfucking bitch, and he's about to find out the hard way. Everyone dies but him. Living with all that blood on his hands will be a fate much worse than death."

At his words, I finally managed to speak. "Your brother was a killer. He wasn't innocent. I know that's what you think, but he killed innocent people, just not my sister."

"You're lying," Keith snarled. "There was no evidence of that. I'd have known. Green would've found out."

"There is evidence, just not at the DOD. My friends can prove it to you, though." Falcon had the files, but I highly doubted this psychopath would hit pause on his plan and let me play the phone-a-friend game.

"You're full of shit," Keith barked out. "Green discovered your brothers took out Bianca's real killer last year, and Rose joined the military to try and right our brother's wrongs, the same as I did. It was all for nothing."

"No, you joined the military because you wanted an excuse

to kill people and you hid behind a uniform to do it. You're sick. A disgrace to our country and to your sister's memory." My lack of filter rose from the dead. The drugs waned, and the words sailed hard, fast, and free.

Keith immediately crossed the room, shouldering past Green on his way to me. "Maybe you're right." His smile was bloody, only adding to the terrifying look. "Maybe I do enjoy killing. But I'm still going to make your family pay." He turned toward Callie, raising his weapon, and Green doubled down on his feelings about the situation by jumping in front of her, spreading his arms wide.

Oh, God. "No," I cried. "Please, don't. She has nothing to do with this."

"Rose would never be okay with you killing these women." Green's voice was shaking hard, and whatever his involvement in all of this, I was grateful he had a spine and clearly some morals. "I can't let you do this."

"Move, or I'll shoot you." Keith kept his arm straight, steadily aimed, only flinching when the lights flickered just before the power went out. A shot was fired, and Green screamed.

"Callie? Are you okay?" I rasped as gunfire exploded from outside the room.

"I'm okay. Not hit," she let me know as Green moaned from somewhere in the pitch-black room.

"I'm going to strangle the life from you." Keith's breath scraped across my skin, and a moment later, I felt his hand around my throat.

I had to believe the current chaos was the cavalry coming; I needed to buy time until they could get to us.

Using all my weight, rocking the chair to the side, I fell over, and Keith lost his hold of me. Precious seconds were purchased with that maneuver before the bastard found me on the floor fast. Two hands encircled my throat this time, and the cry for help died on my tongue, never escaping.

Dizziness started to take over. Oxygen wasn't making it to my brain. But then the distinct sound of a round being fired nearby made its way to my ears, and Keith hissed and let go of me.

The lights came back on a second later as I gasped for air.

"Calliope. Izzy." Alessandro's voice sent a flood of hope and relief to my ears.

I slowly parted my lids, twisting around to try and locate my brother.

Keith was on the ground by my feet, bleeding—shot in the arm from the looks of it—and as he scrambled to reach for his gun on the floor, he took another round in the shoulder. His body jolted from the contact.

I finally spotted two masked men on approach. NVGs on top of their helmets. Skeleton masks on, only their eyes visible.

"Hudson," I mouthed as our eyes connected.

He had his rifle in hand as he came over and kicked Keith's weapon away as Alessandro closed in on Green.

Hudson crouched alongside the chair and helped me upright off the floor. "Give me one moment." And although I couldn't see his mouth, I saw the *I love you* in his eyes.

Tears fell as I nodded, and he brushed a gentle caress along the side of my head.

Alessandro peered at his wife, giving her a hard nod I read as *I love you*, then locked on to Green as he tried to army-crawl away from him. At the same time, Hudson shifted his rifle to his back and faced his target—Keith.

"I have a remote to a bomb. You touch me, and I take us all down," Keith warned, rolling to his back while holding something in his hand for everyone to see.

"Go ahead," Alessandro told him. "It's already been deactivated." My brother swapped his rifle for some type of long chain he'd produced from some-freaking-where.

I suddenly realized the rest of the building was eerily quiet, which meant our guys had control of the situation. Down to two targets. *Thank God.*

My gaze volleyed back and forth between Alessandro and Hudson and their quick movements.

Hudson bent over and grabbed Keith by the ankle, stopping him from trying to get away, then jerked him backward.

Alessandro knelt forward and wrapped the chain around Green's neck and tugged it. "You fuck with my family, you fuck with me." He pulled him up off the ground as Green bled from where he'd been shot by Keith.

"No, wait, stop," Callie cried out, beating me to the words I was about to say, but Alessandro was too focused on his own revenge to hear her. His rage was consuming him the way Hudson's currently was as he railed on Keith with his fists.

So distracted by what was going down before me, I barely noticed we had company.

Constantine crouched before me, lowering his skeleton mask. "Are you two okay?" he asked us.

Distracted by my brother choking the life from Green, holding him off the ground like he had superhuman strength, I sputtered instead, "Stop him."

Another masked man I didn't recognize went around us to Callie as she continued to beg Alessandro to stop throttling the life from Green.

"Alessandro," Callie implored again once freed from the chair. "Don't."

"Stop Alessandro," I told Constantine as he uncuffed me.

"I can't do that." Constantine shook his head. "They deserve to die."

I stole a look at Hudson mounted on top of Keith, striking

him with severe intensity, blood covering his gloved hands. "Green tried to save us," I let him know.

"He took a bullet for me," Callie added, bolting to her husband.

Constantine helped me stand as Callie tugged Alessandro's arm, urging him to look at her.

He slowly pivoted his head and whispered, "Calliope, please."

"He doesn't deserve to die." Tears flew down her face. "I'm okay. Look at me. I'm—I'm okay."

Alessandro bowed his head, finally relenting and letting go of Green to take Callie in his arms.

Green crumpled to the ground, quickly removing the chain from around his throat, gasping for air.

Constantine went over and secured his wrists with cuffs, not taking any chances, and I focused back on our last HVT, Keith.

"I need you." I wasn't sure who Hudson was calling for, and when I faced him, he was still on top of Keith but no longer punching him. The man was limp and lifeless beneath him. "Constantine, I need you to stop me before I kill him." He lowered his mask below his chin. "If you don't physically move me away, I'll do it," he gritted out as if it took all his energy to say that.

Constantine quickly helped Hudson up. "Go to her," he told him, gesturing with his head toward me.

My legs were heavy from the drugs, but I refused to let them slow me down.

Hudson tossed his helmet to the ground, then hauled me against him. "I told you I'd come for you." I felt the tears break free from him as he held me tightly, the emotional dam collapsing. "I'm sorry it took me so long to get to you, but I promise I'll never lose you again." He unwrapped his arms from my body to cup my cheeks, both of us crying. "Are you okay?"

"I am now," I sputtered with a nod, flinching at the feel of something hitting my leg.

I peered down to find a dog's paw on me.

"Fellow frogman," Hudson murmured.

I swallowed the stuttery emotional breath catching in my throat. "Frog-dog, huh?" I reached down to pet him, sniffling as I met Hudson's eyes again. "I didn't realize that was a thing."

"Pulled out all the stops to get to you two." He blinked back more tears, dropping his forehead to mine, still holding my face.

"I'd expect nothing less." I stopped petting the dog and wrapped my hand over Hudson's arm. "You showed mercy."

"No, that wasn't mercy." His brows tightened. "Keeping him alive without anyone here to love him, that's torture. That's hell." His glossy blues held my eyes as he stared at me. "You saved me from the hell I'd been living in, and so help me, Bella, I never want to go back."

Chapter 45

Isabella

IT WAS A LOT TO PROCESS. Like, a lot-a lot. Because even though we were all safe and okay, I'd been on the other side of someone's screen for months. Watched by a madman. My every movement under the scrutiny of a predator. How does one just forget that?

We'd been rescued three hours ago, but without the drugs numbing me, it was hard not to remember the exchange with Keith, and his ugly words. His despicable actions.

I have to forget it, though. I have to. He wins if I let what he did hurt me.

"I should've killed him." From the side of my hospital bed, Hudson was reading my thoughts. As always.

Refusing to be separated, Callie and I were in the same room, her bed right next to mine. Alessandro was currently pacing alongside her while we waited for the doctor to make an appearance and send us home.

I mean, physically I felt okay. The fact I'd been stalked and watched by a maniac would take more time to recover from.

The man had defiled my privacy, and my bear. "No, I'm glad he'll rot in his prison cell instead," I finally answered him.

"He kissed you." He bowed his forehead to our clasped palms, his angry tone jarring loose more emotions inside me.

I probably shouldn't have told you that.

Hudson lifted his head, his sad eyes meeting mine, and I knew exactly what I had to do. What we *all* had to do. Get over what happened. Otherwise, guilt would suck us both into an ugly never-ending vortex of *what-ifs*, and we might lose our happily-ever-after to *what-could-have-beens*.

We were alive and safe. The past finally needed to take its place in our rearview.

"We're going to get through this," I promised. "Dad is okay. Awake and talking. Nothing can take that man down." I forced a smile. "Even that AG is going to live. Only the bad guys were hurt." I'd keep reminding all of us of the facts until we truly absorbed them as true. Baby steps, I supposed.

At the sight of the doctor finally joining us, Alessandro abruptly whipped around and rasped, "Tell me the baby is okay."

Baby?

"Baby?" Callie echoed my thoughts aloud. "Wait, what? How do you . . . ?"

"I found the test you took." Alessandro reached for her hand and dropped into the chair next to her.

"It was positive?" She stared at him in shock. And well, she wasn't the only one.

"I didn't have a chance to see the results before they took me." Callie looked expectantly at the doctor who just might hold the key to us truly letting go of the pain of what went down to move on to something happy and wonderful.

"Both of your bloodwork is good. And as for you, Mrs. Costa, your levels are excellent." She smiled. "My guess is you're about six weeks pregnant. You should make an appointment with your OBGYN when you leave here."

The doctor's words had Alessandro on his feet, bending over the bed to kiss his wife. Then he held her waist and lowered his mouth to her stomach over her hospital gown to kiss her there, too.

"We're having a baby," he said in a daze as he lifted his head, his glossy eyes on his wife. Tears fell as she cradled his face between her palms.

"See." I sniffled. "Everything is going to be okay." I rested my hand on top of Hudson's that held my other palm, meeting his eyes.

He gave me a light affirmative nod that he was on board with my words, and I desperately needed him to be. No going back to any dark places allowed.

"Congratulations," the doctor said after I did, then added, "You can see your father in a few hours. One at a time, though." As she left the room, I caught sight of the governor, still hovering out there despite Hudson repeatedly telling him to take a hike.

The last thing on Hudson's mind right now was any one-on-one time with his father.

At the sight of Constantine heading our way, wordlessly side-eyeing the governor, I sat taller in the bed. "Enzo call?" I'd take all the good news we could get.

Constantine closed the door, pretty much in the governor's face. "Emergency C-section, but Maria and the babies are fine. We have two nephews." He grinned from ear to ear in pride. It was adorable when the grump showed his softer side. "Aldo and Massimo. Enzo will FaceTime us when they're in a room."

Well then. Relief swelled in my chest, and I could truly breathe easily now. Screw Keith and what he did to me. I was stronger than him and what he did, dammit. We all were.

"I, uh, miss something here?" Constantine gestured with his phone back and forth between our beds, reading the room.

Plus, there was Alessandro still glued to his wife, half of his body on her bed as he continued to smother her with affection. "My wife is pregnant."

The way that man said "my wife" had me anxious to hear the same from Hudson one of these days.

"Damn, wow, okay." Constantine cleared his throat. "I'm happy for you." He hugged the both of them, then turned my way, brows lifting. "Don't tell me you have news, too."

I laughed. "None that I can think of, no."

His face muscles relaxed, and it was actually kind of comical.

"You can't get pregnant quite that fast," I teased, and Hudson squeezed my hand, a little, *Don't push your luck with him*, embedded in his touch. *Right.* The idea of us being together-together was still new for my family.

Constantine stared at Hudson, eyes narrowing. "You may not have to worry about me anymore, but let's not give our dad, who just survived two rounds, a heart attack, okay?"

"You have my word on that," Hudson was quick to say. "I, uh, mean it this time." He looked at me, giving me an innocent shrug. "Babies after marriage only."

Marriage. Babies. We'd gone from being held hostage and nearly murdered to celebrating life and fresh starts in the blink of an eye.

It felt like yesterday I'd sold myself on the idea I needed to officially move on from Hudson, worried he'd never feel the same, and there he was looking like he just might drop to one knee any minute.

Before I could make any more comments or push my luck with my siblings, there was a knock at the door. Constantine opened up, letting in Adelina and Sydney. He also went for round two of blocking Hudson's dad from joining with a lovely door to the face again.

"Thank you for your help. And please send my gratitude to Roman's teammates, too," I told them, then zeroed in on Adelina in particular. "Will Agent Clarke give you a hard time about what happened?"

"Clarke's had a change of heart. Which is the only reason why I'm not going to ensure he gets strung up on charges himself for passing the AAR from Hudson's op over to Kit," Adelina answered. "He's assured me the intel has all been destroyed, and she'll be writing a retraction piece."

"We believing him?" I asked, eyes on Hudson.

Hudson's mouth tightened into a firm line, before he remarked, "I'm going to try. He didn't stop us from doing what needed to be done, so."

"At least the AG survived. Seems like, despite Keith's best efforts to bring us down, the only ones that did die were the terrorists." Adelina mirrored what I'd said not too long ago in my efforts to not fall victim to what I'd learned Keith had done.

"How's that boy, by the way?" I asked at the memory. "Will he be okay?"

"Alfie's team handed him over to his aunt who lives in Paris," Hudson let me know. "Found out on the way to the factory, but I was a bit too focused on getting to you to process that development. The aunt seems stable. Safe. He should have a much better life with her and will hopefully not follow in his father's footsteps."

I let go of a sigh, one other thing I didn't need to worry about. "Everyone and everything really turned out okay." Maybe I'd need to repeat that a few hundred more times to believe it.

"Maybe not my ex-husband's job at the Pentagon," Sydney commented in a serious tone. "And he'll have to do some major groveling after hiding what happened from me, but yeah, looks like everything worked out exactly how it was meant to."

"Except one thing," Hudson remarked, drawing my eyes.

"What's that?" Constantine asked before I could.

"The exposé Green wanted shared with the world." Hudson smoothed his free hand over the top of mine. "Maybe that intel should be leaked. All twenty case files. The only way to pressure the government to do better might be to make sure the people know the truth." He added quickly, "Maybe not have Kit write it, though."

A slow smile crossed Adelina's face. "I just might know the perfect journalist for the job. Not really in the media business anymore, but I think my twin could still write the hell out of that article."

"Done." Hudson focused on me next, and second by second, I could see the dark edge and heavy pain losing its hold on him. He was coming back to life. "Maybe we should give your brother and Callie some privacy and get you into your own room."

Ah, he wanted me all to himself, he just couldn't say that in front of my brothers. I was ready to also be smothered in kisses for hours. Hugged for days. "*Or*, after we check on Dad, we could just head home."

"You can't seriously be thinking about going back to your place after what that animal did," Alessandro barked out, and uh, way to remind me.

I needed all new things. Clothes. Perfumes. Furniture. Everything. I'd be hitting reset after this. I angled my head at Hudson. "My *new* home," I said with a small smile. "If you think you can handle me living with you?"

Hudson leaned forward and brought his mouth to my ear, ignoring the fact we weren't alone. "Oh, I can more than handle you. All. Fucking. Day. Sweetheart."

The Art of You

Mmm. Nothing like my guy punctuating sexy words to officially suck me free from the orbit of what was left of my bad thoughts and back to sexy la-la land.

We had a lot of time to make up for, and I refused to let Keith's failed revenge plan stand in the way of our happiness.

I'd been a little nervous after being abducted that Hudson might use that as an excuse to pull away, blaming himself for my being taken. Then I'd have to spend a lot of energy bulldozing through his reservations. But he didn't appear to be pushing back, and instead, was drawing me closer. Quite literally. He had his arm wrapped around me, practically joining me on the bed.

Of course, he'd told me I had nothing to worry about in that hotel in Spain, and he really was a man of his word.

Now I was ready to give him one of my own.

Okay, maybe two. Like as in, *I do.*

Chapter 46

Isabella

Waxhaw, North Carolina - Two Weeks Later

Hudson standing outside the passenger door of our rental truck gave me a new appreciation for the ruggedly handsome cowboy look. *God bless the South.*

"Just a little rain, won't hurt ya, I swear." He gave me a boyish, charming smile, then removed his Stetson and set it over my head. "For protection."

As he stood there, offering me his hand to get out, chivalry became one of my new favorite words. I lived and breathed it every day with how he treated me.

But a few more seconds of gawking were needed. It wasn't like I hadn't already gaped at his backside in our hotel room. Or ran my hands over his washboard abs while we'd showered together.

I sighed, continuing to stare at my Texan in his fitted jeans, white tee, and cowboy boots. The air was misty, and it was hardly raining, but a few drops hit his face as he ran a hand through his hair, mussing it up even more in a ridiculously sexy way.

This was technically our first official date. Well, one that involved leaving his bed where we'd spent the majority of our time since our nightmare ended.

"Ma'am." He held out his hand again, waiting for me to join him in the parking lot so we could have dinner at Maria's sister's restaurant, Talia's Tuscan Grille. Enzo was the head chef here, but he wouldn't be in tonight, still taking time off to spend with Maria and the twins.

We'd flown here to meet the newborns five days ago, and with any luck, my dad would be cleared to travel soon so my parents could join us. I wouldn't put it past him to ignore the doctor's orders and come anyway if he didn't get the go-ahead by tomorrow, though.

Callie and Alessandro would be heading back to Nashville tomorrow, but Hudson and I decided we'd stay a few extra days as a mini-getaway before returning home. I wasn't eager to be back in New York, and the South was growing on me. It didn't hurt that Hudson seemed to be more relaxed down here, too. A little space between us and what happened back home was just what we needed.

"You keep staring at me like that, and we'll never make it inside." He'd laid on the husky drawl that time, and his tone slid under my skin and heated my body.

My ass puckered at the mere memory of Hudson's finger exploring it while we showered. He'd squeezed my ass cheek with his other hand, tonguing my clit, the spray of the water enveloping us. Dirty-clean-dirty-clean. Wash-rinse-and-a-delicious-repeat. I'd never want to shower another way again.

"Mmm. Don't threaten me with a good time," I teased, knowing it was a cliché line, but I didn't care.

Hudson rested his hand on top of the truck and leaned in closer.

The rain was starting to pick up, and I wouldn't so much mind seeing his white shirt meld to his hard frame. But the dress beneath my jean jacket—courtesy of the still warm weather in Charlotte—was a thin material, and wouldn't leave much to the imagination if it became wet.

Already facing him, exposing my cowgirl boots, I scooted forward a bit more and reached for him, hooking my arm behind his neck, careful not to knock my new hat off in the process. "Thinking about what you're going to have for dessert, aren't you?"

He smirked. "Oh, you know exactly what I'll be eating." He playfully lifted his brows twice before setting his mouth to mine in a slow, soft kiss.

God, I was so ridiculously happy. No night terrors had followed either of us after what happened at the factory, which was almost shocking. But maybe that was because we'd kept ourselves busy with happy family news, my moving in with him, and property searches for a new home together.

The sound of an engine close by had us breaking the kiss and turning our heads in that direction. Enzo parked and exited the antique-looking Porsche, joining us by the truck.

"You tell him we were coming?" I asked Hudson. "He's not supposed to be working."

Enzo shielded his face from the rain with a black ball cap. "This isn't mine. Just taking it for a little joy ride." Neither of us had asked him the question he seemed eager to answer, but I'd been a little curious.

"You do need a replacement Porsche," I reminded him. "You ever find out if the airbag really was tampered with?"

"Shockingly, just bad luck." Enzo frowned. "I might buy a

fixer-upper, though, and work on it at Ryan's auto body garage with him."

Enzo's brother-in-law, Ryan, was a retired Navy SEAL married to Maria's sister. That was another long, but beautiful story. They had an adorable son, Dante, who Hudson and I had babysat just yesterday so his parents could steal a quiet afternoon together.

Seeing Hudson with Dante, my niece, Chiara, and the twins . . . just all of them . . . *Le sigh*. He was such a good man and would make a hell of a dad.

"Why are you here?" I finally asked my brother. "You should be home."

"I heard you had reservations tonight, and I can't have you eating here unless it's my food."

"Well, I'm not about to turn down your cooking," Hudson joked, patting his stomach. "We were just about to head inside."

"Mind if I steal a word with my brother first?" I asked him, and he looked me up and down before nodding.

"Maybe not in the rain in that dress." Hudson urged my legs inside the truck so he could close the door. He handed Enzo the truck keys and started for the restaurant.

As Enzo climbed into the driver's seat, I set the cowboy hat on my lap and turned to face him.

"I know what you're going to say." He rested his arm across the wheel. "I'm fine. I'm not going to spiral and blame myself. None of us could've predicted this would happen. It was out of our control." Oh, he'd for sure rehearsed that line. "If you, Callie, and Dad weren't okay, then I'd for sure have lost it, but you're all good, so I promise, I'm doing my best to let go. I have a lot to keep me distracted."

I reached for his hand and squeezed. I supposed that was progress.

He met my eyes and demanded, "Now, you have to promise me you'll try and draw again. I heard from a reliable source you're considering not doing it. And if it's Keith's fault, I will break into prison and kill him myself."

I don't doubt you will. My shoulders slumped. *And maybe I keep picturing Keith's creepy face watching me every time I try to paint.* "It's been so long, maybe I forgot how." Also the truth.

"Nope." His lips tightened briefly. "That'd be like me saying I forgot how to take a life since it's been, you know, like . . . months." He exhaled. "Anywayyyy."

I held back a smile as he took a page from my playbook. *LOL.* And dammit, I did it again. Just thought "lol" in my head. I really did need to disconnect from technology for a bit. Maybe some canvas and acrylics would be the best therapy. "I'll try. You have my word." Since my brothers and Hudson were all about the whole "my word is my bond" thing, I supposed I could jump on board, too.

"It's inside you, I promise." He patted my arm and squeezed my wrist. "You've got this."

I looked over at the restaurant, thinking about our family. "Food is your art. Writing was Bianca's."

"And Alessandro's passion is his wife." Enzo laughed. "And maybe torturing bad guys."

"Same for you, silly. Well, the first part. Your family, I mean." A smile made its way back to my face as I met his eyes again. "I guess I'll figure out if drawing is still mine," I mused. "Now if we could just get Constantine to find his something, too."

"He will." Enzo nodded, then gestured toward the door. "Now, let me cook you two up a meal so I can get back to my exhausted wife."

"You're the best." I leaned over and hugged him. "Love you."

"Love you, too." He reached for the hat and set it back on my head. "The South looks good on you. But so does the whole 'being in love' thing. Glad you finally found your way to the right guy. Bianca would love that you're together, you know that, right?"

I fidgeted with the brim of the hat, sighing. "She'd be happy for you, too," I whispered. "For all of us."

Chapter 47

Hudson

Four Weeks Later

"Thank you, we appreciate the support. Be in touch with more information once the project is ready to lift off," I said after wrapping up my presentation to the last group of investors inside my bar.

Alfie and I walked them out, shaking each of their hands.

I shut the door and faced him, a mix of emotions overwhelming me. Relief. Pride. Exhaustion, too. I'd been working nonstop on this project ever since Bella and I'd come back from North Carolina.

"They're all in, man. We did it." Alfie slapped his palms together as I loosened the knot of my tie.

"It's really happening, then." I was still a bit shocked we'd not only pulled this off so fast, but with so much support.

I went behind the bar and poured us celebratory glasses of Blanton's bourbon. The bar didn't open for another two hours, and I'd been using the space to hold meetings every afternoon of the week.

The Art of You

"All you, brother. Your idea." He clinked his glass with mine and took a seat on the stool opposite me.

"I couldn't have done this without you. Without the support of Matt's family, either." It'd also been an emotional week. Alfie and I had met with everyone from our old team, along with the families of those we'd lost from Echo—Matt and Devon. I'd introduced the guys to Bella, too. She'd won everyone over in the space of a heartbeat, of course.

"So, with all the investors in, including that big whale you landed the other day, The Maddox Group, not to mention the Costas, obviously, I'd say we'll have this project up and running by January 2026." Alfie finished his bourbon and set down his empty glass.

"I really do appreciate your help on this." I added more to his glass and some to my own.

"It's an important mission, and I'm honored you asked me to join you. Stop the flow of fentanyl into our cities as much as possible, and help support those who need help with addiction from the pain the drug has already inflicted. Ensure they get the second chance Matt never had." Emotion choked him up, and he tossed back the rest of his bourbon.

I couldn't take credit for everything. Bella had helped me turn it from an idea into something actually possible. And while I had no plans to reach out to Pablo and personally help him out, I had every intention of working with as many other people who needed support as possible. Okay, that was a partial lie. I did check in on Pablo. More like I was keeping tabs on him to ensure he never bothered Bella again. Some things would never change, and my need to keep her safe would be one of them.

I tossed my suit jacket on the bar top and cuffed my sleeves at the elbows, anxious to call her and share the good news.

I was about to pour us one last drink, but at the sight of my old man walking in, I lowered the bottle. Should've locked the door.

Alfie swiveled on his seat, locating the target I was laser-focused on. "I need to call my wife anyway. We'll talk later." He stood and left without offering more than a passing nod at my father on his way out.

"What do you want?" Bottle back in hand, I refilled my glass. From celebratory drinking to needing to drown out whatever noise would come from his mouth.

He fingered the collar of his shirt as he walked closer. "Tell me you had nothing to do with the story I read in the paper the other day."

My lips curved at the edges as I fought a smile. "Oh yeah, what story?" I couldn't stop it from happening, allowing a full-blown smart-ass smirk to take over as I remembered the article Adelina's sister published, finally exposing the truth.

Congress would now be pressured to implement better protocols to protect our service men and women because of that article. One good thing had come from Green's revenge plan, at least. As for Keith, I still fell asleep to visions of killing that man instead of counting sheep to pass out. What could I say? Golf knocked my girl out and thoughts of murder was apparently now my go-to. Completely unhealthy, but I was self-aware, and I'd work on it. Well, maybe. The fucker did have cameras in my girl's place, set his mouth on hers, and tried to kill her, so . . .

"Christ, what were you thinking?"

Right. You're still here. Another healthy gulp of bourbon needed.

"If the Pentagon connects you to that, it'll be your ass and by association mine."

"I could give zero fucks," I said as casually as possible just to piss him off.

He rolled his eyes. That'd go over real well with his

The Art of You

constituents as an answer to their problems. "And I'm sure you also heard about the deal the government made with Green?"

Yeah, I knew about it. A cushy prison cell if Peter Green would help the Department of Defense identify all of their cyber vulnerabilities and show them how to fix them.

Keith, on the other hand, would be serving a long-ass sentence in maximum security. No cushions, at all. So help me if I heard the man ever had access to a PlayStation. I was all for second chances, except when it came to someone who tried to murder the love of my life.

"I also spoke with Agent Clarke. Seems like he's broken up with Kit, and he's not interested in targeting you to get to me anymore."

"Ah, well, you are in the market for a new girlfriend since the ambassador left you. Maybe a second-chance romance with Kit is on the horizon?" Now I really was just fucking with him, and I didn't feel even a little bad about it. The man had put me through the wringer most of my life for his own benefit, so he could deal with it.

He set his hands on the bar counter, eyeing the bottle. Nah, he wouldn't be getting any of the good stuff. Hell, not even the cheap shit.

"Dean is still planning to run against me next year." That was quite the pivot. "Uphill battle against an incumbent, so I'm not too worried."

Sure. All the worrying. I could see it in his eyes. "I have no intention of voting for him. *Or* you. I'm hoping someone with a little more honesty and decency joins the race."

A resigned sigh fell from his mouth, one I almost believed. "Why do you hate me so much?"

"I'm done trying to forgive you for your constant fuckups," I said bluntly. "I'd prefer you stay away from me for the foreseeable future."

He shook his head. "I heard about your project, and I'd like to support your efforts." Was he kidding? I wouldn't touch a donation from him with a ten-foot pole.

"Nah, I'm good. I won't let you use people who need help as puppets for your campaign or to create a slogan." I pointed to the door. "Time to leave."

"At some point, you will have to forgive me." His brows furrowed. "You're still my son."

"Something I learned in the last few weeks is that family's not defined by shared blood. It's people who stand by and support you through the good and bad times that really matter." And that was the truth. Bella and her family's open arms, and my old Teamguys taking me back in as if I hadn't disappeared for fifteen years was proof of that.

"I won't give up. I'm going to keep trying to earn your trust back."

I swallowed, not liking how those words actually did land, knocking a lump into my throat. "Good. I'd hate for our governor to be such a quitter." I cocked my brow. "I wish you the best of luck in that and your future endeavors." My smart-ass mouth ran again, but in all seriousness, I wouldn't object to him trying to earn my trust if that meant he'd straighten up his act all around. Put others before himself for starters. Like our people here in New York.

My father simply shook his head and left, and I settled back on a stool, much more relaxed with him gone.

At the sound of a text, I removed my phone from my pocket. Seeing Bella's name there changed my mood.

> Bella: Tell me everything. All the good news. I know you have some. I can feel it. <smiling emoji>

I wasted no time and responded, letting her know we landed every investor we'd gone after today.

> Bella: Feel like celebrating now? I happen to be sitting at your desk at our office. I wouldn't mind winding up on top of it, though.

> Me: Already on my way.

> Bella: Good. I've been a bit bratty today (so Constantine said before leaving the office), and you might need to . . . you know.

> Me: Handle your attitude in the way only I can, huh? <winking emoji>

> Bella: Abso-freaking-lutely. But use your words, sailor. Tell me what you plan to do to me when you get here. We have the place to ourselves, so screaming is not off the table. Or the desk, as things may be.

The exchange with my father was now long gone from my mind.

After locking up, I shielded my eyes with my Ray-Bans and went to my truck parked out back behind the bar.

Once behind the wheel, I texted back a dirty message as she'd requested. An explicit, and very direct description of what I planned to do to her.

Kiss every inch of her body. Take each nipple between my teeth. Run my mouth over her heated skin. Spread her legs open. Worship her. Kiss and suck and fuck her with my mouth before I did so with my cock.

> Bella: Getting naked and ready for you now. You better hurry.

> Bella: Actually, I'll leave my high heels on for now. Twist my hair into a braid that you can tug in case I'm a bad girl.

Thank God my bar was near our security office. Jesus, I was unbearably stiff. How the hell had I waited this long to be with her? I had no damn clue, and I'd never find out what it was like to go without her again.

I pulled out of the parking lot and voice-texted her back while driving, offering her more encouraging words while she waited for me to get to her.

When I stopped at a red light, a for sale sign in the window of an art studio caught my eye. Bella was still struggling to draw, even though I knew how much she wanted to. A few times a week I'd wake to her standing in only my T-shirt in front of a blank canvas. A gorgeous sight to open my eyes to, but my heart broke at the fact she'd yet to put the pencil or brush to paper.

I quickly typed the realtor's phone number into the notepad of my phone, an idea taking root in my mind. Christmas was next month, and there was nothing more that I'd like to do than help pave the way for a little holiday miracle for her. After all, her being with me was mine. Having her in my life was like waking up to the best gift every day.

I set my phone aside, and once the light turned green, hauled ass to get to her.

The second I opened my office door, I found her exactly as she'd promised. Naked, in black pumps, on my empty desk.

She was stretched out, resting on her forearms, knees bent. She lazily drew her hand down the center of her body while casually rolling her head to the side to peer at me.

I locked the door and removed my tie, allowing it to hang around my neck as I approached her.

"Mmm. My sexy businessman today," she murmured in a sensual voice.

I reached for her ankles and abruptly dragged her to me. I had every intention of coming inside her one day. When we were both ready for that next step of her having our child. After we were married, of course. No plans to piss off Senior—a.k.a. her father. And especially not her mother. That one scared me more than her dad did.

"Ready to adjust my attitude?" she teased.

"Fuck yes." I was breathing hard as our eyes connected, and I growled out, "*If* you're ready for me."

She nodded her permission, sliding her tongue along the seam of her lips to taunt me.

"Use your words, darlin'." I knelt in front of the desk, leaning in so my breath moved over her sex as I kept her ankles captive in my palms. "Tell me," I began. "What. Do. You. Want. Me. To. Do?"

Epilogue

Isabella

Christmas Eve

"One more step." Hudson kept hold of my waist, guiding me forward since he had me blindfolded with his tie.

We'd cut out of my parents' Christmas party early because Hudson said he had a gift waiting for me. We'd stopped by his bar for a quick minute, then, once in his truck for the short drive, he'd removed his black tie and used it to hide my eyes.

I had to assume the gift would involve copious amounts of orgasms, and I was here for it. What I hadn't expected was the fresh smell of paint when he'd walked me into our mystery location.

"I'm a little nervous," I admitted, chewing on my lip.

"You should be," he joked, then removed his hands from my body and went for the knot of the tie.

I swallowed, keeping my eyes closed as he removed my blindfold.

"Open your eyes."

That husky command compelled me to do as he said. I slowly parted my lids and immediately sought out his hand at the sight before me. Well, *surrounding* us. I did a three-sixty. "Oh my God." *Is this real?* "Did I . . . this is all . . ." Liquid pooled in my eyes, and I suffocated the breaths trying to escape, placing my free hand over my nose and mouth.

"All you," he confirmed, my words still tangled up by my surprise. "Your parents kept every painting and sketch you ever did over the course of your life, until you stopped at eighteen, and they're all here on these walls."

I moved a step forward, and he went right with me.

Another deep gulp to chase down the lump in my throat was needed, emotion continuing to tank my ability to articulate my thoughts.

I couldn't believe he did this. I mean, I could, because this was Hudson—the king of all men as far as I was concerned. Redefining what it meant to be truly loved at every turn.

"This is your studio now." Still holding my hand, he walked around to face me, cupping my cheek with his other palm. "Your art collection. Or, I think it's called an exhibit." He smiled. "I call it, The Art of You." His blue eyes pinned me with a slightly nervous look, like he was worried I'd reject his gift.

Not ever. It was the most thoughtful and amazing gesture.

"What do you think?" he asked when I'd still refrained from speaking.

What do I think? My knees buckled as I let my hand leave my face so I could attempt talking. "I think I love you." I sniffled, trying not to release an ugly sob at how amazing this man was.

"I hope you love me-love me. Not just think." His smile stretched into a handsome grin, one that met his eyes.

"Oh, it's safe to say I love you-love you. With all my heart." Tears hit his hand where he held my face, and he leaned in and pressed his mouth softly over mine.

The noise in my head went quiet, and when he stopped kissing me, I took the moment to peer around the gorgeous space again. Every wall was covered with my art. The unfinished drawing of my sister was on an easel, though, waiting for me. Next to it was another easel that had a black cover draped over it.

"A blank canvas you're concealing there?" I asked him.

He closed one eye. "Not blank. I may have dabbled in drawing a little myself for this moment."

"Really?" I was prepared to make a beeline for my next gift, but he gently took hold of my wrist.

"Not yet." He reached into his pocket for his phone, then a moment later, music began playing from the speakers mounted in the corners of the room.

"Now you see," I began, pulling my hands free so I could set them on his chest and lock eyes with him, "I'd think you'd play 'Unchained Melody' since she's an artist in *Ghost*, and they have that hot pottery scene together. You know, we could make a little art together here."

He pocketed his phone and brought his arm behind my back, hauling me against him in one swift movement. "But he dies in that movie." His brows drew tight. "I mean, I'd haunt the hell out of you like he did, but . . . I'm not going anywhere." He surprised me with a little dip, bending me back. "You did ask me if I could dirty dance, though, and I don't remember ever answering you."

"Artist"—I gestured with my head toward the covered canvas—"and now dancer. Full of surprises, mister."

"For you, I'll be anything you want and could ever need."

He twirled me around, the skirt of my red dress fanning out, then he hoisted me up in the air and I laughed, holding open my arms like Baby from *Dirty Dancing* as "The Time of My Life" played.

Yeah, this was the Christmas of all Christmases. Epic and incredible.

After the song changed, he tossed his suit jacket on the floor by his tie, then dragged his hand down the V-slit of my dress, using his palm to bend me again. The man was all hard lines and sexy masculinity as he took command of my body, taking the lead.

"There's a bedroom upstairs, too," he whispered in my ear, catching me in his arms after twirling me. "I figured you may have some late nights here."

"We're down the street from your bar. Does that mean you'll join me on those nights?"

He stopped dancing and captured my chin with his big hand. "What do you think, sweetheart?" He laid a hot kiss on me, stealing my breath and thoughts along with it.

"Any more surprises?" I asked when the next song began, and he clasped our fingers, walking us around a corner to a private area away from the windows. I honestly wasn't sure how he could possibly top this.

"One or two," he said while we entered a lit-up room filled with art supplies. Like *loaded* with them. He'd gone all out. "Did you know there's such a thing as edible body paint?" He let go of my hand and went over to a table and lifted a small red jar. "Strawberry-flavored dark chocolate."

"Now this is getting even more deliciously interesting."

With the lift of his chin, he motioned to a blanket already on the floor. After unscrewing the lid of the paint, he reached for a new brush. "Get naked, please."

"Promise to lick it off?" I wet my lips before sighing, my heart never feeling so full. "Maybe it should be me with the paintbrush, though. I'm feeling rather inspired now."

"Oh, are you?" He set aside the paint and brush, then worked the top two buttons of his pressed black dress shirt undone. "So, both of us naked, then?"

"Mmmhmm." I unzipped the dress, and the red silk fell to a puddle at my feet, leaving me in only my strapless bra, matching satin panties, and fire-engine-red heels.

"And my job is done. A masterpiece already," he said huskily while turning his clothes into a distant memory. "Why mess with perfection?"

Keeping my heels on, I shed the rest and stretched out on my back, waiting for him to join me on the blanket with the brush and paint, eager to see the new artist at work.

He took a knee alongside my body and spread open my thighs. The brush tickled my skin, making me laugh, as he slowly drew a line in red paint from my belly button to my breast.

"My favorite sound on the planet, a close tie to hearing you moan when I make you come," he rasped before following the path the brush had taken to lick up the red-colored chocolate.

Talk about living art. *Consider me very, very ready to explore my talent again.*

We took turns with the brush after that. I wound up on top of him a few minutes later, perched right on his hard length while drawing little not-so-artistic squiggles along the ridges of his abs.

"You've been a good girl taking your pill, right?" he asked, holding my hips as I ground against his erection. "Not ovulating?"

"Yes to both. I'm good." I set the brush and paint aside,

leaning forward to kiss his chest, offering him the perfect opportunity to slip inside me. "Go ahead. Feel me bare."

"My Christmas present, huh?" he asked with a hearty laugh. "It'll be hard to top that next year. I just might want the chance to put a baby inside you then."

"I hope you do." I swallowed, meeting his eyes, then nodded my permission for him to connect our bodies, letting him take over.

He rolled me to my back, the red "paint" smeared all over us making us somehow a perfect mess, and I loved it.

The moment our bodies connected, he stretched me out, filling me deep. I whispered an *I love you*, that he caught with his tongue before returning the words.

Heaven was truly here. In an art studio with the man I loved. A Christmas miracle. Hell, I might even have to believe in Santa again.

After we made love, and he came inside me for the first time—an experience I'd never forget—he took me upstairs into the bedroom to shower and clean up. We wound up making love again there, too. The man was insatiable and could never get enough of me, and I was *ditto* all the way in that regard.

He had my pajamas already on the bed, little Christmasy ones that were cute but sexy. Just sweats for him. Gray, though, so merry Christmas to me.

We swapped our towels for the clothes, then he took my hand and guided me down the spiral steps to the studio. I still couldn't believe my work was hanging up, framed and displayed like a real exhibit.

He walked me over to the covered canvas, and my gaze raked over the unfinished one off to the right, and my stomach squeezed. Because for the first time, I truly wanted to finish it. It took this very moment for me to understand why I'd left it partially incomplete in the first place.

Because in my head, if I finished, Bianca would really be gone. *She'd* be done.

But I was wrong. I'd left her in limbo. Me, too. Neither of us being able to move on. But it was time.

Tears filled my eyes as I cupped my mouth and Hudson pulled me into his arms, sensing I was going through something. He gave me all the time I needed, and when I was ready, I requested to see his work of art.

"Well, as far as I'm concerned, I'm looking at my masterpiece now." His eyes roamed appreciatively over my body. "But if you're ready . . . ?"

"I am." I nodded, setting a hand over my stomach, a little nervous.

He slowly removed the cover, revealing a rough sketch that I couldn't love more, because he'd done this for me. For *us*.

"And what do you call it?" A flood of tears hit me as I stepped closer to take it in.

"Our future," he said with a lopsided grin as he pointed to a cute one-story home he'd drawn. "We'll build our own place somewhere near your parents' house on Long Island." He gestured to the profile of a woman holding her stomach. "You pregnant with our child."

More and more depictions covered the canvas like the game of Life, only this was going to be mine. And it was real.

"The beach outside your parents' home in the Hamptons . . . I'm thinking that's where we should marry. You love it there, and you feel Bianca's presence when you visit, so—"

"Yes," I cut him off, leaping into his arms. "Yes, I'll marry you." I linked my wrists behind his neck and kissed him.

I felt him smile against my mouth a moment later. "Sweetheart?"

"Mmmhmm?"

"Mind if I drop to one knee and ask you first?"

The Art of You

I sniffled, swiping away tears, while laughing. "Right. I skipped over that, didn't I?"

He bit the side of his lip, which was ridiculously sexy, then reached into his pocket while lowering to one knee. He opened the box, revealing a simple solitaire set in a platinum band. "Will you marry me, Isabella?"

I set aside the ring box on a nearby table, lowered before him, taking hold of his face between my palms, eagerly nodding. "Yes, yes, yes."

He crushed his mouth over mine, and we remained locked into that moment until we were both breathless.

When we finally came up for air, he helped me stand and swept me up into his arms. "Now, I'd like to carry my future wife to bed, because I need to be inside you again if you don't mind." He dropped his eyes to the box. "Want your ring?"

"I'll get it later." I held on to him, lifting my chin to hold his eyes. "I have everything I need right now. Just you." And I meant that. Every word. All I'd ever needed was him and his love, and I knew he felt the same.

Hudson pressed a soft kiss to my mouth, then took me to the loft where we made love again. And after he fell asleep, I slowly crept down the stairs, put on my engagement ring, then began drawing again.

From that moment until the morning, I never left the room. Even with the sun coming through the window, I didn't stop. I didn't lower my pencil until Hudson came up behind me, setting his hands on my arms to hold me.

"You finished." He leaned in, resting his chin on my shoulder to take in the sight of the drawing of Bianca sitting alongside a new canvas I'd begun working on after that one. "Merry Christmas, sweetheart," he whispered into my ear, and I turned to catch his mouth and kiss him.

"Best Christmas ever." I let go of a deep sigh as he changed positions, hooking his arm around me, drawing my back to his chest to hold me.

"And what do you call this one?" He gestured with his free hand to my current work in progress which was of a couple dancing.

I smiled and looked back at him. "The Art of *Us*."

Author's Note

Constantine Costa's book releases next.

Where else have you seen some of the guest characters?

Maria and Enzo's book, *Let Me Love You* (book 1) is a spin-off from Maria's sister's book, the standalone romance, *Until You Can't*.

Calliope and Alessandro fall in love in *Not Mine to Keep* (book 2).

The Echo Team guests are from the Stealth Ops Series. Roman's book is *Chasing Shadows*.

We also had cameos from the Falcon Falls Series.

Adelina is a guest in *The Wrecked One* - where her sister, Mya, discovers Adelina's alive.

Author's Note

Sydney's book is *The Guarded One* where she falls for a small-town sheriff & single dad.

Looking to start the Falcon Falls series from the beginning? Book 1 is *The Hunted One*. The first three books of the series are also available as a boxed set.

Crossovers

Books for these characters are in the "Also By" section

Stealth Ops Echo Team:
  Echo One - Wyatt
  Echo Two - A.J.
  Echo Three - Chris
  Echo Four - Roman
  Echo Five - Finn
  Cyber expert: Harper (married to Roman)
  K9: Bear

Falcon Falls Security Mentions:

Carter Dominick (old rival of Constantine)

Jesse McAdams (friend of Enzo's)

Sydney Archer-Hawkins (ex-husband, Seth Maverick)

Crossovers

Mya Vanzetti (Adelina's twin sister / journalist)

Also By Brittney Sahin

Standalone
Until You Can't
The Story of Us

Costa Family
Let Me Love You
Not Mine to Keep
The Art of You
*Constantine Costa**

Becoming Us
Someone Like You
My Every Breath

Stealth Ops Series: Bravo Team
Finding His Mark (Luke)
Finding Justice (Owen)
Finding the Fight (Asher)
Finding Her Chance (Liam)

Also By Brittney Sahin

Finding the Way Back (Knox)

Stealth Ops Series: Echo Team
Chasing the Knight (Wyatt)
Chasing Daylight (A.J.)
Chasing Fortune (Chris)
Chasing Shadows (Roman)
Chasing the Storm (Finn)

Falcon Falls Security
The Hunted One (Griffin)
The Broken One (Jesse)
The Guarded One (Sydney)
The Taken One (Gray)
The Lost Letters: A Novella
The Wanted One (Jack)
The Fallen One (Carter)
The Wrecked One (Oliver/Mya)

Dublin Nights

On the Edge
On the Line
The Real Deal
The Inside Man
The Final Hour

Hidden Truths
The Safe Bet
Beyond the Chase
The Hard Truth
Surviving the Fall
The Final Goodbye

Where else can you find me?

I love, love, love interacting with readers in my Facebook groups as well as on my Instagram page. Join me over there as we talk characters, books, and more! ;)

FB Reader Group:
Brittney's Book Babes

Facebook
Instagram
TikTok
Pinterest

www.brittneysahin.com
brittneysahin@emkomedia.net

Made in United States
Troutdale, OR
03/17/2025

29805043R00249